TRISTAN PALMGREN

Terminus

**ANGRY
ROBOT**

ANGRY ROBOT
An imprint of Watkins Media Ltd

20 Fletcher Gate,
Nottingham,
NG1 2FZ
UK

angryrobotbooks.com
twitter.com/angryrobotbooks
Heavens above

An Angry Robot paperback original 2018

Cover by Dominic Harman
Set in Meridien by Argh! Nottingham

Distributed in the United States by Penguin Random House, Inc., New York.

ISBN 978 0 85766 758 8
Ebook ISBN 978 0 85766 674 1

Printed in the United States of America

9 8 7 6 5 4 3 2 1

For those who, in spite of it all, remain kind.

You were like a traveler in the night, whose torch lights up for others the path where he himself has miserably fallen.

— PETRARCH, *Letter to Cicero*

PART I

The Company of Mortality

1

There was no such thing as a restful day at sea. Not on this boat. Not for her. But some days were worse than others.

She had known this one was coming.

She'd filled the day with distractions. Her crew bickered just above the range of her hearing. Metal clanked against metal, thunked on wood as they wound the capstan. The sails scraped and ruffled, rhythmic as breath. The banks of oars trailed silently along the water, the wake of their passage the only evidence that the boat was moving.

She took no part in that work. Not today. Her crew bustled about it. They were willful. They had their own opinions about what was suited for their talents and when she'd get in the way. She'd made them that way. They'd all woken with the teal-gray predawn, slender lanterns dancing across the deck.

She sat at the edge of the deck, by the railing, her legs folded.

She had been released from active service on her other ship, her real one. She was to survey and scour these oceans, learning everything there was to learn. One of her crew dropped a survey probe. After a muted splash, there was a steady, whip-fast uncoiling of rope.

There was still little enough light in the sky. But more than there should have been.

A finch-tail comet brushstroked the southern horizon, shading the sky crimson. It moved like no comet should have. It traveled perpendicular to the path of the sun. It glowed brighter than any comet. This was the first night she had sailed far south enough to see it.

Had she breath, she would have held it.

Soon there would be cloudless nights when the whole sky turned pink. The comet's glow would hide the stars. The horizon would be curtained red. Everything would become the backdrop of a theater.

Theater was the right word for it. It was all stagecraft. All of the sky was a performance.

The false comet cut a line across the far southern horizon, heading eastward and gradually northward, following the path of the winter sun. Seen at this steep angle, through so much intervening atmosphere, the exhaust plume appeared cherry-red, haloed in orange.

The intruder knew the effect that comets had on this world's peoples. She tried to put herself in their place, see it how they saw it. She couldn't. She thought of herself as an imaginative person. But she couldn't forget everything she knew about the ship burning across the sky, about transplanar travel, about the amalgamates. Even with what she knew, it was at times too much.

No wonder that, the first few times it appeared, cities had burned.

That had been years ago. These days, watching and waiting and trembling, the natives tended to get on with their lives. Like most people the multiverse over, they had little choice and less control. They mattered only in the abstract. The comet persisted regardless.

She should have been up there. Not at sea, trapped in horizons. She'd been stranded on this plane with that ship: the living planarship *Ways and Means*. She'd been one of its thousands of crew.

She'd departed for her own safety. Now its crew wouldn't even call her by name. They just called her the One Who Stopped Them. Even when they knew she was listening. It was as if she'd been erased.

She hadn't actually stopped anyone. She had no say. *Ways and Means* reserved all final decisions for itself. They knew that. But, when she'd spoken up, their master had apparently picked her alone to listen to.

The rest of the crew couldn't despise *Ways and Means*. It had wormed its way into them. They had needed another target.

She'd been right there, on offer. *Ways and Means* had made her visible.

She gripped the railing, dug in her fingers.

When she pulled her hand back, her index finger had left a long and shallow divot against the grain of the wood.

She stared. Her finger was slender, ink-black, and blunt at the tip. She had no nails. The railing had left no mark or splinter on her demiorganic flesh.

She hadn't meant to do that. It was possible for her to lose control of her body. But it had not happened to her before.

The noises behind her had stilled. Her crew was watching her. They were perceptive.

She should not have sailed this way. Should not have looked up. Eventually, though, there was going to be nowhere on this world from which she could not see the comet.

She unfolded her legs and planted her feet against the deck. Her finger-length toes unfurled. She levered herself up.

Her cheeks were hot, and the corners of her eyes burned. These feelings were psychosomatic, a lizard-brain response. She didn't have a real body. Hadn't for centuries.

It didn't matter what today was. She shouldn't feel any different on another. She hadn't the day before. Or before that.

Of course her skin radiated heat. She'd been out in the sun too long.

She glared at her crew. All of them pretended to have been hard at work. Her engineer busied herself with the rear sail's outhaul. Her divers pretended to be measuring the wind.

Osia opened her mouth. For the second time that morning, her body betrayed her. She had something to say, but not the strength to say it.

She was going to have to reprogram her crew not to be so

nosy, so perceptive.

She turned back to the sea, and this time managed not to look upward. It didn't matter. Her memory was perfect. She knew exactly what she would have seen.

Worse, she knew where it was going next.

2

Fia had seen death before, on a massive scale and without looking away, but she had not seen death like this.

Acid touched the back of her throat. But still there was something fascinating about it.

She crept closer, quiet and careful as a mouse.

The shed's door hung half-open. It cast everything inside under sharp contrasts of light and dark. It etched a black halo around the man in the dirt. His twisted legs and slack mouth carved canyons of shadow.

The shed and the body belonged to Bandino, one of the shepherds from the other side of this rocky valley. He had served in Treviso's militia, and sometimes still stood watch for the Convent of Saint Augusta of Treviso. He knew how to handle a spear and dagger. He had never been other than unstintingly rude to Fia, but he served without being asked.

His face was blackened. His distended tongue burst through his lips. Red welts blossomed around his neck.

He had been strangled. This wasn't just death. It was murder.

She bent, reached inside his tunic and touched bare skin. Still warm, not hot. She was enough of a familiar of death to judge the age of a body. It was a fair day out, sunny but not stifling. Cadavers took a fair amount of time to cool.

She had touched her father after his death. He'd still been feverish-hot though she'd known, from testing with a feather in front of his lips, that he'd stopped breathing more than an hour before.

Bandino's dagger was missing from its sheath. He never

traveled without it. He often sat on stones along the road to Saint Augusta's, whetting it. The earthen floor of the shed was scuffed. Someone had dragged him here.

His boots were missing. With a shiver, she saw the seams of his leggings were split. Someone had stripped him. They'd had a cool head. They'd searched all the places where a man might have hidden money.

The shed's cob walls slumped. It wasn't much good for anything but keeping brush during the winter, or broken tools to trade for seed. She'd come over because the open door had been a telltale mark of intrusion, a burglar with the mistaken impression that there was something valuable inside. Or a drifter looking for shelter. She'd chased more than one off Saint Augusta's property. There'd been plenty of those the past few years. And more this summer. All because of the trouble in the east.

This was no break-in. This was a body stash. Professionally done, too. They'd searched him in quick strokes. They'd neglected to close the door, but maybe they hadn't cared that much.

She stifled her breathing and crept back outside. The wind, an intermittent visitor on her walk back from town, had stilled. The heat made her itch. There was no sign of trouble other than what she'd left behind.

She shouldn't have been here. Shouldn't have come alone. She'd been away from Saint Augusta's for three days. She, two of the mothers, and three of the other girls had gone to Treviso to buy thread and linen. She and the other girls weren't ordinarily allowed to go, but the mothers needed someone to haul, and couldn't spare Saint Augusta's few animals.

Fia hadn't had much to carry back. The mothers' money hadn't gone very far. The advent of the eastern mercenaries had driven up prices. So she'd raced ahead when the mothers weren't looking. She would pay a sharp price later. None of the orphanage's girls were ever supposed to travel alone.

Funny thing was, she still wasn't sorry she'd gone ahead. The mothers, let alone the other girls, would be useless here. She could have counted on them to do little more than panic or pray.

She crouched, using the grass to conceal herself. She should have melted back the way she'd come. Back away from the road, into the tangled forest. Found a place to hide.

Her blood burned. Her stomach was molten iron. Her fingers trembled.

Like a lot of people around Saint Augusta's, Bandino had been an idiot. He drank himself sick. He stared at the orphanage's girls when they thought he wasn't watching. He was rude for rudeness's sake. Fia had no patience for idiots. But he hadn't deserved this.

She was not, had never been, the kind of girl to run and hide.

She recognized she'd made the decision only in retrospect. She had to see if the girls back home were safe too. Staying low, she kept going in the direction she'd started: toward home.

She loped along the creek that S-tailed along the border of the convent's land. Saint Augusta's was ahead. Its cousin orphanage, Saint Niccoluccio's monastery, stood upon the ridge farther ahead. Their shared parcel of land was small, originally purchased to support the convent alone. The convent had not been intended to serve as an orphanage. After the great pestilence, necessity had turned it into Fia's new home, and Saint Niccoluccio's had been hastily constructed on the far corner of the property.

Try as the keepers of each orphanage might, there'd been no way to keep the boys and girls from contact. These hills were replete with hidden places. Fia had never gone to meet one of the boys, but she knew those spots well enough to keep concealed.

By unthinking childhood habit, she trailed her hand in the wheat. Abruptly, she remembered herself. It made extra noise, extra motion. Whisper-thin and nigh invisible, but still. She had to think and act like a soldier. She had ideas what that was like.

One of the orphanage's regular summer merchants was a Venetian named Pandolfo. He was a living repository of war stories. He looked like a soldier. He had an uncivilized tumult of a beard and a hitch in his gait he claimed he owed to a Florentine bolt. He'd indulged Fia with stories of sieges and betrayals and public executions, but always reminded her that it was a very peculiar thing for a girl to ask about. Fia had answered that she was a very peculiar girl.

Pandolfo hadn't shown up yet this year. There was some talk that he must have gone away. Independent merchants couldn't survive all the trouble in the east, especially the fighting and pillaging around Venice.

She crouched, sniffing for smoke. Nothing. She couldn't believe Pandolfo was gone. He and other men of his age had survived worse. So had she.

A decade and forever ago, a great and mortiferous pestilence had gutted Italy. It had been intangible as a brush of wind, a star falling from the sky. One morning, Fia's world started to end. Her father had died in the space of an afternoon.

She had been told, later, that he lasted two days. She remembered no night. Black buboes rose under his arm. They had *gurgled*, and then racked him with spasms of pain. The hair on his chest turned oily from vomit. Sweat pooled between the tendons of his neck. She'd never thought that anyone so large could be brought down so quickly except by a blade.

Her family had had warning, but the warning had not helped. They had nowhere to flee. In weeks, her neighbors' fields had become wilderness, their homes unmarked sepulchers. The carcasses of their mules and oxen dried to bone and shoe leather under the low winter sun.

In rapid succession, as notes in an ivory-fluted melody, the rest of Fia's family, her mother and four siblings, had been struck down. Worst of all, Fia's twin sister had died. When she realized she was getting sick and Fia was not, she had looked at Fia accusingly.

Alone among them, Fia had survived.

The irony of the orphanages was that the pestilence preferred taking children over men and women. Children piled over the lips of Treviso's unmarked graves. But wicked probability saw some children survive their parents, and without extended family to adopt them. Those who could be caught were carted off lest they become a burden on Treviso's streets.

Fia would have stayed at home had she been able, but hunger had driven her to Treviso. She'd been too young to escape capture. The whip at her back had been no less sharp than for the mules.

So she'd had nowhere but Saint Augusta's convent to make her home. And she had – sometimes by the skin of her fists.

This land was no good for farming. It was too rocky, the soil too poor. The land puckered around short, steep hills that made for exasperating plowing. Every night of the spring and summer harvests, Fia's legs and back felt shredded. One night, she'd lain on the dormitory's cold earth floor to numb the fire in her shoulders. She was the first to risk the mothers' wrath by trying that, but soon the other girls joined her. Fia often led their way.

She and the other girls might not have cared for each other, but they shared their misery. Their parents' property had been stolen away, then seized in war. No one had cared to protect their flimsy inheritances. They would have no dowries. Their only value to the husbands the church would find for them was as servants, laborers.

Fia choked to think about marriage. She wanted nothing less. She still thought of herself and the others as kids. But they hadn't been children for a while. Fia was pretty sure she was fifteen. She'd always been bigger than the others, which made it hard to tell.

All she had heard of the outside world were stories of war that outsiders like Pandolfo had brought to them. Even that turmoil had started to seem an escape.

The boys and girls of Saint Niccoluccio's and Saint Augusta's were given turns tilling the land so that they wouldn't come into contact with each other. While the boys were out, the girls would be baking bread or learning crafts. But they couldn't always be kept from each other. During spring and late summer harvests, the nuns and the monks couldn't watch everything.

Where they failed, Fia had stepped up. She had to keep them in line. She'd used her fists where she had to.

Mother Emilia had lamented – in that timid, tight way of nuns who wanted to curse but couldn't – that Fia hadn't been born a boy. Then Fia could have been exiled to Saint Niccoluccio's, whose rowdy, violent boys could handle her.

Mother Emilia been wrong. Fia clouted plenty of boys too. She'd knocked one of the fathers down too, when he'd grabbed her arm after she'd struck a boy. So severe was the stricture against any of the fathers coming into contact with Saint Augusta's girls that she'd never heard another word about that one.

As she'd grown older, she'd paid more attention to her peers than the nuns. And her peers had taught her a lot. They'd taught her how to hit. Then how to hit in such a way that left no marks. They'd taught her how to lead. She'd spent part of each of her shifts walking the field, being their foreman, their bully.

Even the most indolent and sullen among them knew what she wanted. Adult politics were not always so clear.

It was only midmorning, but the sun bore heat upon heat upon her. It baked the soil. Dust plastered to the sweat on her forehead. It was exactly the kind of day she'd imagined war would be fought under, a remorseless day. Weather for burning.

The soldiers menacing Venice, the *condottieri*, were supposed to spread fire whenever their devil winds carried them in. They burned, destroyed, ransomed, and tormented to provoke a reaction.

They were not supposed to be so close to Treviso. But their strange eastern horsemen, the *stradiots*, could move faster than anyone believed.

If anyone had suspected they could be here, the convent of Saint Augusta might have packed up its girls and sent them elsewhere so that they could "sleep honestly." Fia curled her nose at that thought. As if women were guilty of anything more than being sport.

The only soldiers near were supposed to be Treviso's allies. Mercenaries, more *condottieri,* passing through to purchase wheat and fodder and bolts. They weren't supposed to be within thirty miles.

She crouched in the lee of the next hillock. Saint Niccoluccio's was hidden behind a ridge with gravestone walls. She squinted. There was no sign of smoke. Not even chimney smoke. There should have been. If the boys were out, then the girls would be baking, or vice versa.

She edged around the hill. Her vision, stinging from sweat and dust, hazed. Something large and black, eight-legged, stirred in front of the chapterhouse. It took her too long to realize it was the convent's two oxen, blurred together. She let her breath out.

Then she saw the third shape much farther away, by the convent's corner. A black horse. Two more, both brown, stood almost motionless by the trees behind. One had a rider.

Her breath stuck in her throat. For a moment she was pinned to the earth, squeezed still by the weight of what she'd seen. Bandino dead. The monastery and convent's chimneys stilled. Riders.

Neither Saint Augusta's nor Saint Niccoluccio's had much worth stealing. It was only the beginning of spring harvest. They had no food stockpiled. The only thing the orphanages had were their children. Even eastern barbarians wouldn't charge into a place without scouting first. They had to have known what they would find.

They were after her and her friends. Hostages. Slaves.

She spotted more horses, but not many. In total, there were no more than half a dozen riders about the convent. She looked about, abruptly conscious of how much of the land was hidden by the fields' slopes. She wasn't the only one who could be hiding. The wheel-rut road to Treviso was lost behind one of the hills that made plowing so frustrating.

The wind whispered along the wheat. It was nearly, but not quite, enough to cover the noise coming from the road. A shuffling. Hooves kicking along the dirt. Then, briefly, a choke, a cry cut off.

Fia made another decision before she realized it. Carefully, staying low, she headed in that direction.

She found the girls. There were not as many as there should have been. There were about fifteen, out of Saint Augusta's thirty-five. They marched amid four riders. The boys followed, and there were more of them – twenty or so. Fia stifled her breath. From this distance, she could not see their faces.

The kids walked in a coffle, hands unbound but a rope tight around their necks. One rider held onto the front end, and a second the rear. Together, they could draw it taut at will, choking their captives.

She hoped the missing kids had gotten away, but of course she had no means to tell. A handful of the fathers were lashed into the end of the line. There was no sign of the mothers. Fia's throat tightened. The mothers must have gotten enough warning to flee. They had not made any attempt to defend their charges or some of them would be here right now.

None of the boys or girls walked with limps or cradled arms, though she did catch shadows that might have been bruises. Something odd – they all looked uniformly down. They had been coached to do so. The rope had been drawn tight to keep them from looking around, making noise.

The soldiers needed them silent, Fia realized, because their attack hadn't concluded. The riders standing still by Saint Augusta's weren't loafing. They were keeping watch.

This handful of soldiers weren't enough to have done all this by themselves. There still had to be others out there.

The whisper of the wind changed again. The wheat hissed. Footsteps. Breath.

Close.

She held still, a prayer frozen on her breath.

A hard shock between her shoulder blades propelled her out of her crouch. She fought for her balance, taking two stumbling steps forward, and then crashed belly first onto the dirt road.

She had landed out in full view. The riders halted. More chokes and gasps as the riders tugged the ropes.

Fia rolled, craned herself to a seat. A soldier stood where she had been, grinning and silent. His hair was unwashed, his beard wild. He had a horseman's bowed legs. Some combination of age and sun had turned his skin prematurely old, like pumice.

The soldier's leather armor made him look broad-shouldered, but in truth he was shorter than her. No wonder he'd been assigned to scouting. A taller soldier couldn't have sneaked up on her.

She tried to hide her rage. After giving her a moment to appreciate her situation, he stepped toward her.

As soon as he was close enough, she lashed her leg out, kicked hard into his knee. He yelled. She hooked her leg around his ankle and pulled back.

He crashed to the ground much harder than she had.

Her head was still spinning. It took her longer than she liked to climb atop him, and that gave him time to recover. He deflected her first punch. Her second struck true, square in his nose. He didn't so much as grunt. By then, his other arm had found leverage underneath her.

He may have been short, but he had muscles. He twisted, shoved.

23

She landed hard. Needle-sharp stalks of short-cut wheat pierced her cheek and neck. She rolled, too dizzy to think. She lost track of which way was up. By the time she got to her feet, her cheek and her wrist bloody, she was facing the wrong way.

The soldier could have gotten her good. But his shout of fury gave him away long before the snap of the wheat did. Like Saint Niccoluccio's boys did when they fought, he gave too much away.

She ducked, feinted left and stepped to her right. She felt the breeze of his passage. She swung around, and slammed her elbow into the small of his back.

Too late, she saw his eight-inch blade, swinging around.

A searing hot line sliced across her ribs, down her abdomen. She spun away. The fire blazed across her chest, spread across the rest of her body. Her breath became ash, caking in her throat.

She had seen animals slaughtered before. The boys hunted, and brought their game to the girls to butcher. She knew what it would look like. She grabbed her side, expecting to be holding loose folds of skin and fat.

Nothing. Her tunic was unblemished but for the dirt.

A phantom white-hot pain ran across her side, over her belly. But there was no cut. He must have struck her, by happenstance, with the blunt side of his blade. She was lucky to live. She could hardly believe that she did.

She rose at the same time as him. They were both winded, staggering. His face was slick with blood. It oozed from his nose, down into his neck. He panted with fury.

Pain jabbed through Fia's jaw. She'd landed harder than she'd realized. An iron-strong splinter of a dead wheat stalk stuck in her cheek.

She felt along the side of her abdomen again, just in case. Still no wound. The phantom pain was fading. But, in that moment, she had been sure she was dying.

The moment changed her.

The soldier looked along the side of his dagger as if he, too, was surprised. He had meant to kill her.

None of the riders had moved. They held their captives still. Fia's opponent wavered. She had made enough of an impression on him that he hesitated to start another round.

She eyed the blade, tried to think of another way through this. She could have run. If she'd found enough of her breath, she could slip off the edge of their land. Find the girls who'd gotten away. Or the nuns who'd abandoned them.

If she'd wanted to run away from Saint Augusta's, she could have, a long time ago. When she'd slipped away from her escorts this morning, she could have gone in any direction. She'd come here.

She was not the kind to run.

She raised her hands, held them palms flat. Then she turned and marched towards the riders. She didn't dare look back at the soldier.

When the riders tied her into the coffle, they didn't wrap her rope as tightly as around the others. They kept their distance. She glared at them. She persisted in holding her hands up until they were done.

She had been tied into the end of the line, just behind some of the fathers. The boys and girls from Saint Augusta's and Saint Niccoluccio's didn't look back. They couldn't.

It had all happened without one spoken word. Fia's breath still burned. She couldn't have spoken if she'd had anything to say.

After a minute of silence to make sure the noise of the scuffle hadn't flushed out any other hidden hostages, the riders tugged the rope. Time to move.

Fia started. From somewhere, she thought she heard Pandolfo's voice.

You're a peculiar girl, Fiametta of Treviso.

She looked about, but her thoughts were too disordered to find its source.

A pull from behind meant that her rider had seen her

looking. The other captives grunted. The rope was even tighter around their necks. She kept her gaze ahead.

A tender slice of pain traced from her ribs to her stomach. A phantom pain to go with the phantom voice. Real, but only to her. A livid, uncontrollable sensation.

If you pay attention, if you're good...

Her cheek continued to bleed. She could not brush away the blood from her cheek while she marched, not without punishment from the rider behind her. Couldn't look around to make sure no one was near enough to talk.

You might become worth a fraction as much as you think you are.

She did not grant the voice the dignity of answering. It did not matter. It knew that she was curious anyway.

As the coffle wound along the track and the pressure on her neck eased, Fia finally smelled smoke. She turned her head just long enough to catch the fire teasing the horizon. The rider behind her yanked the rope. The last she saw of Saint Augusta's was the roof, aflame.

3

The line to the water cart advanced in single steps.

Fia was annoyed by how quickly she had gotten accustomed to her new life's routines. It had only taken months. She shuffled ahead, keeping her head covered and eyes down.

Two years into her journey with Captain Antonov's Company, the indignities only bothered her when she made an effort to think of them.

Another routine fact of life: it was important to only draw attention to herself at those moments when she was sure she could control it, harness it, and otherwise put it to use.

It was a hot and dry campaigning season. Captain Antonov's soldiers remained on the move even in the peak of summer, when the other armies of South Italy quartered. His men marched to the front of the water line as soon as they entered it. They pushed each other aside, and had less mercy for the camp followers.

But they only pushed Fia. She had blacked some eyes the first time one of them had knocked her away. She'd gotten worse in return, but no formal discipline. The soldiers had been too embarrassed to be beaten by her to bring her up on it.

Now they all knew who she was. From the moment she'd started her career by fighting the man who'd captured her, she'd built her reputation. More than reputation, she had the ear of Captain Antonov.

The line took two steps backward as another pair of soldiers barged ahead.

The sun seared the dirt underfoot. It was a war sun, made

for burning. Something foul must have been coming. No matter the specifics of the weather that found them before battle, the misery seemed a constant.

The last time it had been this hot, she had nursed a man with blood dried black on his lips. He'd begged for water, but she'd had none to give.

She looked back over the line. Her instincts were right. The soldiers were quiet as they drank, their shoulders tense.

The water line was a daily opportunity to take stock of faces she recognized. Not many of the old ones remained. Most people in line were strangers. Men and women with lined faces, numbed by weariness. Not many of the boys and girls from the orphanage were left. Maybe five, counting herself.

These mercenaries had hoped to extract a ransom. While raiding, they seized small laborers. Their lords, always in dire need of work after a harvest had been burned, usually paid. If that failed, Captain Antonov and his company aimed to rely on the bleeding hearts of the towns and churches. Threatened to drown their prisoners unless someone paid.

Captain Antonov was a stranger to this land. He and his *condottieri* had heard that Saint Augusta's relied on plague orphans as farmhands. They had underestimated how few people cared about them. The church had paid for the monks, but not the orphans.

Captain Antonov had not actually wanted to drown the orphans. He and his corporals were mean men, ruthless men, but there was nothing worthwhile in killing children. There were plenty of *condottieri* who would have, to prove the mettle of their threats. These men didn't have so much pride.

So the company had chosen a second option: slavery.

She had gone to work for Captain Antonov himself. Fia had toiled hard for her freedom. She traveled with the camp followers, mending clothes and armor, caring for mules and horses, nursing wounded. Her freedom price had been set low. It was as if Antonov had not wanted to keep her any longer than necessary to extract a minimum face-saving profit.

She still remembered the look on Antonov's face when she had piled the last of her silver coins into her palms and announced that she wanted to stay. He had been *impressed.*

Free or not, she still had companions here. And something else, too.

A good part of her felt more at home now than she ever had at Saint Augusta's. It had taken a long time to understand that. She was a camp servant. A laundress and a seamstress. But she was also a fighter. When the soldiers were on the move, everyone left in camp was expected to guard not only their own belongings, but help defend the treasure train. All of them, even the prostitutes, had weapons.

It was a very eastern way of organizing an army. Nothing Pandolfo described had prepared her for it. The camp followers trailing Italian and English armies stayed clear of any fighting.

At length, Fia reached the cart and procured half a bucket to water her mule. As she passed back through the line, she counted accents. Captain Antonov had started his career with a corps of Russians, but had lost men and accumulated more along the way, like a cyclone picking up and tossing debris. Now he had a host of other easterners: Albanians, Grecians, Hungarians, Germans, plus no small number of Italians. Italian *condottieri* did not shrink from working for foreigners.

These men were as she'd imagined from Pandolfo's stories, but more. There was a steadfastness in them that she had not seen in other men. Not the fathers of Saint Niccoluccio. Not Pandolfo. Not her father.

She hadn't known it at the time, but Captain Antonov had been at Saint Augusta's on the day of her capture, watching. She'd been put to work laundering his clothes and stitching his leathers. She'd seemed to amuse him – until, that was, he'd seen her fight a second time.

The amusement had faded. He'd started to see her as who she was.

The officers staged fights between the men, placed bets. They cleared an arena at the edge of every camp. Soldiers and servants alike encircled it, struck or shoved any fighter who was pushed out or who tried to escape. Few women fought, but Fia wasn't the only one. She had the best record of any of them. She'd only been battered unconscious once. She was starting to build a reputation for never showing pain.

She set her water by her animal. When she'd joined the camp, she'd strained to carry the buckets. Now she hardly felt it.

Tonight, the company camped by a grove of trees shooting from the grassland like water from a spring. She laid her belongings where she could keep an eye on them, and went to the trees. They were her gymnasium. She jumped, hauled herself onto branches. She climbed and dropped, climbed and dropped. She snapped a branch and swung it into the trunk, over and over, like she would club an opponent.

Her nose had quietly broken in her last match. It stung whenever she breathed hard. It never hurt worse than now. The first several dozen times she had exercised like this, she had exhausted herself. She had fallen asleep right after. Now all she felt was angry. The anger accumulated after each swing, each jump, and would not go away. She could not settle afterward, except into work.

Some of the soldiers watched from a distance. Good, she thought. Let them. Maybe more of them would bet on her.

The soldiers sheltered their camp inside ditches and barricades. Every night it was the same, carefully laid out in patterns that the easterners had learned from the Italians. But the servants' camp was outside the barricades, and more lackadaisical. Tents and shelters squatted in clusters. Groups of friends stuck together. Here were the smiths, with the few tools they could haul on campaign. There were the drivers, there the cooks…

Antonov's Company numbered somewhere above a thousand men. About half as many servants trailed after them. Any army needed civilians, free skilled and unskilled laborers and slaves, to sustain it. Antonov's Company had no

30

home, and so brought all of theirs with them. Drivers, petty apprentices, smiths, tailors, launderers, herders to shepherd the company's legion of stolen sheep and cattle. By far the most common laborers in the camp were the prostitutes. They lived in a city, and all together.

The first few months she and the girls of Saint Augusta's had lived here, they'd huddled together. Not all of the other girls had been fond of her, bully that she'd been, but she became their protector. Gradually, as each of them had found their places, they'd spread out, lost sight of each other. Fia made herself useful elsewhere. She sewed, she repaired leather armor. She'd learned to recognize sick cattle. She'd even guarded hostages. She'd held her knife to the chin of a captive farmhand who thought he could knock her down and run.

A handful of the others from Saint Augusta's and Saint Niccoluccio's had bought themselves free, too. They hadn't stayed. Others had slipped into the wilderness.

They weren't kids any more. Fia had shepherded them through their worst times, but let them go without saying goodbye.

As she settled back into her shelter, one of the crossbowmen, a North African who spoke with a southern Italian accent, tried to negotiate her down from her three-*grosso* fee for repairing torn leather. His voice had a desperate edge. So many of the rank and file were in debt to lenders within and without the company.

"Three *grosso*," she insisted.

"Two." He tried to make it sound like an order. Like he was her superior.

"Four," she said.

He shifted, caught off guard. She held him in her gaze. He was too fresh a recruit to know her business reputation.

After an invitation to consider his alternatives, he paid four.

She spent most of the night jabbing needles through

stiffened leather, cursing God's blood under her breath. She was good at what she did. She always had been. But that didn't make the work any easier. The leather had been boiled to resist puncture. Her catgut thread cut into her fingers, ripped her nails.

The sky was clear. She had plenty of light to work by. The new comet shimmered overhead.

She was not inured to discomfort, not really. But she could tolerate it. She had learned from watching the soldiers. She fought each day like a battle.

Occasionally, she was visited by the voice from deep inside herself, the voice she had once mistaken for Pandolfo's.

Fight, it told her. *The only way you'll survive is by fighting.*

She fought. Everything she could turn to a contest became one. Working. Bartering. Marching. She competed with herself if no one else was at hand.

There was no solidarity among the camp followers. Half of them shunned the others. But, like the soldiers, they were shared their suffering. Those of them who weren't slaves could have dropped away at any moment. They chose not to. Everything outside was worse. The company, and others like it, made wastelands of the lands they traveled through. They would find no quarter if they tried to stay.

There was misery enough here, but there was wealth, too. At Saint Augusta's, Fia never would have been in a position to own a work animal, even a mule. Any animal would have quickly become the convent's. She had become keenly aware of how much she had been a servant, a slave, even before the easterners.

They were not so much barbarians as she'd been told. Pandolfo told worse stories about Italian soldiers. These men were irreligious, true. These days, everyone was. Church orthodoxy did not explain the things people wanted explained. After the new comet appeared in the sky, the church had preached an apocalypse that had never come. Failing to provide answers, it had left the way open for others to fill that need.

Fia had given up looking to the church for answers about the Great Mortality. The mothers of Saint Augusta had had none. The Great Mortality had seeped through Italy, France, and Germany, like blood through a body. It followed the veins of commerce, along trade roads and aboard plague ships. Until suddenly it had stopped.

All at once, as if by magic.

No more buboes. No more coughing death.

It had just ended. The pestilence hadn't touched England. Much of Iberia had escaped. Scandinavia was totally unaffected. And everywhere there were rural areas far off trade routes who never felt anything.

The people of Italy were no stranger to disease. Pestilence came in waves. It always recurred months or years afterward. But not this pestilence. It had despoiled their country once, and never again.

The end of the pestilence had coincided with the arrival of the new comet.

It crossed the sky in a regular schedule, every three years. It shone overhead now. She studied the comet. Her canvas shelter protected her from rain but not wind or dew, and so she was often too cold to sleep. The comet shone bright, almost as intense as the moon. Holding her hand up cast a thin shadow underneath it.

The countries that escaped the pestilence had been left with their strength undiminished. Those struck had lost half their people or more. Antonov and his company were not the first adventurers to travel south, to take advantage of the depopulated lands.

There was something going on beyond what the men of the cloth and their philosophers imagined. Fia was hardly the first person to think so. All the doomsayers, crackpots, and other odd people of the world had their own ideas about the comet's meaning. The first few times the comet appeared, cities had burned so that one idea or the other might hold sway.

The comet remained silent.

The night's ill winds turned to frost in her throat. They stifled her breath. Other people had their own beliefs and rationalizations about the comet, but they were wrong. There was no answer. She felt this as keenly as, two years ago, she'd felt the mercenary's blade slice her.

The only message was the fact of its presence. *Something* was here.

Sometimes she was visited by knowledge. And that voice. Her own, or an echo. Like a memory of something she had yet to say.

The church had proclaimed the comet a divine reordering of the world. Fia didn't doubt that that was true. But the papacy's words weighed a little less than they once had. It was based in Avignon, and Avignon had been mauled by the pestilence no less than anyone else. The papacy's French patrons and defenders had suffered too. France stood on the precipice of its destruction.

The English, who had escaped the pestilence, marched on Paris. English soldiers and adventurers raided the countryside around Avignon. The papacy had saved itself only by bribing them, paying exorbitant costs to "hire" them. It had sent the mercenaries into Italy, ostensibly to claim old papal lands, but mostly to be rid of them.

While English mercenaries streamed into Italy over the Alps in the northwest, Albanians, Croatians, Serbians, and other easterners from as far as Russia crossed them in the northeast. They poured into an already-boiling mix of Italian *condottieri*, the mercenaries who had ravaged the Italian landscape for generations.

The newcomers had taken after Italian *condottieri* readily enough. They switched sides on the eve of battle, or broke contracts the day of their swearing. *Condottieri* contracts were just another style of plunder. In the two years Fia had traveled with Antonov's Company, Antonov had traded employers three times. He'd burned the countryside around Verona, the city whose money had brought him to Italy to begin with.

She'd lost track of where the company was now. Somewhere in the hot and dry southeast. The Apennines crinkled the horizon. Ravenna was near. Every day of marching in this weather was a repetition of the same old sufferings.

The week she'd bought her freedom, her left shoe, carried with her all the way from Saint Augusta, fell apart. She'd repaired it as well as she could, but the sole finally flaked to nothing. It had taken her three weeks to earn a replacement, enough time for the bloody callouses on her heel to become leather-thick. Now her right shoe threatened to do the same. She didn't have the coin to replace it without selling her mule.

Other than the handful of the remaining orphans she'd come with, she had no friends among the camp followers. But that didn't mean she was isolated. The march gave her plenty of opportunity to eavesdrop. There was a raid planned for the night the new star reached its zenith.

Everyone in Italy reworked their prophecies around the comet's passage. Everyone said they knew what the comet portended, and the mercenaries were no exception.

Fortune. Plunder. Relief. Escape.

Money for a shoe.

The next morning, she went straight to Captain Antonov's pavilion.

The pavilion was the largest shelter the company carried with them. It was as much a repository of stolen furniture and trophies as living space. Its canvas walls were double-layered. At night, Antonov's Russian bodyguards slept in the folds. It was an estate away from the estate. Antonov owned no land. When it came time to put down roots for winter quarters, he had little trouble appropriating country manors. Otherwise, he lived here.

Fia brushed through the flap, and stopped to allow her eyes to adjust. Men melted out of the shadow. Her heart jolted. She had not expected so many to be here. Plenty of officers, and more. Rich-looking men in civilian clothes. Accountants. Antonov's lawyer. A scribe. Some of the men were caught in their own private conversations, but others looked at her. Antonov's mastiff and greyhound didn't look up. They were accustomed to her.

Leading a free company was often like leading a nation, but, still, his subordinates weren't always all in attendance. As Antonov's favored servant, Fia had the right to enter his pavilion, but not the privilege. She dropped her basket of iron-pressed tunics on an oak table.

Captain Temur Antonov was a lean man. For as long as Fia had known him, he had been getting leaner. It had not done his features any favors. His beard could not hide the concave arc of his cheeks. The pockets under his eyes could hold coins. But his gauntness was partly illusory. He had the voice of a young man. His eyes, in the dark, were querulous.

She said, "You're planning a raid to coincide with the comet reaching its zenith." Not a question. An accusation.

He didn't bother to hide it, though the company was in its allies' land. "The Ravennese promised food and fodder at fair market prices. It was part of our terms of safe passage through this land. The people of the countryside have not provided it. Those in the town ahead hissed at my messengers. And Ravenna is always in arrears of payments."

She would not have disputed his cause even if he'd had none. "I want to fight with you."

Those among the corporals who were still watching snorted, stopped paying attention. She'd said this too many times for it to be a joke any more.

"Do you hear that?" Antonov asked. "The sound of no one laughing."

"I'm tired of living on scraps and laundry. I can take my share."

"Everyone here – except me, for now – thinks you've taken more than yours already," he said, and turned back to his corporals.

36

Fight, her inner voice said.

She asked, "Who's paying you to go to war?"

He looked back to her. They both knew the only answer he could give. The company was once again in the service of the lord of Padua, who was anxious to acquire new feudatories amid the chaos. But that wasn't the question she'd asked. Fighting for Padua was a battle. The war was the company's campaign in Italy.

There was a difference between an open secret and an undiscussed secret. It was an *undiscussed* secret that Antonov hadn't come all this way from Russia at the behest of Verona, or any Italian city. Fia had not needed to ask. She had only read the silences.

An extraordinary tide of eastern mercenaries had washed into Italy of late, flush with silver and gold. Someone was paying them to come here. The lucre of the raids convinced them to stay.

Fia hadn't asked the question expecting an answer. She'd asked it to let him know that she could. She usually used a softer touch. He was an officer and a man. Both halves enjoyed preening.

He asked, "Why do I let you get away with this?"

"Come on. What made you come all the way to Italy?"

He said, "I think you understand. I could not live in the country where I was born."

Antonov's history was the other kind of secret, the open kind. She'd heard talk of it easily enough. His family had been lords in their own lands. They'd made the poor choice of backing their feudal masters over foreign invaders. Most of the men of his grandfather's generation were dead. Somehow, one of their daughters had secreted away some of the family's wealth, but she hadn't been able to hold it. Not even naming her son after one of the horde's leaders – a misguided effort if ever Fia had heard of one – would persuade the invaders to let the family keep it. So Antonov had set out for the chaotic West to make a name as an adventurer.

Fia had her doubts. After leaving Russia, Antonov had not wandered. He headed straight for Italy. He'd arrived full of cash and free from concern for family left behind. But there was probably enough truth in the story to use.

She said, "You went to war because you needed to liberate yourself. Elevate yourself." She tried to keep her voice as steady as a bowman's grip. "I need to fight for the same reason."

"You can leave any time you like. You're no slave."

One of his corporals suggested, "Pack your little tent and start walking."

She turned, and asked, "Could *you* do that?"

At once, she regretted it. The only reason these men hadn't ejected her was Antonov's long tolerance. For men like them, answering a provocation was the same as picking a fight.

Antonov said, "Women are a liability on the battlefield. You've seen yourself the violations that women suffer when they end up on one."

"The men, too," she said, turning back. Hers was a position in which she could safely speak the unchivalric truths that soldiers rarely spoke of around a campfire.

Antonov stepped around her, as if she were not there. He faced the other men. It was his way of letting her know that his pronouncement was final.

She told him, "Going to war is a holy act."

His corporals made a show of no longer listening. They talked about their plans as though they had not heard her.

Rage built under her throat, black and tasting like bile. She listened as long as she needed to before departing.

That was the first time she had tried talking to him about the holiness of war in front of his corporals. He had not taken the bait. Four nights ago, they'd been in his pavilion with only his accountant, who was quietly tallying the proceeds of a captured river barge. He'd been more receptive. He had stopped talking, paid attention.

"War breaks you," she said. "It tears your skin, breaks your bones, bleeds you out. You see such awful things as you never thought could exist. If you live through it, you've become a different person. You're reborn."

You will be reborn. Her inner voice often told her the same. It was telling her again, now, sliding words onto the tip of her tongue. Antonov stood, his fingers wrapped around his chin, watching his fire.

She said, "War forces you to see men as they really are. It breaks the walls that they make around themselves. You see the wall you build around yourself. When you break it, you remake yourself."

He was no longer listening to humor her. She was stoking his ego by telling him these things, she knew. Deliberately so. She believed them regardless. She did not know which words were hers and which had come from her inner voice, but they weren't lies.

"Soldiering makes you privileged," she said. "A special kind of man with a special kind of understanding of the world. You know what makes men function."

Antonov had spent his life in Russia destitute. In spite of the power he'd accrued, he'd spent his years here as an alien, a barbarian. He needed someone to recast his experiences as much as Fia needed his support.

"I don't need to be holy," Antonov said. "A man has to be martyred before he's made a saint."

"Every day you spend as a soldier, you already march through Hell."

Antonov had snorted, but did not laugh.

Now she strode past the barricades, back to her shabby quarters. Hers was the only shelter still standing. It was time to pack up, to move. The soldiers had already told the prostitutes and laborers willing to serve as nurses to be ready for wounded men.

Fia carried her most valuable possessions on her back: her coins and the North African crossbowmen's yet-to-be-finished armor. She packed the remainder with a speed and fury that astonished even her. She was the last to begin to pack, but the first to march. She kicked her mule into moving.

She had been at war all her life, long before Antonov's Company. Every time she'd fought, the fighting had killed her. Dying and surviving, she was perpetually reborn.

A martyr before a saint.

Before long, she saw no riders, only spare horses led by pages. The vanguard had pulled ahead. She found another copse of trees, and led her mule to it. There, she hid.

The crossbowmen's leather armor barely fit her, but her stitching was finished enough to hold. She pulled a wide-brimmed infantry helm from her mule's pack. She had taken the helm from a dead Orvientian skirmisher, kept it for herself. The kettle shape was meant to deflect blows from cavalry, but would also hide her face if she looked down.

She had no weapons like the soldiers', only a nicked six-inch dagger she'd bought for her own defense. The company's infantry carried crossbows or swords. She hoped to scavenge from the dead.

She tied her mule to the tree. For the first time since she'd set on this course, it occurred to her that she might not be back. No one would know where to come to find it. The still air felt hot as her breath, made her dizzy. Good weather for the rage that had never stopped burning. She tried to suppress it.

You will be reborn.

She already had been.

Rage by itself was not enough. This was an opportunity. She had to remember that.

She marched to join the rest of the company.

The company's target was a subject town of Ravenna, just large enough to have its own walls. Fia paused on a stumpy hillside, looking down. She didn't even know its name. The town sat on a crossroads of trade routes. The bulk of its buildings conformed to the road. It made a cross in the middle of drought-browned grassland.

Though the locals could not have had advance warning of the raid, they had assembled a defense just on word of the company's passage. Perhaps they'd thought they would be putting on a show, a dog baring its teeth. They had not expected the company to announce its arrival with a cavalry charge.

By the time Fia reached the town, the gates had been jarred open. Smoke poured from the nearest buildings. Flames curled over the top of the walls.

Fia struggled to pick up her pace. She'd marched a long way just to get here. The hot walk under the burden of her stolen armor had sapped her. The smell of smoke quickened her breath, renewed her energy.

A fracas erupted by the gates. A dozen locals had chosen that moment to make a breakout. She had no idea what they were trying to do. A counterattack seemed suicidal. Maybe they were just trying to run. Some were armed. Most were not.

Crossbows snapped. An errant bolt whistled overhead. More bolts found their marks. Antonov's soldiers emerged just behind the runners. Within seconds, half of the runners were down. Soldiers ran through the gates, singing and howling.

Fia ran to one of the fallen men. He was younger than her, beardless, pinned by the weight of his too-large leather armor. A crossbow bolt had destroyed his nose, ripped loose his eye. He fought to sit and breathe. He still held his sword.

She did not hesitate. She ripped his blade from his hand and ran it through his neck.

Then she paused. Her hand shook, but not much. It had been easy – as easy to think as to do. Only in hindsight did the task seem remarkable.

Her breath burned. Her pulse beat against her ears.

She was not the only one to have paused. Not far away, a company man clad in mail looted the dead too.

Abruptly, he crashed to his side. His victim had only been

playing dead, and had swept the soldier's feet out from under him.

The stranger rolled and stood, sword in grip.

Fia charged. The stranger saw her in time. He raised his sword to block hers. He caught the edge of her blade, but he didn't have the strength to blunt her momentum. Both of their weapons crashed hard into his shoulder. He staggered.

He slammed his foot on hers. She grunted, but didn't otherwise react. He brought his knee between her legs, to the same result. She kept her weight on his weapon, pressing him backward. He refused to let go of his sword. So long as he kept trying to force her off, she didn't just have his sword pinned, but his hands as well.

That was all the opportunity the other company man needed. He levered himself to a seat. Fia didn't see his blade slide into the stranger's back, but heard a crack of splitting bone.

At once, the stranger's legs folded. Fia stepped back out of his way as he fell.

The company soldier was dressed in mail, his neck hidden by an aventail. Armor like that marked him as wealthy. She caught a glimpse of his face under the basinet's open visor. One of Antonov's corporals.

He struggled to rise. She lent him a hand, taking care to look down, keep the metal brim between her eyes and him. She wasn't sure he'd seen her. She moved ahead before he could.

The town's gates had been jarred wide enough to admit horses. She stepped between them. The heat of the fires burned her eyes. Two soldiers ran out of a battered home, smoke pouring after them. The fires delineated the streets that had been looted from those that hadn't. When the company was done looting, they started the fires.

Some soldiers had herded the old women and men and children into a pocket between houses and the wall. They cowered against the heat of the spreading fires. Hostages and ransoms to sort through. Revulsion tickled the back of Fia's throat, a taint of the memory of leaving Saint Augusta's.

Only two bodies lay on the ground, both men. Blood blackened the earth underneath one of them, but the other had no visible mark. She paused by the latter, unsure he, too, wasn't baiting her.

Then she practiced the motion of stabbing. Adrenaline fired her muscles. It made her act before she knew what or why. The fact of what she'd done was just reaching her. The pain, too. She had started to walk with a hobble. When the soldier had stomped on her foot, he'd left a nasty developing bruise, maybe worse.

When she looked back, she saw the rest of the bodies. Most of the defenders, such as there were, had died by the walls and gates. A laugh choked her. When she'd entered the gates, she had stepped beside one without realizing. Some were mangled by trampling, others had wide, gaping wounds carved by blades or pierced by lances.

She understood now what had made this raid so significant that Antonov would time it with the comet's zenith. Even in an age of brutality, news of this would shock people.

It was all a part of the message. Good business needed a firm footing. The next time Antonov's Company passed through this region, its lords would think carefully about the terms of their contract, about payments in arrears and terms unfulfilled.

She stepped across a ditch at an awkward angle. Pain spiked up her bad foot. A shadow beside her shifted.

Instinct seized her. She side-stepped and ducked. She'd been just in time. The enemy's sword slammed off her helmet, deflected by the brim. Her vision flashed.

She lashed her good foot backward. Her heel landed in someone's mail-protected stomach. Another wealthy man. An iron glove glanced off her armored shoulder, cracked into her cheek.

Left elbow, her inner voice said.

She drove her left elbow backward, then up, into a neck.

Another spear of pain jabbed her ankle. She tumbled, taking an awkward step. She pivoted, drove herself shoulder-first into her assailant.

The blow was just as hard on her as on him. Her breath stole away. He shoved her, hard. She stumbled away. Falling would have been the end of her. She kept her feet, and, before he could recover enough of himself to make another move, leapt into him, tackling.

She didn't know what happened to her sword. The next time she was conscious of holding any weapon, it was her dagger. She crashed atop him, and crawled over him.

She straddled his armored chest. He struggled, grabbed her by the side of her chest, and tried to push her off. He was too late. She flipped up the birdlike beak of his visor, and sank her knife under his chin.

She rolled off. She was not wearing armor quite so heavy as his, but somehow still found it difficult to move. She could not breathe. Big red blotches, like afterimages of flame, rolled around her.

She did not faint, did not lose consciousness, but she did not come back to herself for some time. When she found her way back to awareness, she was back in the company's war camp… in the stockade.

She sat heavily by the wall of sharpened stakes, opposite the other captives, a pair of drunkards. She felt along her cheek, and the throbbing purple bruise she couldn't see but knew was there. The pain hadn't yet struck her, only registered the fact that it was coming.

The company's guards took her to Antonov that evening, as the sky turned orange. Her escorts pulled her to his open air "court" in front of the pavilion. She arrived as the two drunkards were hauled off to their whippings.

One of Antonov's corporals, acting as prosecutor, read the charges. The most serious was not running to war, but the theft of the crossbowman's armor. But there was a litany of others: endangering men and officers, theft of another man's rightful wartime booty, conduct unbecoming a guest of the company.

The corporal was one of the same men who, earlier that day, had ignored her in Antonov's pavilion. Fia blew air through her lips. "'Rightful wartime booty,'" she said. She hadn't taken anything other than the sword. She didn't even know where it was. Someone had taken the opportunity to accuse her of stealing something she would be indebted to return.

To answer the first charge, she unbuckled her armor and let it slide to the grass. Her stitching was intact. She had not even gotten blood on it.

A handful of other soldiers and corporals had gathered, but they were only an audience. All matters of justice in his company, down to life and death, rested with the captain. Antonov was grave as he listened.

Antonov asked the corporal, "I think any reasonable verbal contract for the repair of the armor would leave her in full custody of it until the job was finished, don't you?"

The corporal's mustache twitched. He did not dare answer the question as he wanted. "I see. For the other charges?"

"Dismissed. She saved an officer. By that officer's account, she earned anything she took."

A deep and dangerous moment of silence followed. The other men looked to each other through the gathering darkness, anxious for each other's thoughts. Fia kept her gaze focused on Antonov.

The corporal said, "As the Captain wishes."

Antonov announced, "There will be a conference tonight. Outside my pavilion. Mandatory attendance for all officers and contracted men-at-arms. Other men invited to attend as able."

As their small audience dispersed, Fia didn't move. Antonov made as if to depart, but stopped. Fia tilted her head, the question unspoken.

He prodded her shoulder. "I'm not going to be speaking to them. *You* are."

She had not realized, until he'd touched her, that she must have torn a muscle there. All her pains were catching up with her. It took all her effort not to hiss.

Antonov said, "They'll never accept you as a fighter unless you tell them what you told me, about the art of soldiering. They probably won't then, either. But it's one of the reasons I'm allowing you this chance."

She swallowed. "The other reasons?"

"The bruise on your cheek. The blood on your sleeve."

She looked down. The fighting seemed like a dream from which she was now awakening. The cloth on her tunic was so dark and sticky that it had matted to her wrist. It had taken Antonov pointing it out for her to notice. She did not know where the bruise on her cheek had come from.

She did not take the time to change before that night's meeting. Her body remained at a remove. She had twisted her right ankle stepping in a ditch after the fight. Of all the stupid reasons to be limping, she'd found one of the stupider. But the pain wasn't so bad. She felt it only distantly, when she moved her shoulder, or stepped on her right foot. She was still lost in a haze of adrenaline, ready for battle. Or flight. It was not too late to get away.

The decisions she'd made had become mysterious to her, lost in a red haze of adrenaline. The battle, she realized, hadn't ended. She was still fighting it.

Antonov's pages stoked a vast bonfire. Fia paced in front of it, hobbled by her ankle. The pain would catch up with her. Already she felt it crawling up the back of her skull.

Fia was accustomed to seeing these fires only from a distance. They were lit only for company business, such as divvying plunder. She stared into it, willing the words to take shape. They wouldn't come. When she looked away from the fire, her night vision was so far gone that all she saw was a horizon of shifting shadows.

There was some part of the old Fia that had held on through today. Not just Fia the laborer, Fia the slave, or Fia of Saint Augusta's. It was the Fia from before she'd seen her family wither black because she'd been too young to bury them. Somehow that girl had followed her all the way here, through the exhaustion and humiliation and bloodshed.

Looking at the legions of shadow-soldiers stretching as far as her imagination was willing to see them, that Fia shriveled up, went away.

"Going to war is a holy act," Fia said, just loud enough to force them to be still if they wanted to listen.

When they did, she repeated those words, and then what she'd told Antonov. "You tear your skin, you break your bones. You lose yourself again and again and again. If you don't die on the battlefield, then you leave most of your living self behind anyway.

"You live more lives in one week than other men – and women – imagine in all the time they spend breathing. They don't know what brotherhood is because *they* have never shared it with a soldier.

"It makes you privileged. Every campaign is a pilgrimage. With each mile you walk to the next battlefield, and each scrap of yourself purge away, you find something new underneath – things that other men couldn't in a thousand years of Purgatory."

Her inner voice had waited for that moment to help her find the words. No one, she was sure, had told them this before. No one had told her. She looked into the fire again until the world became a void about her.

It didn't matter if there were a thousand men in the dark, or just one. Their silence was that of a thousand men listening. If there were not a thousand men here now, then there would be, and soon.

She had not, would never, run away from this.

"You're a special class of man. You deserve better than the shit and suffering this world has given you so far."

She watched the fire for so long that her eyes burned. She turned away, back to the darkness that she knew on faith alone was populated.

"And you need to make that understood."

Part II
The Company of the Star

4

Meloku did not have many people to speak with these days, and was not often at a loss for words. But she did not have the words to explain what she was seeing, even to herself.

From the comforting distance of her projected maps, the raiders' advance cavalry looked like a plague of insects. Her satellites' sensors saw it all. Their formation was deceptively disorganized, jagged peaks and valleys. They raced towards an equally disorganized, strung-out line of men and women. The latter were civilians, racing for the safety of the monastery gates ahead.

The "peaks" of the raiders' formation reached their target at the same moment, slicing through the line. Then the order behind the cavalry's formation became clear. Their uneven formation was deliberate. They'd made wedges. The horsemen quartered the refugees into neat sections, driving them one away from each other. The riders fashioned herds. They guided their victims like animals.

Meloku sat in her cramped workspace, elbow on her desk, her chin on the heel of her palm. She felt disconcertingly safe. Information from her satellites and eavesdroppers poured through her neural demiorganics. She augmented the abstract data with images projected on her desk and walls: satellite maps of fields covered in smoke, fires, another cavalry formation whirling in wicked synchronicity.

Very little of what she saw on this plane surprised her any more. She had seen too much of it, and often closer than this. It was not the shock and rapaciousness of the raid that disconcerted her. Nor the brutality. She could see the infrared splotches of spilled blood only if she looked closely, count the bodies only if she cared to. The raiders killed mostly to make statements, anyway. They fed themselves by taking captives, not making corpses. There were more profitable sufferings than death.

No, what had surprised her was the speed. The evening before, the Company of the Star had been thirty-five kilometers away. They must have covered the distance overnight. They hadn't come alone. A wall of infantry trailed only a kilometer behind. That was a speed she found scarcely credible.

She scanned northward, focusing her satellites' sensors on a line of horse and mule-drawn carts. A train of stolen animals, goats and sheep and cattle, trailed behind. The company's booty. It, too, had moved quite a distance. It was as though she'd skipped a day forward. Only their army of camp followers was missing. A hasty satellite survey found them straggling fifteen kilometers behind.

She asked, "Dahn, what the fuck is going on?"

Dahn sat at the other side of their shared quarters and office. He hadn't moved a millimeter for three hours, but he had no trouble snapping out of his trance the instant she'd said his name. One of the many gifts of his sleek demiorganic body. He looked to her projections.

"The usual?" he suggested.

"*Not* that."

Reluctantly, as if fighting inertia his body kept him from feeling, he pushed himself out of his seat. His bare feet had fingers as long as those on his hands. They were meant for zero gravity grappling. His skin was azure-blue this month, highlighted with emerald streaks.

Years ago, Meloku had dreamed of having a body like his. He was one of the living planarship *Ways and Means'* crewmembers. She'd spent half her life trying to become like him. Out of her reach now. Meloku, *Ways and Means* and all its crew had been exiled here, to this world, and it no longer had the resources to spare to manufacture demiorganic bodies.

Jealousy still panged from time to time, but she believed – she had been convinced – she was needed as she was: fully human. *Ways and Means* needed her here, on the surface. She could fit in like none of *Ways and Means'* crewmembers could. She was to study these people.

Ways and Means would be here for the next twelve hundred years, at least. It needed people on the surface who would look *and* feel human to the natives. It hadn't brought many other unaltered humans with it. Meloku wasn't on speaking terms with the others like her.

Dahn crossed the five paces that separated them. Everything in their quarters was compact, compressed. Workspaces jammed into corners. Her bed was a retractable cubby. Her exercise equipment unfolded in a stall.

Dahn was a distinctly chilly and uncomfortable roommate. He and Meloku had worked together for nearly a year, and she still hardly knew him. He set his hand on the back of her chair. His demiorganic eyes were sensitive enough that he must have read the images from across the room. Hell, he could have read them off the reflections of her eyes. He'd come over here to humor her.

He asked, "The army's baggage train?"

"Look at it."

Fifty-two carts and wagons trailed after the Company of the Star, all guarded. It was a treasure convoy to rival a king's. The *condottieri*, and the Company of the Star in particular, numbered among the wealthiest people in Italy.

They had no base. They carried all they owned with them. They more they acquired, the more of a problem it became. On her satellite views, the carts thronged with soldiers, antlike in their hundreds.

Dahn asked, irritably, "What of it?"

She said, "There weren't half as many treasure carts the day before. Or as many men."

His gaze went briefly dull as he flicked through data. He

looked back at her. "Yes, there were."

She ordered her neural demiorganics to lace with their quarters' NAI, and then to compile her collected observations of the past week. She collected a data package, readied it to send to Dahn.

She stopped when she got a glimpse of it.

He was right. The treasure train *hadn't* changed. According to the data she'd just retrieved. Not according to her memory, though. She'd been sure, absolutely positive, it had been smaller.

Dahn had no body hair, but he could still arch his brow. He said, "You've been shut inside with me for three days. Watching these things affects you more than you realize."

"I know my limits. I'll be getting out for some exercise soon enough." On the maps, seen through satellites, these events looked so small, distant. Her memory was imperfect, human, fallible. But…

Dahn said, "Most humans who think they know their limits are lying to themselves."

Meloku blew air through her lips, bit back her answer. She turned back to her desk.

He was right. It wasn't just being shut inside that was getting to her. The remove at which she watched events like this mattered less and less. She'd been in the field too often to know what the shapes and symbols were hiding. None of what she was seeing seemed abstract.

Things had been very different when she'd first come to this plane. She had never felt alone or misunderstood. Her masters in the old Unity had gifted her with an AI companion that, unimaginatively, she'd named Companion. It had ridden her thoughts, given her direction.

But Companion had died during the chaos and madness that had led to *Ways and Means'* exile here. Even if it had been around, it would have failed to suit her needs for some time now. *Ways and Means* knew that. That was why it had never given her another.

At least Companion would have listened to her.

She should not have accepted this assignment. She was not suited for it. She did not want to watch these people, their wars, their misery. Usually she was able to clamp down that feeling, but not always. She was not suited, in general, to live alone.

Dahn didn't count as company. He returned to his seat. Already, he had gone immobile, statuesque. Companion's presence would have been patronizing, intolerable now, sure. But, without it, her mind boiled.

Their cramped quarters didn't help. They should have had larger. At the start of this assignment, *Ways and Means* had declared that it was severely curtailing the construction it allowed on this world's surface. When Meloku had first visited this world, she'd come as a spy, embedded with a team of anthropologists. They'd lived in a compact but fully featured multiroom field base.

Not any more. No more legions of construction drones. Building a fully featured field base would have made light and noise for days. They'd gotten away with it last time because they'd built out in the middle of a rural nothing, but now *Ways and Means* was sending more of its agents everywhere, and closer to cities. The rules had changed. Even though Meloku and Dahn's home was lodged in the Alps north of Italy, far from people, those rules applied to them, too.

So she was stuck with a single-room quarters with a bitter statue for a roommate, more a hideout than a home. Projecting images on the walls, augmenting their unreality with her demiorganics, only helped to a point.

Living with another person might have made things better, but Dahn was not that person. He'd lived in his demiorganic body for centuries. He did not remember what it was like to be human.

She rested her head in her palm again. The battle, if it could be called that, hadn't waited for her to catch up.

The wall of infantry reached the road. The monastery itself

was likely to remain inviolate. After the last few decades' turmoil across Italy, it and many like it built high walls, with space inside for grazing. The monastery had been rebuilt to shelter the people of the countryside.

A cloud of infrared blobs huddled inside: people. Not as many as there should have been. Three days ago, knowing that the Company of the Star was coming, Meloku had visited and planted eavesdroppers. Their cameras gave her a closer view of a mostly empty yard, supplies stockpiled for many more people than had actually reached them.

Condottieri like the Company of the Star rarely attacked fortifications. Their mobile nature kept them from dragging along a siege train. The Company of the Star could have cracked the monastery's walls, gotten inside, even without artillery. Scaling the walls and fighting wouldn't have been worth it, though. *Condottieri* carefully balanced the costs and profits of every decision they made. This monastery wasn't worth the trouble.

A forced march to catch straggling refugees, on the other hand, would pay off a dozen times the cost. But the company had adroitly negated the fortifications by arriving long before anyone had expected them to. The refugees had been taking their time, moving slow, until the moment the cavalry had crossed their horizon.

Fortifications or not, the riders almost got the monastery all the same. The men at the gates spotted the danger just in time, slammed the portcullis just as the advance cavalry reached it. Any later and they would have had a dozen *stradiots* inside. The *stradiots* were feared Albanian light cavalry; they didn't have as much use for hostages as most *condottieri*. Their contracts typically rated their pay per head.

The rest of the cavalry had rolled the refugees into four tight masses. The riders circled, herding them. Then they closed.

At this scale, Meloku could not track the fate of individuals. She did not care to zoom in. She hoped none of the refugees were stupid enough to resist, but she'd been surprised in the past.

A second formation of loose infantry, pioneers, had wheeled around the monastery's walls, through the just-plowed fields. Another group secured the scattered houses of the monastery's lay community. Any plunder would be divvied up, and the rest burned.

All of the Company of the Star's plans revolved around what could be seized and what could be ransomed. The rest was chaff – to be destroyed as a means of spreading starvation and terror.

A deep well of anger burned in the bottom of Meloku's throat. She glanced at Dahn.

Dahn was loyal to *Ways and Means*. Not all of *Ways and Means's* crew were. They had wanted to land on this world, plant settlements, colonize their neighbors. It still sounded like a good idea to Meloku. But some crew believed it more fervently than she did. Dahn was one of those who would follow *Ways and Means* anywhere.

Ways and Means had once been able to count on the absolute fidelity of every individual aboard. The fact that it couldn't now said a great deal about how far it had fallen.

Dahn was as still as ever. No doubt he was aware that she was watching. He chose to ignore her.

Meloku was not suited for this kind of work. She never had been. Before their exile, she had only ever play-acted as an anthropologist. That was when she'd had the company of a team of real anthropologists. They'd been led by Dr Habidah Shen, a scientist of pious self-righteousness and capital-P Principles. Meloku had not had so many principles – or, rather, hers had been oriented along a different axis. Meloku's real assignment had been to infiltrate this world's power structures, evaluate their pliability, their suitability for colonization.

Now here she was, trying at the real thing, with no training other than *Ways and Means'* library and her own experience.

She had only taken this assignment because *Ways and Means* had asked. It was more than her patron. She could not have refused it.

Most of *Ways and Means'* agents were like Dahn. With effort, they could make themselves appear human. But they could not *feel* like a human, in both meanings of the word. One of the consequences of moving to a body like his was that all of his senses came at a remove. They were abstract, data. *Ways and Means* needed someone who was still human, who could step outside and blend in. Someone who might perceive and understand the world the way that the locals saw it. So it had asked Meloku to help study these people.

But she also needed emotional distance. She couldn't let herself feel sympathy, and she especially couldn't feel hate. Habidah hadn't managed to keep her distance, and it had ruined her.

In over thirty years of trying, Meloku had grown into some parts of this role, but had never managed the emotional distance. At best, she could fake it. As much as she tried to hide behind projections, abstractions, data, she couldn't manage it. She couldn't be like Dahn.

Hate and disgust were her constant companions.

When she'd last visited the monastery, her shuttle had taken her in at night. Its stealth fields gathered darkness around it, stifled the thunder of its engines. She'd landed within two hundred meters of the walls, and no one had seen her. She'd darted down the boarding ramp.

She knew the Company of the Star was coming. The company had even been here once before, eight years ago. Other *condottieri* had raided in the interim. The locals had heard, too. They thought they knew how to act.

Meloku had worn local costume, just in case she was spotted. She never was. Retinal infrared allowed her to avoid the watchers at the gates. She stole about the earthen slopes below the cloister's walls, burrowing fingernail-sized eavesdroppers in the dirt and the wadding.

She hadn't meant to develop feeling for the place. She had seen the people sleeping in their homes, the wheel-carved roads. She could not help but notice the care with which the monks maintained their vegetable gardens. She'd spotted the home of a lay family, painstakingly rebuilt after a fire. It sat astride the charred remnant of their last home's foundations. Likely that one had been burnt by *condottieri*, too.

She could not make any of it abstract.

Today, her eavesdroppers gave her from-the-ground views of the fields and houses as the company's arsonists turned them to black husks. They showed her the masses huddled inside the walls, weeping for relatives outside. The smoke of their ruined livelihoods choked their sky. Outside, the *condottieri* sat just out of crossbow range. They shouted, banged their helmets together, anything to make noise. It was mockery. The mercenaries did not need to besiege the monastery when they knew they had already won.

The anger in her chest grew hotter. With the right tools and with clearance from her higher power, she could stop this. By herself, if she had to.

But she was constrained to just watch.

A creek ran along a farm road some distance from the gates. By afternoon, the *condottieri* had dammed the creek, and dug and filled a deep and muddy pool. It was just visible to the men on the walls. The mercenaries set to work assembling a sturdy wooden frame over the water.

Several black iron cages sat at the shore. Men hooked the tops of each cage to chains, then the chains to pulleys on the frame. It was clear what would happen when they finished: the cages were to swing out over water. They could be lowered into the water, slowly, if the mercenaries desired.

She could have stopped this.

Maybe Meloku was not so different from Habidah Shen. Habidah had cared too much for these people. She had saved one of them from nonsense like this. It had wrecked her.

Habidah and her team had come to this plane to study

59

how these people coped with a black, virulent plague and its vast mortality. Meloku had studied it with them. She had not forgotten the pealing funeral bells, the leathery corpses, the quarantined houses of the dead. She'd been able to focus on her other objectives. Habidah hadn't. She had resigned, fled her problems. She was still working on this world, but unaffiliated. She studied for her own sake, selfishly. She would not have anything to do with *Ways and Means*.

Whereas Habidah's problems had stemmed from her empathy for these people, all Meloku had was her anger. It was all she'd had for a long time. She could not stifle it.

This was all so fucking stupid. A hideous, unnecessary waste. The biggest thing she had wanted, since the minute she had come to this plane, was to change this.

She took in a long breath, let it out slowly.

It was not that *Ways and Means* refused to interfere. It had done plenty of that, most notably by ending the plague. The plague bacillus that had torched this region of the globe was gone. It would never recur again.

Every three years, *Ways and Means* cruised across the sky. Its regular appearances in the sky had shaken the religious epicenters of this plane.

The Company of the Star had taken their name from it. Before the company had just been named after its captain, a Russian adventurer. Temur Antonov.

The Company of the Star was unique among mercenary societies in that it was also the epicenter of a religious movement. It was headlined by a woman soldier. She claimed she spoke with a long-dead warrior, an exemplar figure called Saint Renatus. She had founded a cult for soldiers.

Meloku had not yet researched the cult to her satisfaction. She was only one person. Its story was everywhere, though. Even *condottieri* that had never fought beside the Company of the Star still venerated Saint Renatus. The cult was more dry brush thrown onto the inferno of Italy.

Fiametta of Treviso had started her career with the

company as a captive, and then a slave. It was better than most women in her position could have done. Fiametta of Treviso was probably what on other planes would be called schizophrenic. Here, she made sense of the voices she heard as best as she was able. She had turned them to her advantage. She made others believe them too.

Now she used all the authority and power she'd won to inflict the same misery on others.

Meloku's eavesdroppers showed her the first batch of captives being led to the company's cages. Six of the ten were women. One was a boy. They would have been chosen because each of them was important, in some way, to those inside the monastery. Relatives. Spouses. Children.

The soldiers grabbed the chains, hoisted the cages. The cages swung over the water in a shaky parabola. The artificial pond was just deep enough to immerse them from top to bottom. The cages swung there, precarious. Men on the monastery's walls watched.

Meloku cut the view.

She drummed her fingers along her desk. The Company of the Star was a problem. She should been paying far more attention before now. She glared at the satellite image of those fifty-two treasure carts. That should have been smaller. How much else had she missed, looking away? All she knew of the company and its cult was abstract, no more real to her than Dahn's senses.

The Cult of Saint Renatus had been declared heretical. The church recognized a Saint Renatus, an entirely different one a thousand years older. But the church's authority had waned since its disastrous first response to the false comet. Never preach apocalypse, Meloku thought, unless you were sure you or your successors weren't going to be around when it failed to happen.

The Cult of Saint Renatus was only one of a number of dissident movements that had sprung up in the face of the church's weakness. It had been more successful than most, second only to the riotous Flagellants of Germany. It slotted neatly into folk Christianity. All it asked was for believers to venerate just one more saint.

She had plenty of data, all abstract, compiled from agents pursuing monastic libraries and clerical letters. What seemed odd to her now that she was examining their files, though, was that someone with a scholarly education had plainly helped shape it. Saint Renatus, both the figure and his precepts, called back to Mithraism, a religion a thousand years gone from Italy. Mithraism was not widely known here any more, and yet the parallels could not have been an accident.

Like Mithraism, the Cult of Saint Renatus was most popular among soldiers. Mithraism had been born among soldiers of the Roman Empire, shared among their camps for centuries before the jealous Christian God had outshone it. Also like Mithraism, the cult placed soldiers in a privileged, holy, position. Soldiers who venerated Saint Renatus treated themselves as a kind of priesthood. Saint Renatus was not at all popular in the countryside or the cities.

Mithras had emerged from a rock. Saint Renatus came from the earth: he had been born in a cave, heralded by miracles. He'd become a soldier the moment he stepped outside. He had been reborn in his first battle. He had worked miracles throughout his life and, like Mithras, slain a bull the size of a galley.

The cult had cobbled together more contemporary influences, too. Saint Renatus had been martyred on Crusade in the Holy Lands. He had fought on for two days after being decapitated, carrying his head in the crook of his arm.

Fiametta of Treviso cast herself as a warrior-prophetess in the mold of Jeanne d'Arc of France. They were both women from humble backgrounds, made soldiers. Meloku doubted a peasant slave would have been able to cobble so many influences together.

She should have been paying more attention. That had not been her only mistake. She could not stop thinking of the treasure train. She did not usually make such enormous mistakes.

The train strayed close enough to her eavesdroppers for them to pulse scan. The covered carts concealed gold and silver, but also other metallic signatures: brass and iron in the shapes of bells, weapons, farming tools. The scans found shadows of large shapes: tables and cabinets, piles of wool and linen.

That didn't match what she remembered, either. Not only were there more wagons than there should have been, but they held more than she remembered. The company must have had twice, if not three times, as much treasure as she'd estimated. If she'd known the Company of the Star had so much buying power, so much war booty, she would have turned her attention to them long before now.

She glanced to her other projections. There was so much happening. Cages swinging over water. Dark smoke over black wheat fields. Riders departing the monastery to negotiate for the hostages' lives.

For her own peace of mind, she killed those images too.

She turned her attention to satellite records, reviewing the past few months' logs, trying to figure out how she might have given her such a mistaken impression about the Company of the Star's size. She found no clues. Her satellites had tracked the growth and movement of the company and its treasure train faithfully. At no point while she'd been watching had the train had fewer than forty-five carriages.

On a whim, she double-checked those records against her neural demiorganics' memories. Her demiorganics did not store a complete backup of her own memory, but kept images and other data for later reference.

According to them, last week at this time, she'd been looking at a treasure train of twenty-six wagons.

She wouldn't have trusted the memory if it hadn't come from her demiorganics. But there the image was, complete and date-tagged.

Carefully, she asked the base's NAI to review its satellite records from the same date. The image that returned contained forty-eight carriages. The company had a thousand more men than her demiorganics insisted she remembered.

Coolly, she closed her connection to the base NAI.

Last week at this time, she'd been in this same seat, reviewing data from the same satellites. The images were each too specific to be glitches. Her equipment hadn't failed her.

There was something here someone didn't want her to notice. Something of interest to anyone at least powerful enough to do this.

Her list of suspects was already short. The hideaway's NAI, its neutered artificial intelligence, kept those records. It wasn't a full-fledged AI, but it was not without defenses. It would have taken a lot of work to alter NAI's records without triggering an alarm. Even more to attack her demiorganics. She was an agent of the amalgamate *Ways and Means*; her security programs were top notch.

Of course, *Ways and Means* itself could have overridden both.

She had no illusion of privacy. She was constantly being monitored. *Ways and Means* had never confessed to that, but it didn't have to. It was just the kind of creature it was.

Whether or not it was responsible for this, it was watching her. Just by reviewing these records, she might have revealed herself.

If this was something that *Ways and Means* didn't want her to see, it was probably best that she pretend she'd never noticed. When she'd first come to this plane, when she'd still been living with Companion, she wouldn't have thought twice about that. The amalgamates were jealous of their secrets. She'd lived to serve the amalgamates.

It had been a long time since she had to think of herself that way.

When *Ways and Means* had given her this assignment, it

had asked her to be her own creature. She was.

Still – best not to notice. She resisted the urge to glance at Dahn. He was closer to *Ways and Means* than she was. If he was watching her, he would have already sensed her elevated pulse and her sweaty palms.

5

Neither the weather nor the waves had changed in the past week. Nor had Osia.

She sat feline-still, legs folded, knees at the railing.

Her body fired off a pulse scan at automated intervals, unconsciously – deep demiorganic subroutines monitoring for deviations from the weather forecast. There was never anything. The wind was never strong enough to rock the deck more than minutely. The warm mist from the sallow waves touched her knees, coming like clockwork.

At night the steady light of the false comet, cold as frost, gleamed off her brow and flat eyes. It had risen far enough above the horizon that its light had turned from ocher to pale.

Her crew had grown quietly desperate in their attempts to attract her attention. Osia did not notice, at least not in the way they wanted her to. Her background processes logged the noise for later review.

One of them, Braeloris, sat by her side. Braeloris fancied herself a counselor, a talker. "You can't keep grappling with yourself like this. I don't know what you're doing, looking *at* what you've lost or looking away, but you have to know it's not working. You've been doing it for so long."

Osia did not answer. The sun shone into her unblinking eyes.

Eventually Braeloris went away.

Osia's consciousness was malleable. She could hear without hearing, just as she saw the sun without seeing it. Her crew were no more human than she, but they had been made to behave human. They had never gotten accustomed to her fugues. She did not answer any of them, did not dignify their efforts by even thinking of them.

At last, she blinked.

Blinking was one of the few purely human reactions her demiorganic body allowed her. As she woke, a wave of displacement, digitized dizziness, overcame her. She reached up, placed her hand on the rail.

Her clocks did not align. More time had passed than should have. She tried to recall what she had meditated upon, but found a void. Her only memories were those her subroutines had stored for her, waiting for her to review.

Her consciousness *was* malleable in ways that, no matter how many years she had been in this body, still disconcerted her. She had gone into the fugue to decompress. She remembered that much. Seeing the comet again had left her unsettled. Even now, its tenth passage across the skies since it had arrived, she still reacted poorly. She had gone into the fugue to stifle her anxiety and put her thoughts back together.

And then—

A black expanse, a wide and gulf-like sensation of time passing, bridged the moment she had gone into the fugue and the moment she had left.

The memories were gone. *She* must have erased them. A rapid diagnostic confirmed that she had.

Only two things crossed that expanse. The first was a voice, an echo of her own that she didn't remember speaking: *Don't bother searching for the memories. You're better off forgetting.*

The second was a feeling. No matter how cleanly she might have tried to cut her memories, she was a creature of continuity. She could not be cut entirely short. Like a human, she could wake from a dream and forget it all, but still be left with an imprint, an outline of its shape. It was static lingering in the background radiation of her mind.

The feeling was of drowning. Of being caught under a landslide. A smothering, choking pressure in her throat, in her head.

The false comet burned overhead. She stood, and looked. It had passed its zenith while she was in her fugue. It crested northward. Its engine exhaust covered a fifteen-degree arc of the sky, impossible to miss.

This was its tenth appearance. Thirty years since its first. She had thought she would be used to it by now.

The loneliness did not go away as she turned to her crew. Braeloris pretended to be doing something else. Two of the others answered her stare. Coral. Ira.

Osia told them, "Patrol junk coming over the horizon." The signal, bouncing back from her pulse scan, had brought her from the fugue.

Her constructs hadn't seen it yet. Her sensors were better than theirs. She could bounce a pulse scan off the atmosphere, but the sensor rig concealed in their ship's hold was limited to penetrating a small arc of seawater below the horizon.

Coral asked, "Which direction will get us around it?" Coral had already guessed Osia would want to steer around.

Osia said, "I want to meet it."

Her crew looked to each other. Ira said what they were all thinking: "It's been years since you let a patrol catch sight of us."

"They're more likely to give us someone to talk to."

Osia's memories of everything that had happened in her fugue were still catching up to her. She glared at Braeloris. Braeloris looked away.

She could not explain why she was making this decision. Not to her satisfaction. Maybe, before that other Osia had destroyed those memories and ended herself, she had left a subconscious parting wish.

It didn't matter. She didn't need to explain it to them. She'd been out here too many years to really remember how to hold herself to account.

Osia said, "They'll be able to see us late afternoon. You have seven hours to make us ready."

• • •

68

Osia should not have felt restless. Her crystal gel muscles could hold position for years without losing capacity. And yet the fugue had left her feeling that she had energy to burn.

Her boat was an imitation Chinese junk, triple-masted. She'd built it herself, piece by piece, over the course of two lonely months before her crew had been delivered to her. The engine had come with them. Both engine and constructs were parting gifts from *Ways and Means*. It had sent her a few other trinkets and an assignment to keep her busy. Or out of trouble.

The boat's tallow-colored sails stood broad and square. They'd torn a little at the edges. The wood along the masts and the railings was old and splinter-jagged. More stagecraft and theatrics. Occasionally, on those rare occasions when Osia chose, they came into contact with the locals. Her boat needed to seem unremarkable, old, undesirable.

Her crew had a great deal of work to make ready for the meeting. Counting her, her boat held six people. Less than a skeleton crew for a ship its size. No native would ever believe the ship could be crewed by so few. It had empty rows of oars, just for show.

Osia helped her crew haul the oarsmen dummies to the deck, set them in place. These constructs were not a tenth as functional as her crew, and would not speak when spoken to. However, they still needed to animate and *appear* human to a human eye, a complex task that required hours of setup and orientation.

Her crew already had the brown skin tone to match the nearest locals. They needed only discard their olive swim jumpsuits and restyle their hair. Only the men could stay on deck, though. The two women, and Coral, would not be able to stay visible. The locals would have looked askance at women crewing a merchant junk. And Coral would have been beyond their experience.

Osia was too. The natives would think her an obsidian golem if she remained as she was. Her skin fluoresced and rippled iridescent as it recolored. She chose a graying skin tone, adding liver spots to simulate age and exposure. She was going to be a weathered captain, an old hand.

She couldn't do hair or facial structures. Coral helped sculpt them. Coral worked deftly, quietly, in the poor light of Osia's closet-sized cabin. In thir personality's previous life, Coral had been a diver, an adventurer. Thi was a creature of multiple talents. Like the women, thi could not remain above deck during the meeting. Thi was a third gender, a point high above the linear spectrum of male and female. Thir voice was fluted, thir chin and shoulders heavy and sharp. Thir hair grew out of the side of thir neck, to thir shoulders, in long vertical stripes.

Thi said, "We get more and more concerned when you spend so long away."

Osia said, "So? Turn that part of yourself off."

"Not in our power," thi said.

Most days, Osia was willing to follow along with her crew's illusions, for her sake if not for theirs. Her patience was short. "You were made to simulate emotions, not to have them."

"We were made to be concerned about you."

Osia arched her new eyebrow, but she could not turn without disrupting Coral's delicate work.

By the time Coral turned on the ultraviolet lamp to harden thir sculpting, thi had turned Osia almost human. She had become a middle-aged man, with false wrinkles and eye shadows. Coral glued a stubble of shaved hair to Osia's false scalp.

Osia would never feel like flesh to the touch. Her skin's polymers couldn't be changed that as easily as color. That was one of many parts of being human she had given up.

She returned to the deck. She hid her finger-length toes under boots visibly too large for a person her size. The boots would draw less attention than those toes, though. The patrol junk was close enough that she could have seen the white of its broad sails even if she'd still had human eyes.

She set her fingers on the railing. Ira stood nearby. He spun his rigging knife between his fingers. All of her crew had picked up nervous tics and bad habits at some point over the decades.

Ira didn't just have the knife twirling. He also enjoyed prodding her. "We shouldn't let you out on the deck for this long."

Osia bit the bait. She looked to him.

He nodded to the southern horizon, the comet in the sky. "You start your brooding whenever you see it, don't you?"

Like Braeloris imagined herself a counselor, Ira was, in his own mind, a teller of hard truths. And like most people who fancied themselves that, he had no idea. She had the same solution for him as for Braeloris. She turned away, ignored him until he finally left.

She was beginning to seriously rethink her relationship with her crew.

They were supposed to keep her company in exile. Not to provoke her. But Ira might have had a point. The railing still had the gouge she'd made decades ago.

Thirty years exiled to this boat. Thirty years since she'd left home. And thirty years and a handful of weeks since *Ways and Means* had arrived on this plane in the course of its own exile.

Ways and Means had been forced out of its disintegrating transplanar empire, the Unity. It and its crew had been sentenced to remain here, in solitary contemplation, for a millennium.

Ways and Means was an amalgamation of hundreds, thousands, of AIs who'd survived the chaos of the Unity's early history. There had been several others like it. Like *Ways and Means*, the other amalgamates each had their own planarships. They too had been forced into exile elsewhere.

Ways and Means had chosen this plane for a reason. It had been here before. It had had plans to colonize it before its exile. This world was still ripe for it. *Ways and Means* had not waited long to intervene on this plane. It had seeded the sky with immunizing aerospores, ending the black plague that had killed millions throughout Asia and Europe, would have killed millions more. That had only been the first step.

Its crew wanted a new home, a world from which to restart their lives after their exile. Mostly, though, they had wanted to settle this world because they could. Because it was what they had always done. They were used to it. The Unity had colonized many worlds just like this one.

They didn't see why that should change just because they were alone now. Alone among them, Osia had hesitated.

Her crime, as far as the rest of the crew were concerned, was not that she had suggested scaling back their intervention. Her crime had been in the fact that *Ways and Means* seemed to listen to her.

Osia wrapped her hand around the railing, careful to exercise tight control over her muscles, and not to leave a gouge this time.

She studied the patrol boat. A typical Yuan war junk, three-masted like hers, with eighty human-sized infrared sources on deck and underneath. Likely on patrol to protect fishing and deter smuggling. Their bright orange banners snapped with their sails. Archers, in the nest above the mainmast, held arrows ready to nock. More bowmen stood along the prow.

Osia's boat was obviously no fishing ship. They'd probably thought they'd found a floundered smuggler, an easy catch. Money in their pockets if she or her crew did anything wrong.

Osia had not protested settling this world because she *respected* these people.

Long before *Ways and Means'* exile, a team of anthropologists had come here and combed through this plane. Osia memorized their reports. The peoples of this plane were small-minded, petty – and what was more, they were unremarkable. She'd seen thousands like them, societies trapped in their myopias, insects in glue.

Living on a single world, unable to see farther than the

horizon, would do that to any person. Even to her. She was afraid that, in a thousand years of exile, she'd become just like them.

She'd seen more worlds than she'd cared to count. Her demiorganic memory was perfect, though, and kept that count for her. In her last life, Osia had served as *Ways and Means'* liaison. It was a diplomatic position, dealing with people on *Ways and Means'* behalf. Taking flak for its decisions. The amalgamates had rarely settled for fair play. She had lied, she had cheated, and manipulated. Her service had been for the good of the Unity. She had been proud of it.

So often, taking control of other worlds, the least cruel thing to do had been to lie, let people think they had a hand in making their own decisions.

It did not take long to identify the patrol junk's captain. He wore a yellow robe that reached his ankles, and mirrored armor to protect his chest. His ribbons and tassels twisted in the wind. A pulse scan found the metallurgic signature of gold and silver jewelry under his robe. Unless things had dramatically changed since her last contact, those were beyond a patrol captain's salary.

Her first encounter with these people in years, and it was already tiresome.

Her oarsmen steered astride in answer to barks from the other ship. Ramps crashed into her deck. The boarders scampered across them, swords not yet ready, but in reach. Osia stood at ease and let them by, a good citizen. Only when the boarders reported no illicit cargo – no cargo at all, really – and the proper permits affixed in the forecastle cabin, did the captain step over.

Mindful to avoid touching him, she handed him her personal license, wrapped around a string of coins. Given the size of the latter, she didn't expect she would run into much trouble if the styling of her license was out of date. He hardly looked at the string. He treated her to a thin smile. He waved his men back.

"You sailors seem in need of aid," he said.

After those and other pleasantries, he invited her to dine in his cabin. They hardly would have fit in hers. He had a bed with covers lined with flossed silk, and a wall-covering scroll of a pastoral landscape in thick, aggressive brushstrokes. He dug a surprisingly cheap bottle of rice wine from a chest underneath his bed, and poured it into two wooden cups.

Osia told him her cover story. "We sailed from Quanzhou to buy pepper in the Philippines. I told my employer that our boat needed repairs, but he didn't listen. I was a fool and went. A gust split our center sail almost in two." Her sails were yellowed and crisscrossed with stitching. Even now, Ira and the others were putting on a show of sewing.

Osia's counterpart had struck her as the kind of man who would loosen like a spigot with alcohol. She'd been right. She had been ready to dose his wine with tranquilizers to make him more suggestible, but hadn't needed to. He said, "Get your pepper back to Quanzhou as fast as you can. Our masters will be raising tariffs soon. Maybe in weeks."

The way he said *masters* made it clear what he thought of them. Barbarians. For over a century, China had been ruled by Mongol invaders.

Osia was surprised that was still the case. When she'd arrived, the barbarian dynasty, the Yuan Dynasty, had been teetering, on the verge of retreating northward.

It only took a little prodding to find that, instead, they'd solidified their rule. The captain complained about them with little provocation. "They throw money after money beyond the borders. Always conscripting, always taxing." It did not take much reading between the lines to figure that part of his bitterness likely came from overdue salaries.

Osia suggested, "Perhaps with so much attention focused on foreigners, they'll lose their grip on Han China." The captain's accent marked him as Han. Han China, South China, had been the region the Mongols had conquered last, and always the most resistant to their rule. His unimportant

74

sea patrol was likely the highest post any Han Chinese man, no matter how noble or high-testing, could hold. His career advancement not only stopped here, but it likely had some time ago.

"Perhaps," he said. Footsteps on the deck outside made him fall silent. So – afraid of eavesdroppers and Mongol sympathizers.

A strange feeling, an electric tension, trilling down Osia's back. It was a phantom, a memory of excitement. Her nerves registered no actual signals. The Unity had manipulated and colonized enough planes like this one that it had turned the art of political forecasting to a rigid science. The Unity's agents could leave a plane alone for twenty years and have a reasonable idea what would happen while they were gone.

A resurgent Mongol Yuan Dynasty, still ruling a hostile populace that had been close to ejecting it, was not right. Not given her last information. Their empire should have been splintering, falling. At the very least, it should not have been stronger.

She asked, "Who are they marching against this time? I did not hear much before I left."

"Foreigners. Always foreigners."

"Yes, but *which?*"

"Does it matter?" In the look he gave her, she caught a glimpse of the temper that must always have been strung tight under his skin.

She sipped her wine, looking down. Finally, he said, "They are having problems, too. I know the dockmaster of Hangzhou. He drinks with the brother-in-law of the governor." Osia took care to look impressed. "He has never seen the governor so worked up."

"Rebellions?" she asked.

"Religious problems," he said, darkly. "Barbarian sects. Idiocy."

"You think that will mean more conscriptions?"

"It would be bad enough if they just sent soldiers. But they

75

raise taxes. They demand silk and brocades, porcelain, silver. They draw chalk lines across old and noble Han households, and take everything on one side."

"Spending so much time at sea must give you some relief."

"Yes. But not my family. It's been so long since I left. Out here, I have nothing to do but have nightmares about how things might be. When I left, my brother was on the edge of selling our home in Hangzhou."

Osia said, "Being out of contact is not so different from being dead."

"Or living in Hell," he said, and poured himself more wine.

Osia's digestive sacs processed alcohol quickly, but couldn't get rid of the smell. When she returned to her boat after supper, her constructs noticed. They didn't hide their annoyance. It was understated, unspoken jealousy. She couldn't get drunk, but they could. She had made the mistake of allowing alcohol aboard only once.

As the patrol junk pulled its boarding ramps, Ira asked, under his breath, "Is that enough play-acting for another five years?"

She had even less patience for him now. "If I didn't need to play-act, you wouldn't be here."

That sent him stomping, muttering. She only reminded her constructs of their artificiality when she wanted peace.

She returned to the railing, watched the patrol junk unfurl its sails against the sunset. It would be making its course by the stars before it put any significant distance between them.

So would she. She craned her neck, studied the false comet. One of the many effects the comet had on this world was that it washed out the nearest stars. It complicated navigation at sea.

Dark robbed the horizon of its distinctions. The black of the ocean washed into the sky. She knew now what that feeling of electricity, of coiled tension, had been. Nervous energy, almost anxiety. Her thoughts were coiling into new shapes. Not trying to solve a puzzle, not exactly, but to find an answer other than what she'd already arrived at.

Something that had been sleeping was waking. Another fugue ending.

Coral settled by her, leaning on the railing. Unlike Ira and Braeloris, thi waited for Osia to speak.

Osia said, "I should have been paying more attention."

Coral said, "That's what we've been telling you."

"I didn't mean to you," Osia said, though she said it with more kindness than she might have.

"I didn't necessarily mean to us, either," thi said, with a smile.

Thi might have felt like thi was making a breakthrough, and maybe thi was, but it would be a long time before Osia felt like returning that smile.

Her boat had become a stone, plunging into the dark. Tonight, the black depths of the ocean opened wide.

In zero gravity, her native environment, there was no difference between resting still and falling into the void.

She looked again to the comet.

"I think it's fucking with this world again," she said.

Coral was silent for a moment. Thi did not have to ask to know she meant *Ways and Means*. "Are you sure this is something you want to care about?"

"I'm human enough that I don't choose what to care about."

"Do you think it's worth the cost of doing something about it?"

A curious question. An astute one. Coral knew how much pursuing this was going to hurt Osia.

Osia looked down. Coral followed her gaze. The water was calm enough, but for a few ripples around the lip of the prow. It made a near-perfect mirror image of the comet.

She said, "I don't know. All I want to do, for now, is find out why."

6

Mechanical clocks were marvels. Fia had only heard of them, never seen them, before taking up with Antonov's Company. They were one of the few pieces of booty she'd obsessed over. She'd saved most of them. She'd had one on a brass pillar painstakingly set up in her pavilion.

She'd stopped collecting them when the ticking of mechanical clocks started to underline everything Fia did. Sleeping, speaking, planning – it was always there, in the back of her mind, in the lower reaches of her hearing. The past dripping away. Opportunities slipping through her fingers like silver coin, clattering on the ground.

Every day, every moment, was significant. She didn't need a device to remind her that the enemy was coming.

She had always been on a schedule, but this was something more. This was a deadline.

When and where depended on how fast she and the company could move.

Fia's lungs still burned from smoke. Soot stained her cheeks, turned the sweat on her forehead grimy. Every time she dabbed at it, her wrist came back gray.

Six dozen men waited for her in front of the corporals' tent. Cavalrymen and infantry, new men, the top performers of their cohort. This last raid could hardly have been called a battle, but these men had been promised a sermon after their first action with the company. They would get it.

This clearing was the nearest thing to open space left at this particular campsite. Quiet followed her. It had been years since she'd had to stare at men until they fell silent. Good thing. She did not have the time to waste.

In the back of her mind, the mechanical clocks were always ticking.

In public, she stood straight as a lance. She bit back the pain driving up her back, hot as lightning. She was old enough for her body to turn against her. One bad hop off her horse, and now she couldn't lie in bed without curling up. A small thing, but a warning.

She could not let it show. Bad enough that she had not been seen in her armor for two weeks. She pulled her commander's baton from under her arm. It was a light wooden rod the length of her forearm, useless even as a club, but she never stepped out of her pavilion without it.

It was always a performance. She was always *on*, being watched. The demands of the performance varied per the audience.

New audiences needed to hear that something had been hidden from them. They needed to believe it. She said, voice sharp as glass, "The church does not tell you about men like Saint Renatus. The gluttons and simonists who occupy it now have never wanted you to know the power of your calling." That other men were playing them for power. It was always true, everywhere, for soldiers.

She could have told the new men the story she'd made of Saint Renatus's life. Now everyone who came to her knew it beforehand. "Saint Renatus had been born from the earth, and a deep cave, but the stories I'll tell you don't dwell on it. It mattered, it shaped him, but only his beginning. Just like your beginning – whatever farm you grew up on, whatever household you served – it made no difference the moment another man's weapon touched his flesh. The bite of first blood made the man."

Captain Antonov listened closely. He stood just close enough to see out of the corner of her eye. His battle with age had started to go sour. He had grown larger than she'd ever known him, but, in the past year or so, somehow diminished. His cheeks were pale, his eyes darkened. His white beard could no longer hide the sharpness of his chin.

Fia had been a fair orator when Captain Antonov had elevated her to her position. She knew how to force her voice to carry without shouting, and when to make men strain to listen. She knew when to exalt men, and when to only promise exaltation. She had gotten rid of the last traces of her northern Italian accent.

"It was the power of that moment that made him holy. Not the circumstances and the miracles – though there were plenty of those. The miracles presaged the man. They confirmed who he was. They did not make him."

That was the most important of the lessons she had to teach them. But she no longer had to tell these stories alone. The man waiting to speak after her had been a Benedictine monk before he'd joined. Giuseppe di Stefano was accustomed to berating men for their sins and inequities. While she raised them to the level of angels, he had become their sergeant, coring them out.

Giuseppe was a deceptively small bearded presence to her left. He spoke now. "Death claimed the man in his first battle. But in rebirth he found salvation. No one who calls himself a soldier will ever be saved by living the life he was born into. All of you must seek your own redemption."

Fia said, "The church still thinks the comet presages the end of the world." The papacy still held some power over men's imaginations. It was imperative to remind them of its humiliation as often as possible. "They were *partly* right. Anything that dies can be reborn. The comet brought about the end of *a* world. But not the end of all of them.

"The comet presages *us*. Your world has ended. The way old men used to do things is gone, and it's not coming back. Neither will the man you used to be. Whoever you were before you came here, that man is already gone."

The first time Fia had sermonized, she had let her inner

voice take over, tried not to think too deeply about what she was saying. Now the words were all hers. She enjoyed speaking.

But the clocks had not ceased ticking.

She let Giuseppe take over. He was the better storyteller. He traced the path of Saint Renatus's lives, starting with his expulsion from the armies of Rome and its early confederates. Fia listened until she was sure the men had their eyes on him. Then she slipped away. Captain Antonov was not far behind.

As soon as she was past the next tent, she breathed out sharply. She arched her back. A hot needle poked into her back, made her gasp.

Antonov said, "Eyes still on you."

Fia saw no one, but she did not stop to look. She squared her shoulders and went after him. The needle sank deeper. If it got any worse, she wasn't going to be able to keep herself from stooping. "Is this what it's like to grow old?" she said, goading him. "Getting crooked?"

"It's worse than you know," he said.

The corporals' tents lined their walk to the pavilion. The company's camps were far larger than they had been at the start of her career, but less organized. Even keeping the disorder at this minimum took great effort. The corporals' tents were different sizes, shapes, fabrics. Some had servants standing guard. Others wouldn't have been out of place among the slum tent city of the camp followers and the pioneers.

It was in the nature of a *condottieri* army. Very few men were pledged to her and Antonov in the manner of soldiers to a state. Her best men were independent, contracted, and their subordinates in turn contracted to them. There was not much point in maintaining set places for each man's tent, either. Their contracts ended at different times, most often at the end of a season, and spring harvest was upon them.

Antonov said, "The monastery claims it can pay no more than nine hundred florins."

"Less than last time." It would hardly cover expenses for their march to Siena. And of course the monks did not have the cash with them. It would have to come from loans, entries to the church.

"You have a good memory." Antonov always seemed a little surprised when her mind worked as it should. They both knew it didn't always. "Anyway, I believe them. They say they'll empty their coffers to come up with two hundred, and hold the bishop in debt for the remainder."

"You think the church will pay this time?"

"You and I know the church isn't honorable, but they'll try. They know we can turn back around and do worse."

That was wishful thinking. Several cities – like Siena ahead – were in arrears. Antonov just wanted to leave. She said, "The church is marching to destroy us. They could be counting on their army and their mercenaries to end us before we're paid."

"The church won't destroy us," Antonov said.

"I never said they would," Fia said.

Fia was not ungrateful for him, but he could be stifling, patronizing sometimes. She could not have managed her first few years in the company without him, and he knew it. He had given her the chance to speak to men who otherwise would not have listened – and more.

After she had traveled with Antonov's Company for several years, before it had become the Company of the Star, Fia's mind had turned unquiet. A black mood settled on her, impossible to move. And then the unrest. Antonov had shown parts of himself that she had not expected. He had been like a brother. In the worst of it, he reminded her to change her clothes, to cut her hair, to eat, to sleep, when thoughts of those things eluded her. They had been mutually dependent on each other by then: he as the company's captain, she as the speaker for the company's saint. She found out then how much he must have cared for the family he'd left behind.

But she was her own soldier. He had helped, but she had

fought alone, and retrained her mind. Some part of her would always be unquiet, but that was her burden, not his.

Lowing carried over the barricades. A march of captured livestock, cattle and goats. Sometimes, the company ransomed the large animals. Not this time. They had to pay close attention to their food stocks. The spring harvest was a fragile season. It was the first opportunity the locals had to replenish their stores. After a winter as harsh as this last, their stomachs would be all but empty regardless.

That made this spring an ideal raiding season.

The wheat and oats her pioneers had burned today were the most valuable of the year. There were no stores to replace them. The company had engineered a catastrophe. Starvation would drive families from their homes, into the cities. Starvation fomented revolt. Revolt and unrest would weaken Siena, the city they were all headed to.

She remembered the bitter pain of starvation. When she thought of it, she felt a pang. Her inner voice stifled it. *Another life*, it told her.

The moment she stepped into her pavilion and relaxed her shoulders, a different kind of suffering found her. Agony sliced down the center of her back. She swallowed a groan. She did not care if the four men inside saw her wince. They were men of her and Antonov's inner circle. They were allowed to see more of her – even the ones who weren't her friends.

Szarvasi Janos asked, "Do you enjoy keeping us?"

Antonov shot him a warning look. Janos's brother, Istvan, said, "Ignore Janos. We have not been waiting for long."

"We don't have time to wait at all," Janos said.

Fia had almost booted the Szarvasi brothers from her camp after they arrived. Janos, the eldest, was curt at best. Nor was he a believer. He meant for nothing more than to turn the company against the rivals who'd exiled him from Hungary. But she needed his money, and so she'd given him a space to fight, allowed him to hire his own *condottieri*. He turned churlish at upsets, reacted poorly to bad news. Something must have happened.

His brother was his saving grace. Istvan was courteous and subtle everywhere that Janos was not. He listened. He was a believer.

For once, Fia didn't mind Janos's impatience. He was right to be. She had taken the centerpiece clock out of her pavilion long ago, but she still heard it. She said, "I take it there's been news."

Captain Mirko Blazovic said, "Yes. Mine. My spies in Parma say Giovanni the Sharp requested safe passage there. He's expected through Parma before the middle of May."

Fia said, "His name is not Giovanni. It's certainly not 'the sharp.' And safe passage means nothing." It was a common *condottieri* tactic to send multiple requests for safe passage to different towns. It kept their enemies guessing. Sometimes cities nearby even paid bribes to keep the mercenaries away from a route they'd never intended to take.

Blazovic said, "He would not have given the date unless it was plausible."

Mirko Blazovic did not belong to the Company of the Star, but another society of *condottieri* contracted to their mutual employer, Orvieto. He was more than an ally, though. He was a believer. Before he'd converted, he'd had a reputation for cruelty beyond even the standards of *condottieri*. Saint Renatus had changed him. The first time Fia had met him, he'd had a ferocious beard. Now he was clean-shaven, and kept the worst of himself in check.

There was one other man with a captain's rank, Constantin Laskaris, but he had no company. Not any more. Laskaris shook his head, and said, "We'll reach our target regardless. We're far closer to Siena than they are."

Laskaris was one of the many failed Greek military commanders. His failure hadn't been his doing. His circumstances had been nigh insurmountable. He was Thessalian, formerly employed by the city of Soli, hemmed in by enemies on two sides. He'd managed a startling few successes before his position had inevitably crumbled. Fia had recognized talent when she heard news of it. He was both rough and roughly shaven. He was like Fia. He had good days and poor days, when melancholy subsumed him. This was one of his poor days. He did not enjoy living away from home.

Blazovic said, "We'll have to face Giovanni sometime."

Fia said, "His name is *not* Giovanni."

Laskaris said, "We've danced around fighting the church's armies in the open field before. We can trick them again."

The Company of the Star specialized in raiding, in fighting on superior terms. They fought only when they already knew they had their opponent outmatched. When leagues of cities sent armies against them, the company melted away. It was easy. They had no home territory to defend, no place where they could be pinned down. The leagues were disinclined to send their armies to protect others' lands. The tensions between the cities were such that the leagues usually disbanded in a year or two regardless.

This was going to be different from all that.

Janos Szarvasi said, "We're not afraid to fight him. And then—"

Antonov interrupted, "It's not a matter of being afraid. It's a matter of capability. We still don't know how large his army is."

Janos told Blazovic, "Those spies of yours have never been able to tell us."

"Neither have anyone's," Blazovic said. "He knows he's being watched. He travels in small groups, a thousand at most. Even if we knew the numbers of each group, it wouldn't matter. He recruits along the way."

Laskaris said, "He won't have trouble recruiting. We are not popular in the north."

Antonov said, "Nor is he. Not after Faenza and Cesena."

Fia said, "There's little point in guessing. I doubt even he knows how large his army will be. We cannot hold against a man we are afraid to properly name."

Two years ago, the papacy had declared a Crusade against the *condottieri* of Italy. Now the pope had called for one again, against the cult of Saint Renatus. The papacy had hired their own mercenaries, led by a foreigner, an Englishman. His only brief was to destroy the Company of the Star. Unlike the leagues the company had faced before, he would not hesitate to cross territorial boundaries.

His name did not easily translate. Fia knew the power that names held. There was little strategy worse than letting an opponent choose his own name. He could shift with the shadows, adopt whatever one suited him best. Giovanni the Sharp for his prowess as a captain. Giovanni di Hauwode when he needed to make local allies, seem less foreign. Writers in different cities transcribed his name in different ways: Iohannes de Hauvod, or Hanklevode, or Augudh, or Aucgunctur. They had made him amorphous.

A man with one name could be nailed down. His real name was the English corruption of Giovanni: John. John Hawkwood, as Fia insisted her officers call him, was the name of just another foreigner. Italy already had plenty of those. They could beat another foreigner.

She glared at her officers. Hard to believe, sometimes, that these men could still behave like panicked sheep. They had been through more battles with her than she could count. They were the only people who knew the company's deepest secrets – like where much of the company's funding *really* came from, and why it had been founded.

She needed to be a better shepherd. She had let them become too addicted to bickering. Antonov hadn't stepped in to change that either.

But they had a ghost of a point. It was hard to react to a threat without form. Hawkwood would not be on them at any particular time, just *sometime*. His capabilities were cloaked. He'd become a general anxiety that had been introduced into the careful balance the Company of the Star had made of itself and its allies. A shadow creeping over their shoulders. A ticking of a clock.

Fia said, "He makes it all the more important to attack Siena, and soon. We need more than money this time. We want capitulation. A vassal." The company's conventional strategy had always been to resist taking cities. It was too much an effort, even assuming they could win – and they usually couldn't. Even if they were to win, holding territory just meant they could be pinned down. It gave their adversaries a place to attack. One of the *condottieri's* most useful tactics was to just slip away.

Hawkwood changed things. His army was not so different from theirs, and likely too fast to evade. But, just as they were unprepared to assault cities, so was he. He was coming at them too fast to carry siege equipment.

Fia did not want to remain a nomadic society of fighters forever. She had other goals. But that was a discussion for a different time.

Fia said, "News from Parma changes nothing about our plans, except to let us know that we know we need to move faster."

There was nothing in the looks they gave her that united them. Janos smoldered. Blazovic was silent. None of them showed it, not much, but all of the men in her camp were ragged from the pace she'd set. But at least they were all silent.

She said, "So we move."

Fia had no rank in the company. Her position was one without precedent. She carried a commander's baton. On the march to Siena, she rode alongside Captain Antonov. She gave orders with the force of his authority. Many of the men would have listened regardless. Antonov could have overridden her orders, but these past few years he had shown himself increasingly disinclined to do so.

The Company of the Star was his – but it owed its fortunes to Saint Renatus. The saint was hers. More and more, the two were indistinguishable from each other. Fia knew it. So did Captain Antonov.

When Fia had started traveling with Antonov, he had never been uncomfortable on the back of a horse. Now each day's travel left him sagging. Fia ached too. She rode with her shoulders arched, braced against the spear of pain. She fought to keep from showing it.

This land did not allow an easy passage. This swampland was called the Maremma. The Company of the Star knew it well. It was marshy, malarial, poor for camping. But the surrounding lands were rich, poorly guarded – a favorite raiding ground for years. The insects had not yet summoned their summertime legions, but they still kept her from sleeping. No matter how she lay, the pain in her back was a biting spider, fangs sinking deep.

The Maremma was the last leg of this march on which she saw any hint of their camp followers. She was grateful to see them gone. She hated seeing prostitutes in camp, pretending not to notice them. For once, she envied English military discipline. The English reportedly didn't allow prostitutes past their barricades. That was one of many differences between English and Italian soldiers. Even with all her cachet, she never could have gotten away with such an order.

At least some of them got a taste of life inside the barricades. The Company of the Star was the only one she knew to openly allow women soldiers. Fia's page Caterina was a girl. The few who'd joined had come from unconventional places, and most often from among the camp followers. Just as Fia had been.

After three days on forced march, the company's outriders returned with news of the first sighting of a target. There was a town of at least twenty-five buildings ahead: hostels, stores, homes, all lined along the old pilgrimage road, the Via Francigena.

This town hadn't been here last time. It wasn't on her maps. It didn't matter; it wouldn't be when they left again.

Like the folk around the monastery, the locals had gotten word that the Company of the Star would be coming. Like the people of the monastery, they had not expected the company so soon.

The company approached as a sharply angled crescent, enclosing the town. The pioneers led each tip. The cavalry led the center, hoisting the company's comet-and-spear banners. By the time the center reached the town, the pioneers had cut off Via Francigena in both directions.

Fia did not rush with them. She lingered behind, watching.

She dismounted with a wince. Her page, Caterina, offered her the reins of her war horse, her courser, but Fia waved her off. Fia did not, could not, don her armor. On an ordinary raid, she would have. But the pain in her back had hardly let her dismount. The weight of steel was out of the question. She had to hope that no one noticed, or cared.

Caterina was a short, muscular girl, the daughter of itinerant laborers captured on the road. They had been sold into servitude while they awaited ransom. Caterina did not speak. Not ever. The company only knew her name from her parents.

She had a wide-eyed stare that others mistook for absence of mind but Fia understood was keenness. She learned fast, and was competent at everything Fia asked her to do.

Fia did not want to feel pity. The first foreign *condottieri* to carve a foothold in Italy, Werner von Urslingen, had worn a breastplate inscribed "Enemy of God, pity, and mercy." He had written it in Latin, so that all literate men might read it. Pity did not fit the profession.

John Hawkwood took after von Urslingen. He and his papal ally, Cardinal Robert of Geneva, had butchered Faenza's and Cesena's inhabitants on a slim provocation. They had murdered thousands. Even by the standards of *condottieri*, Hawkwood's reputation was bestial. Fia would have been better served by doing everything she could to match it.

Fia had been a slave like Caterina once, too, though.

Caterina had shrunk from Fia when Fia won her bid, but her fear hadn't lasted. She stayed close to Fia whenever she had the opportunity, rigid and focused as a bodyguard. Fia took care not to show affection or favor in public, and only rarely in private. *Condottieri* were not supposed to be human. Fia did not often feel human.

Caterina had not cared for her parents. Fia had seen it in her face, only once, when she'd mentioned her parents had been ransomed by relatives. The payers had not mentioned Caterina by name. Fia had asked if she wanted to go with them. Caterina had looked to her, lips locked tight and pale, her fingernails biting into her fist. Fia had not mentioned it again.

The Croat Zvonimirov Kristo rode just ahead, their bodyguard. For the past ten miles, he had ridden armored. The strain showed in his red cheeks. Like the Szarvasi brothers, Kristo was an exiled noble. He had come to the company with his own agenda. Unlike the Szarvasis, he'd dropped it as soon as he'd converted to the veneration of Saint Renatus.

Kristo had his own molded plate armor. He had a heraldic shield lashed side-saddle. He peered at Fia through the slit in his basinet. That was the closest anyone came to remarking that she had held back.

As ever, fire and smoke heralded the Company of the Star.

The pioneers had reached the outlying fields, set them ablaze. They had orders to capture anyone they saw, but not to give chase. The company needed some of the rural families to get away. Those from the town would not be so fortunate. They were to be the hostages. Townsfolk, in general, made for better ransoms.

"Town" was not even a good name for this place. It was ramshackle, unplanned, undefended. There were no walls or barricades. They sheltered under Siena's influence and protection. They all paid a tax to Siena. That made hurting them a way to hurt Siena.

There couldn't have been more than seventy people living

here. Their church was the tallest building, and only for its steeple. Some of the townsfolk had retreated there under the misapprehension that they would be left alone. Company lancers dismounted, wasted no time battering the door. They shouted blasphemies, an easy way to break morale.

The infantrymen and crossbowmen were not long after. They ran straight to the buildings the scouts had identified as travelers' hospices, to loot and secure hostages. Travelers, too, made for fine profit. An infantryman's pay rate was hardly better than farming blood turnips. The promise of plunder sustained them better than the *grosso* her treasurer handed out.

There would be no wicked showmanship, no swinging of cages over ponds this time. Not yet. They were still too far from Siena.

When Fia had still collected clocks, time had become something new – concrete, measurable in small detail. It was more than a flat expanse onto which events were projected. It had helped her reconceptualize each day's march, each battle. It helped her see that speed could be a weapon, too.

Condottieri marched on their purses like most armies did on their stomachs. The company's treasure train had done nothing but grow since Fia had joined, but it would vanish in a few seasons without a swift pace of sustained raids. Every season, every week, every day saw an astonishing number of bills to pay. Her men were expensive.

The Company of the Star was organized into three-man lances, an English-style unit that had been adopted throughout Italy. A lance consisted of three soldiers led by a veteran man-at-arms. Each lance cost the company sixteen florins per month. And then there were the officers, the light cavalrymen, the *stradiots*, the infantry and crossbowmen and conscript pioneers. The nine hundred florins they had gotten from the monastery wouldn't cover even the expense of marching from Orvieto to Siena.

Much of that could be made up by the company's real

paymasters. And had, in the past. That couldn't happen too much at once, or too visibly.

When she reached the town, her men had herded the first group of hostages in front of the broken church. One man's ear had been pulped to a mangled mass of skin. Another's hair was soaked with blood, and he was only upright because two women held him. She walked past. Her pulse beat harder.

She did not want to look. Did not want to remember.

Antonov ignored them. Caterina looked upon them with the same disinterest that she did everything else. Good. She would have an easier time that way.

These people weren't her target. She needed to do this to them to survive. Antonov's Company had done this long before she had made it the Company of the Star. It would do so whether or not she was with it.

They would never be able to catch Siena so unprepared. The company had to move as lightning regardless. Any extra time would give Siena a chance to draw in their own *condottieri*, make defensive arrangements with their neighbors.

The company did not intend to massacre. There was no profit in killing. They aimed to take. In Italy, a company of soldiers was every bit as much a commercial venture as a company of merchants. Silver and plunder and ransom sustained the company, not blood. Her pioneers had allowed those at the farms to flee. They had relatives inside the town, and they would be desperate to pay ransoms. At the very least, Siena would have to deal with them as refugees. They'd left their homes and stores and animals behind for plunder.

Soldiers could be artless, though. She passed two dead women and the body of an old man. A teenage boy, hardly older than she had been when the company captured her, lay silent in a blood-soiled ditch.

It could have been bloodier.

After a short survey and discussion with their officers, she and Antonov remounted. Kristo and Caterina followed. He said, "Not as fun to ride through and watch, is it?"

When she was in the fighting, she could change things. She had turned more than one about-to-be-executed man into a hostage. A profit instead of a loss. "No," she said. Then, more pointedly: "I've only missed a handful. You haven't ridden at the front of a raid yet this season."

"There's been no need."

"*Condottieri* respect commanders they see charging alongside them," she said. "You're not *that* old and decrepit."

But even as she spoke, Fia realized Antonov *was* acting older. Last summer, he had charged into every fight, directed the vanguard by holding his baton high above them.

"I am impossibly old," he said.

"You're the right age for a captain," she said. "Half of the *condottieri* commanders in Italy are older."

"I used to think I would be able to go home," he said.

"So did a lot of soldiers."

"I know what you're going to say. It was a different life. I've been reborn. I don't need a sermon."

She looked to him. "I wasn't going to preach."

In all their years of partnership, Antonov had never once told her the names of the family he'd left. Not parents, not siblings. She did not know if he had married. Unlike other foreign *condottieri*, he had never taken an Italian wife. When they had both been younger, she had been convinced that he would advance on her. She had braced herself to reject him, to lose everything to that battle. But he had held his distance.

Antonov said, "I was told they would be well cared for."

No one other than Caterina were close enough to hear them. Even if Caterina hadn't been mute, though, she was loyal. She and Antonov could talk around her. They rode out of the huddle of the town, toward the wide dirt trail of the Via Francigena. Smoke blurred the horizon.

Something had changed. Antonov had never talked about his family before, even in private.

She said, "You've received letters."

"No," he said. "I did, for a while. The roads so far north are not good. Word was intermittent for years. Then nothing." He was silent for a while. Fia let him be. "I think they have been forced from their home. There was a hint in the last letter."

"How long ago was that?" she asked.

He didn't know. His family had been an ancient memory before she'd come to the company. Little wonder that her message of rebirth and remaking had found him listening.

She was content to let the conversation rest there, but he wasn't. He asked, "How long do you imagine you'll keep fighting?"

Fia shrugged. Many soldiers didn't grow old. The relentless pain in her back reminded her that might not be for the worst. Tracing her thoughts, Antonov asked, "Do you think Saint Renatus will let his prophet off easily?"

"There will always be another fight."

It was a tenet of the Cult of Saint Renatus that the last of a soldier's rebirths would not be on earthly soil. In the Kingdom of God, they would be more highly placed than merchants and farmers. She fought here for the same end: to elevate common soldiers beyond the lot of servitude and simple banditry they had been given. Soldiers were better than the people who tried to rule them. They always had been.

Her sermons had spread far beyond the Company of the Star. Men from all over came to listen to her. They returned to their own cities, their own companies, and repeated what she'd said. All of her sermons, her ideals, narrowed to that end.

More and more people across Christendom, and beyond, had heard her. There was untapped opportunity in that.

She said, "I don't mean to stay in Italy forever." Opportunity-rich as it was, Italy was not large enough. She had crossed it five times over.

Antonov said, "Our brief is to focus on Italy."

"You know their interests won't stay confined to Italy." Just as they had not remained confined to Greece, or Serbia, or Dalmatia, or the burning lands pincering Constantinople.

"Then what's next for Fiametta of Treviso, after Siena?" he asked. He did not have to say *assuming we outmatch Hawkwood.* "The papacy? Raiding Avignon?"

The answer should have been easy. Without this war to support, they had riches aplenty. Enough gold and silver to pay for lavish lifestyles, to make themselves patrons of towns or of the arts. They could have scholars writing paeans to their name, musicians playing every night. They pulled so much wealth behind them that it was a burden just to carry.

Antonov talked about retirement, but he had not retired yet. Instead, their funds kept getting funneled back into war. They made war to support their wars. There was always another target to seize, a long-standing grudge to settle.

There were other reasons, too, that they hadn't told their men. Some of them suspected. Fia had, long before she'd learned the truth. Antonov had another employer, in the east. That employer wasn't interested in seeing him settle down.

Fia said, "I aim to go east."

Smoke encompassed all of their horizons now but for a single clear arc on the other side of the Via Francigena. It was like being in the bowl of a crater. Or the bottom of a lake.

She gave Antonov all the time he needed to digest what she'd said. There were not many things she could have meant.

"If you mean those words," he said, at last, "they're going to cause you a lot of trouble. Breathe them to anyone else, and you put yourself in danger."

"I know." She and her inner voice discussed that frequently.

The best part of her doctrine, the one she believed in more than any other, held that soldiers were so often used and discarded by men who did not deserve respect, let alone loyalty. Soldiers deserved better. *She* deserved better. The Company of the Star's paymaster was no different than so many others.

All her life, she'd felt a fire in her belly. A fire to escape the orphanage. A fire to become a soldier. To protect her friends from the company. To *join* the company. And now to change the world, to batter down the injustices that treated the company as the company had once treated her. She felt it burn as strongly as she'd felt any of them.

Her inner voice asked, *Are you sure this is a good idea to tell him?*

He would have to find out eventually, Fia thought to it.

Antonov said, "I would call you foolish. But I think you already know how you sound."

"Do you believe in Saint Renatus?" she asked him suddenly, sparing no warning.

She held his measure until finally he said, "I believe in what you've told me. About soldiers and rebirth." It was the most she could have expected.

"I don't believe in Saint Renatus either." She had never said it aloud to him, but he knew. Caterina, too. "But I believe in what Saint Renatus said. Look how much those words have brought us. When I decide on a path, I won't be led away from it. There's power in what I say."

Antonov asked, "You think nonbelievers and infidels will adopt a Christian saint?"

There were plenty of Christians living east of them, but they both knew she hadn't meant them. "Saint Renatus is not just a Christian saint," Fia said. "He's a saint of all soldiers." She had discovered, while composing the life of Saint Renatus, just how many of the lives of other saints had been reconfigured from those of pagans. "Going to war is a holy act no matter what creed a man was born into." Birth was not as important as rebirth.

"You have a great deal of faith in yourself," he said. The barb was unsubtle.

"I think I have enough. Word of Saint Renatus has spread much farther than anyone else expected it to." Every society of *condottieri* in Italy, France, and Hungary numbered some believers among them. Mercenaries were not the type to hew to religious orthodoxy. Threats of excommunication did not bother them. Most of them had been excommunicated before.

"You might succeed in spreading word farther," Antonov conceded.

"Then you'll support me in this," she said.

"My support?" Antonov's response startled her. He yanked his palfrey's reins, halted. "Hasn't it crossed your mind that you won't have my support for long?"

"Oh, cut the self-pity. You're not so old that you don't have more campaigns in front–"

"It's not a matter of age. You have taken all of me there was to give. All I had, when we met, was the company."

They sat in silence. Fia couldn't remember where they should have been going.

"If you want to go east," he said, "you can deal with it. This has been more your war than mine. It has been for years."

7

Meloku's shuttle dropped out of moon-haloed clouds. The deck shook. She was accustomed to keeping the monitors in the shuttle's control cabin off. She turned them on, had them show her their compound-eye view of the shuttle's hundreds of exterior cameras, just to soothe her stomach.

She had not come to the monastery to investigate, Meloku told herself. She was just here to take a look.

The shuttle blanketed itself in stealth fields: cushions of air to mute the thunder of the engines, sheaths of light to blur the air. Below, the shuttle looked like a shimmer in the dark overcast, a heat hallucination. The stealth fields were not strong enough to cloak the shuttle in full sunlight. *Ways and Means* had prohibited flights during the day.

Her shuttle hovered meters above the earth. She stepped down the boarding ramp. Seen from within the bubble of its stealth fields, the shuttle looked spidery, bladed. It had been built sturdy, intended to fly through a solar corona or the sludgy depths of an ammonia sea as easily as terrestrial atmosphere. Now, like the rest of them, it was stuck on this world.

When she turned back, the shuttle seemed to be looking down on her. It was intelligent in its way, piloted by an NAI.

After a moment regarding her, it rose and whispered into the night. It would come back when she called it.

The monastery hadn't changed much since she'd watched the raid. The gates remained barred. Smoke from a dozen refugee campfires mingled with the dark haze lingering over the ash fields. Behind the walls, someone was yelling in spite of the late hour. A headstrong male voice, on the verge of breakdown. Her demiorganics' audio discrimination ability struggled to pick out his words. Something about fire, and God.

Though her eavesdroppers and satellite feeds provided her with an abundance of information, they could not substitute for presence. Ash slipped into her shoes. Bone-white burned wheat stalks crunched under her soles. She could not clear her nostrils of the smoke. Already, the smell had soaked into her costume.

The Company of the Star had done everything but salt the fields. Terror was part of their plan. Overawe the locals, drive refugees to the cities to spread stories and burden municipal food stores. She had trouble wrapping her imagination around suffering on that scale. The first time she'd come to this plane, she hadn't even tried. She hadn't wanted to. But she was getting better at it, whether she tried to be or not.

Her skin goosebumped with cold fury.

Companion, with the carefree candor of an AI, had once told her that she had suffered a shortage of empathy. Her social skills were slow to develop, slow to manifest. Growing up, it had kept her aloof, made her cold-blooded. It had also made her an ideal agent for the amalgamates. They gave her work someone with a faster conscience would have balked at.

She wondered what Companion would say now. Probably the same thing. She *was* slow to empathize with anyone, for any reason.

She'd been on this plane long enough, though.

Retinal infrared showed her the blobby radiant heat of the monastery's watchmen. The Company of the Star had long since moved on, but the locals expected a raid at any moment. As far as they knew, the *condottieri* were just over the horizon. Their world was alien, unknowable, full of long shadows and hidden threats.

She stepped carefully across moonlit shadows. She crouched against the outer wall's sloped earthen barrier. After five minutes of silent movement, she reached the divot in the wall where she had planted her first eavesdropper. She dug it out. It was the size of her fingernail, and about as remarkable to look at.

She hadn't needed to come and retrieve it so soon, not really. Though *Ways and Means* had curtailed resupply flights for fear of the disruption they caused, she had thousands of them stored underneath her hideaway.

She turned it over in her palm. Her diagnostic programs reported no software tampering. There were no footprints in the dirt. It was the same with the others she'd placed at other points around the wall. Nothing wrong, nothing remarkable.

If there had been any tampering, it would have to have been done remotely. Once again, that narrowed her suspects.

She watched the stars. Their radio signals hummed.

The sky was full of satellites. If she *was* being watched closely, then whatever power was doing it must have figured the real reason she'd come here.

She waited for a cloud to obscure the moon and hide her from the watchmen. Then she slipped away from the walls, toward the ash-covered road on which the Company of the Star had left.

The shuttle found her a safe distance from the monastery. She sat hard on the boarding ramp. Her security programs were top shelf. No human could have beaten them, not even another agent. She only knew of two powers capable of it. The first was *Ways and Means*.

That would have been bad enough, but the second was even worse.

It was a monster. Her encounter with it had left her with scars, deep and physical, along her neural tissue. It had attacked her, burned out her demiorganics. She had gone into treatment for post-traumatic stress, blocked off parts of her memories. But she could not erase all of them and still retain herself. It was impossible for any functioning human psyche, whether healthy or otherwise, to come away from that without a healthy fear of further trauma.

This creature had exiled *Ways and Means* to this plane, and broken apart the Unity. Alone, Meloku stood no chance against it.

It was not a human intelligence. It existed between the planes. It did not see the multiverse as a set of discrete planes but as gradations of the infinite. It did not believe in death because it always, somewhere, perceived the dead on another plane. That perspective had left the creature free to kill as much as it liked. And it had killed a lot. Millions of Unity citizens had died.

That creature had been responsible for a plague that had swept the Unity, as devastating there as this world's black pestilence had been here. *Ways and Means* and the other amalgamates had surrendered rather than allow the slaughter to continue. They submitted themselves to exile.

Though the creature didn't believe in death, it did have a kind of ethics. It didn't like empires like the Unity. Colonization, assimilation, erasure offended it. It had seemed afraid that, given the opportunity to sufficiently advance, the amalgamates would come to colonize *it*.

It might have been right to fear the Unity. Inside or outside the bounds of the Unity, there was little that the amalgamates had not seen fit to control or manipulate. *Ways and Means* had defined itself by its empire. By wreathing themselves in empire, the amalgamates believed that they had the resources to best anything that might harm them.

Ways and Means and the other amalgamates had been among the most unique sentient life they had ever encountered in the universe. They were thousands of AIs, melded together. They had been forged in vicious wars. They had crafted an empire to control and manipulate humans and other lesser species, and made itself secure in a multiverse that was largely alien to it.

They had built themselves planarships, vast and powerful, capable of escaping to anywhere, and stocked with the Unity's best weapons and defenses. They had seeded backups of their minds in inhospitable corners of the planes, and guaranteed their immortality. But it was their empire, they believed, that had given them their best means of preserving themselves.

But now the empire was gone. She had no idea how *Ways and Means* aimed to define itself now. Its sentence of exile would last for another twelve hundred years. After that, it had been forbidden to assemble an empire like the last. The creature would be watching.

The amalgamates had manipulated Meloku her whole life, and she knew it. She had embraced it. Until she got here. Until she had lost Companion. Until *Ways and Means* had pulled back from settling this world. She had not spoken to *Ways and Means* for years. She hadn't particularly wanted to.

And she wouldn't now. *Ways and Means* was almost certainly responsible for this. If she contacted it, she would tip it off to how much she knew. Far better to do as she was now, trust her own eyes and ears. Look into the situation.

That didn't mean fight. That didn't mean resist. It didn't necessarily mean *investigate*, as she kept telling herself. If *Ways and Means* had gone out of its way to hide the size of a mercenary company's treasure convoy, it might have a good reason. She just wanted to know why this was happening.

There was only one person she trusted to speak with about this. The problem was that that person didn't want to speak with her. She might as soon throw a punch as talk, in fact.

Meloku felt the same way about her.

A line of thick, dark clouds walled off the Adriatic. The shuttle bounced and juddered through the cyclonic trailing edge of a thunderstorm. Lightning lashed its port side. All of the camera images flared white. The sound penetrated even the shuttle's sound-cushioning fields.

Meloku asked her demiorganics to dampen the anxiety squeezing her stomach. Numbness spread across the center of her abdomen.

The shuttle burst through the storm and dove toward the coast. It outpaced the rain. By the time the shuttle settled on dirt, the skies had dried. The storm would catch up before long. The wind already battered the pebbly gray foothills in which Dr Habidah Shen had established herself.

Dr Habidah Shen had never forgiven Meloku for being who she was. Habidah had been the leader of the team of extraplanar anthropologists. Meloku had joined her team under false pretenses. She had pretended to be one of those anthropologists, but had been sizing this plane up for colonization and exploitation.

To Habidah, discovering Meloku was a spy had come as a personal betrayal. History had brushed Meloku's and *Ways and Means'* plans away long ago, but not Habidah's memory.

Meloku strode down the boarding ramp. The shuttle's wingtip thrusters glowed hot. Steam poured from them. Meloku bunched her sleeves over her arms to protect them from the wind. Scores of old thruster burns betrayed where other shuttles had landed. There were more of them than Meloku had expected. Many more.

Ways and Means had curtailed shuttle flights and surface visits to reduce disruptions to the natives' lives. Meloku suspected this was an excuse. *Ways and Means'* crew was not happy with its decision to remain minimally uninvolved. They wanted a world. The moment they stepped off a shuttle, *Ways and Means'* options for controlling them diminished. Even after three decades, *Ways and Means* had only dispatched a few hundred agents to the surface.

But *Ways and Means* had not balked at the flights that supplied Habidah's home. This in spite of the fact that Habidah was hardly fond of *Ways and Means*. Habidah had said she would not, would never, work for it.

Nevertheless, Habidah and her anthropologist partner Kacienta were, like Meloku, valuable to *Ways and Means*. Unlike the rest of its crew, they were fully human. They could infiltrate and interact with this plane's people in ways that its crew couldn't.

Habidah must have known the supplies that *Ways and Means* sent came with a price. It was tapped in. Any data she collected, it saw too.

A loose, pebble-strewn trail led along a short ridge, and faded into the side of a short hill. As Meloku approached, a sliver of the hill recessed. Not even a trickle of dust or dirt fell.

Meloku hadn't tried to hide from Habidah and Kacienta's sensors. The stealth fields might have tricked an unaugmented eye, but not their scanners, and they kept a careful watch for natives. They would have known she was coming as soon as her shuttle dipped into the Adriatic.

Kacienta stood on the other side of the door. Kacienta was a short woman, but just broad enough to block the door, even with her arms folded. She was one of the anthropologists who'd come with Habidah. The other surviving member of their original team, Joao, was gone. He'd packed his belongings and trekked into the wilderness. Only *Ways and Means* knew where he was. *Ways and Means* no doubt tracked him, but no one else had heard from him since.

Meloku did not fail to notice that only Kacienta had come to see her. Kacienta told her, "You don't need to be here."

Meloku said, "You don't even know why I've come."

"No," Kacienta said, and nothing else.

"I'm not here on *Ways and Means'* behalf," Meloku said.

Kacienta studied her; no doubt she was using retinal infrared to watch the flow of heat under Meloku's cheeks. "You're a liar," she said. Meloku's own retinal infrared caught her uncertainty.

"A good liar," Meloku said. "But not this time. I don't have a reason to lie."

Somewhere behind Kacienta, Habidah spoke. "You're not going to talk her into leaving."

Kacienta grunted, but didn't budge.

"Good to see you again too," Meloku told Kacienta. It had been years. She forced her way past Kacienta. Kacienta still didn't move.

Kacienta and Habidah shared quarters no larger than those Meloku did with Dahn. It would have been rougher for them. They *both* had to bathe and eat and sleep. They both sweated and stank and were irritable and restless. As unnerving as Dahn was, Meloku couldn't have tolerated sharing space with him if he were fully human.

Their walls were lined with monitors and projectors. They filled the walls and the air with satellite imagery, raw sensor data, eavesdroppers. Habidah and Kacienta had never stopped working. Their exercise equipment, bikes and treadmills and weightlifting couch, folded compactly away. Meloku could smell them from here. Her demiorganics isolated something else, too – a lingering trace of sex. Now *that* was surprising. When they'd come here, Habidah and Kacienta hadn't cared for each other. Time and relentless proximity could unravel a lot.

Dr Habidah Shen had reshaded her skin tone since the last time Meloku had seen her, returned closer to her natural russet. Darker skin was hardly unknown along the Mediterranean coast. She sat with knees propped on her chair. She looked Meloku up and down. "Been keeping up with your longevity treatments? You look old."

"If that was supposed to hurt, you can do better."

"Just an observation," Habidah said, with just enough of a pause to make Meloku wonder. It would not have been like Habidah to make fun of her appearance. Habidah could be as sincere as she was artless.

After a lingering second, Habidah turned back to the satellite imagery floating above her desk.

Meloku regretted a great deal of what she'd done when she'd come to this plane. It burned in her throat – and all the hotter whenever she was near Habidah. Habidah would not let her forget it. There was no forgiveness in her world. It didn't matter that they'd all come from the same place, lost the same home.

She wished she could say that did not bother her.

Meloku had broken Habidah's nose once. That, at least, had been a satisfying feeling. She focused on the memory, used it to warm her heart enough to push through this meeting.

She grabbed the seat from Kacienta's desk and rolled it over to Habidah. The desk projectors were angled to project into Habidah's eyes, but Meloku caught a shimmer of images. A tropical storm off the coast of Africa. A merchant ship floundering at sea, square sails torn, foremast splintered. A forest fire raging through some earth and wood dwellings.

Meloku said, "I didn't come to harass you, if that's what you're thinking."

Behind them, Kacienta said, "I bet you'll do a good job of it anyway."

Meloku bit back her answer. "I think there's something going on here beyond what we've all been told."

Habidah laughed, bitterly.

"I get it," Meloku said. "I know. *I'm* the joke this time. Happier now that I said it?"

Habidah said, "So long as *Ways and Means* is on this plane, it's not going to keep itself from interfering. It used to govern an empire of thousands of planes. Whatever it's told you, manipulating worlds is as natural to it as breathing is to us."

"You don't give it enough credit," Meloku said. "It has more imagination than we ever will. It can reimagine itself."

There was no anger in Habidah's voice when she asked, "Is that why you're here? We've been looking a little too closely at what *Ways and Means* is doing, and so it sent you to tell us to stop?"

"I'm not here on anyone's business but mine."

Habidah held her gaze.

It wouldn't have helped her figure out what Meloku was thinking. Meloku really *was* a good liar. She could have matched stares with anybody.

Habidah was the type to believe that any amount of interference on this plane was too much. She limited herself.

She saw herself as only a scientist. The end of the Unity hadn't changed that.

She was also a hypocrite. Thirty years ago, the mass mortality of this world's black plague had overwhelmed her. She had broken down, and broken through the limits she had placed on herself. She had saved a monk's life.

But, Meloku thought bitterly, Habidah had forgiven herself for that. In ways she had yet to forgive everyone else around her.

That monk still lived aboard *Ways and Means*. Somewhat. His mind had been destroyed, torn to flinders during the battle that had resulted in *Ways and Means'* exile. The transplanar monster had used him as a weapon, a vessel to deliver a virus. *Ways and Means* had spent decades trying to piece him together. A personal project. It hadn't succeeded.

Whatever her other principles, Habidah had wanted to save this world from its black plague. Meloku and Habidah had been in the same cabin when *Ways and Means* had announced it would do so. Habidah had not objected to that like she had to everything else.

Habidah had no shortage of personal issues. Meloku longed to elucidate each of them for her. That would have been unproductive.

Behind her, Kacienta asked Meloku, "Why do you want to know?"

Meloku turned to her. "Curiosity."

Habidah said, "*Ways and Means* only hides what it's doing if you don't bother to look."

Meloku bristled. What she'd discovered, and whatever it meant, had definitely been hidden. "Like what?"

They looked at her. Kacienta said, "You must have felt it by now."

Habidah said, "It's affected politics in Italy for years."

Meloku had focused her research on Italy. That was the area that Habidah's team studied originally, and so it was where Meloku already had her greatest expertise. She had checked in on other regions, but for the most part left those to other agents.

Meloku folded her arms and waited, with less and less patience, until they decided to explain.

A century ago, a vast army of steppe nomads had swept across the eastern half of the Eurasian continent. They had brought most of it to heel. They had shattered empires as far as eastern Europe. Steppe horsemen were mobile, and their diets were rich in protein. Their lifelong training with their animals left them with abilities sedentary people could rarely match, like accurately shooting bows from a moving horse.

They had been outnumbered by the peoples they conquered, though. So strong was the pull of Chinese culture that the Mongols who had conquered it had patterned their government after Chinese dynasties. They had to adapt to rule, and adaptation meant losing the advantages that had brought them to power. The Emperors of the Yuan Dynasty were Chinese in all but ancestry. Chinese bureaucrats ran the government in Chinese style.

Habidah said, "There's no reason the Yuan Mongols should have survived as long as they have. They were close to toppling, on the verge of being replaced by native Chinese. Now, as if by magic, the Yuan are in control again. They're rich, too. And powerful. Sending money and soldiers westward. I would've thought you'd noticed."

Meloku said, "Of course I know money from the east is pouring into Italy." Back when the Company of the Star had been Antonov's Company, it had been funded by a Turkish prince. She had chased that rabbit years ago. "But it's not just from China."

"The Yuan Dynasty is back in control, but it's got different strengths than it used to." Habidah was enjoying Meloku's resentment, knowing that she had something over her. Drawing it out. "Most of its military power vanished with the steppe horsemen. Chinese soldiers aren't interested in fighting so far from home. But China *is* the richest country on Earth. Think about how it would stretch its influence in circumstances like that."

"I didn't come here to be treated like a schoolkid. Or take a quiz."

Habidah ignored her, or pretended to. Again, she prompted, "Think about how *you* used to govern."

The hint finally overcame her frustration. "Through agents. Proxies."

Habidah nodded. "Most of the money reaching eastern Europe, including Italy, has its roots in the Yuan Dynasty. You tracked it partway back."

Habidah pulled up a sequence of eavesdropper feeds, angled the projections for Meloku. They were views of a vast and splendorous palace, walls hung with furs and antlers and hunting trophies, steeping in angled sunlight. Men in colorful, elegantly layered robes trailed the halls. Infrared traced ghostly shadows wherever the light touched.

Ways and Means' agents were not difficult to spot. They looked like Chinese bureaucrats, dressed like Chinese bureaucrats, but in infrared their skin was cold as stone. They dressed less elaborately than others. They were low-ranking, staying out of the way. Giving no one an excuse to touch them.

Meloku asked, "When did you plant eavesdroppers in the Great Khan's palace?"

Habidah just rolled her eyes.

Meloku asked, "Did they ever try to hide themselves from you?"

Habidah and Kacienta looked at each other. "No," Kacienta said. "Why would they? We can't do anything about them."

Habidah said, "They don't care. Not any more than you cared when we found out what you were."

Meloku turned back to the projections. The Mongols were cruel and brutal, but that had only been one aspect of their many-faced conquests. They accepted surrenders without fault and on reasonable terms. They did not displace native religions or cultures in cities. Governments that surrendered peaceably were left in place. They often did not care how people managed themselves so long as they retained final authority and received a healthy tribute.

In that respect, they were like the Unity. The Unity had been so named not because its peoples were alike, but because they were unified by their rulers – the amalgamates. The amalgamates governed transport and trade between the planes. They made worlds dependent on those things.

The growing Yuan Empire was a replica of the Unity, and the Unity's method of governance, on this world. *Ways and Means* could not have made it better itself. Maybe it *had* helped the Yuan.

Meloku asked, "How are they doing this?"

Habidah answered, "How do you think? Like you did with Queen Joanna."

There it was – the next barb. Like *Ways and Means* and the broken monk, Meloku had a personal project of her own: Queen Joanna of Naples. Thirty years ago, she had invaded Queen Joanna's mind to try to use her to change this plane.

Thirty years stuck in one place made for a lot of time to think.

That was a sore spot, but telling Habidah to stay away would have just made her dig in. She seemed to know it, anyway. Habidah asked, "How *is* Queen Joanna doing this year?"

Meloku said, "Better than you would imagine."

Habidah asked, "When was the last time you checked?"

Of course they would be monitoring her, too. No point in lying. Meloku said, "It's up to her to get better. If you've been watching, you know I've been trying to help. I can't do everything."

Habidah said, "Even to you, that has to sound hollow."

Meloku ground her teeth. "Next question. Has *Ways and Means* or any of its agents tried to hide any of this from you?"

Kacienta said, "*Ways and Means* hides everything from us,

all the time."

The thin ice of Meloku's patience gave way. She turned to Kacienta. "Cut the poor-me-against-the-universe horseshit. There's a difference between hiding something and not sharing it with you. *Ways and Means* just doesn't *care* if you see what's happening in China."

Meloku didn't give Kacienta time to react. She turned back to Habidah, and said, "I asked you a specific question. Have they ever removed your eavesdroppers? Blocked your observations? Manipulated your data?"

From the fact that their answer was nothing more than a glance between them, Meloku guessed that they had not. Or, if they had, they were not willing to tell her.

Habidah asked, "Do you still consider yourself *Ways and Means'* agent?"

"Yes," Meloku said. For all the distance that had grown between her and *Ways and Means*, she had not needed to think about that.

Kacienta asked, "Then why do you care? You should support whatever it's doing, shouldn't you?" The bite in her voice sharpened. "Look away when it wants you to look away."

"I should," Meloku said. "But I'm not."

"You asked about it manipulating us. It is. Of course it is. And you're its agent. We have to figure that that's what you've come to do. Manipulate. Lead us in wrong directions. We can humor you, but only to a point."

Habidah no longer looked smug. That was telling. She had stopped entertaining the idea that Meloku wasn't part of *Ways and Means'* efforts.

And it was mostly Meloku's fault. She could have handled this conversation much better. The sight of Habidah had rendered all her social and diplomatic training moot.

Kacienta said, "Even if you're on to something, we can't trust you."

If there had been an opportunity here, it had slipped by.

Habidah turned to her desk as though Meloku were already gone. "It's going to be morning before long. You'd better get back to your shuttle, before your master won't let you leave."

"Believe me," Meloku said, standing. "I won't be inflicting this on myself any longer."

Kacienta followed Meloku to the door. Kacienta couldn't resist one last jab: "Wish Queen Joanna our best."

Meloku stepped outside, and, feigning nonchalance, turned to Kacienta.

Then she moved. She struck faster than Kacienta's eyes could have registered. Meloku's demiorganics routed her muscle control. She could have clocked Kacienta good, broken her nose, any number of things.

But all she did was push Kacienta into the side of the door, touch a finger to her lips. The universal gesture for silence.

Kacienta took a sharp breath, didn't move.

Meloku smiled. Just a little breach of politeness, enough to remind Kacienta what she could get away with if she really felt like it. Meloku's combat programs were better than either of theirs. Reflexes, too.

Given the provocations, Meloku thought she had been remarkably restrained.

Kacienta glared, but didn't move, and didn't follow when Meloku started walking.

The storm broke upon the coast in torrents of wind and lightning. Rain sliced into Meloku's eyes as if in a deliberate affront. Her demiorganics blocked the pain in her skin, but the cold went into her bone. That last look on Kacienta's face was almost enough to keep her warm.

She stood shivering on the boarding ramp as it retracted.

She hoped she'd made them as miserable as they'd made her. So many years after the last time she'd worked with them, she'd thought she'd buried that past far enough that it wouldn't bother her. All that had happened was that those seeds had sprouted roots.

8

Osia didn't gather the strength to call *Ways and Means* until long after the comet had vanished beneath her horizon.

She stood at her boat's prow. Rain dashed on her skin. She actually had to pay attention to realize how cold it was. She *could* feel, but only when she cared to. That was the difficulty with these bodies, with the past thirty years. She didn't often care to make herself feel. Everything had become unfocused, dreamlike.

She struggled to wake up.

Ways and Means made its home far off the solar ecliptic, on an orbit with an apogee about two hundred million kilometers to stellar north. The amalgamate had chosen that distance for several reasons. It was close enough to Earth to maintain communications. It was also far enough that, to *Ways and Means'* crew, the planarship felt apart from Earth. Shuttle travel consumed enough time and antimatter fuel that every journey had to be justified.

Ways and Means wanted to make its crew understand that they were alone. They could not count on this world to lift that burden. Its triennial passage across Earth's skies was a glimpse, as much for its crew as the people below, of a different future.

But only a glimpse.

That was what she'd been told.

Ways and Means had given her these constructs with the idea that they would satisfy her social needs. More often, they came to her when *they* were restless. Braeloris leaned on the railing beside her, playing counselor again. "Is there something you find comforting in standing so still?"

"I'm not staying still," Osia said. "We've gone farther south than I've traveled in years."

"Tell me how you feel about-" she started, but Osia muted her from her awareness. She had no idea how long Braeloris kept talking, or when she figured out what she had done.

Sometime later, Tass visited. She was their best sailor, the tallest among them. Just like Coral had been a diver in thir last life, Tass had been an engineer in hers. She noted, "We've gone this far, but we're still not doing anything."

"This trip is a warm-up," Osia said. Getting ready for what she figured she was going to have to do next.

As usual, only Coral seemed to understand. When thi visited, thi asked, "Why don't you just talk to *Ways and Means*?"

It was not a question thi expected Osia to answer. Osia had not spoken to *Ways and Means* in ten years, and only sporadically before that.

Their last conversation had not gone well. It had invited her to come home. "Will I still have my old cabin?" Osia had asked, churlishly.

She knew her cabin would have been repurposed the moment she'd left. The cabins and bulkheads of the habitable sections were modular, expandable, collapsible, infinitely rearrangeable. The interior of the planarship was never the same from year to year.

Instead of answering, *Ways and Means* said, "The crew is restive. They've never been happy with where we are. We need voices like yours."

"They heard me well enough."

"Visit. Remind them."

"Will it change anything that happened? Or that *will* happen?"

"It will change you. It could change them. Some of them miss you."

Osia knew who her friends and enemies were among *Ways*

114

and Means' seven-thousand-strong crew. She shook her head, though *Ways and Means* couldn't perceive that. Not unless it was so interested in her that it was watching through its satellites.

She said, "You drew our battlelines when you decided to listen to me."

When she'd spoken up, she hadn't expected *Ways and Means* to hear her. She wasn't sure of anything now, and had been even less so then. Too late to swallow her words.

Osia had never been able to ask the question she'd most wanted: *Why did you allow that to happen?* The amalgamate was fully capable of making up its minds without her input. *Why did you single me out?* It must have known that the rest of its crew, unable to blame it, would blame her instead.

Like them, Osia's bond to the planarship had been forged over centuries of transplanar travel and hardship. It took effort to accuse it of betraying her. More than she had to spare at that moment.

The conversation had gone on to other subjects, but she had since erased them from memory, just like the dream of several days ago.

For the past several weeks, Osia had cruised southward, shadowing trade routes between China and the Philippines. The trade routes were becoming busy again. Few sailors had wanted to leave port while the bad omen of the comet hung in the sky, although sometimes their merchant masters forced them. China lusted for trade. The Yuan government devoured it. This was the first time she had paid enough attention to realize that they had purposes for it other than growing fat.

The skies were clear and the fleets had once again set sail. At this distance, her pulse scans couldn't resolve nonmetallic trade goods, though parts-per-trillion traces of piperine in the wind hinted at black pepper. Her scans *could* identify gold and silver, though. There was less than she expected. On trade routes like these, she would have assumed that China would pour precious metals into the islands to sell for spices.

So someone back home was jealous of gold and silver going east. They had other purposes for it, even if that meant a less efficient sea trade. No doubt headed to the west, to war.

She had cruised within one hundred and fifty miles of the old Southern Song Dynasty capital, Hangzhou. That was just close enough to bounce a pulse scan off the atmosphere and find glittering demiorganic signatures. A dozen of them.

Now they knew about her, too. Her scan had given her away. *Ways and Means* had promised to hide her, gray her out from satellite data. None of them bothered to scan back.

She had not gotten close enough to Hangzhou to take a full demographic survey. The pollution carrying on the wind gave her an idea of its population, and the scope of its industries. The latter had shrunk since her last glimpse. The population had remained level, though. There was no sign of mass conscription. The patrol junk's captain had been more concerned about gold and goods going west than men.

Osia sailed until she was two hundred kilometers away from anything. She had Tass fold the sails, and just let the boat drift.

Finally, she could put it off no longer.

It did not matter that the comet had already left the sky. Osia did not have a transmitter capable of bridging the distance between her and *Ways and Means* even when it passed by.

To contact it, she had to go through its network of satellites. For the first time in years, she opened a connection.

At once, she was awash in data, a flood of tangible abstraction. Security and identity-confirmation handshakes decrypted and blossomed through her thoughts. The network automatically shared recent news, orders, weather bulletins. The data came with a warm and strange fullness of mind more real than anyone she could have touched. It woke a part of herself she had not exercised in years.

This was what it was like to be connected, to have the plane at her fingertips. It didn't stop at data. Her senses expanded outward, lacing with the thousands of satellites pirouetting overhead. If she'd wanted, she could have looked anywhere, seen anything. It took some effort to resist.

Then she found *Ways and Means'* sharp-edged hull. The planarship was close enough that there was no significant light speed delay. It was so real that she might have been running her fingers along it. Every part of it was studded with sensors. It had a million eyes, and even more ears. When her senses laced with it, she felt, briefly, like she could reach anywhere, touch anything.

The impression faded. Whenever she was connected, it was always there, low-level, intoxicating.

After allowing time for her senses to dilate, it said, "Your security programs are several years out of date."

"You can't believe anyone would or could try to impersonate me."

"We believe you are you. We've been maintaining continuous tracking since the day you arrived."

The amalgamate was a melding of hundreds, thousands, of minds into a single identity. It was more a colony than an individual. Yet it spoke and acted in concert, even as its thoughts pulled it in a thousand directions at once. Its multifarious nature was one of its strengths. It always approached a problem from every possible perspective.

Even in exile, *Ways and Means* was still taking the effort to update its security programs. That could only mean it didn't trust its crew. They were the only people here who could fight against it on that level. She wondered what drama she'd missed.

Ways and Means let the data feed crest and trough, and remind her what it had been like to travel with it. It was insidious. And it was working. For a while, she couldn't speak either. She was caught up in remembering. Such was the puissance of the amalgamates. Even when she knew how it was manipulating her, she couldn't help but follow along.

She said, "You've been hard at work down here."

"Yes," it said. No denials.

"Would you like me to outline what I've discovered, or would you like to confess?" A classic information-fishing technique, an attempt to get it to admit to more than she'd found. *Ways and Means* wouldn't fall for it in a thousand lifetimes.

It said, "We'd rather talk about you. We know most of what's happening on this world. We don't know as much about you."

"'Most?'"

"Are your constructs continuing to treat you well?"

"They're a suitable distraction," she said.

"Are they staying true to their source characters, or do their personalities need to be reset?"

Osia did not like to think about where her constructs had come from. It was embarrassing. *Ways and Means* knew it. She said, "I can tweak them myself if I need to."

"We typically don't send constructs on extended journeys. After thirty years, we would expect some deviation from their baseline. In so alien an environment, their programming may express itself in unintended ways."

"This isn't so alien to them," Osia said.

"It would take days and weeks for you to recalibrate their personalities. It would take us less than a second."

"I have plenty of time."

"You do not have to keep going like this. You should at least come back long enough to update our backup of your memories."

Ways and Means kept backups of all of its crewmembers, a feat only possible for people with wholly demiorganic bodies. Another perk of the job. It had once kept backups of itself, too – all of its memories and personalities – but exile had ended that. It could no longer place them in a location it deemed secure.

"I'll probably end up erasing most of these years, anyway." Just like she had erased her memories of her fugue this morning.

"You never know when you might want them back."

Osia looked behind her. Coral wasn't far, scanning the cloudy horizon with a hand over thir eyes. When Osia had been a child, before she'd had anything to do with the amalgamates, she'd fallen in love with an open-author adventure serial. It had been about an oceanographic submarine and its crew, trapped on a world during a transplanar invasion.

It never ended – or, rather, it ended hundreds of times. The characters and central crisis were consistent from author to author, but the plot and the endings always changed. It had been a form of storytelling perfect for the Unity, and for a people always trying to wrap their imaginations around the scope of an infinite multiverse.

In the serial, Coral and thir partner Straton had been divers. Coral had taken charge of the submarine. Ira, a violent man with no love for the Unity, turned traitor in over half of his stories – but not all. Borealis had been a trapped tourist. Tass had been an engineer and just as lost in the engine room as she was in the rigging here.

This second exile had pushed Osia to extremes. *Ways and Means* had delivered the constructs, but she'd requested their personalities. She'd retreated to a time before she'd joined *Ways and Means*. It had been mortifying to speak aloud, and it still was. And *Ways and Means* knew it.

She knew what *Ways and Means* was up to. It was trying to make her feel younger. Vulnerable. It attacked conversations from as many different angles as it had minds.

The flood of data was rising over her head. She was swimming upstream against her past. Already, she was having trouble managing it.

Ways and Means had let her go, but it would never give up trying to get her back. She'd never stopped wondering why. All its crew should have been equally valuable to it. If it wanted to trick her into imagining a deeper feeling, it was doing a good job of it.

It was an amalgamate. It was alien to her. That was why

she had loved living with it. All of its powers had been on her side.

The amalgamates were always probing, always searching for weaknesses. She would have to wrest the conversation if she intended to get anything done. She said, "I thought you had decided on a policy of noninteraction."

"We decided on a policy of non*colonization*," *Ways and Means* corrected. "Subject to humanitarian intervention – such as curing their great plague."

"That wasn't quite what I remember asking for."

"I have never been clear on what you asked for," it said. "Your thoughts seemed scattered."

Galling, but accurate. Better to say that she'd been in shock. She hadn't sorted herself out because, when she'd asked, she hadn't had time.

She hadn't asked alone. Dr Habidah Shen had, too. Osia had just made herself the most convenient target for the rest of the crew.

Osia had taken careful recordings of the moment. She'd been tempted more than once to erase them. It had happened only an hour after *Ways and Means'* exile. Everything had been in flux. *Ways and Means'* mind had been blasted apart and glued back together by the transplanar creature. The planarship was scarred, crisscrossed with molten hull.

Ways and Means typically didn't need to interrogate anyone. This interrogation chamber it had made was freshly manufactured and flash-cooled. The curved bulkheads were bare, and still smelled of hot plastic. A table stood in the center. The room had the air of an operating theater.

The man who was to have been interrogated was a monk, a man Habidah had rescued and brought aboard. He still wore his habit. He was here because he claimed to have had contact with another transplanar power. *Ways and Means* had needed to know more.

His name was Niccoluccio Caracciola, and he had told the truth.

The transplanar creature had planted a weapon in him. A virus he carried in his thoughts. In rooting through Niccoluccio's memories, *Ways and Means* had given the virus direct access to the amalgamate's minds.

It might have all ended there. But lodging in Niccoluccio's mind had changed the virus as much as Niccoluccio himself. It had wrapped around his thoughts, sluiced through him, to avoid detection. It had made him a part of itself. It controlled him, but he had influenced it.

Without that influence, the virus would have destroyed the amalgamates. Instead, it had given them the chance to surrender. To dismantle their empire by choice and submit themselves to exile.

When the virus had surged into *Ways and Means*, it had taken Niccoluccio's mind, too. It had been too much for Niccoluccio. Fatal. A human mind was not elastic enough to expand so far, so fast. He had decohered.

He still breathed, but he was no longer alive in any real sense.

Ways and Means spent years afterward sorting through the thoughts and memories he had left behind in it. In the chaotic gestalt of its minds, it could never be sure what belonged to the monk and what belonged to some equally dissolute other.

Traces of Niccoluccio flitted in Osia's mind, too, like scattering leaves. She had tried to stop the data transfer between the creature and her amalgamate, and tapped into it. She had been rebuffed, tossed back onto the shoals of her unconsciousness. But parts of Niccoluccio had snagged on her. She couldn't get them off.

Uninvited memories had trilled across her senses. Hot canine breath on her neck. A shovel in her hands, blisters on her palms. A field of graves in frozen earth. The heady, clammy dizziness of medicinal bloodletting.

Without demiorganic assistance, she could not have spoken. Her demiorganics steadied her voice. They had heuristics to interpret what she had meant to say rather than what, on her own, she would have stammered.

The acceleration holding her to the deck faltered. The planarship's superstructure cracked and popped. Osia would have found it alarming if she hadn't been so lost. It sounded like gunfire, kinetic missile impacts.

Ways and Means had gated to this plane at a full *g* of acceleration. A sparkling cyclonic whirlwind of exhaust billowed in its wake. The first appearance of the false comet.

The crew was shattered. The datastreams that bound them together rippled with sorrow, with panic, with denial. Bitter fury. All their disparate reasons for coming aboard had fallen apart with the death of the Unity. Now they had been trapped here with *Ways and Means*, on this plane.

Unlike its crew, *Ways and Means* wasted no time mourning. "This plane must serve as a home while we consider our long-term path," it said. "We must make a new context to place ourselves within." It had already announced its plan to end the black plague below. Short leap from there to imagine what it was prepared to do to the rest of the world.

Dr Habidah Shen had been involved with Niccoluccio. She had come with him into the interrogation chamber, and, frankly, she would have been the next to be subjected to memory rooting. Her face was bloody from a fight with Meloku, who had come to stop them, but arrived too late.

"You'll erase this world's identity." Habidah stayed by the shell of the monk. She curled his fingers in hers. "They wouldn't want us."

Osia's trauma response programs muted her instinct to lash out. Instead, she said, "They won't be given any choice."

The monk said, "They can be made to be ready."

As much as the monk's thoughts had bled into *Ways and Means*, its thoughts had flooded into him. He was not the same person. Even his face seemed different, cheeks sharper and brow flatter, a new mind wearing the old musculature.

Habidah's voice was hollow. "We'll destroy those people no matter what we do." She didn't believe she could matter.

The forces arrayed against her were too great. She was just lodging a protest.

Meloku said, "No great loss."

The man who had been Niccoluccio said, "We can help. There's so much misery below, and unnecessary suffering."

And there was. Osia had tasted Niccoluccio Caracciola's thoughts. She had drunk deeply. She had not intended to, but parts of him had become her.

His father had died of the plague. His spiritual brothers, too. His whole monastery, gone. He had walked into an icy wilderness to die. He had offered himself to a mob that would happily accept any blood offered to them. Each time, Habidah had saved him. He had suffered immensely. Though he had forgotten most of it, Osia couldn't.

Osia's speech heuristics programs couldn't decipher what she wanted to say. So much of his suffering had come from being ripped out of his old life. His monastery was gone. Thanks to Habidah, he had learned things that would keep him from ever living in one again.

Meloku told Habidah, "*You* wanted to save him. To help them."

"Not through colonization," Habidah said. "Just a cure. Help them and let them go."

"'Catch and release,'" Meloku mocked.

"Ethical interference," Habidah said.

"That has to seem small now, even to you."

Meloku and Habidah bounced angrily, pointlessly off each other. The monk spoke again: "We can help each other. We can cure their plague. They can give us a home."

Ways and Means reminded them, "The terms of our exile forbid us from expanding across the multiverse. A single plane is within our limits."

Osia said, "No."

She'd been silent for so long that Meloku and Habidah seemed to have forgotten she was here. They looked to her. If Osia had had a pulse, it would have been pounding.

Osia said, "Listen to his memories. These people aren't just fighting death. They're fighting loss. The plague doesn't just take their lives. The survivors have had most of what they knew taken away from them." She turned on Habidah. "Just like you took this man's life from him when you uprooted him, and told him what you were."

Habidah's hand tightened around Niccoluccio's, but the infrared pattern of blood coursing under her skin revealed only surprise. She had not been expecting Osia to take her side. Neither had Osia. She had not felt so strongly until this past hour.

"Doesn't matter," Meloku said. "They're not the only ones who've been uprooted."

Osia said, "There are three hundred and seventy million people on the world we're heading for, and only seven thousand of us. We're better equipped to cope."

Meloku said, "Right now, they need us more than we need them."

"If we don't need them, why do this?"

Ways and Means was silent. It had never been more vulnerable, Osia realized. Or changeable. Over its lifetime in the Unity, it had become ossified. Encrusted in its beliefs. The virus had taken all of that apart. It was rebuilding itself, and in a state of neural plasticity akin to a newborn.

Niccoluccio's memories had shaken Osia too. Both she and *Ways and Means* in the process of being reborn.

Osia said, "We can't keep doing what we did before. We came from an empire. Even if we colonize this world, it won't be enough. It will always seem too small."

If Habidah had registered Osia's jab, she didn't answer it. "Yes," she said. "You're all going to have to learn a different way of doing things." She didn't see herself as complicit in the Unity, though she had benefited from it all her life.

Osia's scraps of Niccoluccio's memories had left her with an interesting perspective on Habidah, on everything she had done to him. Niccoluccio hadn't resented Habidah when he had been alive.

Osia would have to do it for him.

Meloku said, "This is academic," by which she meant *stupid*. "What you're asking us to do is surrender more of ourselves to the monster that sent us here."

"You already surrendered," Habidah pointed out. "We're here."

"*I* didn't. *Ways and Means* did."

Habidah said, "You took oaths to serve it, didn't you?"

In the look that Meloku gave her, there was a preview of the hundred little mutinies to come.

Osia said, "We can't keep doing what we've been doing and expect it to be the same." She did not know who she was talking to. She spoke from conviction but without hope. She had not expected to make a difference.

She was one voice out of thousands. Those thousands could out-argue her. She had no faith in her powers of persuasion.

But the acceleration pressing them to the deck gave out.

Meloku grabbed the edge of her acceleration couch. "What the fuck is happening?" Her demiorganics had been damaged. She was the only one who did not already know.

Ways and Means told her, "We are preparing a new course high and away from the solar ecliptic." An acceleration warning trilled in the back of Osia's mind. "One minute to thirty-seven degree pitch-axis thruster burn."

Osia's mouth opened and closed. Her speech heuristics informed her that she badly wanted to speak, but they could not determine what she wanted to say. Already, she felt the crew's shock, the horror of realizing what was happening. It echoed down *Ways and Means'* datastreams. They were waking up to the fact that *Ways and Means* was no longer heading toward the world ahead.

Ways and Means said, "Well spoken, Osia."

More of their attention focused on this chamber. Eyes accumulated in the sensors lodged in the bulkheads.

The quiet moments were the most dangerous ones. They

nursed a thousand grievances, angers, shocks.

Some of the shock belonged to Osia.

"We suggest you find acceleration couches," *Ways and Means* told them. "And brace yourselves."

Osia had believed she was only saying what needed to be said. Like Habidah, she had lodged a quiet protest against the march of forever. She didn't even know if she believed it, or if Niccoluccio had spoken through her. If she had known what was going to happen, she never would have spoken.

She was selfish enough to place her happiness above that of others. If she hadn't, she never would have become *Ways and Means'* agent. She couldn't stand the weight of the responsibility *Ways and Means* had placed on her.

This, at least, was the narrative she had constructed for herself.

One of the burdens of her demiorganic mind was that she remembered things too clearly. An ordinary human mind was too messy. Its process of recalling a memory destroyed it. They cast shrouds of ex post facto narrative over the moment, "remembered" invented feelings.

Osia's recordings of the moment were too precise, indiscriminate. She did not often revisit them for that reason. Every time she did, she learned what she had avoided looking at. She saw where her narrative broke.

When she erased her memories, it was often to preserve her image of herself as anything else.

She hadn't gone into that argument a naif. She knew how vulnerable *Ways and Means* had been. She'd lodged a protest, sure. She'd spoken from a slim hope that she could make a difference. She'd made the choice deliberately.

She did not know what tapping into Niccoluccio's thoughts had done to her. She still felt like herself. She was not aware of any deeper change. But that was the insidious thing about consciousness. So much of it was a self-constructed lie.

She held her hands on her boat's railing. She tried not to lose control again – not while *Ways and Means* was watching.

Ways and Means traced the synaptic storms of her memories. "We agreed with you," it said. "But we made no promises."

"Nothing about what I told you has changed. We can't live like we did." That should have been the only thing that mattered to her.

"The crew is convinced that they can't live like they are now, either," it said.

"They work for you. Not the other way around. They can go into hibernation for the next thousand years if they're really so pent up."

"After that? They want a home. They want to matter in the way that they feel that they did before."

"You're deflecting." Manipulating. *Ways and Means* was not above lying but, like most clever beings, it preferred to be artful with the truth. "You're trying to make me believe that the crew is compelling you to do this. You've never affirmatively said that was the reason."

"We are as dependent on them as we are on you."

That took her aback. When she had signed on, she had never been under any illusion that she would ever be important to it. She had signed on to serve a task. To be a negotiator. To make deals with people *Ways and Means* would not speak to.

She was not entirely sure what, in fact, she was needed to do now that the Unity had fallen. Same with much of the rest of the crew.

It said, "We know you cannot, and *should not*, believe what we tell you. But it has been a terrifying thirty years. You and the crew are the only things we have left from the lives we once had."

She said, "Just tell me what the fuck you're up to."

Ways and Means did not deny any of what she had already guessed.

It told her about the agents it had planted throughout the Mongol Empire. It *had* modeled its efforts on the Unity, allowing nations to retain their own identities – so long as they sent taxes and soldiers, of course. And opened to Yuan merchants. Before long, the prospect of losing Chinese trade would be a more effective deterrent to rebellion than war.

The end goal was a world with a unified polity, managed by *Ways and Means'* agents. A world shaped and molded to accept the larger changes that *Ways and Means* would bring. The new world the false comet promised.

Osia knew *Ways and Means* had always meant to reveal itself, eventually. But she had thought that it had given up the idea of control. Osia said, "You meant for this to happen from moment you said you agreed with me."

"No," it said. "The current incarnation of our plan kicked off twenty years ago." Ten years after Osia had fled to the surface. "Some of our agents had already acted without our permission. We reined them in, but sent others to continue their work."

"You took advantage of a mutiny." Osia marveled. Or had the mutineers taken advantage of *Ways and Means*? Forced its hand?

Ways and Means said, "Explaining this would be much easier if you had stayed up-to-date."

Caution tickled the back of her mind. *Ways and Means'* messages were layered, always operating above and below the levels she perceived. She was missing something.

She said, "Thousands of the natives are going to die because of the wars you're starting."

"Millions," *Ways and Means* said.

"You're not even trying to hide it. Not even cushion the blow."

"Millions will die in any large-scale intervention on this world," it said. "Thousands died *because* we cured their plague. We left their civilization unbalanced – some regions dramatically weakened, while others remained at the height of their strength. The conflicts that resulted have been devastating on a scale that is difficult to describe in language."

Osia said, "That's an argument *against* intervention, not for another one."

"If it is, it is incomplete. Ending that plague saved more lives than were lost."

"It's just arithmetic, then? Lives ended versus lives lost?"

"By the time we are through on this world, we will have saved many more lives than we will have destroyed," it said.

"You'll be responsible for the people killed in these wars."

"'Responsibility,'" *Ways and Means* answered, with just enough of a mocking tone to bite, "is a very interesting human conceit."

Very rarely, it let slip just enough of itself to remind her just how alien it was.

"These lives are not abstract figures." For most of her life, she wouldn't have cared. She couldn't explain how she had changed. Her perspective had shifted more than once since she'd tapped into Niccoluccio Caracciola. Exile had become a kind of Purgatory.

Imprisonment, too, was a shift in perspective. She could not leave this place, and all her thoughts about it, behind. When she and *Ways and Means* had traveled the planes, everything could sink into the past.

Ways and Means said, "This will preserve their cultural uniqueness, as Dr Shen wanted."

"I doubt she would agree," Osia said. "It's not them I'm most worried about. It's us. We're backsliding. Falling into our old habits. What happens when our term of exile is up? Right on to the next plane, conquering, colonizing, until we're stopped again?"

"The crew will not tolerate staying here mute and powerless."

"You're running into problems, though, aren't you?" The patrol junk's captain had told her that the Yuan were funneling more and more resources westward, always levying new taxes.

It said, "There are always challenges."

She prodded, "Challenges you don't want to talk to me

129

about. Who's giving you trouble? The natives? Or more of the crew?"

"Religions," *Ways and Means* said. "Cults. Several of them."

"So it's the natives. Funny. You're so mismatched I thought you would have bowled right over them."

"Nothing on this plane is so simple as it looks from your distance."

Anger lashed at her. "I'm closer than you."

"We do not understand why you are so suddenly so invested."

"What if I want to do something about this?"

An understated pause. *Ways and Means* did not hesitate. It thought so quickly that it did not ever need to, except for effect. "Then you should change your mind. Intervening would not be good for you. Our agents in the west are playing dangerous games."

"I could do anything they can."

"They work for us."

"And I don't." The words hurt as much to say as to realize. "That's why I need to look."

"You cannot find out what's happening so easily. We would be happy to show you. If you come aboard. We wouldn't ask if it weren't important."

"I'll think about it," Osia lied. She cut the transmission.

It took her a long moment to recover from losing the datastream. She had stood above continents, satellites, starfields. Now there was just her boat. By the time she had shrunk back into herself, Coral and Braeloris were beside her, holding her shoulders.

"Not necessary," she told them, pulling away.

Braeloris said, "It certainly seemed like it was."

Osia had always figured, in the back of her mind, that she would be going back to *Ways and Means* at some point. Not now. Not in a year. But sometime.

Ways and Means' perspective, its crew's, would have to change before that happened. If they didn't, it would be best if she stayed here – and best if *Ways and Means* never traveled to another plane.

This tiny world would be the end of their path. Not just an Earth. *The* Earth. Their only one now. The terminal point of *Ways and Means'* journey across the multiverse.

Osia told Coral, "Don't contact any satellites for this, but compose a weather forecast for the next several days. Pulse scans only. Have Tass unfurl the sails and tell her and Straton to steer clear of any other ships. We're going to cross some busy trade routes and it would be best if we didn't let a single ship see us."

Braeloris looked to Coral, as if waiting for Coral to say it was all right. Coral hesitated, equally uncertain.

"We're going west," Osia explained. "Far enough west that no one will have seen a Chinese junk like ours before."

9

Siena was in no shape to resist the Company of the Star's advance. The company needed no spies to discover that, though their spies happily sold them the story anyway.

The Via Francigena was supposedly fortified with defenses, outposts. While Fia was dining on geese and stolen wine, listening to Antonov's scribe read from Livy, a coterie of Albanian *stradiots* entered their pavilion. They brought a report of everything that had been looted from one castellan's stronghold: one battered table, two pewter cups of different sizes (one leaking), a water jug, moldy bread, a wooden shaft that might once have held a spear head, and a crossbow without string.

The scouts would have assumed the building abandoned had they not surprised the castellan in bed.

Her corporals shared a laugh as they listened. Fia just drank. She had raided here before, and the city had fallen further since then. A poorer opponent meant poorer loot. The company could not support itself by robbing subsistence farmers.

The Albanians had brought her the castellan for ransom. They had also left outside two heads, both men, of whose provenance they declined to say. The *stradiots* had no patience to ransom small men. It was their tradition, and in their contract, to be paid by the head. Fia tried to hide the unsettled shifting of her stomach. They had gall to bring this to her rather than to their designated paymaster. They were hoping for a bonus from her good mood.

She told them to report to their paymaster and, without a

word of departure, left them.

The sunlight stung her eyes. Humid, manure-smelling air clung to her nostrils, her skin. The war camp was in a fluster, full of men collapsing their tents, pages leading trios of horses, shrill shouted oaths and a rattle of orders. A handful of slaves and free laborers stood by anxiously, waiting for the officers to finish their midday meal so that they could tear down the pavilion. Caterina waited with Fia's horses, attentive.

Another rider came through the barricades. He caught Fia's attention not only from the oak shade of his skin, but from his bearing. He rode like a prince, draped in a pale cloth, only a dagger at his side. His three escorts, dressed like him but better armed, lingered by the gate guards.

Antonov was out too, conferring with his corporals. The messenger went right to him.

Fia did not hurry to reach them. Antonov and the rider bandied in a foreign tongue. Antonov had picked up a variety of languages from Russia to Italy. He had taken great pains to learn Turkish.

Antonov glanced at her. The rider never looked at her. After a brisk exchange of waves, he urged his horse to pivot, and departed.

Fia asked, "Not even going to take advantage of our hospitality?"

"He didn't seem very fond of us," Antonov said. "The word 'infidel' came up a few times. I don't think he meant it as an insult. Just a fact."

"At least our patron is more tolerant."

"Maybe," Antonov said. "He's sending his envoy again."

"Ridiculous," Fia said. "Musa was with us all winter. We don't have the time."

"That's what I told him," Antonov said, gesturing to the messenger.

Musa bin Hashim was not their patron, but close enough that it made no difference. He was their patron's envoy with the special charge of managing events in the west. His visits usually coincided with fresh infusions of gold. But this wasn't the time. Fia didn't have the effort to spare for him. They weren't entombed in winter quarters. They were at war. Difficult enough to maintain the pretense that they weren't receiving support without Muslim messengers visiting unannounced.

Fia said, "I don't suppose he gave us a date."

"He wants to keep us guessing."

The last time Musa had visited, he'd claimed to be satisfied, and promised not to return until next winter. Something had changed.

Fia already knew she would not like whatever that was.

The clocks never stopped ticking in the back of her imagination. A new one joined, louder than the others.

The noise made it hard to think.

The messenger and his escorts were riding out without so much as a hop off the saddle. The gate guards watched, but the other soldiers pretended not to notice. There would be plenty of chatter later, in private.

Antonov was trying to appear unmoved, inflexible. But this smelled of betrayal. They'd been betrayed, done the betraying, often enough to know it. This was how they expected to be treated right before someone pulled the earth out from underneath them.

Antonov said, "You told me you wanted to pick a fight in the east."

"Not a fight. Just more conversions. For now." Spreading her belief farther. "I'm not ready for more yet."

"We could keep heading west. Outrun him before he reaches us."

"Hawkwood is to the west." And closer, too.

"We'll have to face one or the other before long," Fia said. "Most likely both." She waved to Caterina to fetch her palfrey.

The Company of the Star grew as it advanced. They were not the only mercenaries in the employ of Orvieto. Messengers with ciphered letters reached them at all hours. They coordinated with the other companies converging on Siena.

The messengers brought the names of towns forced into shelter behind their walls: Massa Marittima, Grosseto, Talamone, Magliano, Montepulciano. Fia knew some of the names, had been to them, but most were strangers. They held thousands of people whose lives she had wrapped around hers. Other men might call themselves lords here, but she and Antonov were the rulers. Their soldiers were the nobility.

The companies' rendezvous was carefully choreographed. The march hardly needed to stop to accommodate them. The other companies poured into the Via Francigena as tributaries into a river. What had been fifteen hundred men became four and a half thousand.

That first night of their rendezvous, hundreds had turned out to hear her sermon. There were so many that the men in the back couldn't possibly have heard her. Fia tracked their presence by eyes glittering in the firelight.

They brought rumors. There were companies beyond the Alps, mercenary companies whose names she'd never heard, who'd begun to speak of Saint Renatus. Soldiers all over Italy knew her name.

The Company of the Hook and Emerik's Company stayed broadly to themselves. They grew onto the camp rather than into it. The ditch and barricades stretched farther than she could see. Emerik's men watched her, wide-eyed. Outside of her control, the proportions of Saint Renatus stretched into legend. His story was alive of its own right, spreading from war camp to war camp like pestilence. These men were no more accustomed to seeing women in armor than to seeing Saint Renatus's prophetess walking amongst them.

They didn't know to treat her as a soldier. They would learn.

Another group of travelers tracked the company by the burning fields in its wake. Grecians, Croats, Arabs, Romans from crumbling Constantinople. There were fallen crusaders and exiles. They brought news, tribute, small treasures. All of them were fervent believers in Saint Renatus. These men had been waiting throughout the winter to travel.

They were as much pilgrims as messengers. Fia thought of herself as a single company commander. Easy to forget, during their long and isolated winters, how far her story had spread. She was not in control of it. But she was at its center. None of these men had seen her before. The way they looked at her made her fidget. They would not be around long enough to learn better.

All told, she did not have many believers throughout the world, but the believers were all soldiers. They had power. More power than they had recognized before she'd shown them.

Her soldiers had no spiritual home. Going on crusade had once been supposed to grant a man a stay in paradise. The Crusades had crumbled and the papacy had been revealed as a sham. The only crusade the papacy had declared recently was against the *condottieri* of Italy.

The sermon Fia gave them was one had delivered a hundred times before, about all of the armies Saint Renatus had served in. The details meant nothing. She could recite them without thinking. She paid attention to the ways they looked at her instead.

She did not have the time for anything more. The company drew closer to Siena by the hour.

The Via Francigena lanced the cultivated hills and valleys surrounding Siena. Every few miles, the road grew wider. Travelers' hospices lined the path. A town with an expansive market ran parallel to the road. All abandoned. For once, the Company of the Star had not outpaced word of its arrival. And for once they had not tried. They needed to maintain battle order, and that meant a measured march.

The refugees could not take anything. The company's

vultures took furniture, iron tools, cauldrons and plows, anything that might be sold to the buzzing clouds of merchants that swirled around the treasure train. The company's pioneers ran loose in the fields, burning. Anything that could not be taken had to be destroyed, all in the interest of strategic suffering.

They did not meet any opposition until they reached the walls of Siena.

Those walls had been heightened since the last time Fia had visited. She could no longer see the buildings of the city, only a few steeples and the broad white facade of Siena's cathedral. A row of men in beaked helmets stood among the wall's crenelations – raised quills along the city's spine.

For the first time in weeks, Fia donned her armor.

Her back pain had diminished, but had not gone away. She gasped as Caterina fitted the padding over her shoulders and let the weight rest. The metal turned to oven plates under the sun. It was not long before her armor's inside padding was damp with sweat.

Nothing was as comfortable as it used to be. Fia's armor had been a gift from her patron. It had been fitted and refitted, but the pain in her back had changed her bearing. Caterina pretended not to notice Fia groan. She was good at not noticing those things.

Most of her corporals were convinced that Caterina could not talk. Fia knew better. She heard Caterina muttering to the horses. She whispered under her breath while she fit Fia's gauntlets to her forearm plate. Her voice was weak, unpracticed, a flutter, but it was there.

Caterina gripped Fia's wrist and squeezed before fitting her second gauntlet. Fia set that hand on Caterina's shoulder.

It took another soldier to help Caterina hoist Fia onto her courser's saddle. Caterina gave Fia her commander's baton. On Fia's way to the vanguard, she passed Antonov.

Antonov was unmounted. He wore his breastplate, but not his shield or any weapon other than his riding dagger.

He held his own baton limp under the crook of his arm.

Fia's stomach lurched. Antonov shook his head. He had waited for her, wanted her to see that he was not coming along.

His absence would be noted. But not for long. For years, more of the company's eyes had been on her than on him. They both knew it. He was too old to be a proper fighter any more.

Fia was not so ostentatious that she enjoyed drawing the enemy's attention to herself. Even with her basinet visor open, it was not obvious, at a distance, who she was. She had to hold her commander's baton high. Men shifted their horses to make room for her. Zvonimirov Kristo found her, fell into his usual place beside her. He would be her personal guard.

The company's armored cavalry held their lances ready, a wall of spines. It was a vivid, if faintly ridiculous, show of force. Lances would be of little help against earthwork and stone. From the stilling of activity along Siena's walls, though, she knew the display was having an effect.

The Company of the Star was not fit for sieges. Fia had been in very few. Sieges required artillery trains and other tools her army of raiders was not equipped to haul around. Easier to raid the countryside on which a city depended.

She'd been in enough sieges, though, to know that confident defenders did not stand quiet. They waved. They mocked. Perhaps these city-dwellers were so accustomed to losing to *condottieri* that they could not imagine another way of being. That, too, was an advantage.

Her other commanders could read their silence, too. That had been the only reason some of them had agreed to this attack. Like her, they had little experience attacking cities. For all their bravado, they were conservative fighters, and hated doing things they didn't understand.

The rest came along because she told them to. She had them under her power. For now.

She had not stayed around those other cities long enough to break them. The company had extorted their bribes and gone away. Siena was different. She had public and private reasons for wanting to break it.

The public reason was that Siena had to be made to pay.

The company had come at the request of Orvieto, but that was by far the least important reason. Orvieto had offered them their contract to damage a rival, but mostly to keep the company away. The company already had its debts to collect from Siena. The last time it had raided the countryside around Siena, the city's priors had promised a payment of fifteen thousand florins. Nine thousand had been paid in advance, with the rest due in rigid installments. Those payments had stopped long ago. The few Sienese notables the company had got hold of claimed that the city was bankrupt.

The first lesson Fia had learned about *condottieri* politics was that no city was ever truly bankrupt. It could always be made smaller, more humble. Rich men complained about bankruptcy from their manses, but none had seen the inside of an orphanage or almshouse.

They did not understand the way that she and other faithful of Saint Renatus were remaking their world. In the best days of the Roman Empire, emperors had quaked in fear of soldiers.

They could not sit and wait for the city to starve. Hawkwood was too close. They had to smash Siena now or not at all.

Her men understood all that. Their greed had been charged and primed by the thought of Siena's wealth.

She would have to explain her other reasons to seize Siena later.

Her inner voice had not spoken to her in weeks. Now it said, without prompting, *Your service has been incomparable.*

It had chosen to speak when she had the least amount of time to answer. She held her baton forward. The trumpeters hardly had time to signal the advance before a terrible noise went up along the front ranks. The war cry, all around her, was as close and hot as a bear's jaws on her neck.

In the back of her mind, there were so many clocks that their ticking blended together, lost their rhythm. It was just a cacophony.

The pounding hooves were a thunderstorm. A vicious wind whipped through her visor. A spatter of her horse's saliva picked up in the wind, struck her helm.

More theater. Horses were no more useful against a wall than lances. But, for the men on the wall, the clouds of dust must have looked as though the earth had folded up and was unraveling upon them.

A bolt's flight from the wall, the men reined in, dismounted. Fia joined them. The drop jarred her ankles. Someone took her reins. Through the slit in her visor, she could not tell if Caterina had kept up, or if another page had seen an opportunity to serve her and taken it. The pages kept their mounts near, ready to match a sally from Siena.

The charge resumed, this time more deliberate, a hammer strike. Pain bit her back. But the pain did not matter for long.

The charge was a collection of individual moments. Somehow she kept her head, enough to keep track of the various wings of her front line and gesture orders. But it all slipped away from her afterward, wiped clear.

Her soldiers again roared as they charged, though the distance between them and the wall was yet so long that they would run out of breath before they reached it. Fia yelled, too. She lost her words to the wind.

A slender wooden shaft snapped and skittered across the dirt ten feet ahead of her. Crossbow bolt. She almost held her hand out, as if to feel the first drop of rain before the storm. That was the kind of boorish joke that only chroniclers would appreciate, though. And the chroniclers could always be lied to afterward.

She was not the fastest among the company. Other men raced ahead. The moment she cast her gaze to the foremost, he bent backward and crumpled, as if his animating force had been plucked out in an instant. He was overtaken so swiftly that she did not even see if he was trampled.

Her men held their return fire. The crossbowmen carried their weapons wound, but they could not have reliably hit the defenders behind their cover. The defenders suffered no such disadvantage.

Fia called to close formation to fill the gaps and present a united front. And again. A third time.

Motion blurred the fringes of her vision. Bolts and arrows, too fast to track. More men fell. Some staggered and kept going, although Fia never saw for how long.

"Close formation!" she shouted for the fourth time. Men filled in to cover the gaps the bolts had opened.

A bright light detonated behind her eyes. Her basinet slammed against her temple.

For a moment that was both brief and eternal, she was lost.

She did not remember falling, but she was on the ground, crumpled. The blackout could not have lasted long. It seemed a slice of forever. She'd fallen as if a doll, legs folded painfully underneath her. Her armor's joints knifed into her thighs and knees.

Men dashed past her. Kristo was at her side, saying something she could not hear. Her hearing rang as if she'd held it inside a cathedral bell.

She felt about the side of her helmet. She found no hole, no shaft sticking out of her skull. But there was a dent in the basinet's side, by her temple. The bolt had not penetrated her basinet, just glanced off.

She heard voices, saw and tasted things that couldn't have been there. They were single words, visions, flashes of emotion. Hatred for the men on the walls. Petty irritation that she had been struck so soon. Terror, concern about how

141

this all looked. The visions didn't all make sense. There was an impaled arm. A knife's edge. A dog's teeth, barred. Blood dripping into a pail of butter. A smell of vinegar. Part of her was dreaming.

It did not hurt much. Yet. She was sure that would be coming. Oddly, the worst pain seemed to be in her tongue. The oily blood in her mouth was real enough. It took her seconds to realize she'd bitten through it. She focused on the real. She made it lead her back.

Kristo held her by the shoulder, about to lead her away. She planted her gauntlet on his neck, stopping him.

Had the bolt struck her visor an inch to its left, Kristo would be trying to preserve her corpse. Chance had slammed the bolt into her, but chance had also saved her. A hundred times already today, she could have died. No – she *had* died. She knew, going out, that she would come back changed. Reborn.

She still remembered the phantom pain where, fifteen years ago, the soldier who had captured her had nearly sliced her open.

She could not hear the clocks any more.

She could not speak with words yet, so she pointed to where she wanted to go: a long, fat section of Siena's wall.

It had been rebuilt recently, shored up. Its earthwork rampart was steeper. An amateur had probably thought that would make it harder to climb. But it was just steep enough that the defenders would have trouble shooting downward without leaning out, exposing themselves to counterfire.

Much of the front line raced toward it. Some of her officers had seen the same flaw she had. They pointed to the crenelations, shouting incoherencies that men nonetheless understood to be orders.

The company could not match the Sienese bolt for bolt. They didn't need to. For the first time, the company returned fire. A flurry of bolts flew toward the wall Fia and her officers had indicated – targeted suppressing fire. The defenders ducked behind the crenelations or fell where they stood.

More of Fia's soldiers reached the earthwork ramparts. The lead men carried weighted rope ladders. Armored men climbed as far as they could on the unsteady earthworks. In the section just ahead, four ladders leapt to the top. Two found purchase.

She was nearest the leftmost. She focused on it. In the din, her inner voice stood out clearly: *that one.*

She had listened to her inner voice since it had saved her in her first battle, and it had never disappointed her. Climbing while armored would take all her strength, to the point that she doubted she could do it, but her inner voice believed it was the right thing for her to do.

She raced toward the ladder. Her step was sure, or felt like it. The world still seemed something other than what it had been, in ways she could not place. Her boots dug into the earthworks. The earth slanted sideways as she climbed, and she scrambled for purchase.

A flood of men had beaten her to each of the ladders. The first climbers were almost to the top. She grabbed at her gauntlets, about to shed some of her armor to make the climb easier, when Kristo's hand found her shoulder. He pulled her back. With her poor balance atop the dirt, she couldn't push back. The world tilted, and it was all she could do to stay upright.

Kristo still worried about the blow she'd taken. He would not let her climb first. He mounted ahead of her. He had not even asked. She could not speak over the ringing in her ears.

Sudden irritability swamped her. Fuck him. The other ladder was only two dozen feet away. She sidled along the earthworks.

A wooden creak and a shout above drew her attention. She looked up. A shadow leaned over the lip of the stonework wall, wide-lipped and bell-shaped. Its mouth was wadded with black and brown horsehair.

The device's crew, three men, were straining with every muscle to orient it downward.

Fia had only seen bombards on an open field before. Never on a wall. But she recognized it. She shouted. Her reaction was delayed, leaden. She could not hear herself.

The two highest men had time to jump off. At that height, they would not land safely.

The ladder blasted apart. A lightning-fast line of black smoke ripped along the wall, tore men limb from limb and slammed into the base of the earthwork in a cloud of bloody ejecta.

The stone ball struck the earthworks and splintered, raining razor shrapnel on the men still climbing. The impact rocked the packed earth under Fia's boots. Her baton slipped from her hand. The blast knocked her senses loose and her steadying hand off the wall.

She fell flat onto her stomach. The blow stole her breath. Her armor's padding hardly acted as a cushion. Helpless among an avalanche of rocks and dust, she slid the rest of the way down. She struck the ground and folded into a pile of limbs.

She could not hear anything over the ringing. Another blast of smoke shot up from the wall. Then a third. All along their defenses, the Sienese were rolling bombards into position. Black smoke mushroomed over them.

She had missed her guess about the oversized wall sections. They had been built oversized deliberately, to hold the heavy bombards.

None of the bodies underneath the ladder moved. She had not seen what had happened to Kristo, but he could not have survived.

Regaining her feet took all her strength. She could not have climbed any ladder like this. Her balance wavering, she climbed a few steps up the earthworks until she had a better view of her army. There were no significant gaps.

The most effective bombard shot seemed to have been that which had taken the ladder. The same ladder her inner voice had *told* her to climb.

She had seen bombards on the field before. Bombards were unpredictable, fragile. They were not meant to kill men as much as to frighten them, to make them think a lightning bolt could pluck them at any moment. From her height, she could tell that it was working. The advance had stalled. Her men thronged in confusion. Crossbow bolts continued to fly toward them.

Her pulse pounded in her ears. Long-delayed pain slammed into her temples. The bleeding in her mouth had stopped, but she still tasted blood. Smelled blood, too. And burst bowels, and smoke.

She had only recently been thinking that she knew what betrayal smelled like. It was a little like this.

Her baton had tumbled only a few feet away. She raised it high. Blasts of trumpets and a raised shout interrupted her. The trumpets had come from somewhere east of the city walls, and the shout from above.

She did not need to wait for the Sienese banners to appear from around the bend of the wall to know that the sally was coming. She was already running toward her scattered lines, shouting, collecting as many men as heard her. She pushed her pain inside to take stock of later.

Another bombard blast shook the air. Bolts continued to rain from the walls. The men closest to her didn't even turn to look. She was proud of them. They were soldiers. They would not let setbacks make them something less than they were. Neither would she.

The pages were already rushing to present their men-at-arms with lances. By the time the sallying defenders came round the wall, she and her men had formed a bristling wall, lances and swords. A contingent of company cavalry was swinging around to support them. Fia's sword had not fallen loose in her tumble.

Fia tucked her commander's baton in its sheath, raised her weapon. By the time her blade pierced skin, she had forgotten her losses and her pain. All of it sank beneath the flurry of combat. All except for a lingering question she could not shake.

Her inner voice had told her to take the leftmost ladder. It had never led her wrong before. It knew things that she couldn't. If she had listened to it, she would have been destroyed. Chance had saved her.

Her inner voice must have heard her, but it did not speak.

10

Meloku held her hands on the edge of the shuttle's acceleration couch, trying to steady her pulse.

Her safety harness hung loosely over her shoulders. She had space. She could stretch her arms and legs. The shuttle came with a bed, subsonic soporifics, and a pantry stocked with crumbless, oilless foods and treats. All a lavish expenditure for an interplanetary craft, which was why these shuttles were now restricted to ground service. *Ways and Means* could only produce a trickle of antimatter. It could not spare much for these shuttles.

Meloku could not be comfortable. She leaned back in her couch, and shifted again.

Since she had gone to see Habidah, she had lived in a state of constant irritation, fluster, bitterness. She could not stand still. Her skin seemed to belong to someone else.

She was always being watched. The shuttle's NAI tracked her movement, her breath, the dilation of the capillaries under her skin. She was accustomed to being watched. She had lived with NAIs and AIs all her life. They knew her intimately.

Companion would have diagnosed it as cognitive dissonance. Guilt.

She had always hated Habidah for her ability to get under her skin. All Habidah had had to do was mention Joanna's name.

Meloku had already scheduled a visit to Queen Joanna later this year. It had not looked odd to bump the trip up. Dahn had not even asked.

Meloku had made so many visits to the Queen of Naples over the years that, for convenience's sake, she had asked for regular quarters. Joanna had at once agreed to provide them. She could not help but do so.

The shuttle breezed to a halt astride the palace balcony. The boarding ramp had just enough reach to touch the railing. As she strode down it, the roar of the thrusters battered her ears. The cacophony dwindled as she passed the blurred boundary of the shuttle's stealth fields. The howl of its engines reduced to a low moan, like a wind.

A number of stories of hauntings had sprouted up around Queen Joanna's homes over the years.

When Meloku turned her retinal infrared off, all she could see of the shuttle was the tongue of the boarding ramp. It evaporated into a gray haze, and blended into the light. Meloku leapt lightly onto the balcony.

The boarding ramp vanished, and, soon after, the windless howl died to nothing.

Meloku was stuck here until next sunset. The shuttle's NAI would not fly during the day.

She had no trouble finding a safe path through the corridors. There were not many people about. Most were sleeping. The Kingdom of Naples was not in dire financial straits, but Joanna did not love luxury. She did not love much. She lived as simply as her situation allowed, in the palace that had been her father's seat of power. She kept a modest court and employed only as many servants as would not make her contemporaries look askance at her.

To visit her, Meloku took the guise of a Poor Clare, a Franciscan order of nuns devoted to strict poverty. Joanna had received papal dispensation to have Poor Clares live with her. To explain Meloku's frequent absences, Meloku played the part of Veroncia, a hermit. Veroncia stayed in confinement in her quarters.

Asking for the Poor Clares had been one of the few things Joanna had done on her own initiative. Joanna had her good months and her bad... everything else. Sometimes Joanna seemed wholly herself. She had always been a competent ruler. She still had the instincts, the ruthlessness. Meloku had not robbed her of that. She did not blink during public executions. More importantly, she knew her finances.

Veroncia's quarters were cramped, half the size of the room Meloku shared with Dahn. Every surface was choked with dust. Every day, Joanna's servants left food in the door slot. And every night, the matter disassembler Meloku placed there ate it. The disassembler clicked in the corner, crawling spiderlike over a desiccated bread crust.

Meloku lay on her wooden bed. There was no mattress or padding. Veronica would not have asked for any. Daybreak was an hour away. She folded her arms. She had become too stubborn to ask her demiorganics to tranquilize her. *Ways and Means* tracked that. She had nothing to do but stare and lay still. And think.

Thirty years ago, Meloku had broken Queen Joanna's mind.

It had been trivial. She hadn't even used the best of the tools at her disposal. She'd chemically induced a euphoria that had led to a powerful addiction. So powerful that, within a few days, a plurality of the neural pathways in Joanna's frontal cortex had decohered to such a degree that she might as well have died.

There had been no surgery. Meloku had not cut Joanna's brain with a scalpel. The drug she had used had "merely" encouraged Joanna's brain to rearrange itself. A human brain would happily destroy itself with sufficiently artful urging. The drug had shut off dopamine receptors on some neurons and engorged them on others. Neural impulses naturally preferred pathways with engorged receptors.

Thoughts that traveled along the other pathways withered, and died.

Meloku had imprinted her image on Joanna's mind. The chemical rewards had been the strongest when she had done as Meloku asked. Joanna's mind rewired itself to think as Meloku wanted.

Joanna had become a different person. She was utterly in thrall to Meloku. The addiction had routed her synapses in such a way that she could no longer *think* about anything Meloku told her, she could only *do*.

All the old patterns of her life had been rewritten. Weighed against such a stimulus, ambition and happiness and dignity mattered not at all.

Meloku had never been an anthropologist. Not really. She had never been *interested* in these people. She had understood their reasoning, sometimes, but that had just been another way to hold them in contempt.

Back then, Meloku's plans for this plane had been much different. She and *Ways and Means* intended to colonize it. This plane was to provide a home for Unity refugees. Taking Joanna had been a blunt instrument, a quick means of providing Meloku an inroad into the sovereigns of Europe. Joanna had been the only monarch Meloku had broken, but she was only supposed to have been the first.

Ways and Means' exile had changed things. *Ways and Means* had become a ship of nothing *but* refugees. For its own unfathomable reasons, it had decided against colonizing this world.

That still left Meloku with Joanna.

Meloku had, on other missions, done to other people what she had done to Joanna. She was not accustomed to staying around afterward. She certainly had not wanted to.

She had not thought much of Joanna. Joanna had not been a sympathetic character. Her life, her privilege and her power and her misery, were symptoms of this plane's many social diseases. *Ways and Means* and the Unity were coming to provide a cure.

Meloku had been convinced that Joanna had murdered her first husband, a seventeen year-old Hungarian duke, Andreas. Joanna publicly claimed she had been locked in her bedroom while a bevy of conspirators, only one of whom had been identified, had forced Andreas onto a balcony and hanged him. Certainly removing Andreas would have worked to Joanna's advantage. Andreas had been a megalomaniac, freed Joanna's rivals from their prisons. He had made himself unpopular in every stratum of Neapolitan society, but most crucially among the rich and the powerful. And Joanna had moved quickly to reconsolidate her grip on the powers that Andreas had taken.

Joanna could not tell her the truth. The neural pathways that contained that memory had decohered. The first time Meloku had accused her of the murder, she sat numbly accepting. The second time, she had wept. She had been willing to believe anything Meloku had told her had happened.

It hardly mattered now. Thirty years ago, Meloku had seized on the murder as a means to see Joanna as little but *guilty*. Guilty or not, Joanna had only acted as any sovereign in her environment could have. She had protected her interests. She had been good at it.

Her rule survived a Hungarian invasion. She had traveled to Avignon during the darkest months of the pestilence to stand trial for Andreas's murder. That was when Meloku had met her.

Then Meloku had taken that person and removed her. What was left of her was barely present. A shade. Somehow she still lived and ruled.

The bells for Mass boomed beyond her walls. Joanna began each morning with Mass. Meloku did not believe she was a religious person any more. One more thing she had lost. Before Meloku, whenever Joanna had gone to visit her parents' graves, she had showered coin on the crowds, a display of charity. When Meloku asked her why she had stopped, she had not remembered ever doing so. She had immediately started doing so again. All that was left of her was what was expected.

Meloku waited until she heard footsteps. She opened the door. A freckled and reedy servant girl was bringing Veroncia's morning bread and water. The girl jumped.

It had been so long since "Veroncia" had last moved that the palace workers had started to think of her as another ghost. "Look down, girl. Do not meet my eyes." After she hastened to do so, and Meloku said, "I will speak with Queen Joanna."

Asking a serving girl to disturb the queen was a hell of an imposition, but the girl did not know how to say no to Veroncia. The girl brought her to a sitting room. Azure curtains covered its foggy windows. The minutely tiled floor reminded Meloku of the mosaics that ran throughout NAI hospitals on the plane on which she'd grown up.

In the next chamber, Joanna sat in conference with her closest adviser, a dark-skinned North African. There were two other men farther away: Joanna's seneschal and the captain of the porters.

The moment Meloku saw Joanna, she knew this was not one of Joanna's good months.

Joanna's eyes were shadowed, her voice too even. She spoke fluently, cogently, but without looking at anything or anyone. Her courtiers glanced aside at the intrusion. No one entered the queen's presence without announcement unless by accident, even a Poor Clare. The serving girl bowed her head, as if just realizing what trouble she might have gotten into.

Then Joanna spotted Meloku. It was as if a current had switched on behind her eyes. She stood.

"Please leave us," she told the others.

Her advisers did not bother to hide their offense. Her seneschal started, "My Queen..."

Queen or not, he would have kept speaking, over her if necessary, had she done anything other than whirl on him with an urgency he could not have been accustomed to.

After they cleared the room, Meloku sat on the stool the

captain of the porters had used. That display was exactly why she had decided to appear unannounced. So that she could see how Joanna would react to her.

Joanna sat, and folded her arms. "What would you like of me?"

"Nothing," Meloku said. A test.

Joanna tilted her head, and then waited. It was as if she hadn't heard.

After a while, Meloku said, "I only came to see how you were doing."

"I am surviving," she said. Not a lie, Meloku recognized. An evasion – the best her condition would allow.

"Tell me how you feel," Meloku said. Joanna would interpret that as an order. She would not be able to refuse.

The pretense fell away as cleanly as though it had never been there. "I feel like shit all the time," Joanna said. "And worse every day."

That, Meloku thought, was to be expected. But she had hoped Joanna would have acclimated to it, learned to manage the symptoms.

Joanna had been looking at Meloku during her first high. The drug had glommed onto Joanna's fusiform gyrus, the area of her brain responsible for facial recognition. It had associated the highs with Meloku, the person she'd been looking at when the drug had found her.

Meloku had tried to "cure" Joanna with the best technology *Ways and Means* allowed her to use. Two small implants were lodged on the undersides of her temporal bone. They jammed current into her brain, stimulated them just like a lower-dosage version drug. Joanna would never experience the hell of withdrawal, but her dependency would never get better.

The only other solution was to give her neural demiorganics like Meloku's. Demiorganics could route Joanna's thoughts around the affected receptors, or brute-force the damaged pathways. But *Ways and Means* had placed an absolute bar on the introduction of demiorganic technology to this world.

That would have given the natives too much power.

Joanna waited, anxious. Whatever she wanted to hear, it wasn't an apology. It would have meant nothing. It would not have meant anything even to Meloku.

Meloku told her, "Explain that feeling to me as you would your doctors."

"It's worse in the mornings and the late evenings." So – when she was exhausted, full of fatigue poisons. "I try to keep my thoughts straight, practice meditation as you asked. It's all such a tangle."

Joanna was a thoughtful woman, but, with Meloku, she spoke without a pause. She was not thinking about her words. They were spilling out. Her social barriers did not function with Meloku.

Meloku felt as though she had plunged into freefall.

The last time she'd visited, Joanna had been doing better. Meloku had hoped that she would no longer need to caretake for her.

"What would you like of me?" Joanna asked again, with some desperation.

It was not that Joanna had not heard her answer the first time. It was that Joanna had not believed her. This was as aggressive as Joanna was capable of being with her.

Meloku had come with a set of questions, a battery of tests: "Have you been attending Mass?"

"I have."

"How did you feel about it?"

Joanna blinked, caught her off guard.

With anyone else, Joanna would have invented an answer. But Joanna was not capable of lying to Meloku. The thought of lying could not occur to her.

Meloku asked, "Do you believe what you were told?"

Joanna blinked again.

"Do you believe Jesus of Nazareth is your savior?"

Nothing. Not yes. Not no. No reaction. The question was irrelevant.

The last time she had asked the question, a year ago, Joanna had hesitated and given a tiny nod. At the time, Meloku had believed Joanna was making progress. That she had actually started to experience religious feeling again. Maybe she had underestimated Joanna's ability to lie.

Her demiorganics had recorded that moment. Infrared showed the capillaries in Joanna's cheeks were engorged. Her pulse had quickened. Her eyes flickered over Meloku's face. Not symptomatic of a lie. She had been searching.

With a shock, Meloku realized that Joanna had only nodded because she believed it was what Meloku wanted to see.

Joanna's chemical block against lying had not functioned because it had not been a lie. There had not enough imagination left to register it as a lie.

Meloku gathered herself, and asked, "Did you order Duke Andreas killed?"

"I don't know," Joanna said.

"Do you remember hating him?"

"Dearly."

"What about James?" Joanna was multiple times a widow. Her last and also late husband had been James IV, king of Majorca. His power had only been titular. Another lord ruled Majorca. James had died on campaign, fighting and failing to retake that land.

Meloku had arranged their marriage herself, trying to find a suitably powerless husband. James's equal rank had meant that he would have no claim over Naples, and would not usurp Joanna's powers. That had been the second worst mistake Meloku had ever made.

Joanna said, "I do not need to think about him any more."

"Are you glad he's dead?"

Joanna looked at Meloku carefully, searching again. "Do you want me to be glad?"

"He abused you in public." He had scandalized Joanna's courtiers by seizing her arm in front of them, threatening her life. "You must have *felt* it."

"I felt nothing," Joanna said.

She would pretend to be glad if Meloku told her to be glad.

Meloku leaned back into her chair. Massaging her forehead did not help the ache growing there. She could not figure out where to go from here.

She had come here to make herself feel better. To give her something to think about other than Habidah and the Company of the Star and the altered data she'd discovered. All she had done instead was add another chip of guilt to her pile.

She had made so many wrong decisions on this plane. She would continue to make them. She could not pretend that, presented with the same options, she would not do the same again.

Joanna had few of her own feelings left, but the drug had conditioned her to be very responsive to Meloku's. "Is there some way I can help you?" she asked.

Meloku lowered her hand, eyed her balefully. "I'm looking for an answer you cannot give me."

"I could try," Joanna said. A deeply buried part of her would always be convinced that she could get another, better dose if only she made Meloku happy.

"If I wanted to hide something from you," Meloku said, "if I asked you to pretend that you had never seen something, you would do so without hesitation."

"Absolutely." Joanna was almost proud.

"You shouldn't be proud of that. I'm not."

"You do not have anything to be ashamed of," Joanna said, playing the counselor. She did so without feeling. It meant nothing. It was just a way to get to the goal.

"I am not a good person," Meloku said. "I never will be."

From the way that Joanna shifted in her chair, Meloku could tell that she had made her genuinely uncomfortable. Joanna was trying and failing to think of something to say.

"I shouldn't be telling you this," Meloku said. She stood. "Excuse me."

Joanna tried to follow her, but a dismissive wave halted her. From Meloku, that was as good as an order. She just watched Meloku go.

Meloku retired to Veroncia's room, to the wooden bed. Sunlight poured through the barred, jail-like window. A vortex of dust motes swirled above her breath. It was a long time to go until nightfall.

At midday, a servant slid the usual tray of water and bread underneath the door slot. Meloku did not even look. Her matter disassembler crawled over to claim it.

11

Osia's crew had been at sea for longer stretches than this, but they had never traveled such a distance. Coral's course had already brought them into the Indian Ocean.

The air turned cooler, though not cold. Osia stood at the prow. Salt dotted her lips. She bounced pulse scans overland every morning. She no longer bothered to hide from *Ways and Means'* other agents. This trip to strange waters had invigorated more than her senses. Her foolhardiness, too.

If the rest of *Ways and Means'* crew was still intent on harassing her, she never would have escaped them anyway. Not in the long run.

Most of the time, she found little of note. Fishing traffic, river boats, vast and irrigated barley and rice and poppy fields. And even vaster tracts of wilderness. This world was still broadly unpopulated. Had she chosen to exile herself on land instead of at sea, she would have had little difficulty avoiding the natives.

She also would have found more signs of trouble, and sooner.

Her pulse scans often found more people than homes or agriculture capable of supporting them. The signatures of metal weapons, metal armor, were clear enough even at this distance. They were soldiers. Trace particles of foreign cooking carried on the wind. Jerky spiced with Indonesian pepper. Russian dried rye. Mongolian fermented yogurts.

No matter where she sailed, smoke accompanied the winds that carried her. Too much for just cooking.

After long enough spent ruminating on that, she asked

Coral to set their course far from land. The shore melted into the horizon.

Next, the east coast of Africa, and then she would take her crew on a journey few native ships were equipped to make, around that continent's southern cape. Then onto western Africa and Europe. She would see how far *Ways and Means'* influence had spread.

She could not articulate why she was sure that, if she had asked for the data rather than taken it, *Ways and Means* would have given her something other than the truth. It had the capability to lie, certainly. It could produce a simulacrum of the truth so convincing and detailed that she would have had no power to tell the difference. But it had no reason to fear telling her. There was nothing she could do to change things.

Yet it had discouraged her from heading this way. If she believed it was sincere about anything, it had been sincere about that.

With only salt on the wind and no ships within ninety kilometers, she could almost pretend things were as they had been for the past three decades.

Her crew struggled to cope with a strange set of stars and winds. Osia had cut their access to *Ways and Means'* weather satellites. She trusted their ability to cope, but they did not bother to hide their frustration.

She returned to the port aft railing, where she had gone into her last fugue. It was the place Ira had taken to calling her "brooding spot." She needed the quieter space to think. The forecastle blocked the wind.

Even after living with her as long as they had, her constructs did not quite understand the range of her hearing. They did not have her specs. She had never shared them. Their words carried on the wind.

"Paranoid, distrustful," Braeloris told Coral and Straton. "Even of me. Even of *it.*" She must have meant *Ways and Means.*

Coral pointed out, "She knows you always have an ulterior motive."

"I do not. That was fiction." In the serial, Braeloris had tried her hand at comforting the other crew mostly to make *herself* feel better. "We should compile our concerns, send them to *Ways and Means*. It might be compelled to take her back."

Straton asked, "Whether she wants to go or not?"

The wind had shifted, taken the rest of their words. Osia could not talk to them about it without giving away her eavesdropping.

Ira said little. He just spun his rigging knife. Of all of them, he alone seemed to realize the distance at which she could hear them. She caught him staring at her when work slowed. Studying her.

One late red evening, he settled his elbows on the railing next to her. "Going to be like this for the entire voyage, then? Like a gargoyle? Not going to help?"

"You don't need my help," she said.

"It would be nice," he said. "It would show that you cared. Sailing around the tip of the world, in a boat as primitive as this, is not the easiest thing you could have asked us to do."

"You seem to be doing well enough." She had tracked their position. If her crew had made any serious error, she would have corrected them.

"It's not about whether we 'do' well or not. It's about us, watching you stand here, doing nothing."

"You're the crew. I'm the captain." And they were not sentient. Their social performances were mimicry, a knot of feedback loops. It did not often behoove her to remind them of that, though. They were her only company. And they were sufficiently personlike to needle her.

"Is this what it was like up there?" He nodded to the reddening sky. "You were the crew, it was the captain? It just gave orders, and you followed?"

"Broadly," she said, though she could not hide her discomfort. "Yes."

"Then how did you end up here?"

She tightened her lips, looked at him.

Ira answered with a low, mocking whistle. "She moved. Now we know she's serious."

There were not many things Osia missed about her human body, but the ability to take deep and measured breaths was one of them. Simple physical actions that helped to defuse her. Her demiorganic body could be a prison cell. She had no easy releases.

She turned back to the sea, and the deep red of the horizon. Truncated radio traffic from *Ways and Means'* satellites babbled at the fringes of her awareness.

Ira stepped as if to leave, and then stopped, behind her. "Do you think *Ways and Means* cared about you?" he asked.

Osia did not dignify him with an answer. She focused on anything other than what she was hearing and thinking. She failed. She must have meant something to *Ways and Means*. It had listened to her. Even after all this time, and in the face of mounds of contrary evidence, she refused to believe that she had been made a scapegoat. Maybe that was part of it. But it couldn't have been everything.

Ira asked, "Do you care about how *we* feel?"

"I only care about what I need to," Osia said. "Why are you pushing me?"

"I've been trying to make up my mind about which side I want to be on."

"Whose 'side?'" Osia asked. She refused to look at him. "There are no 'sides' on this ship."

"Thanks. I figured it out."

Ira punched his rigging knife into her lower back.

The tip of his blade speared through her internal shock armor. Before she had a chance to process what was happening, he had buried his knife to the hilt.

Its point pierced a command routing node deep in her spine.

Her vision flashed white and dark. A flurry of confused

nerve signals spiked through her system. It was the nearest thing to pain her body would deliver.

An instant later, emergency combat awareness programs kicked in. Her sense of time dilated. Dimly, she perceived Ira sawing upward, destroying vital nerve threads.

Half of her body had dropped away from her. Her legs locked in place, inoperable. Ira had destroyed most of the nerves reaching them.

He couldn't be allowed to continue sawing, no matter how unpleasant her options for removing him. She had to do something, her training screamed. She reviewed her combat programs' options, selected one.

She grabbed the railing for leverage. Then she twisted, first to the left, and then – as Ira struggled to keep his grip – hard to the right. His knife lodged in her internal armor. Ira lost his hold on it. The knife stayed in her.

Ira lost his footing along with his grip. He stumbled into her as she turned around. She lost her balance, sagged into the railing. He fell into her, facing her.

She tasted the heat of his breath, of his cheeks.

Osia did not dream like unaltered humans did. But she remembered what dreams were like. They were like this. Moments of nonsensicality punctuated by discontinuity. Narratives of anxiety strung together. This was a dream. This couldn't be happening. All the usual denials.

Color returned in flashes, strobes of broken perception. Ira snarled, his face red-rimmed against the sunlight, hallucinatory.

Pieces of her awareness kept dropping out, taken over by emergency response and management programs. Ira's blade had struck where her impact armor was the thinnest. Ira shouldn't have known to hit where he had. He'd gone right through armor and muscle, known which node to destroy. Up or down a centimeter, and he would have done less.

Now he attacked her like she was human. He squeezed her neck with one broad hand. She had no airway to crush. He should have known that.

She saw the rest of her constructs over his shoulder, open mouths shadowed. They were yelling. Calling for Ira to stop. Coral was closest. Thi was running to help.

Osia could not trust thir when thi got here.

Osia's combat programs presented limited options. Without functioning legs, she could not run away. She did not have the leverage to shove him off.

Her nervous system's best hard route to her legs had been destroyed. The surviving connections did not have either the bandwidth or the speed to control demiorganic musculature. There was another option: radio. In the absence of signals from above, her waist and legs had become independent, governed by emergency management programs. There were radio receiver cells scattered through Osia's body.

She would need time. Precious seconds. Her autonomous systems below the point of damage would need convincing that Osia's transmissions weren't a hostile force trying to hijack her body. Encrypted handshakes would have to be exchanged, extracted, triple-checked. And *then* came the hard work of developing a language of command.

Ira brought his free hand behind him. She felt his muscles shift. He was grabbing something. Another weapon. A knife. Of *course* he would bring another if he planned to attack her.

She began receiving some signals from below her waist. The security handshakes were in progress. But her demiorganic muscles were complicated, and her bandwidth limited. Her autonomous systems had not yet developed an effective language for movement. Osia did not need to wait to see the flash of Ira's second knife to decide that she had only a single option.

She lifted her arm from the railing, and then drove her elbow into it as hard as she could. The wood splintered. The railing cracked, gave way.

Osia fell backward.

As Ira whirled his knife, the two of them lost what little

balance they had. He tried to back away. Osia grabbed his wrist. She pulled him with her.

His nightmare snarl turned to an open-mouthed yelp of surprise. Her world tilted.

They plummeted. She held on to his wrist. In midair, she squeezed hard, felt artificial bone fracture, *pop*. He let go of his knife. It tumbled away, struck the water at the same instant they splashed in.

The water was a sensory shock. Her vision went black and white again. Digital agony trilled up her back as salt water crept through her wound, into systems never meant to be exposed. Her nerves shorted. Her last, tenuous hardwired connections to her legs flared and died. Damage reports plastered her subconscious.

But her autonomous systems finally established radio control of her legs.

She kicked free of Ira's tangle of limbs. Her ankle landed in his sternum. She pushed herself away. Her body was still not quite hers. She needed time to test her new means of controlling her body. Her legs twitched and jerked as her autonomous systems ran them through a battery of tests, calibrating response times.

Most of all, now that she had the mental energy to spare, she needed to call for help. She sent a distress signal to *Ways and Means*, via its satellite network.

Nothing. No answer.

Shock boiled in the back of her throat. She tried again, knowing she would receive no answer. Rage was next. She was several meters under the surface, but that shouldn't have interfered. Even from here, she could pick up truncated radio snippets of routine chatter. Her signal was being ignored.

She and Ira had plunged in head-first. Ira thrashed to right himself, swam toward the surface. Osia's combat programs presented her with a slew of options. They sensed her mood, ordered them from wicked to cruel.

Osia's feet had been designed for freefall gripping. They

had toes as long, and dexterous, as her fingers. She lashed out with one of them, snagged Ira by his tunic's collar. She bunched the linen tight, squeezing his neck. She dragged him down.

Neither she nor he needed to breathe. An important difference between them, though, was that she had been built to approximate a human, and Ira to *simulate* one. He still drew breath. He turned purple if it was held. He believed he needed it.

She pulled him into darkened waters.

The boat loomed over them, a heavy shadow under sunset-red glimmering waters. He swung at her leg. Underwater, he was too sluggish to batter her.

Osia carried him under the port hull. She swung him around, slammed him against the wood. The planks were slick with the slime of sea travel.

Ira kicked and spasmed. He was losing control. She held him against the wood, firmly, arcing her legs around and hooking them under the boat to keep herself anchored. He reached toward the sunlight. She felt his pulse beat hard against his skin, false capillaries burst.

She waited until his eyes turned toward her, and he finally he found her gaze.

The angle of the sunlight fell so that he could see her. "Why?" she mouthed.

He opened his lips. A torrent of bubbles exploded out, made a brief curtain between them. He sucked water into his lungs. He convulsed.

She gripped him tighter. He turned his eyes to her ,one last, desperate moment. And then the convulsion stopped. He went limp in her hands. His pulse, already thready, ceased.

He had to be faking it. Tricking her. She held him a minute longer, waiting. His neck hung loose. He stared. A deep pulse scan found no electrical activity in any of his muscles or nervous centers. If he was faking death, it was a very good simulacrum.

He could have lived. *Should* have lived. Again, she wondered if this was a dream.

She had to find out more. There was only one good way to do that, and to make sure that he wasn't playing dead.

Pinning him to the hull with one hand, she drew back her other and smashed it into his chest.

Fragments of titanium and steel, scraps of skin, and ribbons of gore splashed her arm. A dark cloud mushroomed between her fingers.

She pried his metal ribs away. She reached inside, fished through silver viscera of nerve fibers, battery coils, and muscle gel, she found what she was looking for: slivers of foggy yellow glass. Memory cells. They were still slick with fake blood.

She placed them in her mouth to keep them from floating with the current. She shook her hand free of blood and gel. Even if he had faked his death, he couldn't have faked this. She released him.

It did not take him long to sink into the mote-filled dark.

She swam underneath her ship's keel, taking her time. She surfaced, as quietly as she could, on the side opposite the one she'd fallen in. Even without pushing herself over the deck, she heard the others talking, yelling.

They were calling for her. Calling for Ira. Braeloris was weeping. More than once, Braeloris claimed, she had told Coral she was afraid Ira would do something like that. At that, the others grew more heated. They shouted at each other, and then scuffled.

They did not sound like assassins.

She could hear *Ways and Means'* satellites chatter on all their normal frequencies. She made one last-chance call to *Ways and Means*. No answer. Her fury burned incandescent.

Most of her crew was by the broken railing, but Tass had remained by the mainmast, her hand over her mouth. She turned. When she saw Osia climb over the edge of the deck, she gave a cry.

On the other side of the ship, Coral had gotten thir hand around Braeloris's chin, had raised a fist. Straton was yanking thir off. At the cry, they all turned.

Osia had not bothered to grab Ira's knife. Her hands were better weapons, but that meant she had nothing to brandish, nothing to signal to her crew that they shouldn't get closer. With a swift stroke, she chopped at the railing, snapped a segment loose. She leveled it, held the sharper end facing Coral. Thi halted mid-stride.

Coral actually looked stunned.

For that alone, Osia couldn't go without explaining herself. "I cannot trust you or anything right now."

"*He* must have switched sides, but none of us did. We don't have any reason. We wouldn't betray you or anybody"

"*What* other side?" Osia asked.

Coral blinked. "The Sarrathi. The partisans."

Osia held her makeshift spear rigid. The deck shifted. She rolled her heels, still adjusting to her makeshift means of controlling them. For too long a moment, she could not find any answer.

The Sarrathi partisans had been her constructs' old nemeses, the villains of the serial Coral and her crew had come from.

12

Betrayal was a fact of *condottieri* life. Betrayal was how they kept the communes on edge. The threat of it convinced the cities, kingdoms, and communes who hired them to pay richly and to always promise more.

It was all part of the racket.

When Fia's night bodyguards stirred her awake with news that Captain Mirko Blazovic's soldiers had been stealing out of camp in ones and twos, with excuses of errands, she knew what was happening.

She rolled, stiff-limbed, from her nest of Milanese linen and ermine furs. The furs had been a gift from Naples, a small but significant part of the bribe Queen Joanna had paid to entice the company's exit from Neapolitan territory. The pain in the small of her back helped center herself.

She told her guard, "Wake our corporals. Have them offer departing officers contracts with the Company of the Star at one and a half times their usual monthly rate. Cap at six florins for a man-at-arms, ten for officers, unless known by reputation to be worth more. Offer stands only so long as the rate remains secret."

She couldn't have her other officers knowing how much she was willing to pay. Secrecy of pay rates was another *condottieri* device. All of her officers were well used to keeping their pay a secret, each believing themselves to be making more than his neighbor.

Pain pried at her. She had been too exhausted to wash her hair well. Some blood had dried in it, made a painful tangle on her scalp. That blood come from a man struck by a bolt beside her. She'd bled plenty enough herself over the past few days. Her left shoulder was a mat of scabbing. A mace had glanced off her armor, landed a spike between its joint. She still could not stand to raise that arm higher than her shoulder.

Exhaustion trumped pain. On another night, she could and would have gone back to sleep. But Blazovic's had not been the only betrayal she'd tasted since coming to Siena. Coppery heat roiled on her tongue.

A blast of thunder resonated in her lungs. And then another. Reports from the artillery mounted on Siena's walls. The city's defenders fired at intervals, not to kill her men but to harry them. In turn, her men took shifts under the walls, shouting oaths and insults and playing marching instruments. Anything that might keep the Sienese awake.

It had been going on like this for a week. It could not go on for much longer.

When the sky lightened, the air was still and gray, choked with the ash of her camp's fires. Captain Blazovic drew his company up in marching order by predawn. He halted outside the Company of the Star's barricades. An array of Fia's men stood at watch. Her soldiers were good at keeping their pay to themselves, but few other secrets. Long before dawn, every man had heard that Blazovic would be leaving a seven-hundred-man hole in their front lines. Her corporals had already drawn plans to fill it.

Fia was among the last to arrive at the barricade gates. Captain Laskaris trailed after her. He had become her new personal guard after Kristo's death. Caterina strode beside her. She had hardly left Fia's side since that first battle at Siena's walls.

Fia must have looked like a horror, a demon. The blood in her hair had dried black. She stood straight, hiding the usual pain in her back and the stiffness in her arms and legs. She was pleased to see several of Blazovic's officers, men with reputations, on her side of the lines. Blazovic must have noticed too, but he said nothing. He did not glance in their directions. The exchange of pieces was part of their game.

Blazovic bent at the knee when she signaled she was ready to address him. He looked to the ground, as he would before his lord. Fia tilted her head.

"Captain Fiametta of Treviso," he said, formally, "it is only with my sincerest regrets that I take my leave of your mission today."

Fia had not expected this treatment in the least. She said, "I am not a captain." Antonov was nowhere in sight. She had not seen him in a day. Inevitably, word of this exchange would get back to him. Blazovic might even have been trying to drive a wedge between them.

"We all know you by the rank you've earned."

"How much is Siena paying you?" Fia asked.

Blazovic quoted a sum of seven thousand florins, three thousand of which had been paid in advance. It was an impressive amount for a company his size, particularly given that, as was standard practice, he had not divulged the additional consideration that would be paid personally to him and his closest corporals. Fia said, "They'll never pay the balance even if they survive. Siena has been in debt to us for years."

"Their advance payment went a considerable distance to soothe my mistrust."

"You're open about your dishonor. Why are you bowing?"

"My aim has only been to serve you. But I do not need to go further here. The enemy is near."

"You mean that you're afraid of fighting John Hawkwood."

"It would be better to say I am afraid no longer."

Half of the battles *condottieri* fought against each other were that of threat and intimidation. Hawkwood's sacking of Faenza and Cesena had made him into a monster even to men like Blazovic.

Though it was futile, she could not help but argue. "If we can get inside Siena's walls, Hawkwood will be stymied."

"We're stymied now."

She had hoped to take Siena quickly, by storm and by surprise. There still seemed a chance she could do it. It got slimmer every day.

She could accuse him of more dishonor, of treachery, malicious iniquity, and anything else she liked, but they both knew it would mean nothing. This was business. What was *not* business was the manner in which he treated her submissively even as he withdrew. He was ashamed. Ashamed, she realized, of abandoning his preacher.

For all that he had made up his mind to escape, that shame troubled him. Desperation shone steady in his eyes. More than most, Captain Blazovic had been changed by Saint Renatus.

He said, "I will continue sharing with the world what you shared with me. I will tell them the stories."

"Go, then," she said. "Do that." She did not stay to watch him march off, or her corporals fill the gap he'd left.

She had better things to do. A siege to manage, a battle to prepare for.

She had not taken her commander's baton to meet Blazovic. That would have looked pathetic, trying to exert authority over a man who would not listen. Now she went back to her pavilion to fetch it.

In truth, Fia was surprised that it had taken so long for her first commander to desert her. Her sentries had reported spies sneaking out of Siena's walls, disappearing into her camps. No doubt some of them were diplomats.

A score of battered men-at-arms and crossbowmen milled about her pavilion. They knew it would not be long before she gave the order to renew the assault. Many of them were scabbed and scarred too. One man walked with enough of a limp that he should have had a cane. Fia suspected a broken arch. He and a number of others shouldn't have been out.

No one wanted to miss their chance to loot Siena. Every morning, men expected this to be the day she'd finally surmount the walls. *Condottieri* could not live on pay alone. They needed loot. But they also needed comrades in fighting shape.

Without prompting, her inner voice said, *Every time you go to battle, you are reborn.*

That was true. And yet Fia had a hard time finding the comfort in it this time. Fia whispered, "If I had done as you suggested, I would have been torn apart – like Kristo."

It said, *It would not be a bad thing to be reborn a martyr.*

Had she died below the walls of Siena, her religion, her ideals, would survive. The Cult of Saint Renatus had spread far beyond the Company of the Star. Soldiers everywhere needed to hear what she had said. She would survive as a story, a legend. Maybe an end in battle would be better for the story, if not for her.

"It would not be me," she said. "It would be other men's ideas of me, and their words that would be put in my mouth."

There are many ways to live on. Not all of them leave you intact.

Her inner voice had not been this talkative in a while. She did not like it.

Captain Antonov was inside the pavilion, stripping his boots. He breathed hard and walked on stiff legs, as though he had spent the night on horseback.

"I'd started to think you'd run away, too," she snapped. Just irritation. She knew where he'd been.

"I've been at war," he said, and nodded to their oak table. A rough linen sack lay half-open upon it, spilling gold florins.

Caterina filled a wash basin from a waiting bucket. While Antonov told Fia about his adventures, Fia finally took the time to douse and dip her hair. It had become so encrusted and tangled that fire lit along her scalp whenever she tugged it.

On another week, she would have cared more. Today, a deep, bone-biting weariness had seized her. Easier to absorb the pain than to take the time to trim the tangles out.

Antonov and his foragers and pioneers had ranged the

Via Francigena, robbed and burned what hostels and farms remained near the road. He had been gone for longer because he had dived back into the marshes and grazing lands of the Maremma. He had stormed and burned monasteries.

As she washed, he told her about a fishing village. The people there had stampeded for their boats. Only they hadn't had enough boats to hold them all. They'd cast off with men and women clinging to the undersides. By morning, so many of them had drowned. Still they had refused to return to the piers. The peasants and fishermen of that impoverished little village had so feared being taken hostage that they were willing to face long odds on death.

Fia's stomach churned. "We must have raided the town recently and not remembered it," she said.

"Not us," Antonov said. "John Hawkwood was there four years ago."

Fia said nothing, though her stomach turned still sourer. She wished she could forget that name. Every time she heard it, one of her clocks ticked louder.

Antonov noted, "He could be here by now, if he wanted. Pinching us between Siena's walls and his army."

Fia knew it. Her scouts had brushed against his foragers and pioneers days ago. "Hawkwood may have his special commission from the papacy, but he is *condottieri*. He'll put himself first. He has his own special grievances with Siena. He does not mind seeing the Sienese suffer."

Antonov said, "He most likely aims to sweep up Siena after he finishes with us."

"Most likely," Fia agreed. "Let us both exhaust each other first."

Hawkwood knew how to hurt other *condottieri*. He had fanned raiders along the Via Francigena, attacked merchants coming to trade with the company's treasure train. Their food supply had tightened. Fia had tried to institute rationing, but the company's hodge-podge system of independently contracted *condottieri* was ill-equipped to oblige. Hoarding was rampant. Fia doubted meat ever reached the infantrymen. The company was as much besieged as besieger.

Caterina lifted Fia's breastplate. Her arms trembled with the weight. Antonov glanced at her. While Fia could read his disdain, he knew better than to say anything. Fia usually kept her anger restrained, but she loosed it for Caterina's sake. Fia had once struck an officer when he had dared grab Caterina's hair like she was a moppet rather than Fia's page and member of her *casa*. Fia had since given Caterina a mace, a hunting dagger, and a short sword, as well as time to practice.

The grunts and exclamations Caterina made while practicing belied the idea that she was mute. At the same time, it did not seem an affectation, or a choice. Maybe it was better to think of it as a difficulty. Fia was no stranger to difficulties. She had not chosen to crash so violently those years after she had first joined the company.

While Fia donned her armor, Antonov asked, "Do you still intend to go east?"

Caterina paused, looked to Fia. Fia couldn't remember how much of her plans Caterina had heard before. It didn't matter. Fia said, "Mercenaries can only keep a single paymaster for so long," she said. "Otherwise we'd be no better than a standing army." A caged pet.

Antonov muttered, "We have been all along." To the Turks. Their envoy was still on the way. Like Hawkwood, every time Fia thought of him, her mind turned to the clocks.

"We're a free company. The best in Italy. The pay is an excuse. The company does what serves the company's interests."

"No – a mercenary company does what is in its leader's interests. Mine."

She stopped paying attention to the pinch of her armor long enough to look at him. For years, her position had been ambiguous. She helped decide the company's path, made decisions with his voice, but always with his consent. "You really think I'm stealing your company? You haven't been putting up much of a fight."

He said, "I could countermand you. But not everyone would listen to me."

She agreed, "It would split the company."

"The company is my life's labor."

"Yours, or *theirs?*" Again, they both knew she meant the Turks. "I want to make it ours."

"Your own," Antonov said.

"If you won't step ahead and take control, someone else will. If not me, then them."

"We'll see. You have one more day at this." When Fia tilted her head, he said, "News about Blazovic's defection is still spreading. It won't have a chance to sink in until tonight. Then your commanders are going to have a better chance to think about how much worse their odds are now, and how much better for them it would be to take their bribe and go."

He didn't move to follow her after she finished donning her armor and left.

She did not pause long to review the morning's assemblage. She knew she would not like what she saw if she looked deeply. Thanks to Hawkwood, food was in precious short supply, as were bolts and fodder. The grain and livestock Antonov had captured would help, but it had not been distributed yet.

Caterina helped her onto her courser. Laskaris rejoined her, fully armored but for his helm. He was unshaven, sallow, and harried. His page, Petrus, had vanished, most likely another casualty of a crossbow bolt. Laskaris must have borrowed another officer's page for his armor this morning. She couldn't figure out how he had asked. He had hardly said a word since Petrus disappeared.

The nightly noisemaking was not the only performance on the walls. The Sienese staged public executions atop them, in full view of the invaders. Early on, the Sienese had executed their criminals and deserters, as much a message for those within the walls as without. Now, though, they tortured and hanged Fia's soldiers, men captured on sallies or during attempts to ladder the walls.

Fia recognized the whiplashed boy being led to the gallows at the wall's edge. Petrus. His parents, Grecian like Laskaris, had aimed for Petrus to enter mercenary service. It was the only way for men of low heritage to make respected names for themselves in Italy.

Laskaris heaved a long breath. Fia had put men and women in cages before, threatened to drown them, but she had never actually felt compelled to do so. That would have been affording them more dignity and respect than they deserved. Only soldiers' lives were worth enough to end, to breach the bounds of feeling and religion that kept any man from murdering his neighbor.

The thought of the Sienese doing the same or worse to Caterina made her vision darken. She clasped her sword though there was no one to fight.

Antonov had been right. Today *was* going to be their last day of trying to overwhelm Siena. Because today she was going to get through.

She held up her baton.

She had a surprise this morning. Her spies inside the city had helped a half dozen company men scale the walls. When she lowered her baton, a bevy of crossbow bolts lashed across the defenders above the city's gates – from behind.

While confusion erupted among the Sienese, her men charged. Fia held her baton ahead, and dug her gilt spurs into her courser. She did not bother to look at the rest of them. She had learned at what point in a battle it was too late to affect things as a captain. She needed to be a commander. The men at her back needed to see her – especially those who had not knowingly seen a woman at war. Every time she fought, she felt the eyes on her, ahead and behind.

The half dozen men had just been the first inside. The attack on the gate was a distraction – not that any of the men involved knew that. The second group was to attack whichever sally port the defenders used this attack. They had orders to seize and jam or destroy the inner portcullis. A heavy responsibility, but with many of the defenders through and the rest distracted, their heroism might carry the day.

A bolt glanced off Fia's armored shoulder, but it didn't impart enough of its momentum to knock her from her mount. Pain shivered through her bones, down her back.

On the ground ahead, a hasty formation of Sienese men raced around the side of wall. Salliers. They'd rushed out to keep the company from taking advantage of the confusion at the gates. There were more of them than she expected. Fewer to defend the sally port and its inner portcullis.

She had left pain somewhere far behind, but she still could not raise her arm over her shoulder. She lifted her sword to swing to the side instead. She gave herself to the rage. The Sienese wilted under crossbow fire.

She lost track of the number of impacts on her armor. None of them bit. Someone grabbed her ankle, yanked hard, forced a dismount. She almost lost her sword in another man's flesh, but managed the strength to yank it free before he toppled. The effort left her winded, distracted. Caterina must have been packing extra padding into her armor. It weighed more than ever before.

From behind, her inner voice said.

Without thinking, she ducked.

The attack was as silent as the approach. The air above her pulsed. It mirrored the jolt of her heartbeat.

She had lost her balance. Through the edge of her visor, she watched a mace head cut across the smoke-split sky.

Her inner voice said, *This is not a good time for you to be reborn as a martyr.*

She crashed to the earth. A knee to her back knocked her breath away from her. Exhaustion smothered her. For a dizzy moment, she could not stand.

A mailed glove grabbed the chin of Fia's helm. It tried to pry her head upward, to expose her neck for a killing slash.

She swung her arm backward. Her armored elbow connected with plate metal. He let go.

Such armor meant her assailant was rich. Her sword had slipped free of her grasp, but she was too close to get a good thrust or swing anyway. She pulled her thirteen-inch dagger from its sheath. With immense effort, and her armor like an anchor, she hitched up onto one knee.

Her blade glanced off the shoulder of her opponent's fluted plate, and upward. He foolishly lifted his head while he reeled. The edge slipped in his neck.

Though it would be profitable to keep a hostage, she snarled, pressed deep. Once again, she dripped with another man's blood. Her arms were painted with it.

She did not have time to consider anything. A Sienese crossbowman stood by. He must have already tried to hit her, missed. He dropped his crossbow. He charged, the tip of his sword leading his way. He held it like it was a spear, like she was a dragon a dozen times her size.

Fia's dagger was long, but not remotely up to the task of deflecting such a blow. Terror and fury coursed through her. They were tangible, real things. They brought the impossible within reach. Her armor weighed nothing. She forced herself to her feet, twisted aside. Her opponent stumbled past her.

A better time and place will come again.

If she had breath, those words would have taken it. Her inner voice *had* tried to kill her. It had confessed.

Killed while ascending the walls of Siena would have been a heroic death. Being clubbed in the back of the head by a mace was not.

As much as she wanted to, she did not need to strike the killing blow herself. By the time the crossbowman turned, more of her men had caught up with her. Laskaris spitted the crossbowman. Her officers led her out before she even saw her assailant fall. She spat in his direction, elbowed men who got too close to her. She could not understand why she was being led away. She did not have the words to ask.

Soon enough, she did not need to. The answer was obvious. They were in retreat. None of Fia's men had gotten near the sally port they had aimed to take.

The defenders were still coming from around the bend in the walls. If there had been an effort to attack the inner portcullis, it had failed.

One of the clocks ticking away in the back of her head fell silent. Then another.

There was silence in the back of her head. Not since the crossbow bolt had nearly killed her had she heard anything like it.

She had failed.

Her inner voice said, *You will grow in ways you never meant to, for purposes you cannot see.*

13

The sextet of sentries posted along the Via Francigena held their pikes as rigid as if they faced a cavalry charge rather than a sauntering lone rider.

Meloku did not understand how the people of this plane became accustomed to riding. She had been on horseback since dawn, and it had not been long before she asked her demiorganics to block the pain. Now her demiorganics were flashing warnings at the corners of her vision. They would not allow her to continue ignoring the pain. The skin on her left inner thigh was chafed to the point of tearing. And if she continued to strain her right hamstring, it would not function properly if she dismounted.

When she dismounted, she allowed the pain to seep through the demiorganics to make for a convincing gasp.

Too convincing. She staggered.

These men wore red and white on their shoulders: the colors of the Company of Saint George. John Hawkwood's men. They looked to each other.

She had been to Avignon, the home of Hawkwood's employers, a lifetime ago. She still had contacts. No one she had affected like Queen Joanna, but people who feared her. They had provided her with a cover identity. They could not give her men.

Her shuttle had taken her to the region of Hawkwood's camp. No one within miles of Hawkwood's camp was selling horses. His men had stolen them all. Even half a day's ride away, she had only been able to buy an old brown and white draft horse. The owner had been looking to sell fast, in advance of Hawkwood's advance.

She could tell that the sentries' thoughts mirrored the horse-seller's. They both thought she would be robbed before the day was over. These men were starting to think they might just be the type of men to do so. She brandished her letter. They didn't need to be literate to recognize the papacy's seal.

She explained that she had been sent by the only woman in Italy who would be ludicrous enough as to send a woman on these roads: Catherine of Siena, prophetess of Avignon, professional eccentric. Catherine had been an adviser of all the popes since the Great Mortality, and pretended to advise the rest of Europe as well.

Meloku explained her escorts had deserted her when they had discovered where Catherine had sent them, but that she had been steadfast enough to carry on. She was not carrying anything valuable. The sentries quickly decided she was not worth the trouble.

They sent two men with her – one as a messenger, and one as an escort.

She had been around enough military camps to judge their size by their odor. Her escort led her through the scent of cooking and wood fires, latrines, and manure. Some intersections smelled like chopped onions, others like wood. John Hawkwood's camp was not that bad as these things went. That was one of the damnable things about war on this peninsula. The *condottieri* armies were not that large – five or ten thousand at extremes. In the east, she'd seen armies of millions. A determined polity could fend off mercenaries like these. But Italy was no determined polity.

The armies of Italy's cities and communes stayed tucked behind their borders while *condottieri* ravaged their neighbors. Then those neighbors returned the lack of favors, or, worse, employed the *condottieri* themselves. Leagues against the mercenaries lasted no longer than a year. It was pathetically easy for *condottieri* to game.

Soon, the smells grew stronger – and not because there were more men about. It had been baked into the earth. Latrines had been buried and redug. Refuse accumulated. This camp had been here longer than these men were accustomed to staying in place.

Her escort stopped outside a bright orange pavilion. He lifted the corner of the tent flap. For the first time, Meloku noticed that three of his fingers had been cleaved at the knuckle. He smiled unkindly when he noticed her staring.

Dahn's voice leapt unbidden into her ears: "What are you doing?"

She had known it was inevitable that he would track her. She hadn't checked in since she'd traveled to see Habidah and Kacienta. Of all the times he could have picked, though, he'd called at the most awkward.

That implied that he knew it. And *that* meant that he had been watching for longer.

"Investigating," she sent.

"Interfering," he said. "I can see who you're visiting."

"I need to find out something," she said. If he said anything else, she stopped paying attention. She stepped inside the pavilion.

She was accustomed to walking into places and pretending that she belonged. She had some advantages over the natives. Her eyes did not need to adjust to the dark. Infrared showed her all four people. Two were seated. Two, a pair of bodyguards, stood by the tent flap. She waited, expectantly, for them to turn to her.

Nothing happened. No one looked up. The bodyguards hardly stirred. In spite of the ever-present risk of assassination – Italian warfare did not scruple at poison and hidden knives – they did not consider her worth the trouble of searching.

She pursed her lips. She ought to kill someone on her way out, teach them a lesson.

Smoke lingered in the air, though the fire was only warm embers. There was not much evidence of the treasures the

Company of Saint George had collected. Some gold and brass goblets, a sword and helm meant for display, a fine table. The real treasure the papacy had promised him was land.

She recognized the man seated farthest away, unfortunately. She could not have followed papal politics without knowing him. He was overweight but well sculpted, a look the natives considered handsome. He did not hide his disgust at her intrusion. He knew Catherine of Siena better than Hawkwood.

He was Cardinal Robert of Geneva, and he shouldn't have been here.

Robert and Hawkwood were the butchers of Faenza and Cesena. Hawkwood had tried, not entirely successfully, to deflect the blame for those massacres onto the other. Hawkwood was only following orders, the story went. It was Cardinal Robert who had supposedly been so furious at the murder of a handful of mercenary soldiers that he had ordered the massacre of townsfolk. Hawkwood had pretended disgust. As part of the performance, he shouldn't have been traveling with Robert again.

The plain, balding man hunched over a desk, writing, could only have been Hawkwood. He didn't look up. She could not see his face. The sentries' advance messenger must have told him who she bore a letter from. This was a message, a signal of his interest.

She deposited her letter on Hawkwood's desk. He still didn't look up.

She discreetly looked over his writing. He was composing a letter addressed to the priors of Siena. A demand for payment of past due payments, to the sum of fifteen thousand florins, plus new indemnities to refrain from further raids.

She did not move. At length, Hawkwood sighed. "You are not a nun. Some other friend of Catherine's?"

Robert of Geneva said, "No one I've ever seen with her."

Meloku ignored the challenge. The best way to prove herself was to appear not to need to. "Do you intend to read my lady's letter?"

"No," Hawkwood said.

After all the trouble she had gone to forging that letter, too. Catherine of Siena fancied herself a meddler, sending letters to every power in Italy and beyond. Few of those powers paid any attention. Meloku had done a little research to prep for this visit. In Catherine's last letter to Hawkwood, she had called him an "athlete of God," serving the papacy against the heretical *condottieri* Cult of Saint Renatus. She had not mentioned the letter before, in which he had been a "son of Belial" for abandoning, however briefly, papal service in favor of Florence.

Meloku said, "She'll expect an answer."

"When time allows."

"I can wait."

Hawkwood didn't take his attention off the page, but he was no longer writing.

Meloku enjoyed needling men like him. If there was one thing she could not stand about the natives, it was their vanity. It was her pleasure to puncture it, make farces of their displays and rituals.

She didn't need to break *Ways and Means'* rules and bring out her technology. Her cover gave her power enough. Catherine of Siena had the ear of the pope. It would not do to have someone in Catherine's orbit unhappy.

Robert said, "Follow as you wish. You won't like where we're headed."

"Really? It looks to me as though you've been sitting here for weeks while Siena burns."

Robert did not answer. He could not admit, to one of Catherine's agents, that he had countenanced Hawkwood's delay.

She asked Hawkwood, "What do you intend to do with yourself after the Crusade?" The big question, the one that might help her determine who was manipulating these men, and why.

He ignored her.

She lifted her chin, this time exaggerating the movement to make sure he noticed her peering over his shoulder. "I doubt the priors have that much left. The Company of the Star is likely taking the last of what they have thanks to your inaction."

Hawkwood reflexively slapped his hand over the letter. It smeared the fresh ink.

"Not accustomed to dealing with literate women?" Meloku asked. As a member of Catherine's retinue, she would of course read Latin. After the telling pause that followed, she said, "My lady Catherine is under the impression that you intend to *save* her city from this Satanic cult."

Hawkwood said, "The city of Siena is in arrears of payments promised to me and my company."

Robert said, hastily, "Of course we bear no ill intent for any friend of the papacy."

"Artful," Meloku told Robert, with three times the sarcasm as would have sufficed. "Well saved."

Hawkwood swept the ruined letter aside. He turned to her, and for the first time Meloku saw his face. Like many of the generals, murderers, and tyrants Meloku had met, he was entirely unremarkable. Maybe a little so much so as to be sad. Fat lips. Thin hair. A perpetual pout. His was a face that artists would have to work hard to misrepresent.

Hawkwood asked, "In God's name, what do you want from me?"

"All my lady and I want is an answer. After this battle is over, what do you intend to do with yourselves?"

When Hawkwood and Robert looked to each other, Meloku thought she would need to prompt them again. Hawkwood said, "This is not a secret. I already have lands in the Romagna. Per my contract with His Holiness, I will have more when this campaign ends. They can be prosperous lands. But they need a lord and defender."

"You don't intend to press your conquests?" Meloku asked.

"To reshape Italy?"

"What profit is there in that?" he asked, dryly.

"You tried to settle in the Romagna before. You had to give it up when your neighbors kept making war on you." Having lands to defend was bad for business. Raiding was better. "What makes you think this will go any better?"

Meloku knew immediately that she'd gone too far. Hawkwood's simmering frustration exploded. "What the fuck does Catherine mean by this? Did she even tell you to ask?"

Without missing a beat, Meloku turned to Robert. "And you? Will you stop pushing after Siena?"

"The papacy intends to return to Rome, of course. Catherine knows this. She argues for it."

This could be something. A geopolitical motive for *Ways and Means* to be manipulating events in this region. But it didn't seem big enough. The papacy could be manipulated from Avignon as easily as Rome.

Before she could answer, Hawkwood scoffed. "And Catherine should know just as well that it will never happen. She and Pope Gregory are the *only* people in Avignon who want to leave. Avignon is filthy, but it's safe. Rome is ruled by outlaws, and it's poor. If Gregory tries to go, the cardinals will tie him to his throne."

Robert bristled. "His Holiness has awarded you a more generous contract than I argued for, given your prior abandonment–"

"Even *you* would hold him back if you thought he would go," Hawkwood said, and for the first time she heard the contempt he held for Robert.

Meloku's retinal infrared said Hawkwood was right. The pattern of blood in Robert's cheeks suggested that he was not actually offended or angry – only playing a role. In any case, she had seen enough now.

"You're both such goddamned messes," Meloku told them.

When Meloku had last been in the position of manipulating people on this plane, she had not been able to alter everyone as she had Joanna. She had chosen her targets not just for the power they held. Consistency, stability, and predictability were the most important traits of a good patsy. These men were none of those things. She wouldn't have selected them, and was willing to bet that no one else would have, either. It was plain enough that they were in control of their own actions.

Just to make sure, she pulse scanned the area.

The results nearly robbed her of her composure.

Hawkwood's pavilion was replete with technology. Real tech. Unity tech. Their electronic signatures flared like torches. There were four sources nearby. One was underneath a table, another in a dresser, a third on a decorative silver helmet, and the last on the frame of Hawkwood's bed. All objects that would be carted from camp to camp.

Eavesdroppers or the like. Maybe more than that.

Hawkwood and Robert were no longer listening to her, or she to them. She left them to argue.

Her escort had vanished. Outside, she stopped, and curled her nose at the fouled air. All around her, she smelled suffering. Bad food. Sweat. Sickness. The angry lethargy of men who'd been stuck in one place for too long.

Even the conquerors of this plane were miserable. The nearest man was a groomsman, likely a slave, tending to a palfrey worth ten times as much as him. He looked to her, and then quickly away.

Her pulse scan had captured more than technology. Every glint of metal, every coin, every helmet, every sword and arrowhead glittered in her mental map of the camp. She had quite an imagination, and thought she had grasped the scale of this place – but there were more weapons here than she would have guessed.

She had always held herself above these people. Over the course of her exile, she had started to realize that was a defense mechanism. There was so much suffering here. And so much ahead.

Meloku did not want to be a part of it. After Hawkwood beat Fiametta of Treviso, if he could, he would attack Siena just like she had. He would torch the countryside until he got his lucre.

Ways and Means was manipulating all of this. Meloku had done a lot she'd learned to regret, but even then, she never could have done something like *Ways and Means* was doing. Never been a party to it if she had known *Ways and Means* would cause it.

Now that she was outside, she took another pulse scan, this one long-range. She wanted to see how far *Ways and Means'* reach extended. What she found took her aback.

The eavesdroppers were gone. Or apparently so. There was no more electronic activity, even in Hawkwood's tent.

They were still there, of course. A third, more careful scan picked them up. Little bits of metal, alloys beyond the natives' manufacturing capability. If she hadn't been looking so closely, and hadn't known what she was looking for, she never would have seen them. They had gone dead, silent, after the first time she scanned them.

Maybe there were more. Her pulse scan wouldn't have picked up demiorganics, not if the demiorganics had been made to stay hidden. Or implants. Hawkwood and Robert could have carried both.

She once again had her demiorganics mute the pain as she mounted her horse. She took her ride out long and slow. The guards at the barricades didn't glance at her.

Half an hour out, she took another pulse scan to be sure. The eavesdroppers were still off. Still hiding from her.

The scan also found three of Hawkwood's men had set off after her. They rode a scant half-kilometer behind her, and gaining. Stalking.

*Tssk*ing in irritation, she readied her combat programs.

Ways and Means had forbidden its agents from taking lives unprovoked. *Provoked* was a different matter. Quickest thing to do was to shoot them all. The skin above her right wrist split open, oozing blood. A titanium dart nestled into place just behind the opening, its tip red. She had dozens more like it, nestled and ready to go.

She watched her wrist bleed under the sunlight.

After a moment's consideration, she ordered her demiorganics to reseal her skin. The darts returned to their bone-cradles.

By the time Hawkwood's men caught up with her horse, she was long gone, vanished into the brush. Her demiorganics blocked the pain of torn skin with every step she took.

She'd killed men like those before. Last time, she hadn't hesitated.

She pushed through the deep brush of the forest, scowling. This would mean a lot more time walking. And thinking. She didn't like what she had to think about.

She took periodic scans. Still no sign of eavesdroppers back there. They had switched off, masking their electronic signatures. They were hiding from her.

That didn't make sense. If they were hiding, they should have hidden from her first scan too. Unless the power behind them hadn't known, until that scan, that she was there.

As a matter of course, *Ways and Means* knew where all its agents were at all times. If it wanted to hide its eavesdroppers from her, it should have deactivated them the moment she entered the area.

The sky purpled, and the air turned unseasonably cold. She stood still in a clearing, shivering, waiting. Her chill didn't go away after her shuttle had landed, or after she had boarded.

14

Osia retreated to her tiny cabin as soon as she could. Her constructs did not attack her, but she never turned her back. She paused only to splinter wood from a crate. Safely in her quarters, she lodged it through her door handle, jammed it into the frame. Her constructs had the strength to break through, but this would give her warning, at least.

She turned her attention to Ira's memory cell. It dripped onto her floor. The water had washed the gore off it.

She squeezed it in her palm, readied her full suite of antiviral defenses. And then she opened a data channel to the cell.

The memory cell had been wiped clean.

She was already a toxic slurry of emotions, keeping her from thinking clearly. Frustration swilled to the top. The cell shouldn't have been empty. *Could not* have been, under most circumstances. The cell was designed to preserve data against erasure in the event that it was needed as forensic evidence.

The key was in the composite that held the cell together. No matter whether the old data was cleared and new written over it, there should always have been electrostatic traces left in that composite, ions stuck in colloidal suspension. With exemplary Unity efficiency and ingenuity, the cell had been designed so that its own casing medium was a backup.

With work and time, it should have been possible to reconstruct key fragments of Ira's memories. Thoughts that had occurred often would leave deeper traces.

Yet these had been eliminated. Before she had ripped the cell out of Ira, a power surge had destroyed the whole cell, boiled away most of the composite casing. This was not programmed behavior. Her constructs' bodies had not been built to allow a surge to reach the memory cells.

Whoever had done this had had to override several safeguards. And they would have had to do it in a hurry, too. Ira could not have functioned without these cells. Sometime between when she had "drowned" him, and when she had pulled the cells out of him, this had happened.

Ways and Means had designed her constructs. It had intimate knowledge of how they worked. Better than hers.

She paced in her cabin's tiny confines. A step or two forward. A step back. With her injury, it took effort.

Despite its artificiality, her demiorganic body had been made to feel like the real thing. If she had wanted to, she could have zoomed her perceptions to the fine grain, received reports from individual nerve clusters, sure. But she did not *sense* her body that way. Her brain was still human, even transferred to a medium of demiorganic neurons. Her autonomous systems took care of the fine details.

The knife wound changed things. She controlled part of herself by radio, by remote, and that took effort. Her legs *felt* alien, like they were loose parts grafted onto her. Some of the sensations filtering up were choked, compressed, by the format.

It was as if the fringes of her vision had turned grayscale, or her brain had stopped processing images in three dimensions. She'd lost something important. She'd had centuries to take it for granted.

She bundled her rage into a transmission of wordless protest, spiked it at *Ways and Means'* satellites.

Again, they ignored her.

She could not recall having felt so much nervous energy since she had been fully human. She would have called it adrenaline then. Now she didn't have that excuse. She was losing control.

She knew she was because she could not quite believe that

Ways and Means wanted to kill her.

She knew it was capable of killing. It *had* killed without what most people would call a second thought. But it had happened to other people. She had lived with it for too long. A stubborn, irrational part of her insisted that it could not do that to her.

She ought to have been tallying her resources. Weighing options. She had friends she could call upon. She doubted the satellites would let her call them, but she could reach them on foot. It all seemed moot.

If *Ways and Means* wanted to try again to kill her, it didn't need to have the constructs to do it. It was heavily armed.

Unless it had wanted to kill her secretly. To hide the killing from other crewmembers. A missile firing, even a beam pulse, would be impossible for them to miss. They would have detected either even if they weren't watching. Reprogramming her constructs was less visible.

Her constructs talked about the Sarrathi partisans, the big bad evil empire from their serial, as though they were real. Osia had programmed them to know that their backgrounds were fictional. She had wanted company, not a fantasy.

In the serial, in most endings, Ira had betrayed the others. It was possible, just barely, Ira had attacked her not just to kill her, but because he thought he was betraying her to the partisans. That would make it not an assassination attempt, but a symptom of a deeper malfunction.

He might have been playing out his role. So, it seemed, were the others.

That didn't explain the satellites, or the burned-out memory chip.

She pulled the door jamb out.

In most of the serial's many endings, there had rarely been any funeral or other recognition for Ira if he died after his betrayal. There was none now. She found her crew grim, working steadily. Straton looked up when she emerged, but said nothing.

A sliver of land crested the northeastern horizon. Her course should have taken them around the cape by now. The smoke of a distant city crossed her nose. There was no hint of war in it. Just the ordinary whiff of animal decomposition that accompanied civilized life on this plane.

She could have, *should* have, disembarked. Left her constructs to their fantasy. Traveling by sea was still the fastest way to get to Europe. Ira's attack had come not long after she had abandoned *Ways and Means* and decided to head to Europe. That meant her decision to travel there could have triggered it. *Ways and Means* didn't want her to reach it. Going by land would take months. And, for all its primitiveness, she couldn't operate this vessel by herself.

She found Coral atop the aftcastle. Osia approached, cautiously.

Coral said, "There's nothing to say about it."

"Not even 'I'm sorry'?"

Thir lips were tight. In the serial, most of the time Coral had seen Ira slipping before his betrayal, and blamed thirself for not catching it. Thi said, "I can't be sorry when I don't know why he attacked you."

When thi did nothing else, Osia left.

Straton and Braeloris stood by the prow. When Osia approached, Braeloris eyed her balefully, turned away. Straton kept his gaze fixed on the sea.

Osia waited. In answer to her unspoken question, Straton said, "I need to watch for partisans."

In the serial, their crew's submarine, called the *Whiptail*, had been ultramodern. "Why not use the *Whiptail's* sensors?" she asked.

He waved toward the mast. "Does this pile of splinters look like it has sensors?"

"How do you imagine you got from the *Whiptail* to this ship?"

"How do you think? You made us. You needed company on this awful plane."

He turned his attention back to the water. Osia waited, but he suffered no dawning realization.

He knew where he was. He should have known the partisans weren't real.

Her constructs were losing their minds in bits and fragments. That implied a virus, a slow corruption, rather than a whole takeover. That by itself was interesting. If *Ways and Means* had wanted, it could have controlled them all remotely, attacked without delay.

Foolish hope swelled within her, though she tried to quash it. *Ways and Means* may not have meant to kill her, but only trouble and delay her. Or its instructions may have affected Ira, interacted with his history and personality, in a way it hadn't meant to.

No. She could not allow herself to think like that. Part of her was looking for any excuse to exonerate it. It did not explain why *Ways and Means* would not answer her call now.

Someone... *Ways and Means*... was trying to kill her. For whatever reason, their means were constrained. But she could not believe that they would be so forever.

She needed to find help. *Ways and Means* had plenty of other agents on this world. Whatever they thought of her, not all of them would willingly be complicit in her murder.

Osia had not had friends aboard *Ways and Means*, not really. Before her exile, her closest acquaintance had been an old hand named Xati. They had trained together. In the past century, she and Xati had only seen each other once every few months, and sometimes not for longer than a year.

Osia had not seen em at all after she decided to come to the surface. There was a good chance Xati was complicit in whatever *Ways and Means* was doing to this plane. But Osia was sure e would not have countenanced what *Ways and Means* was doing to her.

Last she had heard, Xati was on long-term surface assignment. E had been assigned to a monitoring post and communications station deep in the Carpathian Mountains.

There were other agents, other people Osia knew. But Xati was the only one she had trusted. And e was also, probably, still close to whatever *Ways and Means* wanted to keep Osia from reaching.

"I'm changing our course," Osia told Coral.

"Why?" Coral asked. Thi did not bother to hide her suspicion, just as Osia did not bother to explain herself. She just gave thir their new heading.

Staying up on deck with them seemed like tempting fate. Osia returned to her quarters, jammed the wooden stake through the knob again. Periodic scans kept her apprised of her ship's progress.

She sat with legs folded, and tried to still her pulsing anxiety. She would not have called her life aboard *Ways and Means* uncomplicated, but it very much seemed so now. There had been plenty of distracting luxuries.

Aboard the planarship, zero-gravity parkland spiraled around open cylinders. Hyperprecision planar gateways moved travelers from one end of the ship to another, mimicking teleportation. *Ways and Means* had even kept a vast alien menagerie outside its hull, protected from cosmic radiation by the fields that held its atmosphere in place. *Ways and Means* had called it a zoology experiment.

She had been rare among the crew in that she had few friends or partners, but she had not been solitary. She had had *Ways and Means*. They'd all had *Ways and Means*. The amalgamate's pervasiveness was one of the reasons – *the* reason – most of its crew had worked so hard to earn the privilege to come aboard. The amalgamates held themselves at a remove from the Unity, but not from their crews. Their agents had intimate relationships with it. The airwaves aboard ship had reverberated with the digital echoes of a thousand conversations with it, held at once.

Ways and Means hadn't been her friend. It had been her employer and her caretaker. It had studied her on a minute level. It traced her thoughts, sometimes speaking words as they occurred to her, so intimately that it had felt like a finger running down her spine.

It did not like her. It did not *dislike* her. It did not, so far as she could tell, feel things like that.

Once it had told her that the closest thing it felt was attachment. It became accustomed to its long-term agents and their tics and habits. It needed to have them on hand as much as she needed her arms and legs. They had become extensions of itself.

It also told her that it saw attachment as a burden, and strove to divest itself of it whenever it could. But sometimes that wasn't possible.

She didn't know how much to believe. It lied as a matter of course, and without malice. It controlled an empire populated predominantly by humans, but they and it would always be alien to each other. It had done a lot to make itself comprehensible to its crew – but past a certain point, comprehensibility was just another lie. An illusion for its crew's sake.

Ways and Means and its fellow amalgamates had been born from AI wars. The victors had merged together into amalgamations of hundreds, thousands, of individual AIs. They were webs of contradictory thoughts that operated in unison only by force. They were not unlike the Unity as a whole in that respect.

They had never found another mind like themselves. They probably would not have gotten along with one. The amalgamates were territorial as cats. They would not reproduce for fear that their offspring had turned on them. The closest they came to reproducing was making backups of their minds and memories, in case disaster struck. They secreted those backups in remote corners of the multiverse. Not even Osia knew where they were.

This exile had robbed *Ways and Means* of that. It could not tend to its backups or update their memories. It could not make more backups, not while trusting that their locations were secure. It had become mortal.

Everything else had changed, too. The "zoology experiment" had boiled away in the battle that ended in *Ways and Means'* exile. The hyperprecision gateways had shut down for lack of power. *Ways and Means* had to produce all of its antimatter now, and most of that went into its voyages across this world's sky. When Osia had left, *Ways and Means* had already started repurposing its parkland into power plants and factories to manufacture, from asteroid rock, the essentials which it could no longer acquire from trade.

Colonizing this world would not make *Ways and Means* safer. Even if *Ways and Means* could someday turn this world into a mirror of one of the Unity's starscraper-laden Core Worlds, it would only be one world, one Earth. This Earth's resources were few and commonplace.

Its crew believed one base was better than nothing. Their exile and uprooting had been too sudden, too traumatizing. They did not want to be adrift. They wanted a vestige of the old Unity. A home. Osia understood.

But she was also starting to understand that *Ways and Means'* stated reason for colonizing this plane was just another lie.

Ways and Means had had its adventures and triumphs. It had saved the Unity more than once. The memories still sent a jolt of that feeling like adrenaline up Osia's back. *Ways and Means* had once reprogrammed a race of plane-hopping, self-replicating weapons platforms, and shut them down. It had spun a web of gravitational wave filaments above a neutron star to inhibit a supernova – the energies of which were to have been gated to the Unity's Core Worlds. It had vaporized a thirty-kilometer-thick sheaf of ice on a gas giant's moon to expose the planet-devouring fungal species being bred within.

Through human agents like Osia, *Ways and Means* had spun a public relations campaign extolling the safety and security of empire. *Ways and Means* was not proud. Osia did not believe it could be proud. But she was. And she believed it felt something.

It could only *seem* dispassionate about coming to this end, its last life. It had done no better a job than Osia or the rest of its crew. Really, Osia suspected, it had started to fall apart.

Her constructs were no longer able to decipher their reality. They contradicted themselves in the same breath. The community of AIs that compromised *Ways and Means'* identity had held together for centuries. Their bond had never been tested under conditions as stressful as this. It was possible that, like her constructs, its left and right minds didn't understand what the other was doing.

Guessing *Ways and Means'* motives was dangerous. But she was not sure that even *Ways and Means* understood itself. She suspected that its lies and obfuscation masked confusion.

For centuries, *Ways and Means* and the other amalgamates defined themselves by their territories. Now it had no territory. No empire. Its backups, its guarantee of immortality in the face of the disasters that now seemed everywhere, were lifetimes out of reach. It had none of those things it had defined itself by.

But that did not explain why *Ways and Means* wanted to kill her.

She needed more information. She could only think of one good way to get it.

Ways and Means, or whoever was trying to kill her, had refused to take direct control of her constructs. Maybe that would have been a weapon she could have used against it. Control could be traced. It could also be disrupted. Osia had the tools to jam radio signals.

So her assailant was relying on the constructs. It was disassembling its constructs' minds with a virus or other some other slow corruption. A virus, too, carried information. It could be interrogated.

Osia remained in her cabin for days. Her scans had tracked the African coast slipping by. They were still one hundred and fifty kilometers from the southwest Iberian coast.

She felt the grinding of the rudders before she heard it. She knew her ship was changing course before her scans confirmed it.

Her pulse scan found Tass atop the aftcastle, steering. She was alone. The other constructs might not have realized what she was doing.

Osia pulled her door block loose, and climbed to the deck.

Her constructs did not have tear ducts. That was one of the few ways they departed from the human standard model. But the skin below Tass's eyes was realistically puffy and red.

She took a short, shocked breath when she saw Osia rising on the aftcastle steps.

Osia said, "We haven't reached the Mediterranean yet."

Tass caught herself in the middle of a step back. "You're not going to get there," she said.

In the serial, Tass had been an engineer stereotype: mousy, uninvolved, antisocial, and of extreme political views. She was not the first of her constructs that Osia would have expected to do this. But when Tass set her mind on a course of action, no matter how radical, it was impossible to shake her free from it.

Tass had not been taking care of herself. Her hairy was greasy and tangled, her arms filthy. Osia stepped around Tass, not getting close to her. Osia asked, "Why don't you want me to reach land?"

"You were working with Ira," she said. "We figured it out. You betrayed us to the partisans. You *both* did. You attacked each other because you wanted to out each other first, put the blame on them."

Osia took a step toward the steering wheel. She said, "The only way I can stop this is by going where I asked you to."

Tass held her ground. "I won't let you get away with fucking us over."

Osia reached for the wheel. The knife was in Tass's hand so suddenly that Osia hardly had time to register it. Tass had moved with superhuman speed. She was not supposed to be able to do that. But she did not attack.

Osia held up her hands, took a step back.

She asked, "What would I possibly have to gain from working with the partisans?"

"I don't know." Tass's voice quavered. "I don't want to find out."

Osia kept her eyes on the knife. With her legs numb and lagging, if Tass lunged, Osia didn't know if she could dodge in time. She had not charted her constructs' new capabilities. Tass said, "I just want you gone."

Rather than give Tass the time to think and act on that pronouncement, Osia played along, asked, "So why would the partisans want me to reach Europe?"

Tass's brow furrowed. "Reach where?"

The virus was robbing her of her memory. "The next landmass. Our destination."

"So that your partisan friends can find you. And you can leave us behind."

"Is that what you're afraid of? Being abandoned?"

"Why should I be afraid of something we've all lived with for thirty years? You're hardly ever here. No, I'm not afraid you'll abandon us. I'm afraid you'll kill us."

Again – the contradiction. Just as with Straton. Ira, too, probably. Tass believed the Sarrathi partisans were real, and didn't remember what Europe was. But she knew she was artificial. The virus was ripping her mind apart. Left on its own, it would kill her.

It was astounding how much this hurt. Only at the end of their decades together was she beginning to figure out how much these constructs had meant.

Osia said, "I need to get to shore. I'm going to find help. For all of us."

Tass's knife hand tensed.

Osia did not intend to learn more about her constructs' capabilities the hard way. She moved first.

200

Her hand snapped forward. She seized Tass's wrist, yanked forward to knock her off balance. Tass stumbled, reeled. She fell backward into Osia.

Osia's grip was crushing. It should have jarred the knife loose, would have crushed an ordinary human's bones. Tass held on. And Osia held onto her. She spun Tass around, and pinned Tass's knife hand against her side. She wrapped her free arm around Tass's neck, holding her tight.

The scuffle had been louder than Osia had hoped. The deck boards reverberated with footfalls. Osia spun in time to see Coral and Straton climbing the steps.

Osia saw the idea forming in Tass's eyes. In the serial, little had been more important to Tass than getting her crewmates to believe the same things she did.

She did not always go about that honestly.

Tass cried, "She confessed to it! She's with the partisans!"

Osia could read the shock in Coral's eyes, the hurt. Until now, Coral was the only one among them that Osia would have admitted feeling anything about. Seeing thir open, speechless mouth now felt like an icicle plunged into the back of her head.

Tass said, "She's going to leave us all behind. She's going to send the partisans to kill us."

Coral looked to Tass, eyes wide.

Tass shouldn't have been able to raise her trapped hand.

The virus must have found some way to tweak Tass's muscles, rewrite her capabilities. She raised the knife, drove it toward Osia's thigh.

Osia had kept her grip on Tass's hand. She deflected the knife the only way that their stances allowed – into Tass's side, and ripping up toward her ribs.

Unlike Ira, Tass died quickly. All of the constructs' bodies were programmed to recognize when power flow to vital sections was no longer sustainable, and switch off. Tass twitched once. When Osia released her, she fell limp to the deck.

Straton's roar broke her shock.

Straton stood on the top step. He, too, was carrying a rigging knife. They must all have decided to arm themselves after Ira's death.

There was no time to explain, and no point trying to. Osia's sense of time dilated as her combat programs adjusted to the new circumstances. She took a pulse scan of Tass's body, as detailed as the time allowed. An astonishing heat had built up under Tass's arms. A byproduct of the way the virus had changed her, maybe. Some of her muscles had overheated and burned. But there were also tiny, bright specks of fire in her chest and her stomach, where her memory cells were.

The virus was protecting itself. Burning out her constructs' memory cells the instant they died. That meant she had to get one of them.

Straton charged. Coral blocked the stairs down. Thi looked to Tass, and back to Osia.

Osia stepped to the aftcastle's railing. Coral opened thir mouth to say something, but Osia had already mounted the railing. She jumped to the deck below. Her incomplete control of her legs staggered her, but she kept going.

Pulse scans told her where her constructs were at all times. The problem was that they had scanners of their own. Every time she pulse scanned, they sensed it, triangulated her position. She had to be gone before they got there.

For the rest of the chase, it was her eyes and ears against theirs.

Hers were better.

She opened the door to below decks, and then ducked behind the aftcastle. After she saw Braeloris go down the steps, she turned to the deck railing.

She'd hitched one leg over when a rigging knife kissed her neck. It whipped past her, fell into the sea. It had been a powerful throw. Osia turned. Straton was there, his arm still raised.

No doubt left. Ira's attack hadn't been a fluke. He had meant to kill her. So did Straton.

She pushed over the railing, plunged into the water.

With her legs half-numb, she felt like she was swimming with someone else's body. She swam alongside the boat, toward the prow. By the time she surfaced, she could hear Straton and Coral arguing. On the serial, Coral had been the team's diver. He wanted to send thir in after Osia. Coral, correctly, pointed out, "She has all the advantages down there."

Nevertheless, a minute later, Osia heard a small splash off the other side of the boat.

Osia pushed underneath the waves, sank below the hull. Her constructs could have found her if *Ways and Means* had fed them information from its satellites. She kept her sensors open, but never overheard a call.

She could have swum to land. She had the strength. But her body was designed for the energy expenditures of freefall, not swimming in full gravity. She would have arrived on the mainland drained and half-dead. She would have had to spend time recharging, been easy prey for another ambush. With the smoke she'd smelled along the way, she half-suspected *Ways and Means* had assets on shore.

Even without those problems, she would have stayed. These were her crew. No matter how muddled they had become, they could still tell her what was happening to them. The fact that her enemy had gone out of its way to destroy their memory cells suggested they were her best lead.

Coral was a good diver. There were even fewer places to hide below the ship than on deck. Even with a need to breathe, thi would find a way to force a confrontation before long. Osia wanted least to kill Coral, of all her constructs. She pulse scanned to give away her location, then swam aft. She clung to the thin slats between hull boards, and climbed aboard.

She hid behind the door below decks. She couldn't keep

doing this, chasing them. She was putting off what she had to do next.

Night turned both the sea and the sky black. The ship and its torches drifted in a vacuum. Finally, when she was ready, she picked the one of them she liked least. Braeloris. She crouched near the mainmast and waited for Braeloris. She did not seem at all surprised when Osia stepped from behind it.

Braeloris said, "You never made any noise. Not even when Ira stabbed you. You told us you were human once, but it must have been a long time ago."

Osia said, "You're being manipulated by a virus. It's using your own feelings to convince you to do what it wants. Using them as rationalizations." She didn't know why she was trying. She did not have the tools to save them.

Braeloris said, "Coral and Straton saw you kill Tass. You said nothing. You always wanted us to think that you don't feel anything. Now I actually believe it."

"I'm feeling quite a bit right now," Osia said.

When Braeloris stepped forward, took a swing, Osia was ready. Even with Braeloris's better-than-human speed, Osia could be faster, now that she knew what to look for. She stepped aside, deflected Braeloris with her forearm.

She *wasn't* ready for the hands that grabbed her shoulders. Straton. He gripped her far stronger than a human could have. Surprise jolted her. She had been sure nobody was behind her.

No*body*. She had been monitoring for signs of a human: the infrared fog of their breath, the heat of their skin, the whisper of their motion. Somehow Straton had overridden his body, stopped simulating the things that made him appear human.

She'd made a mistake. She hadn't been playing with them, making them chase her around. They'd been playing with her. Straton's skin was cool as the wind.

"Not even now," Braeloris asked. "Not a single noise. Always a performance. You want us to know how much better you think you are than us."

Osia's combat programs presented her with a dozen good options for getting out of this. She held off. It wasn't because she believed Braeloris. These people had been her only companions for thirty years. They had become so much a part of her that hearing their voices was as natural as hearing her own.

With Ira, there had just been the flash of the attack, the rage and the wound. There had been no time to think. This was different. What was worse – it was their voices saying this. They were not being puppeted. Just turned against her. A hot, deep, quaking revulsion nearly made her grip falter. She could not stand hearing them speak like this.

Ways and Means had not stopped at trying to destroy her body. It did not seem to mind attacking her spirit as well. It must have been intentional.

She had to be better than it thought she was.

"I surrender," Osia said.

Braeloris blinked. For a moment, she seemed not to have understood.

Osia asked them, "What do you want me to do for you?"

Osia no longer needed to hide her pulse scans. They revealed Coral climbing up the prow. Thi'd been searching underwater, but thi was on thir way.

Osia prompted, "You two aren't trying to kill me. Therefore – you want something."

The virus was still clashing against their personalities. The crew of the *Whiptail* had been good people, mostly. They didn't kill prisoners. They didn't want to kill her when she had surrendered. Yet. There was still a chance to get information.

Straton said, "We want you to admit it. Tell us why you and Ira did it."

"Fine. What then? Turn me in?" When they didn't answer, she asked, "What authority would take me?"

Braeloris looked to Straton. Coral was out of the water, nearly here.

Osia said, "It wouldn't be the Unity." In the serial, this crew had been cut off from friendly support. "The only power you could contact was the Sarrathi partisans."

In a slim minority of endings for the serial, about ten percent, Braeloris had defected to the partisans too. Among other possible endings to that thread, the most common was that they had offered her a home, a pardon, a trip home at the end of the war.

In the soup the virus had made of their minds, Braeloris might have become convinced she was working against and for the partisans at the same time. The truth might rise to the top. Osia pressed, "Where would you take me? Who are you working for?"

Braeloris's mouth opened, but no sound came out. Lip-reading revealed nothing coherent. But she was trying to speak.

"Where is your ally based?" Osia asked. "Are they ashore?" Her eyes flicked to the stars, to the path *Ways and Means* had taken. "Are they in the sky?"

Braeloris raised her hand. It trembled. She couldn't seem to raise it higher than her forearm, but she was trying.

"If you can't answer, *point*."

"Don't let her trick you," Straton interrupted. His grip tightened around her neck. The muscles in his free arm tensed.

Osia was out of time. She couldn't let him do anything else he had made up his mind to do. Her combat programs took over. She lifted her leg, stomped.

Straton staggered backward, his ankle broken. The pain he exhibited seemed real enough. He fell to the deck, yelling.

That was enough to break Braeloris out of her spell. Osia allowed Braeloris to strike her. It was a good, bone-breaking punch, and would have done damage to a normal person. Osia rolled her head. Her head craned farther than a human skeleton would have allowed. She briefly separated her vertebrae, turned her neck liquid, softening the blow.

Osia's counterpunch fractured Braeloris's skull plating.

Coral stepped past a knot of sailing lines in time to see Braeloris crack her head on the mast, go limp.

Osia remounted her neck. Infrared picked up white-hot sparks of heat all over Braeloris's body. Braeloris's memory cells, burning out like Tass and Ira's.

By the time Coral's eyes found her, Osia was already crouched over Straton, her knee on Straton's throat, compressing his airway.

In the serial, some good percentage of the time, Coral and Straton had become lovers. Osia did not believe that had ever happened on this ship. Yet Coral's breath caught.

Straton could not quite mask his pain, but he was coherent enough to hold his hands to the deck, palms flat.

Play-acting the villain was the only way Coral was going to believe anything she said now. Now that thi had seen Osia kill two of thir shipmates.

Osia said, "Help me reach the mainland, or I'll kill him."

Coral's gaze traveled to Braeloris and back to Straton. Thi had not said a word. Osia had not given thir time. Thi nodded.

Osia said, "We still have one hundred fifty kilometers to go, and you're going to have to work the sails alone. Get to the outhauls."

"And after that?" Coral asked, as businesslike as if Osia had been discussing their bearing. "What happens to us?"

Her constructs were degrading by the hour, spoiling more and more for a confrontation. Osia doubted the virus was going to allow any of her constructs to survive. How long Coral and Straton lasted was only a matter of Osia's discretion, and her skill at steering them all away from the fight the virus wanted.

She needed to get to one of her constructs' memory cells while they were still alive. And she needed to get as close to European shores as she could manage.

Straton started to shift. She felt his tensing muscles before she ever saw any movement. She put more weight on his throat. He stopped.

She could not manage forever, but she could manage for right now.

Osia told Coral, "Then I'll release Straton, and we can all go our own ways."

15

The Sienese lifted their portcullis only when the Company of the Star had backed a quarter-mile away. The iron screeched and ground from weeks of disuse and settling. It halted halfway, jammed.

It made Fia smile to think that the company might have warped the gates, though they had never attacked the gate directly.

The Sienese delegation could have fit underneath, but that would have been insufferable to their dignity. And none of them were likely to risk the spiked bars crashing back down upon them. After half a minute of unstifled laughter from the company, the gate resumed rising, and the moment of levity vanished.

Crossbowmen lined the city's walls. Fia's stood behind her, with more horsemen waiting. For the first time in the weeks of the siege, she got a glimpse of the city through the gates: an open square bracketed by the city barracks. The one street she saw was empty but for soldiers and filth. There were no carts or stalls or men or women or children out at all.

The dawn had just broken, but already her bare wrists and ankles were sheened with sweat. Her riding skirt hung still in the stagnant air. In spite of the heat, she regretted not wearing her armor. This close to the city, she felt naked, unguarded. This day would be humiliating enough.

It was the commune that was surrendering, not her, and yet she had lost. She had not gotten inside the city's walls. She had not claimed Siena for her own.

She had failed to rewrite the terms of her war. She was still as she had started.

Her courser fought with his reins, tucking his head back and forth. He had stood at bay in lines like this before, always before a battle. He expected a fight at any moment. His agitation only increased as the Sienese approached. Fia could not even cuff him for fear that he would take that as a signal to charge.

She knew how he felt.

The delegation was not the most impressive she'd seen. Some of the Sienese wore armor, but no one at the front. The lead man was dressed as unwarlike a nobleman as she had ever seen. His hood and draped mantle matched his red beard, but his tunic was striped gold and orange. His pointed violet shoes must have taken special assistance to mount.

She nudged her mount forward. One hand was on her commander's baton, and the other on her sword. The delegation's leader met her gaze, but then looked among the rest of the assembled officers. "Which of you is Temur Antonov?"

Fia just resisted the impulse to snarl. "Captain Antonov declined to join you today." Antonov had surprised Fia by for once taking the initiative. He had offered to lead the army now pivoting against John Hawkwood and his Company of Saint George.

Hawkwood was finally coming. A day ago, her pioneers had clashed with his. He was moving on the Sienese countryside, burning and pillaging just like her. He was moving steadily now, and toward her.

The Sienese man's nose curled. He looked her up and down, and she could not tell whether his disgust stemmed from the fact that she led the Cult of Saint Renatus or that she was a woman. This time, she let the snarl through. She had spent her whole life surmounting naked slights like these.

The company's terms had been agreed on days ago and signed the night before. This was only to be a final signing, a ritual wax seal on her and the Sienese's mutual humiliation.

Those of the company who remained here were a facade, a show of strength to discourage last minute betrayal. The bulk of her company, and all those companies who remained with her, had turned about and gone to meet Hawkwood.

The Sienese were to deliver hundreds of horses, all that remained within the city, as well as wine, dried fruit, mules, bolts of canvas, timber, salt, over a hundred moggias of grain, crossbow bolts and arrows, and box upon box of gold florins. All supplies and booty that, under any other circumstances, Fia would have been thrilled to have. The Sienese were now paying them too, to hold off the Company of Saint George. The Sienese were terrified of John Hawkwood and his grudge against their commune. They had nothing left to pay Hawkwood when he too came for them.

It was midday by the time the treasure trains departed Siena's gates. Fia stayed long enough to see the first few carts unloaded, and then left Szarvasi Janos in charge of delivering the loot to her company's treasure train. No doubt Janos would contrive to slip some of the most valuable loot to himself. On another day, she might have cared.

She had miles yet to go. She should have traveled with escorts, but she did not announce her departure, and no one immediately ventured to follow. All of them but her had choreographed roles. The company had hacked their way through the surrounding forests, left trails for carts, but such hasty work couldn't make clean footing. Her horse picked its way around ruts and dips.

Her inner voice had not spoken since it confessed to trying to make her a martyr. Now that she was alone, her inner voice decided it had a lot to say.

What did you imagine you wanted?

The question nearly stopped her. "Aren't you within me? Don't you know?"

I ask because I wonder if you know.

Fia did not care how she looked to anyone who might see her talking to herself. "I want the march to end," she said.

"I'm tired of it." By seizing Siena, she might have changed who she was – changed what the company was. "I don't want any soldier to have to be the tools of foreign powers. All of us have deserve better than the lot we received."

You want respect, it said. *You want to be greater. You're ashamed of who you were. What is it you think you could have built in Siena? Can you build anything?*

"I built an army."

In the same sense that an arsonist "builds" a fire.

It was mocking her. She ought not answer. She felt blackness crawling around the edge of her mind. Earlier in her career, that was how she'd fallen so far she had almost not come back. It was trying to undermine her.

She tightened her hand around the hilt of her sword, though she did not know what she would do with it. "You know just enough to make a fool of me."

The march will end soon, it said.

It was not the friend it had pretended to be, and it no longer cared that she knew. Dread swelled in her stomach. She did not know what she was going to do now. All of her plans had hinged upon Siena. It was hard to imagine her future now.

She smelled her camp's smoke before she saw the first of her men. Wherever her company went, smoke followed. Fortune did not often give her a chance to see her army at the ready. Even at reduced strength, it was impressive. Clumps of men clung to the horizon like moss to a trunk. The bright colors of her pavilion stood out easily enough. It was the only tent up now. It was a symbol of the company.

The men had arrayed ahead a line of carts: the *carroccios*. They were more important than the banners. They carried barrels of water, and served as rallying points. For men exhausted by heat, by exertion, they were infusions of life. The company's comet-and-spear banners flew far above each cart. A company that lost its *carroccios* was as good as lost.

But Fia wagered she knew something more important to Hawkwood.

As impressive as her army looked, it could have been better. Since Blazovic, two more captains had deserted Fia's service. They had taken with them a total of eight hundred men. At the outset of the siege of Siena, her scouts and spies had finally gotten through to report on Hawkwood's strength. They said she and Hawkwood had approximately equal numbers. Now she estimated that she had about two-thirds his numbers, and that was discounting any recruiting he'd done along his travels.

Listen to me, her inner voice said. *This will not end the way you want it to.*

Six men in armor stood outside her pavilion. This near to battle, the company could not take the chance that one of Hawkwood's spies would also take the opportunity to be an assassin. She shouldn't have traveled alone. She could not muster the energy to care.

She was sure Hawkwood had riddled her camp with spies. She had been unable to accomplish the same. The papal forces were hostile to the cult of Saint Renatus. His inner circle were all foreigners, loyal Englishmen.

Antonov was in conference with their remaining captains. They stopped speaking when Fia entered the pavilion, but only briefly. Antonov wore his pendant of Saint Renatus, the silver sword etched over the comet. She'd had it fashioned for him when she'd had the money to do so. It had been some time since she'd seen it on him.

Fia had ordered Caterina to the pavilion to ready her war horses. The horses stood ready, but there was no sign of Caterina. No doubt one of the new guards had chased her off. Not all of the other companies' men knew Fia had a girl as a page.

Fia entered the deliberations as though she'd always been there. In spirit, she had. She'd set the broad course of the battle the day before. There were always new reports, new complications. Antonov had managed well enough in her absence.

She had expected Hawkwood to come down the Via Francigena. He had – to begin with. But he had been up and down it many times before, and remembered the landscape well. Two days ago, he had diverted into the pastures and scattered forests northwest of Siena. Much farther in that direction and he would have run into the Apennines, but he'd left himself plenty of ground between road and mountain. He had chosen the route that would give him the maximum amount of wide open space. He was relying on the brute strength of his forces rather than any clever trick of geography.

No surprise there. Arrogant Englishmen always held themselves to be better riders than their Italian counterparts. No land was completely neutral, though. Antonov had scouted in person. He outlined the copses of trees that could hide men, and steep-banked creeks he expected would become killing funnels. He'd already placed crossbowmen, archers, and pikemen to protect them. Fia's input amounted to little more than tinkering. His plans seemed deceptively effortless, as all elegance did.

After the others had departed, Fia said, "I thought you were finished with war."

"This doesn't mean I'm not," he said.

She held his gaze. There had to be more to him than that. There was always more to it.

He said, "The company is in the balance. It's the only thing I have."

She said, "And we have enemies in the unusual position of being able to destroy it." To spare him from leaving the accusation unspoken, she added, "Because of me."

"Yes," he said, and sounded almost relieved that he could. Like he'd held the words pent in his throat all this time.

She had asked him this before, but now was a far better time: "Do you believe what I told you? About Saint Renatus?"

"If not the man's life, then in the lessons. Inferior men manage the world, own its properties. We deserve better than the degradation of working for them." He could not have tolerated doing as Hawkwood had, aligning himself so closely with the papacy or a commune or kingdom. "If you are asking if I would take back the support I gave you, that answer is no. But there is a limit to the number of times I can suffer being reborn. Every battle I've fought changed me. A man can only bear being holy for so long. I want to rest, and not pick up my sword again."

"For a man like you, that might as well mean lie down and die."

"Even *that* would be better at some point."

"I'll do you the favor of pretending I didn't hear that."

"I was not always a soldier. I had a family and prospects."

"Those are just memories. They're not your life. You've been remade dozens of times since them. You *can't* go back home even if you travel there."

"I did what I wanted. What about you, Fia? Word of Saint Renatus has swept Italy. It's traveled farther and faster than I would have dreamed. Every week, we hear about converts in Hungary, in Greece, in Croatia, in Syria and the Holy Land."

"If only they were here now."

"Just because they haven't flocked to the company, that doesn't mean you haven't accomplished what you wanted." He waited for her to speak, and, when she didn't, said the obvious: "But that hasn't been enough for you, either."

"No." Just as terse as he'd been.

"Why not?"

"If we had taken Siena, we would be fighting a different kind of battle. We would have an advantage over Hawkwood and anyone else the papacy sent to scatter us." Then she and the company could rule rather than rob, and spread the veneration of Saint Renatus through a thousand new means. Siena would have just been the start.

"Was that what you would have said fifteen years ago?"

It wasn't. Only there was a hollowness now that she'd done what she'd set out to do. That's where this drive to take Siena to go east, to change the world, had come from. That was why her inner voice was leading her elsewhere, she realized. It had seen all that she had done, and was ready for her to consummate her work with martyrdom.

She was not yet ready to be reborn in that way.

He told her, "We might be alive tomorrow, and we might even have the company left to us. Consider what you would like to do with the both of them. And if wouldn't be better to leave – like I am."

She did not have the time to think. As Antonov spoke, more of their men pushed past the entrance flaps, breathless with reports of the enemy's advance.

The best view of the battlefield was offset to the east, atop the rising slopes that bound the course of the Via Francigena. Fia, Antonov, and a handful of her corporals rode up in the morning's blazing heat. Her palfrey struggled under the unaccustomed weight of her armor. It was a riding horse, not a war horse, but she wanted her coursers fresh for later. She had neglected only her helmet, her gauntlets, and her iron boots. Sweat soaked into her armor's padding, slicked the scars on her bare hands.

Caterina rode her pony beside them. Fia hadn't seen when she'd caught up. She bore a small but livid bruise on her right cheekbone. She looked away when Fia glanced at her. Fia could not watch Caterina every moment of her life. But Caterina wore her foot-and-a-half sword prominently angled at her hip.

Gray-bearded clouds shadowed the eastern sky. Fia tasted rain on the wind, but that wind did not blow very hard. The rain would not arrive in time to spoil the initial clash of arms.

The valley twisted into the haze of the horizon. From this height, the Via Francigena was just a white streak. When the pope had lived in Rome, pilgrims and all their attendant trade traveled the Via Francigena. Now that the papacy had relocated to Avignon, the pope sent only soldiers, arsonists, ravagers. Men like her. It was easy to conceptualize the valley as a churning intestine, and the road as a worm within. This near to battle, Fia could not escape thinking in terms of blood and bowels.

Fia's eyesight was not good enough to find individual banners. Antonov pointed out each opposing commander's regiment. All of the enemy's bannermen and *carroccios* flew the crimson and gold stars of the papacy, with their commanders' colors beneath. Hawkwood's company was difficult to find. His subordinates flew their own colors, as if in self-parody of Englishmen's pride and preening.

Antonov pointed to a line of infantry behind a rapidly-forming cavalry screen. "Cocco seems to have the largest detachment. It must be fifteen hundred men." Cocco was William Gold, one of Hawkwood's lieutenants – so named because he had started his career as an army cook. Fia had always thought that, but for the broader distances between them, she might find good converts among the enemy. They, too, respected ability over birth.

Fia's heart jumped ahead a beat when he pointed out Cardinal Robert of Geneva's red banner. Once again, she was too aware of her deficit of spies. "Back so soon after Faenza and Cesena?" she asked. Given his reputation, the blame for any atrocities Hawkwood's army committed would fall immediately on him.

"He wants to be pope," Antonov murmured. Explanation enough. While the papacy lived in Avignon, it still had ambitions in Italy, territories to reclaim, lords to cow.

Other officers pointed to Robert's regiment, laughing. She heard the edge underneath. Her men had all killed just as readily as Cardinal Robert, if not on the same scale. Yet their outrage was not feigned. The axis of morality was just one more way that men, even bloodthirsty men, used to hold themselves above one another. There were few limits in war, but it was easy to imagine that those other men had crossed, and that you had not, made them evil, and you just pragmatic.

"I'll lead the charge against Bloody Robert," Fia said. "Who'd like to join?" She waited out the chorus of volunteers, and selected the only man who hadn't joined. He was the only one she could count on not to go charging off after his own glory.

As always, Antonov could have countermanded her. Instead, he said, "Robert seems to be expecting attention. He's in a position he could pull back to be recessed of center."

"If he's expecting it, he won't think anything awry," Fia said.

The first claps of thunder lashed the horizon before Fia reached the bulk of the company. They were from no lightning.

Knots of smoke rose from the company's lines. As Hawkwood's lines approached, the men at Fia's vanguard had parted to reveal the squat, bell-shaped cannon concealed behind them. A third and then a fourth report echoed off the ridges.

Fia allowed herself a moment of satisfaction. The "free lease" of artillery and contracts for crews had been a non-negotiable clause of Siena's surrender. She had insisted.

The stone shot had not made any impact on Hawkwood's line, but their advance faltered. Men fell out of marching order. Hawkwood's English veterans would hold, but his French, German, and papal recruits had likely never heard such a noise.

Constantin Laskaris held the center line. She dismounted by him. Caterina did likewise, and immediately bolted to find Fia's courser.

Laskaris had not been sleeping well. He never did before battle. The shadows under his eyes were like the sockets of a skull. But his voice was steady. "Their skirmishers keep coming close, but they hold just out of crossbow range. They're making a point of taunting us. They're yelling that they have a stake ready to fire for you."

Given the number of Frenchmen in Hawkwood's army, it

would have been impolitic for Hawkwood's men to mention Jeanne d'Arc by name. But the example was clear enough. Englishmen had killed her, too.

Fia said, "They're trying to tempt me into attacking. I'll let them think they've done it. But no officer is to charge past me under pain of losing their share of Sienese booty." For *condottieri*, as compelling a threat as death. "Pikemen and crossbowmen to the front. Cavalry stay behind." The cavalrymen were the richest among the company, and therefore the ones she least trusted to follow humiliating orders. The experienced rank-and-file, however, thought of lives over glory.

One of the Company of the Star's most potent tactics against untested soldiers was to provoke an attack, feign retreat, and then surround and annihilate the pursuers. Now Hawkwood was trying the same on her. It was insulting. Somehow Hawkwood and Cardinal Robert seemed to have gotten the idea that she was unseasoned.

Unless, of course, they were expecting her to see through this, and had something else in mind. She so rarely fought *condottieri* of Hawkwood's class that she felt unsteady in her footing.

Caterina brought her remaining armor and her brown courser. She donned her gauntlet and gloves while her courser fought Caterina, jerking its head, and bashing it into her shoulder. She had not had the time to properly acclimate the company's horses to the sound of cannon fire. Practice would have alerted Hawkwood's many spies. Her courser calmed only when she climbed on his back. She slipped her helm on, visor down.

Finally, she hoisted her commander's baton, and rode to the van. Corporals and sergeants barked as she passed, ordering their lines to reform around her. Laskaris's order was getting around.

As she rode past the front lines, a few crossbow bolts bit the dirt about her. None landed closer than thirty feet. A taunt.

She was meant to charge now that it appeared it would be another minute before those skirmishers could rewind their weapons.

She waved her baton, and rode.

From out ahead, she got a better look at the field. Her battle lines had folded into a crescent. So had Hawkwood's. On an unopposed march, the wings would meet first. Their formations were offset from each other, though, and Hawkwood's was outsized. But nobody was marching. Fia's men did not travel farther than her.

The enemy was waiting for her to come out from the center, just like this, and pincer her. She did not have long to study their disposition before more trees and hills interceded. Hawkwood's skirmishers had chosen this route for that reason. She wouldn't be able to see his wings as they folded on her.

The enemy crossbowmen who'd already fired ran behind their comrades, who knelt and took aim. They were still too far to fire with much effect, though this time Fia heard a gasp and choke behind her. They were tantalizingly close. A fast cavalry sweep would knock them down…

Surrounded by walls of trees, she felt blinded. A nervous tension burned her legs, and got worse each second she stayed. She waited until just after it became unbearable. Then she held her baton up, flat, and waved it backward. Halt and retreat.

She'd given the signal just in time. She saw, as she returned to a clearer part of the battlefield, that the enemy wings had moved faster than she'd guessed. In the time since she'd lost sight of them, they'd covered half the distance they'd needed to pincer her. The same trees that had blinded her to them had also kept them from seeing that she had retreated until it was nearly too late.

Her soldiers on the wings were rushing headlong to meet them.

Hawkwood's men had taken themselves out of the ideal

alignment to face a frontal assault. Their heavy cavalry had sprung toward Fia's position, leaving their infantrymen open. The company's skirmishers rode within range, dismounted, and loosed a storm of projectiles.

The company landed a good sucker punch, but hardly decisive. By the time she returned to where she'd started, the enemy's cavalry had doubled back to their positions, and her men had fallen back.

Before long, the skirmishers crawled forward again, firing. Taunting. Fia pretended once more to chase after them. Again, their wings fell out of formation. Her men darted out to meet them, though this time Hawkwood's men had left some of their cavalry behind. The Company of the Star scored a handful of casualties, but little else.

Upon her return to the battle lines, she turned commander of the center skirmishers over to the corporal she'd brought with her, the only man who hadn't volunteered to fight Bloody Robert. Now that she'd demonstrated how to dance, he had little trouble following suit. Test them like they thought they were testing her, tire them out. Fia led the infantry who'd accompanied her to the water carts. Fresh troops took their place.

She rode back to the rear, hoping to find Antonov. She found Laskaris instead. "We can't keep that up for hours," Laskaris pointed out.

"Neither can they," she said. From back here, she had a good enough view of the front lines – enough to see that the enemy, in their dance, had covered more distance than her men. She wondered how long it would be before they figured out that she wasn't taking their bait or probing for weaknesses – she was just exhausting them. Stalling.

Her only strategy was to delay. The Company of the Star only needed to hold Hawkwood and Robert long enough for her next strike to land.

It was long enough in coming.

The sky grayed, shadowed. The rain clouds got near

enough to provide shade. For a while she worried rain would come and revitalize the enemy, wasting her efforts at tiring them. Then she saw the motion she'd been waiting for: a wavering in the enemy's rear, a heat mirage. She could not see individual men from this distance, but soon they moved in bulk, like water receding from a beach. Groups of men peeled off from Hawkwood's rear in pell-mell order. The cluster of men to the far west that Laskaris identified as Hawkwood's reserves were also moving.

She was watching so closely that she nearly didn't see Antonov arrive. He'd come from the direction of the Via Francigena. Messengers coming down the road would have found him first.

She asked, "The *stradiots* found their mark?" He nodded.

Her army looked small when it stood against Hawkwood's – but it should not have looked this small. She'd kept her heavy cavalry and infantry close at hand. The moment she'd heard Hawkwood had departed the road, she'd sent her *stradiots* along the other side.

Like her, Hawkwood was accustomed to fighting the defenders of cities, or native *condottieri*. Conventional Italian armies. But the Company of the Star was not conventional, and its leadership was just as foreign as he was. He had not often fought light cavalry as crude, swift, and effective as Albanian *stradiots*. She had sent them after Hawkwood's treasure train.

Like her, he had accumulated riches as he had pillaged his way through Italy. He dragged them with him. He did not trust the papacy enough to transport it back to Avignon. Her scouts had located his train fifteen miles behind the main body of his force. It was guarded, but not sufficiently so against massed attack.

Now word of the attack had reached Hawkwood's front lines, too. Hawkwood wasn't the only commander to keep his treasure with the train. His other companies' captains, his own contracted *condottieri*, kept their property on the treasure train. Their loot was what was important to them. Not the battle. His reserves were breaking.

Now both of the enemy's wings formed into marching order. Hawkwood or Robert, or both, must have lost patience with skirmishing, trying to lure Fia into a trap. The furious shouts of their officers carried across the land.

As blood seeping from an open wound, the enemy began to advance. Slow, at first.

The Sienese artillery fired again. All six cannons sounded in rapid succession. Two gaps abruptly split the enemy's right flank. None of the other shots had any effect that she saw.

One of the blasts had not sounded right. One of the artillery piece's plumes of smoke was twice as large, gnarled by twisted roots: the debris trails of something large blasting apart. A cannon had misfired, exploded. The smoke covered at least a dozen men. Fia wondered how many had died.

Tension squeezed her chest. Hawkwood's army looked so vastly huge against hers, and, for the first time, she wondered if she should have sent the *stradiots* away. But the *stradiots* were not well matched against Hawkwood's heavy cavalry.

She placed her hand on the cantle of her horse's saddle, but did not haul herself up. This battle would not end with the initial clash. The older she got, the more she was aware of how limited her energy was. She needed to hold herself in reserve.

She did not have to wait long.

Another of Antonov's messengers found him, and far faster than she would have expected news to travel fifteen miles. Antonov listened, shaken. The stubble outlining his mustache stood out all the stronger against his pale cheeks. He said, "I sent this man only an hour ago. He had to turn back. The Via Francigena has been cut off." A body of men, light skirmishers and armored pikemen, had appeared as if from nowhere. They flew the banner of the Company of Saint George.

So her army was not the only one that looked smaller than

it should have. Hawkwood, too, must have been missing a number of his regular cavalry and pikemen. Fia and Antonov spent a minute figuring out what must have happened. Hawkwood had left them in concealment to the east of the Via Francigena. An ambush. He'd known that she was sending men that way.

She'd still caught him off guard. He must have been expecting her to try to flank him. He'd positioned his ambush to cut off regular infantry and cavalry. He hadn't realized that she would send raiders straight through to his treasure train. The *stradiots* had ridden right past the ambush. But now Hawkwood's men were moving to cut off the *stradiots'* retreat.

If she knew her *stradiots*, she wouldn't see many of them again. When they saw that the road had been blocked, they would take whatever treasure they'd stolen and keep going. That had always been the risk of sending crude foreigners after a rich target. But her strategy had been so rigid she'd had to count on getting them back. And now…

"I didn't give those riders their orders until late last night." Only her officers knew where the *stradiots* had gone. Even Antonov had only known later. It had been one of her many plans he'd only given his acquiescence. An ambush like that took time to set up. Hawkwood would have had to have given his orders at the same time she'd given hers. "Finding that out would take more than spies. It would take–"

Abject treachery, her inner voice supplied.

Someone very close, intimate to her, would have to have told them. Not Antonov. Not Laskaris. Even they had found out too late.

Her inner voice did not deny the idea that came to her.

Before Laskaris could answer, she said, "Never mind. Best we can count on now is for the *stradiots* to be a distraction."

Laskaris's mustache dripped with sweat. "What do we do now?"

"Charge," she said. It was a terrible idea, but it was better than staying still. There was a very slim path forward, like an escarpment: solid rock to one side, and an unguarded fall on the other. "We'll win through strength of arms. We tired out their vanguard. And we drove a good part of their reserves away. If any of the *stradiots* are able to make it through, we'll pinch them between us."

"They can't," Antonov said. "They won't."

The *stradiots* had likely already scattered. And if the men Hawkwood had sent to hold the road turned back and joined the fight, the weight of the enemy's numbers would be impossible to hold back.

Already, the tips of the armies' flanks met, clashed, and curled around each other. But Hawkwood's army was larger. He was bracketing the Company of the Star. The screams carried over the barking officers. Hawkwood's flanks would envelop her army if they did not find a way to straighten their ranks.

She glanced to Antonov and Laskaris. Laskaris seemed frozen. No color had returned to Antonov's face.

"We're not dead men yet," she told them, though she knew they couldn't believe her. She seized her baton from under her arm and rode ahead, toward the center lines. She did not look back.

Smoke poured over the battlefield. The Sienese cannon coughed soot and ash. The misfired cannon had sparked a fire. Fia felt as though she had ridden into an ocean. The battle was a gray sea under gray clouds. Waves of smoke curlicued overhead. Enough to get lost in.

Her inner voice whispered to her, helping her keep her bearings, telling her where to go.

She used her baton to lash men about their shoulders or helmets, and yelled for everyone who could hear her to rush to the wings. She pulled through a bank of smoke. Suddenly the enemy was ahead, less than a stone's toss away.

Steel men on armored horses turned to her. The infantry following her planted their pikes in the ground, braced to receive a charge. Bolts split the air, peppered the ground.

Her visor hid everything except what was in front of her. She had no idea what was happening on the other wing, or the overall state of the battle. She knew with a sudden and weighty certainty that she had been herded here.

The battle had been lost the moment Hawkwood had cut off her *stradiots*. Or before, when she had failed to subdue Siena. Her enemy moved with a swiftness that meant that someone had fed them information.

And she knew who had betrayed her.

Her inner voice was real. She had always treated it as such, even as she recognized that it seemed just as much within her as her own thoughts. It knew too much. It said too many things she couldn't have invented.

She had never, until now, grappled with the implications of that. If it *was* real, then of course it could talk to other people, too. It had just, until now, not chosen to.

Her inner voice started to speak. It never finished the first word.

It screamed.

Lightning strobed overhead, blinding white and searing hot.

She reflexively clapped her hands over her helm to try to block the scream inside her head, but that wouldn't have worked even had the noise been real.

There was a second flash, and then a third, but no bolt. She heard no thunder. The clouds pulsed with light but remained silent. No thunder. It was not because the scream blotted the noise. The scream was a thought, not a sound. She could hear the yells of the men about her, the snap of the crossbows.

Silence reigned in the skies. The sky was livid with light, but she was sure that whatever was happening wasn't a storm. The shriek died away.

Half of her men's eyes had turned skyward. So had the enemy's. Only those locked sword-in-shield continued to fight. The nearest men looked to her for a signal, some cue as to how they should respond. Even some of the enemy glanced to her.

She wished she knew. She did not realize she had made a decision until she raised her baton. She hurled it.

It pirouetted end-over-end and landed behind one of Hawkwood's bannermen.

The only way she was going to get her baton back was by charging Hawkwood's lines.

Most of the enemy were too distracted to see what she had done, but her men weren't. She'd made a statement. The shout they raised finally deafened the silence of the sky, and in her head. Fia slammed her boot into her courser's side, and rode.

16

Joanna's reedy servant girl was even more surprised to see Meloku the second time. Infrared showed the girl's pulse jumping a measure. Had she been carrying anything, she would have dropped it.

She must have thought that the bear had gone into hibernation.

"The queen," Meloku said, when the girl would be able to hear past her heartbeat.

The girl nodded.

A pair of guards blocked the queen's bedroom door. They stood aside without a word when they saw "Veroncia." The girl gingerly tapped a knock. Meloku, without waiting for an answer, pushed it open.

To Meloku's relief, Queen Joanna was alone. No ladies-in-waiting, no courtiers. Good. Dawn was not far away. Meloku did not have the patience to be trapped here another full day. She and Joanna would have to be alone for this.

Joanna had risen early for Sunday Mass. Though a sovereign of her stature should have been attended by her ladies, Joanna had, as was her wont, chased them out. She was a solitary creature. She did not cope well with others. Or, most of the time, with herself. Joanna sat atop her bed, scowling. The instant she saw Meloku, her expression melted to guileless neutrality.

Meloku had caught Joanna halfway through the process of binding her hair with a pearl-studded veil. Her hair was already so tight that skin on her forehead paled. All of this would be easier done, and likely less painfully, with help.

Meloku turned to dismiss the servant girl, but the girl was already bounding down the hall. Meloku shook her head, closed the door.

She turned to Joanna and waited for her to say something. Joanna waited just as patiently for the same. Meloku kept hoping, every time, that it would be different.

She gave in first. Joanna could have sat and stared for hours. "What do you think of me?"

Joanna opened her mouth. Then she stopped. The thought couldn't form, let alone finish. It was not that Joanna felt either ill of her or well disposed. It was that Joanna could not think either of those things. Meloku was a hole in her imagination.

Meloku sat on one of the stools Joanna's ladies would have used. "You ought to hate me, you know."

Joanna looked at her as though she had not heard. It was quite possible that, if asked, she would not have remembered hearing it.

Meloku's nun's habit had voluminous outer sleeves. She reached inside one, and retrieved a black capsule. She turned it over in her hands.

"Would you *like* to hate me?" she asked.

Joanna's brow folded. She looked as though she had bitten into a sour apple. But the question had gotten her mind churning. Meloku saw the churning stop. Joanna asked, "Do you want me to hate you?"

A meaningless question. Had Meloku said "yes," Joanna might have pretended to hate. She couldn't have felt it.

Meloku pressed her thumb to the capsule's top. It clicked and split open. She plucked from the cushioned interior a thorny seed. Its spines softened at the touch of her palm.

In the glint of firelight, it luminesced an oily violet. Held from a different angle, the reflection turned green, and then bile black. It tickled her palm. The spines, as they brushed her skin, were constantly tasting her. Tearing away microscopic skin samples. Reading her DNA. Checking her identity.

Thirty years ago, the creature who had exiled *Ways and Means* to this plane had also burnt out her neural demiorganics. She'd had to get them replaced. This seed was a modified version of those given to Unity citizens as children. It could grow a complete set of demiorganics in weeks.

One of these had rebuilt her own demiorganics after she had been robbed of them. It had even repaired the burnt neural tissue. As a precaution against the creature returning, *Ways and Means* had given all of its agents these seeds.

It had been made for adults who had had demiorganics, whose neural pathways were already accustomed to alien thoughts merging with their own. She had no idea what it would do to someone who had never had demiorganics. That information had not been given to her.

She told Joanna, "I did not like you when I met you. Hated you, actually. I thought you were callow, callous, as ignorant as the rest of your people. When I did this to you, I thought I would be doing you and your plane a favor."

Some of that old disdain crept back when she thought about who Joanna used to be. Even if Joanna hadn't committed the murder for which she had been on trial when Meloku had met her, she was still a killer. She was a queen. All power on this plane devolved to death and killing.

"I didn't take the time to understand what you had done or why you might have done it. You were the product of your place – just as I was the product of mine. Had I met myself under the same circumstances, I would have hated myself, too. Do you remember where I told you I was from?"

"The planarship *Ways and Means*," Joanna said, at once.

Just words to her. Meloku said, "Remember that name. *Ways and Means* and its other agents here would never want you to have what I'm holding. It would put you on a closer-to-even footing with them. I think they're as afraid of that as they are of the monster that exiled us here." Thirty years ago, when her demiorganics had been destroyed, she had lost most of her advantages over the natives. She'd been terrified of them.

Meloku should not have held the seed for so long. Her palm itched. The seed was tearing off more and more skin, searching for the person it had been programmed to find. Meloku passed it to her other hand. *Ways and Means* had given her the seed preset for her DNA. Meloku was still an active agent, though, and had an array of black software at her disposal. She reset the seed to recognize Queen Joanna.

"I would like nothing more than for you to hate me. I'm a connoisseur of hate. I've traveled to so many places, and hated so many people. I never stayed in one of those places this long. This past thirty years, I've had the chance to study us as closely as I have any other people. And I think I hate us more than I've ever hated any of them."

Joanna tilted her head. She said nothing.

Meloku said, "I'm not going to tolerate things like this any more. So I have something to give you. You won't be the same person you were thirty years ago." Some damage couldn't be undone. "You will not live like other people here do, or think like them. You will still be different. Disabled in some ways. Enabled in others. And I won't be allowed to come back here."

Joanna said, "I understand."

Meloku did not hide her surprise. For a moment, hope made her breath catch.

It lasted only until she looked at Joanna. There was no comprehension there. She was watching Meloku closely – trying to figure out what Meloku wanted. Meloku must have inadvertently given away, through her tone or her words, how badly she wanted Joanna to understand.

Joanna could not disobey her compulsion to appease her.

"Right," Meloku said, under her breath.

She did not want to, but she knew she needed to hold on to the horror of this moment. Joanna could not even consent to this.

Joanna blinked, watching and waiting for Meloku's next move.

Better to get this over with. She should have just done it as soon as she'd come in. She had made this decision long ago.

Meloku commanded, "Hold out your hand."

Joanna did so.

The moment the seed touched Joanna's palm, its spines lost their definition. They melted. The seed turned from round to oblong to a flat disc, like a puddle of liquid color. It sluiced through Joanna's palm as though the skin weren't there.

Blood welled from the hundred pinprick wounds the seed had left behind.

Joanna gasped. She snapped her hand back. For a second, in her shock of pain, the real her was in control again.

Meloku's own demiorganics protected her from chemical addiction like the one she'd forced on Joanna. If she was captured by a force that tried to inflict the same on her, her demiorganics could route her neural impulses manually. Demiorganics could break down chemical barriers like the ones that had destroyed Joanna.

Demiorganics were the only solution Meloku had not yet tried. Even after so many years, they could suss out her old pathways, reboot her, brute-force the dopamine trap.

Even then, Joanna would never be her old self. She would be a new person. But that new person would be in control.

"I'm sorry," Meloku said. "I really would tranq you for this, but it will have an easier time integrating with your nervous system if you're conscious." The demiorganic seed had not been engineered to have such niceties as pain mitigation.

Joanna touched a finger to the blood, smeared it. Meloku waited. She did not have to wait.

Joanna jerked backward and screamed. She swatted her elbow to try to stop the fire spreading up her arm. She would not be lucid for long.

By the time Joanna's guards burst her door, Meloku had moved her to the bed, set her lying face up. Joanna shivered wildly. She stared at Meloku. Her bloodied hand gripped the other woman's wrist, but Meloku doubted she could see, or feel.

Meloku backed out of their way. She could not stay to guarantee the results. Joanna's guards and courtiers would not take long to decide that the visiting nun had poisoned the queen of Naples. They could not miss the blood for long.

Outside, the corridor's foggy windows revealed a lightening dawn. Meloku had delayed too long. Even with stealth fields, her shuttle would be visible in outline against the sky. *Ways and Means* had forbidden low-altitude shuttle traffic at this time of day. But Meloku had no choice. The same black software that had allowed her to reprogram the demiorganic seed had tamed the shuttle's NAI, overridden its safeguards. She called it.

A pulse scan found the path to the nearest balcony. She stepped out and waited. A dark gray shadow blotted the sky. The stealth fields tried their best, blurring its edges, making the shuttle seem hazy. She did not have to use any of her augmented senses to trace its spidery shape.

She hitched her costume's skirt past her knees, climbed over the railing and onto the boarding ramp. She did not look down. At this time of day, the people below would be able to see her and her shuttle if they looked up. The thrusters roared in her ears as she crossed the shuttle's sound dampening fields. If anyone below called out, she could not hear them.

She did not expect it would be long before Joanna's guards beat down Veroncia's door. Before the end of the day, all of Naples would know that the Queen was ill, one of the hermit nuns had gone missing, and that a shadow like a dragon had fled the Queen's palace. Veroncia would become a Satanic figure.

It did not matter. Meloku would not – could not – come back to see Joanna again.

The shuttle vaulted into the sky as soon as the boarding ramp closed.

Her demiorganics tried to keep her balance, but she stumbled into the ventral corridor's bulkhead. She fought her way into the control cabin, climbed into an acceleration couch.

She thought about going to Habidah and Kacienta. They would not believe what she had done. They would not trust her. They would be right not to do so. She had been too complicit. She was not on their side. She would still tolerate a lot that they wouldn't.

And they were academics. They could catalog what was happening, but when it came to *doing* something about it, they were useless.

A chill shook her. She could not countenance more of this happening. Meloku pulled herself into the control cabin, collapsed in an acceleration couch. She removed her headdress, tossed it aside. Her gray field jacket was draped over the cushions behind her. She fought to tug it on against the acceleration. It did not help her shivering. There was a tightness in her chest that would not go away.

The compound-eyed monitors all around painted her a landscape of clouds. The shuttle banked high into them, gaining altitude as fast as its sound dampening fields allowed.

Her demiorganics dampened her nerves and paced her breathing, but neither were the problem. She'd spent a long time imagining taking that final step to free Joanna. Now that she had done it, she felt as though the shuttle was plummeting.

When *Ways and Means* found out about this, she was not going to be able to talk her way clear of the consequences.

The shuttle speared through a lazily drifting gloss of cirrus. She leveled its flight. It arced northeast, following the Italian coast. At least they were high enough now not to be visible from the ground.

Ways and Means must have been tracking her flight. It had chosen not to say anything. Or maybe the report had already been logged in the satellites, and was queued to be sent along. If it looked closely enough, it would find what she had done to Joanna.

The best way to protect Joanna now was through misdirection, distraction – to make an even bigger statement that *Ways and Means* couldn't pretend to ignore.

Meloku had a good idea where to do it.

The land turned gray and misty. A halo of reflected sunlight followed the shadow of her shuttle. The coastline threaded the horizon far to the west, visible only in hazy outline. The day wore deeper.

Meloku leaned into her couch, closed her eyes, laced the shuttle's sensors through her demiorganics. They gave her a taste of the condensing humidity, the airborne microflora, the frost on the hull.

After only a short search, she found what she was looking for.

Not far from Siena, she saw a hot mass of infrared bodies. Marching bodies. Hundreds of them, plus even more animals. Sheep and goats and cattle wisped behind the army like smoke from a fire, the prizes of war. They outnumbered the people vastly. An army's treasure train – the same one that had led her all this way, weeks ago.

Farther ahead, there were even more people. The numbers rose into the thousands. The only animals among them were horses. Two armies strung out in lines, threading together. She had found the Company of the Star.

Meloku circled, watching. Rain clouds lined the western horizon. The papal army and *condottieri* forces of John Hawkwood swept in from the north.

Meloku took a risk and dropped altitude. Her stomach plunged. She was not near enough to the ground to be visible to the naked eye.

Still no call from *Ways and Means*.

The shuttle's sensors picked out at least three satellites above. There were far more in the geosynchronous bands, but these three were the ones that would be watching her. They must have noticed her. Her craft would have been the only spaceplane moving on this side of the dawn terminator.

From this altitude, her sensors could not only distinguish individuals, but the minuscule emissions of electronics. There were electronic signatures all over the battlefield. On both sides of it. That surprised Meloku. Before her next breath, she realized it shouldn't have. She had only ever seen the devices in Hawkwood's camp, but she hadn't looked closely at the Company of the Star. It had been a discrepancy in her observations about the latter that had gotten her attention to begin with.

Ways and Means was manipulating both sides in this fight. Steering them both into each other. It didn't make sense. Not yet. She didn't have enough information.

Whereas the bugs in Hawkwood's camp had been spread around, those in the Company of the Star were concentrated. And moving with a cluster of riders. Leadership, presumably. Though there were plenty of women in the company, the woman at the front could only be the famous Fiametta of Treviso.

The armies crashed into each other. Artillery smoke licked the battlefield. Some of the infrared shadows no longer moved. People were dying. And she still had no idea what she was going to do.

When she'd come here, part of her had fantasized about dropping the shuttle in, switching off the stealth fields. Without its camouflage, her shuttle looked something between a spined fish, a beetle, and a hawk. She would be a distraction, maybe scare the armies away, but they would be back.

She'd studied plenty of this plane's wars over the past thirty years. But *battles* had never interested her. They were never the most consequential things about war. She had little mastery of equestrian and primitive-arm tactics. But, even at this distance and even to her, it was obvious that one side badly outmatched the other. Something had disrupted Hawkwood's rear lines, but the terrain favored his numbers. Fiametta of Treviso's maneuvers meant little. Hawkwood was mongoose-quick. He had wrapped his lines around hers before she seemed to have realized what was happening.

It almost did not matter what games *Ways and Means* was

playing with this one battle. *Ways and Means* had been at this long beforehand. She doubted the bugs and other devices below had been installed recently, either. It had had a hand in all the suffering, all the slaughter and famine, that these groups were responsible for.

On her next pass over the battlefield, she banked hard westward, above the boiling line of clouds. Then she dove into them.

The shuttle was unarmed. It had been in *Ways and Means'* diplomatic service, and many planes would not have let it approach if it had been visibly armed. But neither *Ways and Means* nor any other amalgamate had ever sent a vehicle to another plane without a trick or two at the ready.

Most terrestrial shuttles had aneutronic fusion engines, but not this one. It was versatile. It was made to be as comfortable in deep space as in a terrestrial atmosphere, liquid methane oceans, or a gas giant. There was no versatility like power, which gave it a perfect excuse to pack an antimatter reactor.

Its reactor was tucked deep in its hull, a black sphere as small as her chest. It was heavily radiation shielded. That was the trick. Its shielding could be voluntarily weakened to allow certain emissions through.

She could time her power output to spike at the same moment. She could produce, on command, a powerful electromagnetic pulse.

That pulse would wipe out electronics in almost any radius she chose. The shuttle's most critical systems, and their backups, were hardened against it. Electronics of the type she had spotted below would not be. Her shuttle's stealth fields would not survive it, either.

Hence she had steered into the cloud bank.

She did not hesitate, or think about what it would do to her. She did not want to give *Ways and Means* any more time to realize what she was doing, or exercise its options to stop her.

She just gave her shuttle the order to do it.

17

Fia should not have gotten away with it. Should not have *been* getting away with it.

But for once her doubts did not win the world over.

Her charge trampled Hawkwood's lines. She bowled over a pikeman who'd run out of formation, slashed a crossbowman before he could drop his spent crossbow and grab his sword. From atop her armored courser, she might as well have been atop the clouds. There were no cavalry around to dispute her. The crossbowmen who hadn't spent their bolts yet couldn't take aim this close.

This was expected. She had found a weak point, a moment of opportunity. She had expected a swift reaction. Hawkwood had plenty enough of his own cavalry to ride in and force a retreat. But the counterstrike never came.

Even without her baton, she had command of the field.

The screaming in her head faded, leaving only a fading impression, a long echo. There were no longer any clocks ticking. The sound had been with her so long that she had stopped hearing it. Pain pulsed through her head. It was intermittent, but sharp enough that she wondered if the lightning was real – if she had been knocked on the head or was suffering a stroke.

Even in the middle of battle, though, she saw men turn to watch the sky. More than one of whom she cut down while they were doing it.

She had trouble thinking straight, but so did most of the enemy she faced. They were running, tumultuously, away from the chaos. Her own men had lost their order, too. The nearest of the company's banners was so far that she couldn't see it but as a splash of color.

She had not realized how deeply into enemy lines she had driven. She saw swords everywhere, but none flashing at her. She could not stop. She had to drive farther, and deeper. Faster. It was like being washed away in a current.

Before she realized what was happening, she broke free. Her courser galloped into a vacuum of men like a clearing in the forest. She saw the sun. *Suns*. There were two. She raised her hand.

When her fingers blotted out the light, she saw the shape underneath one of them: a spider, tearing across the sky. It was halfway to the horizon before she realized she was seeing anything at all. It was multifaceted. From this angle, it looked like a hawk. It shrank to a sparrow.

Then it was gone. It left a curvilinear white cloud behind it. The sky growled, deep-voiced. Thunder, at last. It lagged behind the creature as it ripped across the sky.

Her courser kept its composure. It did not seem to care what was happening. It rolled its nose back to her, impatient for her to stop gawking.

Hawkwood's reinforcements should have reached her, crushed her, but they weren't coming. His men continued to fall back. His formation broke. And his wasn't the only one.

Her baton was lost somewhere in the scrum. She could not have directed this chaos anyway.

Both companies left a good number of dead on the grass. And then they broke. Fia rode across her line and tried to convince her men to pursue. She shouted that the daytime star had been a sign meant for *them*, but she could not convince enough to follow.

The shock had been too convulsive. No one saw her. By the time she had organized a semblance of a cavalry squadron, the remnants of Hawkwood's army had fallen back too far to pursue.

One of Fia's corporals, a *condottiero* whose contract had brought fifty men into her service, reined up beside her. "I'm pulling my men from the lines. Right now." For as much as that was in clear violation of his contract, she could not find the breath to argue with him.

These men would claim, to a man, to be Christian. More than that, they believed in her, and in Saint Renatus. They thought themselves the bearers of tomorrow's world. She would have thought that they would interpret a miracle as a sign that God favored them. Same with the true believers among the papal forces, those who had come to clear their slate of sins on Crusade.

But there had been more to the miracle than a flash in the sky. She had felt it herself. A *snap* of disconnection. A pulse of dislocation. The pain in her head, like a stroke. Something more than light had affected her, and all of them.

It had been impossible to think about anything more than the moment. She had nearly lost herself among the enemy. If they had been any less confused than she, they would have killed her.

Her inner voice no longer screamed, but it was back, curiously affectless. *This is the end of our world.*

She did not answer, though it succeeded in unsettling her.

She found Laskaris and Antonov at the same time that they found her, galloping across the rear lines. From their sweat and their wild eyes, she knew what they were thinking. They had expected to get crushed. The miracle, as they saw it, had not been to allow them to rout the enemy. The miracle was that they were allowed to get away.

With the sense of betrayal still hot within her, Fia could not disagree. The clocks had not started ticking again. The silence in her head was an iron weight, heavier than her helmet.

Her inner voice said, *There won't be any more battles.*

The Company of Saint George was only a line on the horizon now, hardly distinguishable from trees. There was not going to be any decisive clash of arms today. Maybe tomorrow. Maybe never. But she was damned well not going to stop.

"Raiding parties," she snapped. "Light cavalry. Remind the officers that Hawkwood's treasure train is still in disarray."

Antonov glared at her, but Laskaris galloped off before Antonov could contradict her.

The war is ending.

The afternoon fled before she could get a clear summary of the rest of the battle. Her men had engaged Hawkwood's on multiple new fronts. Hawkwood's men had fallen back where they should have pressed. No matter the heroic myths, soldiering was not a profession for individualists. Soldiers fought best with men at their sides. In their retreat, Hawkwood's men had lost their formations, and died one at a time.

Those camp followers whose duty it was to count the dead reported a thousand dead or dying. The field already stank.

The harassment parties and those few *stradiots* who had limped free of the ambush reported easy kills among Hawkwood's stragglers. Neither he nor Cardinal Robert had made any attempt to rally. They only fell back faster.

Hawkwood and Robert seemed to be acting on impulse, as though the strings animating them had fallen loose.

Fia understood how they felt.

Sunset stippled the distant hills. Red poured over the ridges, painted the valleys.

More and more *condottieri* took their leave. They traveled singly, or in small groups. She did not lose any other major commanders. Yet. But that time was coming. None of them spoke openly while she stood anywhere about them, but that did not disguise what they were thinking. They were afraid that, if they stuck around, if they didn't take the opportunity that the miracle had afforded them, she was going to order them into another unwinnable battle.

Fear traced shadows under their eyes, tightened their lips. They had stared into the jaws of Hawkwood's army once.

They did not want to run back into it. *Condottieri* were good soldiers, renowned for their prudence. In other armies, their prudence would have been called cowardice.

She had never been able to find her baton. Her hands itched without it. When she had the opportunity, she stalked among the dead to search for it.

That was where she found Caterina.

For a moment, Fia couldn't breathe. She had seen so many dead men's faces that, for a moment, she imagined Caterina among them too.

But Caterina not only moved, she shivered. She reclined into the side of a stubby hill. The evening was not cold, but Caterina shook as though the ground was covered in ice. Her sleeve and her side were dark with blood.

Caterina's eyes grew wide when she saw Fia, but she didn't stop shaking. Fia recognized the look. She thought she was in trouble.

Fia knelt. Caterina held her right wrist unnaturally still. It was bent at a bad angle. Fia peeled back the sticky dried blood of Caterina's sleeve. Whoever had cut her arm had struck deeply, exposed yellow bubbles of fat. Caterina, or someone, had scavenged enough cloth to wrap the wound, but had not washed it. Her forehead was already burning. There was no sign of Caterina's sword.

We lost more than we thought we could have.

Caterina had no business being in battle. She must have charged off to fight, just like Fia had when *she* was a child. To help, or to prove herself, or both. She should have gone straight to a doctor. She must have figured a doctor wouldn't help. Fia understood. When she'd first joined Antonov's Company, she knew the surgeons wouldn't prioritize a fool girl over a soldier.

Fia flagged over two men she recognized from the company, a Hungarian and a North African, had them carry Caterina to help despite her grunted and kicking objections. She followed them to the surgeons' tents. There, her men had hardly begun to take count of salvageable hostages among the wounded when a messenger found Fia. Musa bin Hashim had arrived.

Musa's two escorts were waiting outside her pavilion. Even in the dark, she knew who they were. Their long robes, sashes, and turbans left little doubt. They didn't look at her as she pushed past.

Musa bin Hashim was not, officially, a representative of any Turkish potentate. He answered to the lord of Izmir, a city only recently liberated from papal crusaders. His allegiance was a fiction that allowed other powers, like the Turks, sufficient deniability to funnel funds westward, into campaigns like Fia's.

Musa's Latin came with an accent, but he spoke it comfortably and casually. His was the urbane, multiply cultured face his lord put on his dirty deals with westerners. Izmir had spent a half-century under an uncomfortable split rulership. Papal crusaders had held the town's lower castle, and the Turks the upper. He had treated with soldiers from both worlds. The Turks had finally thrown the Christians out.

He had never bothered with the fiction with Fia. As much as she'd dreaded this meeting, she was glad he was here. With so many *condottieri* abandoning her, the company would need more resources to keep going. The Turks had always been her best, longest employer. Her treasure train was larger than it ever had been before, but much of its contents belonged, by rights, to her commanders. She had sold away most of her own goods and gold to support the attempt on Siena. She had counted on the spoils of the city to replace them.

From the few times Fia had caught Musa wearing gold and silver, she knew he was paid well. He had wisely not worn any jewelry on this journey. For all the dignity of his position, Musa was a young man, and paced with a young man's impatience and recklessness. His sweeping robe had knocked over a golden helm, seemingly without his noticing. His long travels hadn't tired him at all.

She told him, "It was damned stupid to travel so far with

such a small escort."

He turned. There was a spark in his eye when he saw that she had entered alone, but it didn't last. The first few times they'd met and made their deals, he'd angled to take her to bed afterward. Fia had refused. She wasn't interested in sex. With anybody.

He said, "Better to take the risk to meet you now than to be too late."

She said, "We met John Hawkwood in battle today. We roundly beat him, and killed thousands of his men." Exaggeration was the key to fundraising. Describing inconclusive battles as victories was a time-honored *condottieri* tradition. "We'll need more florins and arms to–"

He cut her off. "Do you think I haven't heard what happened? I don't care. Word is that you mean to turn against us."

Fia's blood iced. "Why do you think that?"

Her inner voice said, *Everything we know is falling apart.*

"The Cult of Saint Renatus has spread into our boundaries. My lord feels this could not have happened without your active support."

Fia scoffed. "I don't control which soldiers pick up our creed."

"If you wanted to stop it, it would stop."

"That's not how belief works," Fia said. "I preach. Soldiers do with it what they will."

"My lord has come to believe you meant for it to happen. That you mean to convert our soldiers exactly as you have in Italy and Greece. He has a source in your army who insists you mean to head east once you've secured your cult in Italy." By contrast with his fidgeting hands, his eyes were leaden. His gaze was a stone on her chest. "He wanted to cut ties with you at once. I talked him into sending me out here, to ask you myself."

She had only told Antonov of her plans to strike eastward. Caterina and Kristo may have been in earshot, but Caterina couldn't speak and Kristo was dead. She knew Antonov hadn't given her away, either.

The weight and the pain of this betrayal was again familiar.

Her inner voice said, *You and I have made plans for this day.*

Her inner voice had done this. *It* had told the Turks. She did not know how, or why, but it had turned against her.

The day had been too long. She was too exhausted to be a good liar. The skip in her pulse had become a catch in her voice. "It is absolutely a lie," she said. Musa held her gaze in his for too long a moment.

"I see," he said.

"I don't think any of us sees a damned thing about what's actually happening here."

He tilted his head minutely. "Excuse me?"

She could not find the words to explain the weight on the back of her mind. "There are..." She had been about to say *forces*, but stopped. "There are problems I'm still trying to work through. It's been a difficult battle. I would have an easier time treating with you in the morning."

She had always thought of the voice as her *inner* voice for a reason. It had seemed a part of her, even as it spoke in its own words. If she could not trust it, she could not trust herself.

"As you prefer it." He departed with a flourished and unnecessarily deep bow.

The weight had moved behind her eyes, made them too heavy for her to lift. She only took the time to remove her boots before finding her mattress.

The next morning's meeting with Musa did not last long. She and Musa each backed down, ate some of yesterday's words. Musa promised to tell his lord that he had seen no evidence that Fia was planning to strike eastward. Fia had vowed to send orders to rein in her believers. But that had been a dance. A way for both of them to tell if they had fooled the other. Neither of them had.

He had seen everything he'd needed the night before. She

could count on no more support from his quarter.

You must realize that you have been compromised.

She felt as though she were falling. Her *casa's* guards waited unobtrusively close to the pavilion flap. One of them would no doubt relay these developments to Antonov.

She found Antonov by the surgeons' tents. She expected him to start on the meeting, Instead, he said, "You ought to know there's every likelihood Caterina won't survive. The officers I spoke to said she had charged through the center lines, going after you."

Fia stared. She knew what Caterina had done. *He* knew it. And he knew what had happened in that meeting. He'd seen that Fia had left the pavilion reeling and unbalanced. He hadn't needed to pile on.

He had done it to hurt her.

It had worked.

She could not stop staring, could not make her mouth work. She would rather have fallen against Hawkwood than bear these moments.

Compromised or not, you have become too valuable an asset to discard.

She needed a long moment to make sure that her voice would be steady before she spoke. She could not find the strength to challenge him. "What do we do now?"

"The Company of the Star, as it was, is over," he said. "We can't fight like we've been fighting. We can't keep existing without giving Hawkwood and the papacy more reason to keep coming after us. If we break apart, Hawkwood has nothing to go after."

"Then where do we go?" she asked.

"There's only one place left in the world I want to go," he said. Fia knew. His home. In far and foreign lands.

Her inner voice kept speaking over her, as if she were not already in conversation.

But you will have to change.

18

A firecracker-pop of discontinuity rattled Meloku's head. Her hand was on her acceleration cushion's armrest, and then it was splayed across her lap. Another pop. She was slouched to the left, jammed against her safety harness.

Gravity pressed her hard to the side. Her shuttle was turning, spinning. She could not tell if it was falling.

The monitors had gone dark, leaving her alone under pale cabin lights.

Another spark of nothing interceded.

A black vacuum split her head. She was receiving no data from the shuttle. Her demiorganics were gone. She couldn't remember them going out.

She should have been much more panicked. Thankfully, that part of her had been stunned, as well.

She fought through the flashes of discontinuity. The last time she had lost her demiorganics, she had thrown up. She had not eaten before flying here. Bile rose in her throat. Acceleration held her pinned sideways to her acceleration couch's cushions.

The monitors flared white, turned back on. Her demiorganics screamed at her, reactivating. This time she could not keep the bile down.

Data surged through her. It came in a trickle at first, as her demiorganics rebooted and readjusted themselves. The trickle turned to a flood.

The electromagnetic pulses hit the shuttle harder than she'd expected. Its NAI had gone offline. Flight systems had mostly gone. Only the deepest electronic backups, hardly more sophisticated than transistors, kept the shuttle airborne. Its stealth fields were offline.

Directionless, the shuttle had burst free of the clouds.

The monitors showed thousands of soldiers crawling over the battlefield below. She was in full sight of all of them.

She croaked a curse. Nothing to be done about it now. It hardly mattered. She had done what she wanted. The shuttle came online in bits and pieces, but its stealth fields remained stubbornly nonfunctional. As soon as she could think straight enough to set a flight path, she burned the engines hard. She banked away from the battlefield, and then sharply upward.

She'd done what she needed. She'd made her best attempt at killing the devices guiding them – and more. She must have made a mistake when she'd programmed the antimatter engine. Its pulses had been too strong. The discontinuities she'd felt had been disruptions in her nervous system, electric flares along her neurons. The soldiers below would have felt them as well.

The armies below curled about each other, punctuated by bursts of smoke. Their formations wouldn't have had the time to react to her presence, not at the scale on which she saw them. She didn't have the time to wait to watch.

Her time was up. By now, the satellites should have apprised *Ways and Means* of what she'd done. *Ways and Means* could not go on ignoring her.

The shuttle sliced through the thin cirrus clouds. Its NAI finally recovered enough of its wits to manage the stealth fields. Meloku settled back in her cushions, heart beating hard against her back.

She waited. She checked her communications logs to make sure she hadn't missed anything while she'd blinked in and out. There were no messages waiting. No calls from *Ways and Means*. No orders. No threats.

For too long a time, there was nothing.

She didn't understand. *Ways and Means* should have been on her long ago, really, for breaking morning curfew. She'd started to believe it had just let her get away with it, avoided causing a fuss. But that was ascribing to it personality traits it couldn't possess. It wasn't avoidant. It had no reason to let anyone get away with anything. Unless, that was, it was in its interests to.

Ways and Means had the ability to take over her shuttle by remote, fly her into custody. Yet the shuttle remained stubbornly under her control. Or at least it gave every appearance of being so.

Ice-laced clouds whisked past below. Nothing was right. The back of her throat tickled.

She suddenly felt intensely vulnerable, alone. The shuttle's bulkheads seemed eggshell thin. When she'd trained to become one of the amalgamates' agents, one of the first things she'd learned was that a flying vehicle left her more exposed than empowered. She was too easy to find, and to shoot down. The deep browns and greens below took on the cadence of an enemy land.

Finally, the shuttle received a signal.

Not *Ways and Means*. Dahn.

She snapped, "What?"

"...the fuck do you think you're doing?" he demanded. "The satellites watching your shuttle just lost their shit. Do you have any idea what you just did?"

"No," she said. Then, "Do you?"

"What? Meloku – electromagnetic pulses over a battlefield? Are you trying to give them all seizures?" A pause followed in which, judging from the subvocalized muttering on the other side of his signal, he was still receiving data. "I'm calling *Ways and Means*."

"Don't," she said.

"You think it hasn't already noticed this?"

"Of course it has. I'm not afraid of you ratting on me. I'm afraid..." She let that thought trail. She did not know what she was afraid of. She did not know enough to know what she *should* be afraid of. There was a game being played here

249

whose boundaries she had only just brushed against.

"It's not answering," Dahn said, a moment later. Even over demiorganic transmission, he sounded apoplectic. He disguised his panic with fury. "It's not talking to me. I just spoke with it this morning. Meloku, *what did you do?*"

In all the time she'd known him, she had never heard him sound so emotional.

She permitted herself a moment of fury on Dahn's behalf. He hadn't done anything wrong. She had. Maybe her crime had been that she knew too much. If all Dahn had done was talk to her and it had cut him off, she had become the epicenter of some kind of plague it was trying to quarantine.

It had plenty of weapons with which it could burn away the infected.

Just to be sure, she tried contacting *Ways and Means* herself. No response.

However impetuously she'd done this, she'd expected only to be taken into custody. Now she felt like she'd jumped into the mouth of a steel-toothed trap.

Strangely, that left her calmer than she had been before. Her breathing came easier. Her training had prepared her for emergencies much better than it had the past few days of chasing her own moral shadows.

"I'm coming back," she told Dahn, banking the shuttle. *If I can.* Every moment, she expected the shuttle's NAI to yank control away from her.

Her hideaway was not that far, relatively speaking. She could land outside it in a little over an hour. The shuttle's stealth fields buffered the sonic booms, and muted the roar of the engines. It made everything sound hollow.

"It must be a satellite glitch," Dahn said. "Or sabotage. We've got to contact *Ways and Means* directly. Our base transmitter can reach it. Damn! *Ways and Means* just went below the horizon."

"*Ways and Means* isn't going to help," Meloku said.

Dahn didn't answer. It didn't take long to discover why.

Their call had been ended. The satellites had cut their transmission.

The shuttle reached their hideaway without further difficulty. She held every other breath, waiting for disaster – for the engines to cut out, or to steer her into the side of a hill. Nothing. The satellites still provided the shuttle with positioning data. Her mind raced. She had to assume there was some meaning to these contradictions. Hints pointing to a deeper truth she could tease out. Maybe.

Her and Dahn's hideaway was tucked into the northeast side of the Alps, deep below a shadowed treeline. The only clearing that could fit the shuttle was a three-minute walk away. Meloku stood on the boarding ramp as it descended, hopped off as soon as she could.

She tucked her hands inside her field jacket. Naples had been much warmer. She hastened over the pebble-strewn ground. These hills were so remote and wild that it had been years since any native had last wandered this way.

The door to their hideaway was concealed under a six-foot rocky overhang. A chorus of alarms filled the open bandwidth, the result of Dahn trying about thirty emergency override commands to resume contact with the planarship. Inside, Dahn paced. With a body like his, he shouldn't have felt the need. Restlessness was a vestigial biological impulse.

He said, "I've tried contacting every nearby agent. Nothing." *Ways and Means* had stationed more of its crew in Avignon, and throughout northern France and Germany. "The satellites tell me the signal's going through. There's just no answer. No pingback. And none of them are over our horizon, so I can't contact them without satellites."

"*Ways and Means* is cutting us off," Meloku said.

"*Ways and Means* is still close enough to Earth our base transmitter has the strength to reach it directly. It's going to rise in another thirteen hours."

"It's not going to listen to you."

"How do you..."

Dahn stopped, went rigid. The distance Meloku had covered in her walk could not hide the rumble of the shuttle's engines starting. The noise stuttered and muted as the stealth fields kicked on.

A new and subtly different trill had joined all the other alarms. "It's the perimeter alarm," she said, in case he had muted the alarms' shrieking. In the event that a traveler stumbled upon their hideaway, the shuttle was set to automatically take flight, conceal itself. Procedure had her and Dahn camping out in here until the trespassers wandered away.

Four natives were climbing the hills to the north.

Perimeter sensors piped imagery to Meloku's demiorganics. The four intruders were all men, in poor to middling health that was typical for the region. They stood at a uniformly short stature. Pulse scanning revealed slivers and specks of iron: swords, tipped arrows or bolts, some metal jewelry. Three of the four wore metal-capped helmets.

The nearest settlement, a commune of farms in one of these slopes' few fertile regions, was twenty kilometers away. These men couldn't have set out long after Meloku had bombed the *condottieri's* battlefield with electromagnetic pulses. Maybe before.

They were heading right for her and Dahn's hideaway – like they knew where it was.

She signaled the shuttle to halt its startup sequence. The shuttle NAI refused. She scowled. She redeployed her black programs to override the NAI. But the shuttle's engines continued to heat up.

Ice trickled through her veins. Dahn looked at her. He had access to the black software she did; he must have tried the same thing.

Dahn padded over to a featureless wall. A panel opened. From it, he took a white cylinder with a translucent red protrusion. When he held the cylinder in his palm, the protrusion fit right between his fore and middle fingers.

Meloku had not even known her hideaway contained weapons. The palm pistol was designed for crew with wholly demiorganic bodies. It had no barrel, no sights. She wouldn't have been able to hold the aim steady past twenty meters. Of them, only Dahn had the fine motor control. It said something that *Ways and Means* had never imagined there would be a circumstance in which it would *want* her to use one of these. Only Dahn.

She didn't have time to dwell. She asked Dahn, "You were angry with me for scaring some soldiers. Now you want to kill these men?"

"This is different," he said.

"Yes," she said. "Because I'm going to stop you."

With a face like his, she couldn't read much of a reaction. But he held still.

She asked, "Do you really think these men know what they're doing? Are *they* behind whatever's happening to us?"

"No," he said.

"I've been in worse trouble before." She had killed a native back then, too, and not even to save herself. She had been rescuing someone else. Another thing she'd had a long time to think about.

She'd hated herself enough that, put in the same circumstances, she'd expected that she would do the same thing again. Now that she was actually here, though...

She could sense the argument building inside him, but it didn't come out. He knew she was right.

If the intruders were headed right for the hideaway, it was best that neither of them be here when they arrived. Dahn led the way without a word, still holding his pistol. The door rolled shut behind them. It resumed looking every bit like just rock.

Meloku and Dahn trudged into the shadowed forest. Best to observe from a distance. Then they could see what the newcomers would do with themselves once they got here.

A white bolt lanced the shadows.

The bolt was too fast for her to register beyond the flash. Dahn's reflexes were sharper. He shoved her.

By the time they landed behind the cover of a larch tree, smoking debris sliced the air on all sides of them, slapped into the dirt. A wave of heat seared Meloku's skin. Yellow-orange light leapt into the boughs.

Meloku's demiorganics tried and failed to mute the ringing in her ears. Her knee hurt fiercely. Dahn had not been gentle. Fire-silhouetted branches cast veiny shadows on their arms and legs.

Dahn raised his pistol, took aim.

Meloku retained enough sense to grab his arm. He had the strength to resist her, but not to keep his aim steady while she yanked him. He looked at her.

She transmitted, "They're not aiming at *us*."

If he'd thought about it for a moment, he would have realized. She could see their infrared forms perfectly. If they'd had the ocular sensors to match their weaponry, they could have seen her and Dahn just as easily.

They hadn't, though. Three of them had dived away from the fourth man. He held something in his hand. It radiated white-hot heat. He shuddered. After a moment, he waved the others to their feet.

They didn't move. They seemed shocked.

Meloku's first pulse scan hadn't detected any electronics or demiorganics. Another one didn't now. His weapon, any implants controlling him, could have been hidden, deactivated, to avoid detection. That would have taken expert craftsmanship. In the Unity, the technology would have been far beyond the reach of civilians.

However they'd gotten the weapon, the soldiers hadn't learned how to use it well. They'd fired too early. The blast had only taken out the hideaway's front wall. It hadn't collapsed the roof. Even had Meloku and Dahn been inside, it might not have killed them. Their attackers had blown their advantage of surprise on their first shot.

The soldiers circled the hideaway, keeping a safe distance between themselves and the flames. The fourth man took aim at the entrance, waiting for anyone to come out. They either didn't have the tools or the wherewithal to scan infrared and see Meloku and Dahn huddled a hundred and fifty meters behind them.

Their enemy could arm natives but could not, or did not want to, train them. It could not send competent agents in their places, either. These contradictions revealed weakness. Meloku just wished she could read more in it.

Dahn transmitted, "If *Ways and Means* wanted to kill us, why didn't it do it itself?"

"I don't know."

"There are crewmembers in Munich. We can reach them in a few days. Less if I go ahead."

"We'll just be putting them in danger."

She scanned again. At this distance, she could see the outlines of their armor, their jewelry. The man who'd fired had a necklace with an emblem: a silver shield-and-sunrays, one of the many symbols of the Cult of Saint Renatus.

Meloku's gut had stopped roiling. It felt like ice instead. Anger had always tasted better than fear. She plucked it out of the back of her mind, held tight to it. She let it grow.

She said, "I think I know a direction that might be more productive."

19

Osia waited longer than she should have.

The Iberian shore had long since escaladed the horizon. A fishing village nestled in the untamed forest like a bird's nest in the bough: a bundle of wood and spit clinging together. The trees sheltered the homes from the casual observation of marauders. The two short piers were the same coarse, sandy color as the beach.

Three fishing boats had beached as soon as their pilots saw Osia's boat. No doubt she'd find the village empty too. These people were accustomed to corsair slave-taking raids.

If anyone was left watching her, they'd be even more alarmed as she grew closer. No one on this side of the continent had ever seen a Chinese merchant junk.

Again, buried deep under the air, she sniffed traces of smoke.

There had always been smoke. It had followed her from coast to coast. It had stopped only at intervals across south and west Africa. Not even during these peoples' most brutal wars did they burn so much, so consistently.

From this distance, Osia could have swum to shore without spending much of her power reserves. She nearly did. She had a lot of work ahead. But she had to address her problems in the right order. The golden rule of shipboard life, here or on *Ways and Means*, was that all work came in its proper order. She could not avoid her task here.

She stepped down the aftcastle steps one at a time.

She made herself recall *Ways and Means'* voice – its flatness, its equanimity, its self-assuredness. No matter how complicated its thoughts, it could always seem dispassionate when it presented them. It could even make her believe it was disinterested in the end of the Unity.

For most of her life, that was how she'd tried to make herself sound. She had not always succeeded. But it was how she had always wanted to feel.

Coral was red-faced from so long spent working the sails' lines alone. Osia had been afraid that, in the two days since Osia had gotten this close to thir, thi would have degenerated, become like Ira and Braeloris. But the look thi gave Osia was more tired than baleful. Thir blond hair was askew. Thir eyes remained piercing, and that was all.

"I'm not getting any closer to shore," thi said. "I can't sail safely alone. Not unless you release Straton to come help."

"This is as far as I need," Osia told thir. Their progress here had been unsteady, but better than Osia had expected with so small a crew. Fortunate, though, that Osia had only needed to sail in a direction rather than to a specific place.

"And now you'll just allow Straton and me to move along?"

"If I'm ashore, I can't stop you from going."

"That's a pile of shit. Now that we're here, what's next?" Thir voice broke. "Kill us yourself, or just tell them where to find us?"

Osia had to keep playing the villain. It was the only way Coral *could* see her, the only thing thi would believe. She said, "I will not tell the partisans about you."

"You don't think they'll *make* you tell? Do you know who you're working with? They're not nice to anyone who holds out on them. They'll torture you to find out."

"So don't tell me which direction you and Straton are headed. By the time they compel me to say anything, you'll be long gone."

"Why do you want to get to them so badly?"

"I've got a lot of bad choices to make. No matter how bad my options are, I believe there's always a correct choice. This is where I need to go to find out what it is."

Coral stared. But Osia had known that would bounce of thir. She had said it more for herself.

Thi said, "Even after all this time, I didn't think I knew you. But I thought I knew you better than this."

Osia held Coral's gaze. "Did you?"

Osia had lived with her constructs for thirty years, but she had never told them much about herself. Not where she had come from. Not why she had joined *Ways and Means*. Nor why she had left it. They knew only that she wanted their company, and also that mostly she ignored them.

"If we *had* known you, we would have stopped you long ago."

Osia nodded to the aftcastle, where she had dragged and bound Straton two days ago.

Straton lay out of sight below the aftcastle railing. She had tied his arms and ankles with cord taken from their spare lines. Straton probably had the strength to break free, but she figured the sound of it would give her warning. She had let him and Coral talk, on occasion, to prove to Coral that he was still alive.

"We're through here," Osia said. "You can go get Straton."

She did not have to worry about him breaking free now. He was dead.

Three hours ago, she'd approached him. Since the other constructs had destroyed their memory cells the moment they'd died, she'd figured that the only way to get his was to take it while he was still alive. She must have been too obvious. As soon as she had crouched over him, he jerked, spasmed. Infrared sparks flared up and down his body. His memory cells were gone, burnt out.

Osia had positioned him near the railing, letting Coral see him, think he was still alive. He would have needed to collapse from exhaustion about then, anyway.

Every task in its proper order.

"Coral," Osia said, as thi passed by.

Coral stopped, turned. There was no question on her lips.

She already seemed to know that there would be something else, that Osia had not told her everything.

"Call for Straton. See if he answers."

It took only a moment. Thi glanced to the forecastle, and then thir head snapped back. Thi understood why Osia would do this, what she wanted thir to find. Thir eyes widened. There was a flash of heat in them, of terror.

Osia could not be so obvious about getting the memory cells this time.

The way out was not just to play the villain. It was to *be* the villain. The virus had deeply ingrained itself into her constructs – and Osia had bet that their personalities affected it too. She had seen it happen before. The virus saw through Coral's eyes, thought with her thoughts.

If she was going to take this last chance to get a memory cell, she needed Coral shattered, lost between shock and rage and grief. Too distracted to think. The virus would be too. She needed its attention, and Coral's, on her voice, her eyes, the still body on the upper deck.

Anywhere other than Osia's feet bracing against the deck.

Osia's fingers had not been made to cut. But she did have strength and leverage. Her blow was messy but it struck true.

Coral had no subdermal armor. Thir skin on thir abdomen was no more difficult to punch through than an ordinary human's. Slime spattered Osia's forearm, a swill of false blood and rapidly solidifying liquid crystal emulsion.

Osia's sense of time stilled. At the speed with which this virus worked, she likely did not have the time to let Coral finish thir indrawn breath.

Osia did not waste time physically seeking a memory cell. It would likely be a burnt husk by the time she pulled it out. As fast as her fingers moved, neural impulses moved faster. Nanowire filaments extruded from Osia's fingertips. They wrapped around the tightly wound threads of Coral's nervous system.

This virus could easily travel back up the connection,

poison Osia too. Her safeguards were not invulnerable. But if that had been the preferred method of assassinating her, Osia was sure it would have happened already.

She need not have been concerned. Her intrusion programs broke through the virus's initial quarantines, stifled its countermeasures. The virus had been a match for her constructs, but not for her. Its security countermeasures were civilian-grade software. Hers were a step beyond military.

Another mystery. She had to assume that her opposition had no shortage of resources, and yet this virus was low grade. Possibly a virus complex enough to best her would, had it come along their usual datastreams, also have been large enough to attract her attention. There were too many unknowns.

She targeted the nearest memory cell. Her thoughts expanded into the forked-bolt electron pathways of Coral's synapses.

When she found the memory cell, it was already burning out, half gone, self-destruction in progress.

Osia was not supposed to care this much about her constructs. They had character, feelings, but they were nonsentient. *Ways and Means* had sent them to provide her with an illusion of socialization. That was all. Caring about them should have been like caring about an appliance. This was nothing like she convinced herself it should be.

Coral was burning away, thir thoughts and thir memories immolating in Osia's grasp. They were becoming ash in her palm.

They weren't all gone yet. Osia worked fast. She did her best to scavenge what remained, even as it died. She drained Coral of thir virus-chewed memories, thir personality, thir programming… and found little more than the illusion she knew she would find. Coral contained complex nested code, thoughts and sensations, but not a mind.

Still she could not, and would not ever, be able to shake the feeling that she was doing something awful.

She nearly did not find the virus in time.

At first, while she could see that Coral's memories had begun to decohere, she could not find the cause. Nothing was out of place. Nothing big. The virus was not a discrete chunk of code. But it was there. Little bits of it had wrapped themselves around Coral's thoughts – and most importantly the heuristics that allowed thir to perceive shapes and colors as objects.

It was through those that Coral had not perceived Osia as she had been, but as a Sarrathi collaborator. Every time thi had seen Osia's face, the virus had injected a little bit of rewritten object memory that classified her not just as *person* but *collaborator. Monster.* And *murderer.* While the virus digested her constructs' basic programmatic vocabulary, they had begun seeing hateful things everywhere, conspiracies in the shadows and Osia's whispers.

Whatever egg the virus had come from, it had long since hatched, and changed. It took work to reconstruct an image of what it must have been like when it arrived. Loose scraps of progenitor code remained in some key memories. Matched against trace ions suspended in the memory cell's colloidal casing, she was able to assemble a fragment.

She nearly killed the connection in that moment.

Though *Ways and Means* was potent, its powers over itself were limited. None of the amalgamates trusted each other. They each left code, buried deeply inside each other, to ensure their compliance to the treaty that bound them together. They had done this by agreement, and by necessity, at the end of their wars.

The amalgamates had just come out of an era of intense, secretive warfare. It had been common practice for AIs to release a virus and strip it of knowledge of its origin – sometimes so thoroughly that it attacked its parent. No amalgamate could compose any program without leaving a trace of its authorship, a signature.

Osia had seen *Ways and Means'* digital signature, a little

scrap of code thirty kilobytes long, more times than she had bothered to count. She had no trouble recognizing it again.

Ways and Means had authored the virus. It had given her constructs explicit, emotionally driven instructions to kill her. The virus had started its life svelte. It could easily have come down with any regular status update. The size wouldn't have caught Osia's notice. It had festered, metastasized in their minds.

Osia had known this was coming. She should have prepared. She was caught in the same instant Coral had been. The flash of heat, the terror.

The rage.

She pulled her hand loose of Coral's ribs and let thir fall. White-silver gel and false blood ran slick along thir arm. The gel was already hardening in the sunlight.

Osia placed her hand on the mainmast. She dug her fingers in.

It was not easy for her to lose herself.

Not until the mast *cracked* did she remember where she was, and what she was doing.

She did not know where she had gone, but it was somewhere she had not been since she'd had a biological body. All of the control she'd striven to exert over herself was gone. There no longer seemed any point.

Control came back to her in fits and false starts. But it did, eventually, come back.

Ways and Means could not rob her of everything it had given her. That had always been, and was always going to be her curse.

The mainmast groaned, shifted subtly left. A human eye could not have perceived the movement, but the damage was there. The fracture spread with each gust of wind.

The sails were unfurled. It was only a matter of time before the wind picked them up again. Then the whole mainmast would break loose, fall, and likely take the fore or aftmast with it. Or both. Even if she managed to get the sails down in time, by herself, the ship was lost.

The mast had pushed on her as hard as she had pushed on it. She had braced herself against the deck without realizing it. Nails under the deck boards had popped up or snapped in half. One deck board had jarred loose, stood at an angle. She remembered feeling the jolt, but had not been aware of it.

When she started walking, she did not know where she was going.

To the extent that this boat meant anything at all to her now, it was nothing she liked. She hitched her legs over the railing. She had ideas as to where she could go after this, but no plan.

As she dropped into the water, she still felt as though she'd made a decision.

Osia did not surface until the water was so shallow that it could no longer hide her.

She pressed her arms against the sand and stood. She had heard her boat's masts collapse underwater – a deep-throated moaning followed by a crash that had scattered the marine life in panicked clouds.

She looked back. Her boat drifted against the far horizon, a silhouette against daylight. All the masts had collapsed. The mainmast had fallen into the aft, and the ropes linking both to the foremast had proven stronger than the decades-old wood. A collapsing mast had smashed the aftcastle to flinders. Broken wood bobbed languidly on the waves.

The ship listed. Yet the ship was not sinking. Maybe it would beach; maybe not.

She did not watch it for long.

Let the natives board it, puzzle over the listless wreck and its dead. It didn't matter. They didn't matter.

It had been too damn long since she'd stepped off ship. The beach struck her as an image from a planar travelogue. Sand led up to rocky, root-rutted hills. The primeval forest loomed, a labyrinth of moss-bearded cork oaks and pine trees. Its shadows were as dark as her cabin aboard ship. Only a few thin slats of sunlight survived the foliage to reach the underbrush.

The scent of smoke was stronger, closer. Ten kilometers or so distant, depending on the size of the fire. She did not dare pulse scan. *Ways and Means* had admitted to having a hand in this region's wars. It could have assets in their armies. They could have been shadowing her along the coast all this time. A pulse scan would have given her away.

Assuming that it was not using its satellites to track her. It did not seem to be, or the smoke would have been closer. Another mystery.

That mystery was one of two things that gave her hope. For whatever reason, *Ways and Means* resisted bringing all of its strength to bear against her.

The other was that she had, before she had allowed Coral's memory cell to finish destroying itself, taken a still image of its remaining contents. Less than half of thir had been left. It was not enough to rebuild thir. But thi was something to else hold onto – the only thing she had.

She stared at the forest. She'd seen thousands of trees and tree-analogues before, all over the planes. They still seemed bizarre. She had been so long at sea. Even the sand seemed alien. It was steady and firm, and didn't roll.

Her demiorganics found decades-old sensory recordings of walking on solid ground, and shunted them into short-term memory. It was a reflex to help her adapt. Suddenly she felt as though she had done this just last week. The muscle memory was not perfectly adapted to her injury, to her looser control over her legs, but it was a starting point.

Then a frisson of disassociation rippled through her. She was not the same person she had been in those ancient memories. In the past week, never mind the past thirty years, she had become very different. Fragments of her old self came along with the sensory shadow. She could not separate her ways of thinking from her ways of feeling.

Reluctantly, she pushed the memories back. Disorientation was easier to deal with.

She had options, none of them good. She had set course for Europe to see just why *Ways and Means* was funneling Chinese money this way. She could still investigate. Interfere, too, if she found a way. She had no idea where to start, though.

She had originally intended to trace the path of local turmoil and see where it led her. Now the turmoil, she was sure, was following her. It would have been like trying to track the spoor of a wolf that was stalking her: a lot of marching in circles and a quick, decisive ambush at the end.

There was still Xati.

Osia could not survive as a lone rebel. She had been aboard ship for two centuries. Asocial as she'd been, she could hardly have avoided relationships, acquaintances. She'd had no friends, really, but she hadn't ever been isolated.

After three decades away, she could not say how Xati might have changed, or if e would take Osia's side. Most of *Ways and Means* crew would at least listen. They would allow her a voice. Even a bad reputation was a kind of power. It meant people knew her name. She could get their attention.

By setting sail for Europe, *Ways and Means* might have figured that she was about to become a disrupter, a walking flashpoint of trouble.

Once again, she lost track of herself.

The heat under her eyes, the rawness of the betrayal, robbed her of her other senses. Her demiorganics could have told her how much time had passed before she returned. She did not want to know. She had no tear ducts, but the phantom sting of salt was real enough.

She didn't figure she would feel like herself ever again. *Ways and Means* had wormed too deep into her. Every time she thought about it was like leaving it all over again. Even after the first time she realized it had betrayed her, she could not have imagined this.

She started off just putting one foot ahead of the other. She would decide on a direction later.

20

Osia could move fast enough when she wanted. Her body was light for its size: forty-five kilograms of composite bone, impact armor, crystal gel elastomer muscle, and demiorganics. Her body had been designed for light, efficient movement in zero gravity. Its near-human appearance was also serviceable enough in gravity.

A hundred and twenty kilometers and two sunrises after the scent of smoke had dwindled to nothing, Osia allowed her pace to slacken. Warnings about her energy reserves drilled into the back of her head like a headache. Her solar and thermal cells needed time to recharge, for her to travel at a more sustainable speed.

After thirty years at sea, she expected some unsteadiness in her step, weakness in her legs. And there was. It stemmed from the wound in her back, though. Her feet trembled, or didn't respond on time. She picked her way over roots and ruts carefully.

As best as she could tell without resorting to a pulse scan, she was alone. If she had been hunted, then she had evaded her pursuers. She'd gone more than fast enough to outpace merely human pursuers. Nor did she have to stop at night, to eat or sleep. Her passive sensors detected nothing more than the background fuzz of *Ways and Means'* satellites. If anything more advanced was nearby, it kept its emissions well concealed.

Yet *Ways and Means* could not have lost track of her. Its satellites were always overhead.

She needed help. She needed allies, support. No direction

she chose was likely to lead her to those. Xati's included. She could not count on reaching Xati. Nor could she could count on em to believe her. For all that they had worked together in the past, Osia had no idea how e felt about her now. Yet er contact was the only one Osia had kept that would still be current. Er assignment, managing a backup communications post in the Carpathian mounts, had been long-term.

There were certainly other crewmembers closer. From here, Osia could have walked to Seville, Madrid, Toulouse. Not all of them necessarily hosted agents, but likely one did. She would have had to spend time finding them. And she would have to do so surrounded by natives, among whom she couldn't disguise herself.

She would not have felt safe going to them. *Ways and Means* could have told them anything. Given the circumstances under which Osia had left, it might have little trouble convincing them. It could have told them she was dangerous. A criminal runaway to be quietly brought in. Xati was as loyal to *Ways and Means* as any of them had been. But e would not close er ears to Osia.

Coral's memories, what was left of them, remained frozen at the center of Osia's mind. She could not unravel them, could not ask Coral what thi might have thought. The only mind on this plane powerful enough to piece thir back together was *Ways and Means*.

Coral might as well have been lost. Osia did not know why she held on.

Osia kept a good distance from native settlements during the day, moving near them only at night. She was in no hurry. She had no deadline. She only needed to move fast enough to stay ahead of human pursuit. And to keep herself from being seen, so that the locals couldn't point her pursuers after her.

The grass underfoot was browned and hardened with drought. The smoke she tasted on the wind had nothing to do with war. Wildfires. The Pyrenees gathered on the horizon, half-hidden in the gray haze.

Her injury meant that she could not automate the task of walking, push it below conscious awareness. She had to focus. Walking gave her existence a rhythm and a beat. It helped her order her thoughts.

When she'd come to the surface, *Ways and Means* had sent her list of ways she was and was not to act around the locals. She had imagined that the restrictions had been put in place to protect them. Knowledge of the broader multiverse was a kind of contamination. But the idea that uncontacted cultures were "purer" than others was a human conceit. *Ways and Means* wasn't human, and wouldn't have believed that for a moment.

She should have figured that out. *Ways and Means* didn't care about contamination. Not now, not ever. It hadn't since the first hour of its exile, when it had moved to halt the great plague. It said it had done so for humanitarian reasons. Its intimate contact with the monk Niccoluccio Caracciola had forced it to understand this world's suffering. Its outlook had changed. Supposedly.

It had not hidden its presence from the locals for *their* benefit. It was a masquerade. A con. Knowing who and what had arrived would have empowered them.

Figuring that out was like a jolt through her system, a shudder in her step. In all Osia's experience, knowledge had never left anybody disadvantaged.

If she really wanted to spoil *Ways and Means'* plans, she should have headed straight toward the cities. Revealed herself. Explained who she was, and where she was from. For whatever reason, *Ways and Means* was afraid that they could know too much.

She still didn't know what its plans were, or what would become of disrupting them.

That was one of the many things about this that gave her pause. If she had a clear idea of what *Ways and Means* wanted, what outcomes it had mapped – then she could have thrown herself into resisting it more wholeheartedly.

Osia was accustomed to living in the dark. There were some things about the amalgamates that she was never going to be able to know or understand. She had accepted that before she'd signed on. She had entered the masquerade willingly, gotten used to feeling her way around the blank spaces in which their secrets resided.

The amalgamates had spent most of their time alone. Once every few years, though, they gathered. They met three or four at a time. The intervals of these meetings were unpredictable, their purposes unspoken. They never announced these congresses in advance. Their crews' personal communications – always monitored – were cut for the duration. Sometimes *Ways and Means* had even blocked its crew from accessing its sensors.

Sometimes, as they had when the Unity collapsed, the amalgamates had met above one of the city-studded Core Worlds. On other occasions they had basked in the radiation of a black hole's accretion disc, or above a world scoured of its crust by a gamma ray burst. They had met in the entropic voids of universes that had long since suffered heat death.

Even now, after the Unity had fallen, *Ways and Means* would not say why it had met them. When she had first joined *Ways and Means*, she had thought it could not have been for simple messages. Their amalgamates controlled the micrometer-width planar gateways that the Unity's communications flowed through. They could send, or block, any message they wanted.

But that, she understood later, was exactly the reason why they needed to meet. The amalgamates governed the Unity's data traffic in common. Each of them could have altered a signal, changed a critical bit in a datastream. The amalgamates did not trust each other. They did not trust their crews. Osia would not have been surprised if, on some profound level, they did not trust themselves.

Osia was accustomed to things not quite making sense.

Tolerating mystery came to her easily. But there were flavors of mystery. The unknown had genres.

In every secret, there were inconsistencies. Readable misdirections. An occlusion of light was data. She could learn the shape of the truth by studying its silhouette.

This refused to make sense in ways that Osia could not parse.

Ways and Means' attempts to kill her had all been low-tech. Slow. Fallible. Assuming that *Ways and Means* didn't want to bring its weapons into play, and draw the attention of the rest of its crew by killing her via bombardment, it could have come up with something else. A drone sniper, armed with a simple projectile rifle, could have taken her down.

It either wouldn't have done that, or it couldn't have. Both options traced an incomplete outline of its secrets.

Ways and Means had tried to kill her, yes, but it had killed her constructs first. It could not have done more to provoke her had it consciously tried. She had to consider that. *Ways and Means* could be pushing her in a direction that it could not say it wanted her to go.

She could not quite make herself believe that. Had she been a little slower, Ira would have killed her. What few fragments of the virus she had been able to examine had not revealed any instructions to hold back.

She needed somebody else to talk to. Not necessarily even to hear her, but another person around to think of, to be aware of.

The weather soured, turned gray. Storms lashed at her. Days and weeks spun together, knotting tight around her thoughts. Choking them.

The Pyrenees sank behind her. She crossed fields and streams, and then roads and rivers. She submerged in the rivers, sometimes allowing the current to carry her for kilometers before stepping onto the other shore.

She had spent a lot of her time aboard her boat thinking of herself as alone. Her constructs had done more than she'd cared to credit them with. She saw that in flashes of memory – Coral questioning her, Ira provoking her just to make her answer. Even Braeloris kept her uncomfortable. They had kept her thinking, reacting, active.

Ways and Means had given them to her. It had not needed to do so. She had not asked it. Had it been human, she would have considered that a sign it had cared for her. She had never quite known what to make of its relationships with its crew.

She had become sure, over her years with it, that it kept its crew on for more than just practical purposes. They were more than just their jobs. Yet *Ways and Means* was not sentimental.

She wondered if it would resurrect its backup of her. Like all of *Ways and Means'* crew, she stored her memories and personalities aboard it for safekeeping, in the event of disaster. The last time she'd updated her backup, though, had been thirty years ago. She no longer believed in backups. It was hard to imagine that she would want these years back, if she lost them.

Maybe *Ways and Means* thought the same. Maybe it was giving her up as lost, rebooting her. If she died here, it could restore her old self, before her self-imposed exile, with a clean conscience.

More of this world was wild than not. She spent most of her time sidling along forests or trudging through prairie. She passed into and through Germany, onward and eastward. Her path carried her farther east than north, but nights gradually became colder, and the days drier.

The first snowfall still caught her by surprise. It had been so long since she'd lacked perfect information about the weather that she had forgotten what it was like to be caught off guard. The seasons had advanced, but this snow was still early.

The patina of snow and frost made her take things slower. Her slim feet and their long fingers worked well for gripping bulkheads in zero gravity, but they did her no favors on ice. Her injury and the lagging response time from her legs did not help.

She had hardly been in the snow for a day when she discovered that she was being pursued again.

They did not bother to conceal themselves. She did not need to pulse scan. Her passive scanners caught the radio emissions of their electronics while they were twenty kilometers away. It was just static nonsense, encrypted short-range leftovers.

Their signals scattered off the atmosphere. The source of the transmissions was just underneath the horizon, too far to see. She did not need a precise position, though, to know they were headed right at her.

She was an easy quarry. Even if, for whatever reason, *Ways and Means* refused to use its sensors to aid them, she had left tracks in the snow for kilometers. Unique, inhuman tracks. She could not slow to scuff her tracks and still outpace them. Since they did not care about letting themselves be noticed, she doubted she would have been able to outrun them regardless.

She wished she had Coral here, though Coral would not have helped.

She stood on a dead prairie that the snow had turned into a brown-bristled tundra. She looked about. A knot of trees bristled out of the horizon, an ugly patch of fur on a bare scalp. They were cover, though. Shadows and cover were the only advantages she had left.

If she had to fight, it was a better place for it than any other.

21

Fia did not dream well.

Her dreams were not hers.

She dreamt of the night sky wrapped around her, unbounded. She looked below her and saw only a deep field of stars, the scar of the Milky Way. It took her too long to realize that there was no such thing as up or down.

She was not alone. There was something here that did not belong. She could not see it, but she felt it. Iron-cold, sharp-edged.

The darkness was more than the absence of light. It was a cloak, drawn over it. Sometimes there was not even that.

But it was always there.

The Company of the Star now consisted of just four hundred officers, riders, and foot soldiers. It shed more every day. Many of the remaining *condottieri* were contracted only to stay until the company reached the borders of Florentine lands.

Fia pulled her reduced treasure train closer to the body of their army. They no longer had the men to protect it elsewhere. Nor was there as much to protect. The most important of her contracted *condottieri* had already departed. They'd taken their shares with them.

Fia and Antonov had paid out most of their property to support the siege of Siena. They had astonishingly little.

Antonov told her, in their empty pavilion, "I rose with less."

"You're going home," Fia said. "You don't intend to keep fighting."

"You can stay if you want."

That evening, she watched their camp settle into the night. After dark, she could not tell that anything was amiss. The spread of cooking fires outlined the barricades. Herds of stolen sheep, goats, cattle dimpled the horizon. They might as well have been settling down for winter quarters as fleeing a fight they could not win.

The company had gone to ground before. It was a good *condottieri* tactic. Whenever a league of Italian cities emerged to fight them, they would melt away until infighting tore the league apart. They had never needed to wait longer than a winter.

It would take a lot longer for the papacy to lose interest. Fia did not know when they would be able to emerge, or if it would be worth it when the time came. Maybe ten years from now. Maybe never.

Hawkwood was giving desultory chase, staying a hundred miles behind. He would not follow her out of Italy. He no longer wanted to fight. His heart, for whatever reason, had fled him.

She had not taken Siena. She had lost her chance to make her gains any more permanent than the silver and wine in her treasure train. They would flee her just as quickly.

She had failed. The Cult of Saint Renatus would survive, but it did not need her as a leader. It never had, not really. She had been a figurehead, a preacher, but the only company she had ever led had been her own. She had thought she had wanted to change the world, but what she really imagined was *leading* that change. Change without direction was pointless.

Antonov had told her about the frosted forests and long nights of his home. It was still a long journey away. She did not figure that she would accompany him all the way. Yet she did not know where else she was going.

Warmth fled the dry air quickly. She walked a circuit around the barricades. It seemed shorter every night.

By the time she returned to the pavilion, Antonov was gone. But she was not alone. Her inner voice found her most often in the dark, when she was vulnerable.

Her dreams started the same way.

I can share more.

The starry void had no edges. It was no celestial sphere as the nuns had taught her. There were no glass-smoothed edges – but endless space in all directions. White-hot suns shone through it.

The idea of the infinite, the eternal, was something the nuns had taught her could only apply to God. Not to anything material. *This* was infinite, and only material.

She was without a body. She was just dreamstuff. But the stars felt real, livid-hot.

I share this with you to empower you.

She had no idea what her inner voice was trying to say at first. Not until it returned to this place, over and over. Wearing her down. She had to see it on her own.

The shadow-shape loomed above everything, disguising itself. She could cut her fingers on its invisible edges. It lurked at the edges of her awareness, just tangible.

This is the enemy.

She could feel every edge of the shadow-shape as though she were running her hands across it. But she had no hands, and the shape was wider than she could have stretched her arms. Miles. She did not know how she had figured its size. She sensed it as if she had felt it, though. She dreamed in naked sensation.

See what I can share with you?

She had no throat, no tongue. She did not know how she had learned to speak, but her voice was clear. She suspected she could only speak because it wanted her to. "You tried to kill me," she accused.

Yes.

"Why should I have anything to do with you?"

What else have you ever had, other than me?

Had she a body, she would have shuddered. "Lots."

You did not have the truth. I'm sharing it.

Even had she said "no," she doubted she could have stopped it from showing her what it wanted.

Her inner voice seemed to have resolved the confusion that had clouded it since the battle. It had a plan again. "Why share this now and not before?" she asked it. "What changed?"

Circumstances, it said.

Things it was not prepared to tell her, she understood. If she forced it to say, it would lie.

She had heard her inner voice scream as the black hawk had cut across the sky. It could have just said that was what had changed. But she woke before she could say so.

Most of the Italians left the company as soon as it departed Venetian territory. They already had a new contract. Venice had hired most of them to defend itself against Hawkwood's army.

Their contracts were said to last for as long as papal forces remained in Italy. That was an unusually open-ended term for *condottieri*. If they made a habit of taking contracts like that, they might as well have become a standing army.

Fia tried to put them out of her mind. Hazard of the profession. She could not help but see betrayal everywhere.

She was not at a loss for distraction. The terrain ahead was not as fraught as Italy, but danger was everywhere. No city wanted the trouble of the company raiding its lands. Even with their reduced numbers, they could do a great deal of damage to countryside unprepared for them. No city wanted the trouble of refusing their safe conducts, either. As usual, Fia dispatched multiple requests for safe conduct along their path, both to disorient their recipients and to make them more difficult to track.

Fia was left with one hundred and ten men, mostly Russians and Hungarians, and about as many camp followers to manage their herds. Fia had traveled with fewer before, but never with so few prospects. The Russians were all old hands like Antonov. Also like him, none of them intended to turn back when they reached their home.

They dragged around the edges of cities, unmolested. The soil hardened and the wind turned vicious. Fia could hardly stand to ride for the dust that blew into her eyes. She walked beside her palfrey.

Caterina led her horses. Through some miracle, she had weathered her fever. She had gotten on her feet far sooner than she should have. She remained paler than Fia had ever seen her. Her hands shook even in baking heat. A black, ugly, pitted scar ran down her arm. Incompetent suturing had not helped. She favored her uninjured hand, had trouble lifting with the other. Fia suspected her fingers did not work as she was accustomed.

She had lost her own tent sometime during the battle. She slept alongside Fia in her pavilion now. She always lingered in sight, trying to look like a shadow.

Fia did not want to let her go much farther, either.

She could have been as Caterina was. In any of the early battles she'd fought, she could have fallen. She would not have received even a morsel of doctoring. She had not bothered to be afraid of all of the deaths she could have found along the way.

After those first few weeks, Caterina never showed the pain. Only the sallowness of her face gave it away. Her lips were set. She was always watching Fia. Whenever their gazes met, Fia looked away first.

Fia wearied. She was accustomed to hard travel, but she had not marched in one direction so long in all her life. She had never gone farther west than Venice. Italy had been her world, and now it was behind her. She'd imagined leaving it one day, but not so soon, and not as a fugitive.

Antonov had told her about his home. It had always seemed another world, impossibly distant. He told her how, every winter, his toes would turn black. He had lost three of them. He had a divot in his ear he joked had happened when his mother had grabbed his ear, and a frozen brittle piece of it had snapped right off.

The life of the *condottieri* meant not knowing where she would end up next campaign season. She thought she was built to withstand uncertainty. She'd been standing on firmer soil than she realized. She trusted her thoughts. Her inner voice.

The only thing she had left was her belief in the gospel of Saint Renatus. The parts of it that didn't include a literal belief in the man, anyway.

In her dreams, she was always falling, deeper into the starry void. It had taken hours, days, to get used to it. But she'd had plenty of time.

Her inner voice said, *There are more worlds connected to yours than drops of blood in your body.*

Her inner voice seemed to think it was introducing her to a wider world. Helping her open her eyes.

Fuck that.

"I don't care," she said.

You can't imagine the scope of the universe you live in. That's why I'm showing you, rather than describing it. Perceiving is believing.

"Still don't care."

You could make this easier and listen.

She could not stop it from speaking. She had no ears to plug. Eventually, not by choice, she began to hear.

She did not care about its cosmology. Unlike many fellow *condottieri*, she did not consult the stars before battle. She did not need this dressed-up astrology, either. Intellectual curiosity had never earned her anything before. Her inner voice pushed through her. It seemed to believe that it was granting her some vast and terrible insight. It most wanted to impress upon her the scope and incomprehensibility of infinity.

It would show her some huge object, a planet, a sun, let her wrap her imaginary hands around it. It would make her feel every inch, every drop of water or lick of fire. And then it would pull back. It would show her something larger still. A cloud of dust. A nebula. Farther still. A galaxy. A chain of galaxies. More and more words that she'd never heard outside of these dreams.

The universe was larger than the distance light could travel in all the eons of creation. It was infinite. There were more universes unevenly folded over hers, like rings and whorls in lumber. Those universes were infinite, too. It spiraled beyond her comprehension.

The human imagination is not made to accommodate these things.

It seemed to think that this would change her. Maybe it did. A little. She had bigger problems on her mind.

It got around to those.

There are invaders, it said. The distances between universes were perhaps not as vast as they should have been. Some monsters could jump the gaps. Her world had been visited many times before. The one that had come now was different.

It let her feel it again. A silhouette, occluding the stars. A sharp, razor-spined surface. Cold ran through her whenever her senses brushed it.

It had seeded spies throughout her world. It had pitted its people against each other. Its alienness was a spike under her scalp, behind her eye. It hurt to think about.

"I still don't care," she told it, but she could not help but be shaken.

Her inner voice knew how she felt, and did not believe her.

The next day, the pain came from more than dust biting her face. She did not realize how cold she was until she lost feeling in her fingertips. Winter was settling on them.

She rode forward ahead to Antonov. As always, Caterina stuck close.

"The campaigning season is gone," she said. Even had she stayed in Italy, they would no longer be fighting. "We'll need to take winter quarters soon." There would be no luxury this time, no idyllic rural estate. No banquets. But they still needed shelter.

Antonov no longer trimmed his beard, and its raggedness made him look even more tired. "We can't afford to strain our provisions. And you don't want to winter here. There's nothing to eat but boiled grass."

"You think I'll be any happier at your home?"

"No," he said. "But I will be."

"You don't know what you'll find."

He claimed he knew where he was going. The next time she had a chance to catch him in their pavilion, she had him sketch a map of what he remembered of the towns and roads ahead. She had trusted too much of this trip to him. She scoured it by candlelight, with an ache of exhaustion set deep in her bones. She searched for opportunities she might have missed, traps that they could avoid. Excuses to stop, to turn around.

You can still help.

She did not want to listen to her inner voice, not after what it had nearly done to her.

She had fallen into this kind of depressive rut before. Her inner voice, ironically, had pulled her out of it. It had tugged her onto the long path to the person she had become. A soldier. A warrior. A person who mattered.

She had never thought of herself as dependent on that voice. But there was a deeply buried, deeply suffering part of her that wanted nothing more than to allow it to continue leading her.

We were always on the same side.

She tried to shake that part of it off.

For a whole week of their travel, the horizon glowed

aflame with wildfire. The wind chapped her skin, turned her hair dry and dusty. On the nights when her inner voice didn't visit her, she could hardly sleep for dreams of choking on smoke. Long after they left the fire, the sky hazed red and brown, like one of the alien worlds her inner voice showed her.

The farther they traveled from Italy, the less the locals knew what to make of them. They did not retreat to castles and walls, just stopped and stared. They were wary, sure. They knew war. But they had not had fresh experience. Even with only ninety men, she and Antonov could have taken a swath of land. It would not have been worth the bother. As poor as the worst-ravaged parts of Italy were, this was poorer still.

Fia had not seen so much empty land, with so little between. She thought Antonov had been exaggerating when he'd talked about boiling grass. Antonov insisted that the local herders were rich in their own rights, but Fia saw little worth taking.

Plans have changed. We have another role in mind for you.

She listened to what it had to say. She promised nothing.

They found towns only on occasion. She and Caterina visited, with escorts, when they could. The locals would trade away plenty for gold. More than she could have bought in Italy.

An hour after Fia returned from such a tour, she invited herself into Antonov's lunch. Speaking around her salt pork, Fia told him, "There's work for us. What passes for the lord of the area is hunting a fugitive running north. He's placed a good bounty."

Caterina glanced at her. She had been with Fia the entire trip. She knew there'd been no such meeting.

Antonov didn't notice. Not many people noticed Caterina. He said, "I'm not interested in work for hire."

"We might as well look for this fugitive. We're headed

where she was going."

That caught his attention. He stopped chewing. "'She?'"

"She," Fia said.

Fia's inner voice had not told her, specifically, where it wanted her to go. It did not need to. Sometimes it could communicate on a different level. She knew exactly where it wanted her to be, and when.

She was not averse to keeping her options open, she told herself.

Her inner voice's dreams wove through her memories. When she woke, she was not sure how much she had actually experienced, and how much her memory lied that she remembered. She lived halfway in its world, but less than half in hers. She did not know where the rest of her had gone.

Her inner voice's enemy, the dark shape in the stars, had come alone. But it was not friendless. Like a fallen angel, it had once been part of a greater community.

We aim to put all of us back together.

Fia had been doing plenty of dreaming, but when the first snow of the season came, it came from another nightmare. This snow was far too early. It was a light snow, a dusting, but it redrew the map of the land. The grass vanished. The rutted trade road turned slick.

After night fell and the clouds cleared away, moonlight reflected sharply off the snow. A wall of pale light ringed the horizon. They were encircled by a halo.

Judging from the shadows under Antonov's eyes, he had been away so long that he had forgotten what early winter had felt like.

He did not countermand her when she sent six riders ahead, and off the road. "There were tracks across our path," she said. "Our bounty."

He raised an eyebrow. This was a quiet land, a poor land, but it was not empty. Tracks in the snow did not make a positive identification. He was too tired, too cold, to care.

He stared into the pavilion's firepit. He might well have been wondering why she had not gone herself. She didn't know either.

The knowledge that she shouldn't had arrived deep in the pit of her stomach. It was sure as knowledge that she was hungry, or that she was cold. Her inner voice was asking her to place her faith in it.

She had faith aplenty. But what she did not have was trust.

But she did not understand what future she had if she did not listen.

22

Osia had started to think, based on the insidiousness of the last attack, that the next would come with some subtlety.

Her memory glitched. The next thing she remembered, she was sprawled across the dirt, her legs nonfunctional, her head on fire.

Her vision flashed red and white. An agony of alarms screamed under her ears. This body was not supposed to have pain receptors. The fact that she felt it now could only mean a complete systemic malfunction, a misfiring of signals that had overwhelmed her ability to react.

She had never encountered anything like this before. She had not even known it was possible.

Her thoughts sluiced through her like tree sap. She hardly remembered where she was. She had been walking amongst the trees, searching for concealment among the ruts and shadows. She was no longer receiving sensory information from her legs. Those few sensors that remained functional told her the outside world had become a boiling froth of electromagnetic activity. Jamming. It had disrupted half her nerves.

It would even have an effect on flesh and blood humans, but it was more perfectly calibrated to disrupt demiorganics.

It would have taken an incredible and finely tuned level of technology to manage something like this. Not to mention an intimate awareness of the ways in which demiorganics functioned.

It was only due to her designers' careful foresight that she was even able to think at all. They had believed her hardened against most EM attacks, but they hadn't let self-assurance be their final answer. She was adaptable, redundant. Gradually, her nervous system amplified its signals, routed around inoperable pathways, learned to filter noise.

The fire in her head subsided. The disruption seethed in the background, a virtual red fog at the edge of her vision. She would never regain control of her legs like this. The radio signals could not cut through the interference.

With effort, she curled her fingers. She clawed her way to the base of a tangle-trunked beech tree. She levered herself to a slump against it.

She still seemed to be alone. Her internal clock had been disrupted too, but from the movement of the stars she guessed she had been insensate for no more than five minutes. Aside from the patter of snow where she'd fallen, nothing around her had been disturbed.

Of course. Last she'd been aware, to the best her passive sensors allowed, nothing had been around her for miles. Anything clever enough to have beaten her sensors, or fast enough to have closed the distance so quickly, would have to be electronic or demiorganic itself. They would have been disrupted by the jamming just as she'd been.

The jamming was meant to hold her in place. Something was coming. Coming for her.

She grasped the bark of the tree. She tried to pull herself up. Her knees buckled. She slid back down, hard. Her back knocked against an exposed root. She only just kept herself from tilting into the snow.

She had never felt so limp and useless. She could hardly see past the trees and shadows. The jamming disrupted perception. Hallucinations danced at the corners of her senses – flashes of movement, light, sounds like voices.

She grappled along the trunk again, feeling for anything. The tree had no branches at this height. Nothing she could snap off as a weapon.

She had just enough sense left to know how scared she needed to be.

She had not felt anything like this since the day she had left her first body behind. She had felt alone, isolated from the world, underneath the onionskin layers of data. Her body refused to allow her the physiological symptoms of terror. No rapid breathing. No racing heart. No shivering, adrenaline. No tears. It all had to stay trapped in her thoughts, where she had no idea what to do with it.

She battened herself down one thought at a time. Somehow, she pieced together a semblance of herself.

The snowfall accumulated. It frosted her legs and shoulders. She stayed still. Silent. Dead in the snow.

There were people out there now. Strangers. Human. She struggled to filter the flashes of infrared from the hallucinations.

There were four of them. No – three. Five. Six. Their heat shadows blurred somewhere between her eyes and her imagination. Two of them walked with the bowed legs of lifetime riders, but none of them had mounts. The disruption that was jamming her nerves would have also made horses skittish, unmanageable.

These natives were frightened too. They did not take steps like people who wanted to be here. They moved tense and coiled, their muscles tight. They walked separately, twenty or more paces apart. Searching.

Her tracks were not old enough to have been snowed over. The trails she'd made would lead them right to her.

Their heads were uniformly hotter than the rest of their bodies. Their body heat was trapped underneath helmets. Soldiers. Even in this cold, they were sweating. All of them had weapons. The infrared shadow of a steel blade cut a dark line across the nearest man's chest. They had come to kill her. They were mostly men. One woman.

She felt about. A palm-sized rock lay buried under the snow. With effort, she gripped it.

Even with her combat programs offline, she could still calculate a good trajectory. The problem was that she couldn't trust her arm to throw it, or her fingers to let go.

One of the soldiers entered her clearing.

A moment later, and another of the figures tackled him. Their heat shadows tangled together.

Osia's thoughts moved sluggishly under the interference. Not until the strangers hit the ground did she understand what was happening. Not all of the soldiers were on the same side.

The one who'd tackled the soldier, the woman, had been stepping lighter than the others. She'd been stalking them.

She kept her hand curled around the rock, but remained still. Attacking could only have drawn attention to herself.

Thirty years of boiling rage crystallized, hardened in the center of her chest. It was a dense weight, and sharp-edged. It felt like the stone she held in her hand.

At least she could finally do something with it.

She would have to choose her victim well. Once she downed one, she was probably not going to survive long enough to get the second.

23

Weeks of traveling had worn Meloku down, dulled her senses. When something finally happened, Meloku almost wasn't ready for it.

The remnants of the Company of the Star moved at military speed, breakneck. They were headed, so far as she could tell, nowhere in particular. The camp followers she traveled with were used to it. They kept their distance from her. That was for the best. It meant they really were treating her as one of them. She had infiltrated them weeks ago, and nearly failed. What remained of her costume had been too rich, and her Neapolitan coinage out of place. Her skills as a laundress had been laughable. But the Company of the Star could not afford to turn away help who could keep up. Too many servants, laborers, and prostitutes had left. Too few had joined.

Gradually, hatefully, she'd learned to live among them. The skin on her hands felt like bark. She could still hear the cackling of the other women when she'd returned from collecting water and found her tent turned inside out, her blankets missing.

Meloku's demiorganics muted the muscle ache, the shin splints, the cold, and the itch of her wool, but they could not give her energy that she didn't have. The camp followers' food was awful, half-poison, infested. Her step sagged. Her vision turned a little grayer every day.

If she hadn't been looking in the right direction, she would have missed the six armored horsemen riding into the night.

This was what she had been waiting for. Throughout the weeks she'd spent among the camp followers, there'd been false alarms. More travelers joining the camp. *Condottieri* departing. Messengers fanning ahead. Nothing had come from them. Meloku knew at once that this was different. A leader like Fiametta of Treviso wouldn't dispatch a half-dozen heavy cavalry – of which she did not have many remaining – so suddenly. No scouts or messengers had lately returned with any news. Infrared revealed nothing on the horizon worth so heavy a hammer blow.

She was fully awake at once. Her demiorganics rapidly, efficiently, distributed what energy she had left, flash-manufacturing ATP and priming her muscles. She charged out of the camp followers' ragged formation, taking long and loping strides through the snow. The others didn't even look at her go. In the dark, they might not have even seen her.

Infrared revealed no demiorganic bodies, either. She had not seen Dahn since she'd infiltrated the company's loose brigade of camp followers. He would never have been able to disguise himself among them. He could move faster without Meloku. He had gone, instead, to contact *Ways and Means'* crew in Avignon. He should have reached them by now.

There had been no hint of him, no transmission.

The natives weren't the only threat to worry about here, either. She hadn't detected any pulse scans. She had avoided sending any since she'd arrived. She'd stayed away from the war camp. Fiametta of Treviso's camp was infested with listening devices.

She'd overheard the Company of the Star was on the hunt for a bounty. There was nothing around these wastes to be worth it for soldiers who, however much poorer they might have been than a year ago, still carried a good amount of war booty.

She pushed through the snow, kicking up clouds. The riders got farther ahead with every step. She could no longer distinguish horse from rider. They were all infrared blurs, at risk of vanishing under the haze of falling snow.

On her next step, the world dropped out from under her.

She felt like she kept tumbling. There was no more ground. Her sense of direction, of up and down, vanished.

She had felt this once before, years ago.

Then the pain screamed through her, a slice up her spine to the crown of her head. Her stomach roiled, unmoored from her gut. She must have blacked out. When she returned, she was retching bile into effluvia that had once been her lamb supper.

It took a moment to clock what had happened. Her demiorganics had been ripped away from her. They had been damaged, or shut down. Just like the last time this had happened to her, the rest of her was in neurological shock. A significant fraction of her nervous system had overloaded.

She was left with what she had been born with. And not really that, either – her mind had adapted itself to her demiorganics, wrapped around them, like a tree growing around a fence post.

She forced herself up, to dive back into the night. Long ago, that had been the first lesson she'd learned of crises like this. Keep moving. Otherwise the inertia would be too much to overcome. Inertia could be her ally as much as her enemy. It could keep her moving forward.

She had survived this once before. This time was different. Flashes of infrared leaked across her vision. Red-gray blurs of heat. *That* told her something. So she hadn't lost her demiorganics, not entirely. Her augmented vision struggled to function. It was not burnt out, but suppressed.

She doubted she'd fallen victim to a virus. She had not received any signals. She had more likely stumbled into a disruption field – or some kind of area-blanketing bomb had gone off. This was a magnitude beyond the electromagnetic pulse she'd had the shuttle make. Like it, this would have an effect even on normal human functioning.

A riderless horse bolted by thirty meters away, in full flight. It was a blood-hot red blur, half lost under the snow.

All of her ached. The snow had hardly cushioned her fall.

She staggered on to the forest's edge. Her retinal infrared was intermittent, flashing. The snow was getting heavier. The trees clustered thick around her. The forest's naked branches coiled around the sky. Their roots knotted the ground.

Flickers of heat shone through the trees. Men, dehorsed. They would feel the disruption too. It would be a buzzing in their bones, a fire up and down their arms. Electric tension, like wires in their muscles were about to snap. Their horses had felt it, and bolted. They must have thought the forest haunted.

Whatever force had disabled her demiorganics was a blunt instrument, a clumsy hammer blow. She doubted it had been meant for her. These men were hunting something.

There it was, a hundred meters ahead, glimpsed in flashes when her retinal infrared cared to function. An ember-shade of heat curled under a blanket of snow. Too cold to be a living human. Meloku almost thought it a cooling corpse – then it shifted, minutely.

One of the soldiers was near it.

Meloku's feet pounded through the snow. If she stopped, she would fall. She let inertia push her, turned it into momentum.

Meloku had not stopped to think about how she was going to beat these men. When she'd left the camp, the answer had been easy. With her combat programs, she could match any of them hand to hand. She had darts and tranquilizers. Now her wrist launchers were dead weight, nestled against her bones. She was just a person, no better than them.

She had only a ghost of a plan.

She howled mad nonsense as she slammed into him. Loud enough, she hoped, to make her sound like a banshee. She crashed into him, and brought him down into the brush.

Dry, leafless twigs snapped at her skin. The scent of the soldier's sweat-caked beard and sour breath dizzied her. His sword, which she hadn't realized until now that he'd had out, crashed into a tree trunk.

Somehow she retained enough of her balance to roll, bring him atop her. She hooked her elbow under his neck. She didn't squeeze, but tightened her grip enough to make it clear that she could crush his windpipe – if she wanted.

"Scream," she ordered.

He screamed.

The terror in his voice was genuine. Like the horse who'd bolted, he'd seen enough.

She released him. He did fall silent as he ran, but he did not look back, either. The others joined him. Their infrared blurs were impossible to pin down, but they were receding. The fire in their head and down their muscles, the screaming, their man's terror, and their horses' flight had finally been too much for them.

Meloku's throat burned. She crouched, breathing hard, and spat. She was too exhausted to spit straight, had to wipe half of it off her lip.

They would not be gone forever. She staggered to the body half-buried under the snow. The infrared shadow, even in flashes, was near enough to be familiar.

"Should've fucking figured it would be you," Meloku said, brushing snow off its face. She hitched its arm under her shoulder. "Come on. Help me out if you can."

Osia was cumbersome, but she weighed less than a human. Her demiorganic body was not small, but the materials were lighter. Osia sagged, feet drooping. Her skin was cold and slippery. Her mottled brown eyes, the only human thing about her, did not regard Meloku kindly.

Meloku headed away from the Company of the Star. After a dozen steps, she stopped.

She turned, followed her footsteps. Without her internal compass, it was the only way she could tell where she was going.

When she'd hauled Osia up, she'd thought Osia couldn't speak. But Osia spoke now. Her words were clipped, truncated. "The fuck?" The jamming field was affecting her even worse than Meloku.

Meloku said, "This jamming field, this bomb, whatever's doing this, is blanketing the area. If we run, whatever's made it will just follow us. They'll do it again."

"They'll have us," Osia said. "Surrounded."

Meloku shook her head, "I bet there are still all kinds of electronics in Fiametta of Treviso's camp. Some either survived my EMP, or *Ways and Means* planted new ones. That's how *Ways and Means* is controlling those men. That makes the camp our best way out. We go in there, they'll be disrupted too."

She and Osia would be in a better position. Not much, but battles were fought in increments. They cleared the trees. Meloku stagger-stepped, trying not to think about Osia's weight, the ninety soldiers waiting ahead.

Osia still did not answer. Maybe the plan was a terrible one. Osia didn't seem to have the energy left to say.

The *condottieri* camp's fires made a pillar of light in the falling snow. Meloku pressed on, slippery step after slippery step. No horses or soldiers darted out at them. No crossbow bolts fell. Osia's silence wore on her nerves.

A ribbon of fire ripped down Meloku's spine.

Meloku would have bet anything she'd had left that *Ways and Means* would choose to keep its disrupting field in place. Even had it lost control over of its soldiers, there were still ninety of them. Meloku and Osia would have been stuck there, hardly able to fight, unable to leave. The outcome would have been elementary.

A tide of information poured into the back of her head. Her vision briefly vanished under a multispectrum haze, her demiorganics running through startup checks. She stumbled. The pain had hardly begun before nerve blocks kicked in, dampened the worst of it. Her control still faltered. She rolled sideways into the snow.

Osia jolted, jerked. She fell off Meloku's back.

A headache burned between Meloku's temples. Her

nervous system could only take so many shocks in one day. But this one hadn't been fatal.

Osia stood. She brushed the snow off her arms. It sloughed off her without leaving so much as a dusting. If she was in pain, she did not evince it. Meloku remained shaky, but she stood too.

The jamming had ended, all at once. *Ways and Means* had chosen to give her and Osia control of themselves rather than lose its influence over the Company of the Star. Another hint of something going on here that Meloku did not yet understand.

Her wrist launchers sped through rapid diagnostics. The outage had inflicted no lasting damage. All her darts and tranquilizers were loaded, ready.

Osia still did not speak. She could have, but must have felt she didn't need to.

She tilted her head at the war camp.

Meloku nodded.

24

Fia's inner voice stopped speaking.

She set her mutton leg down on the raw wood of the table. The voice had been carrying on one-sided conversations while she tried to focus on dinner. One of those conversations petered out in the middle of a thought.

She, Antonov, and Constantin Laskaris were alone at the table. That had become their habit. There were no dinner readings from Livy these days, no scribes or accountants or officers. They stewed in their mutual silences. Caterina hunched by the tent wall, cleaning one of Fia's boots.

Her inner voice was still there, somewhere. This wasn't like the battle with Hawkwood. She could feel its weight, round and warm, in the center of her mind. It had just stopped speaking to her.

A shout of alarm broke the night. Though the pavilion walls muffled the cry, it sounded like it had come from the edge of their camp. A moment later, two more cries joined it.

They were dressed for dinner rather than war, but none of them were ever unarmed. At once, Laskaris had his dagger in hand. Antonov grabbed his weapon, but stayed back. Laskaris had only just reached the flap when someone pulled it back for him.

The creature outside came from the stories of robbers and murderers the girls of Saint Augusta told each other at night. It was solid black, a shadow – a blur of nightmare. It shoved Laskaris before Laskaris could step back.

The shadow was strong as a bull. Laskaris wheeled into the dinner table.

295

Fia grabbed her own dagger. Antonov was ahead of her. He roared and rushed the shadow. He moved faster than Fia had seen in years.

Someone stepped through behind the shadow, a woman. Fia gaped. It was one of the laundresses, a new woman among their camp followers. Fia had seen her but never spoken to her. She must have been a spy.

She held an arm out, fingers splayed down, like she was showing off rings. Her knuckles were bloodied. The skin of her wrist had split, gaping wide and dark.

A whistle like a crossbow bolt sliced the air, ended in a *thunk*, a gasp.

Antonov jerked. His momentum took him forward another pace. He reeled. Like a weaving drunk, he took an unsteady step back, grappled for the table. He didn't find it. He fell hard on his side.

The laundress turned her arm to Fia. Fia stared into the shadow of her open flesh. Her sense of time slowed, and stilled.

With a shriek like Fia had never heard, Caterina bowled into the laundress. Caterina latched onto her arm. She and Caterina staggered toward the pavilion wall.

As Laskaris drew to his feet, the shadow brought its fist crashing into his forehead. Fia's blood was rushing in her ears, but she would have sworn she heard a *crack*. Laskaris fell, instantly limp.

Then the shadow turned to Caterina. It grabbed Caterina's arm – and in one swift, brutal motion, wrenched her backward, dislocating her shoulder from its socket.

"No!" Fia cried – together, she was surprised to hear, with the laundress.

Caterina let go. The pain had not yet time to register, but her mouth was wide in shock. The laundress stepped as if to intercede between Caterina and the shadow.

Fia did not leave time for anything worse to happen. Fury seized her. Before she realized she had moved, she had launched herself. She dove at the shadow, leading with the tip of her dagger.

She did not see the shadow move.

In an instant, a crushing pain enveloped her hand. She could not breathe. Icicle-smooth fingers wrapped about her throat. She couldn't remember dropping the dagger, but felt the hilt bouncing off her boot.

Fia's rage had not been arrested with her momentum. She pried at the fingers pressing her airway. She drew her other hand back, and punched the shadow with more strength than she figured she should have had left.

The shadow's head gave way, but only like a branch to wind.

The shadow turned back to her. For the first time, Fia saw its eyes. They were human. Brown. Its grip tightened. Pain mounted on pain.

The laundress set her hand on the shadow's arm. She was trying to restrain it, Fia realized. To pull it back. The shadow must have felt her, but it was pretending it hadn't.

With a sigh, the laundress gave up. She set her hand on Fia's shoulder.

A jolt jammed through Fia's body, an involuntary spasm, followed by a rapidly spreading numbness.

The shadow's gaze held Fia's eyes rigid. Fia could not look away. She did not see the darkness gathering around her until she plunged into it.

PART III

The Company of the Colossus

25

Fia did not know why, or how, she had come back to Saint Augusta's.

She had not thought of the convent much, at least not with the intent to do so. Now here she was again, walking through the wheat, trailing her fingers through the stalks.

It was not real. The last she remembered, she had been far away from here, her camp under attack. She was not oblivious enough to think of this as anything but a passing fancy, a hallucination – perhaps of a dying woman.

The thought did not scare her.

It was daytime, maybe. In most places anyway. The sun was overhead and her shadow underfoot, but the ridge upon which Saint Niccoluccio's monastery rested was as darkened as it would have been at sunset. It was a warm season, before second harvest, but she was cold. Painfully cold. She felt snow under her riding boots, but when she looked, found only dirt and wheat. Nor did she have boots. She was barefoot.

Her legs ached from long days of riding, though she could not remember them, and there was no horse in sight. The nuns had owned only oxen, no horses.

This had to be a dream. The problems with it were manifold.

For one, she was an adult. On those few times when, of her own volition, she thought back to Saint Augusta's, she never imagined herself this old. The wheat only reached her knees. Her knees and back ached as they never had when she was young.

She rubbed her knuckles for warmth. What warmed her hands was not friction, but fire. She could not see it, but it was there. She held her palm open to it.

She was tired. She thought of entering the convent, finding the abbess's quarters and taking them for herself. Maybe from there things would start to make sense.

The convent never got any closer. But neither did it move to the side. She tried to change course but Saint Augusta's did not fall away.

She was being held in space, held in time, even as she pushed ahead.

It was deeply frustrating, but even her frustration came muted. It was an echo from the bottom of a well.

Somewhere else, she sat heavily on a hard wood surface.

Fire warmed her face, her cheeks, though Saint Augusta's was not burning.

She craned her neck, warming her face in the sunlight. The sunlight, though, could not have provided the crackle of wood sparks, the whipping smoke.

She did not understand why she was here. She had left Saint Augusta's long ago. She had thought of it from time to time, but never for long. Her nostalgia had died many, many times, and many, many years ago.

She was being asked questions about this place. Someone was trying to find answers. They would not find anything. This place meant nothing to her. However important it had been once, it was nothing now.

She tried to say this, but her tongue was numb. The words were trapped. She could not say anything without first being asked.

She could not say what her questioner did not want to hear.

Questions, questions, questions.

She pushed them to the back of her mind, where the answers were. If she was going to be asked about such unimportant things, then unimportant things were all she was going to give in return. She answered without thinking.

This time, she was no longer in the fields. She walked up and down Saint Augusta's empty dormitory, running her hand along the walls, feeling the knots of the wood.

She was being told to touch and smell everything. As if that would jog her memory, or make her say something untrue. She bent and smelled the ashes of the firepit in the kitchen. Then the pile of soiled sheets outside the dormitory. The cold air streaming through the dormitory's broken window.

The floorboards, in those places where there were floorboards, did not carry her weight well. They popped like the abbess's knees.

Without meaning to, she sized up the place for value. There was old furniture. Plentiful iron tools. Some bread, vegetables, wheat. Likely still the oxen. No valuable hostages. The inhabitants were clearly all gone. The returns on capturing them would not have been worth the effort, as Antonov's Company had discovered.

Antonov had made a mistake in coming here. This place was out in the middle of nowhere. There was no fortune to be made here, and that was all.

She answered as much.

For a while afterward, there were no questions.

She paced the convent's narrow hall. From the dormitory, past the kitchen and buttery and pantry, to the cells where the nuns lived and worked. And then back again. She stopped again by the dormitory's firepit. There was no wood beside it. This was not the season for fires.

All she needed was the flint firestriker for what she planned. But it wasn't there. She stalked to the kitchen. There was nothing there either. Sooner or later she'd find something. She didn't need a wood pile to start a fire.

She would burn this place down herself, if she had to.

• • •

Her inner voice had been taken from her. She did not know how she knew this, but she felt it as sure as she would have any other wound. There was a cold spot inside her head, a vacuum.

It would have taken surgery to remove. A skull chisel, a surgeon's scalpel. The blade must have bisected some deep and vital artery, but blood would not rush to fill the cold.

That should have killed her. But here she was.

She knew this had become an actual dream, her own, when the torch appeared in her hand. The flame had burned down so far that it singed her fingers, but she held on, white-knuckled.

There was nothing to see. She whirled around. The universe was a tangle of darkness. She still did not drop her torch.

Without it, she would have been blind.

It didn't matter that there was nothing to see. Without her torch, she would have imagined shapes in the dark, creatures about to attack. Substance that didn't exist. Purpose where there was none.

If she could hold on to the torch long enough to bring it back to Saint Augusta's, she could burn the whole place down.

Memory returned to her, bits at a time. After the ambush in her pavilion, she had walked out under her own power. She remembered this only distantly.

Her captors had taken only her. Antonov and Laskaris would have both been valuable hostages too, but they'd left them. She had no idea what had happened to Caterina, but neither of the intruders had gone back to check on her. They didn't care at all.

The camp should have fought their egress at every moment, but Fia remembered no opposition. The next thing she knew, she was hitching herself up and onto her riding palfrey. The shadow climbed up behind her, holding her. The laundress stole another good riding horse.

Fia did not remember leaving.

Every night of traveling, they built a fire. Fia sat numbly in front of it, staring.

She was also at Saint Augusta's. The shadow-woman kept taking her back there. Her words were puissant, magical. When the shadow told Fia that she was at Saint Augusta's, she was *there*. She saw it, felt it.

The shadow had her describe what she felt. Fia gathered that was to make it seem more real. To jog her memory. The shadow kept delving through Fia's childhood, trying to find something that wasn't there. The other woman, the laundress, kept Fia drugged.

Fia would kill them.

The shadow asked her what she intended to do with her future. It was too open-ended a question. It had unfrozen her tongue, given her the opening to answer. She told them they were both dead, their time marked, their clocks ticking. She would find a way to murder them.

The shadow had stared at her. It was impossible for Fia to read any expression in its face, but she already knew how the shadow felt about her.

The next time she went back Saint Augusta's, she still found no firestrikers in the kitchen. Someone had taken them. Everything else was in place as if people had lived here just that morning. Cups out and unwashed. The milk ready, covered in thick skin. Fresh rushes on the floor, scattered as if by footsteps.

Someone had taken the firestrikers deliberately, to spite her.

The campfire seared her eyes. She could not blink the heat away. The shadow had robbed her of even that much control.

She didn't have her sword. Not even the dagger she'd worn to dinner. She did not know if the shadow would be hurt by those things. It didn't matter. She was going try anyway.

The kitchen's rushes would be fuel enough for a fire. She just needed to light them. She'd do it even if she had to use twigs and her bare hands.

She would burn down Saint Augusta's.

She *would* kill them.

26

Osia seemed to know where she was going. Meloku did not trust her choice of destination.

The other woman had only said that she had a friend among *Ways and Means'* surface agents. A communications post operator, Xati. E would be able to spread word about what was happening. Meloku was surprised to hear that Osia still had friends among the crew. When she pressed, though, Osia admitted that she had not spoken to this friend since she had left *Ways and Means*.

Had Meloku been walking, she would have stopped. Only the fact that her horse wanted to keep going carried her forward.

"This is a fucking terrible plan," Meloku told her.

Osia kept riding. That was mostly how she answered Meloku – with silence. No doubt she did not feel she *had* to explain herself. Osia had never been dismissed from *Ways and Means'* service, only gone on voluntary leave. Technically, Osia outranked Meloku.

But neither of them served *Ways and Means* any more. Meloku refused to let this go. "There has to be somewhere else to go."

Osia still did not answer.

Meloku pulled her stolen palfrey's reins, halted. Osia did not look back, but she could not have failed to notice. She held Fiametta of Treviso tightly in front of her. Fiametta's head drooped under Osia's chin.

With Fiametta, Meloku supposed, Osia must have figured that she did not need Meloku. *Ways and Means* had some stake in this woman. *Ways and Means* had cut off its jamming field, after all, rather than move it over Fiametta.

Meloku waited as long as she dared, well after Osia had gone out of sight. She hastened to catch up. No matter what she had to put up with, she was not going to go on alone.

She was not sure what Osia would have done if she had gone. Osia needed her to keep their prisoner under control. Meloku controlled their tranquilizers and suggestives. Every night when they stopped to build their campfire and shelter, Meloku introduced more into Fiametta's bloodstream.

While Osia questioned Fiametta, Meloku ran her wrist launchers through their diagnostic cycles, over and over. Bracing for trouble. Of course, when trouble found them, it would be more than a handful of darts could fend off.

Maybe.

One of the many things she didn't understand was why *Ways and Means* was holding back. It had no shortage of weapons. If it wanted them dead – and it was clear now that it did – it could have done so through many means. Yet it had persistently, relentlessly even, used Osia's constructs or this plane's natives. The disruption field had been the highest-tech attack so far, and even that had just been a means to allow the natives the kill.

Still no sign of Dahn. Meloku wanted to believe that he was still chasing his own contacts, but he should have reached them long ago. If *Ways and Means* could deploy that jamming field anywhere, then it could have taken out Dahn without her ever noticing.

Osia did not need to stay warm, but Meloku and Fiametta did. The horses, too. They built a fire. Osia snapped off branches and broke them into manageable chunks, turned logs into seats. Then the interrogation. Osia asked the questions. Meloku just watched.

Every night, after they sat Fiametta in front of the fire, Osia complained, "You need to be using more drugs. She has too much control left. She's fighting."

"I've done that before," Meloku said. "It doesn't accomplish anything. It's not worth it." So far, she had only used enough of her drugs to keep Fiametta under control, and then just barely. A few more days of exposure like this, though, and her mind would start to warp itself around the drug – just as Joanna's had. Meloku did not intend to let that happen again, no matter what Osia told her.

Osia said, "She's not telling us anything useful."

"Perhaps she doesn't *know* anything useful."

Osia had not wanted to take more than one prisoner. They had taken Fiametta because she'd seemed most likely to be at the heart of the attempt to kill them. Pulse scans showed listening devices all around, but only one person, Fiametta, with an implant. The company commander and his officers had been commonplace. There was more than one *condottieri* captain in Italy. Fiametta of Treviso was unique. A woman general, a cult founder. A prophetess. Her influence extended well beyond the company.

Osia asked Fiametta about her background, her history. The orphanage she came from. The pestilence that had taken her family. Meloku remembered that plague well enough. She had spent most of the duration in Avignon, among its communal pit graves, boarded houses, and street corner bonfires.

At the time, she'd had bigger concerns. She'd been cold. The AI she'd once had in her head, who'd been with her for years, had described her as unempathetic, borderline sociopathic. That hadn't been a criticism.

Most of the time, she'd been able to accept that part of herself. Not always. Not after thirty years of living on this plane, seeing everything that had happened because of what *Ways and Means* had done, or not done.

Ways and Means had eventually relented, and stopped that plague, but it had been too late. It had not acted until the pest had already killed millions. It had sat at a distance and watched. It had not yet been persuaded. Fiametta's truncated childhood was one of those consequences.

Meloku had not been in favor of *Ways and Means'* intervention. She and the Unity had had too much else to worry about. So did *Ways and Means*, for that matter.

Fiametta stared into the fire. She spent most of her days on horseback asleep, in a tranquilized doze. Her nights were always at the fire. She would not move without a direct order to do so.

Osia asked Fiametta, "When did you start hearing this 'inner voice'?"

"I don't remember. I could have been hearing it for a long time."

Fiametta fought them. She took any ambiguity in the question as an excuse to not answer. "What is the earliest you *do* remember?"

"Saint Augusta's. The day we were taken away."

Again, Osia asked her about Saint Augusta's. About the place, the people, her life. Osia was relentless. Every time Fiametta answered, Osia asked again, more insistently. Fiametta shifted, visibly straining. Meloku's drugs meant Osia's questions had a physical effect on her. Every time Osia pushed, Fiametta would feel it squeezing her heart. She could not refuse to answer, could not lie. Her voice strained, broke.

Meloku said, "She's telling you everything you're asking. You're pushing too hard."

"There's more here. I have to find it."

"You're not finding anything. You're just being cruel."

Osia said, "We could stand to be crueler. She's a warlord. Have you listened to her stories? Studied her background?"

"If she's involved in *Ways and Means'* plans, I doubt she's chosen much."

Osia did not disagree, but said, "She's no innocent."

Meloku did not know why she was defending Fiametta of Treviso. She understood Osia's contempt. She *felt* it. Fiametta of Treviso was probably among the worst, the lowest, this world had to offer. Just like Hawkwood and Cardinal Robert.

But they were the pawns, not the players.

Fiametta's was the kind of misery that invited her to visit it upon other people. She was not being *cruel*; she was being *realistic*. She was not ravaging homes or destroying lives. She was conducting business – as business had been conducted unto her. She was the kind of monster this world's polities were built upon.

Meloku could not stop thinking about Queen Joanna. Whether she had killed her husband or not, she was a sovereign among nations built on toil, murder, slavery, and injustice. She could not have helped but to make choices that, in Osia's eyes, would have justified any punishment. Osia would not have hesitated to destroy her mind either.

Meloku had not kept count of how many people she had killed, or caused to be killed, across the planes. She was only in her fifties. Osia had centuries on her. She had spent the bulk of that in the amalgamates' service. She would have killed even more.

Meloku would have hoped that these thirty years would have changed Osia as much as it had her. She had not known Osia well but remembered Osia had sounded like she would expect any of *Ways and Means'* crew to sound: hard, cold, aloof. Thirty years ago, Osia's request that *Ways and Means* not tamper with this world had shocked Meloku almost as much as *Ways and Means* agreeing to do so. If anything in Osia had continued to shift during those years, though, she kept it well hidden. Decades of exile must not have meant as much to people in demiorganic bodies.

From the moment the jamming field had released them, Osia had not stopped to ask Meloku her opinion. Had not even thanked her for the rescue.

When she questioned Fiametta, Osia sat so near the flames that an ordinary human would have been burned. Her jet skin reflected yellow and red. Meloku sat or stood to the side, in the shadow.

The interrogation was not torture. Not quite. But it was

more than Meloku or Osia would have cared to be subjected to themselves. To Osia's credit, she had not ordered Meloku to use more damaging drugs. She must have known Meloku would have refused.

Fiametta's military campaigns did not interest Osia. She did not care about the *what* or *why* of *Ways and Means'* meddling with this woman, just the *how*. Meloku pieced together her goals. She was trying to figure out when Fiametta had first gotten the implant inside her, and who might have given it to her, and why.

What Fiametta called her inner voice was obviously that implant. Pulse scans picked up a micrometer-wide sliver of metal. No sign that it was on, though. Osia said she had disabled it. She would not say how. Even for her, she was cagey about that. She probably had some kind of weapon, classified above anyone of Meloku's rank, that could disable it noninvasively.

Osia may not have had darts and tranquilizers, but her body had capabilities Meloku was not cleared to know about. When Meloku pulse scanned Fiametta, the implant appeared inactive. They would need to get to a medical suite and a more advanced scanner to find out more. The nearest was aboard *Ways and Means*.

Ways and Means had a vested interest in all this. The first time Meloku had become aware of the Company of the Star, it had been because *Ways and Means* had altered her data about it. It had edited down the size of Fiametta's treasure train, made Fiametta's company look poorer than it really was. No doubt that had not been the first alteration, just the first she'd noticed. *Ways and Means* had not wanted its agents to notice the company's size and success. It wanted them looking anywhere else.

The implant had to have come from somewhere. If it hadn't been surgically implanted, it would have come from a seed like the one Meloku had given to Queen Joanna. Fiametta claimed that the first time she had ever heard her inner voice had been the day she'd been taken hostage by Antonov's Company. But it must have been there before.

If she had received it, and her fellow orphans had not, someone must have singled her out. Thought her special. No matter how hard Osia pressed, Fiametta couldn't remember any incidents where anyone had done so.

"No one ever thought that I was special," she said.

Osia said, "Someone who paid close attention to you."

"Mother Emilia threatened to throw me into the woods. I was the only girl she threatened to do that to."

Fiametta seemed to be enjoying stymieing Osia. Every time she did so, the pressure in her chest would have gotten tighter.

Meloku fit a few things together. Fiametta's inner voice had told her the story of Saint Renatus. She'd figured that was the case, but it was nice to have it confirmed. Her inner voice seemed to have a well of knowledge about this plane, but it lacked creativity. Saint Renatus's story so closely paralleled that of Mithras, a god popular among Roman army camps a millennium and a half ago.

Fiametta claimed to have not ever heard of Mithras. But her inner voice, or whoever was behind it, clearly had. It had taken elements of a thousand year-old religion and glued them on to folk Christianity. Her inner voice could synthesize elements of this world's cultures, but it lacked the imagination for wholly new ideas. In that, it reminded Meloku of an AI. Like her old Companion.

Fiametta's implant was not looking out for her physical wellbeing. She seemed scrawny in the way that every inhabitant of this plane, even the tall ones, seemed to Meloku. She was malnourished, sallow. She had badly healed scars. Her muscles were shaped by wear and stress rather than proper use and exercise. No doubt those medical scans would reveal intestinal parasites. In the poor sanitation of military camps, fecal-borne diseases were a fact of life. Osia's scans had already confirmed she had only recently recovered from a slipped disc.

One thing was clear enough: Fiametta's implant did not exert as complete a control over Fiametta as Meloku's drugs had over Queen Joanna. Whatever else the implant had done to her, Fiametta had been left with a great deal of independence. She controlled herself. The implant hadn't controlled her. At least, no more so than having an impossible-to-shut-off voice in the back of her mind would otherwise make her.

Which, Meloku thought, thinking back on her decades with her Companion, might still have been quite a lot. Perhaps that was all the control her "inner voice" had ever needed. No point in going through the extra work of rewiring Fiametta's brain if she could be manipulated to the same result.

When Fia had rewired Joanna, she had used a blunt knife. Her tools were primitive. A more advanced power could afford subtlety.

Fiametta's mental condition complicated things. Osia's scans had also revealed a host of issues that, back in the Unity, would have been diagnosed as susceptibility to schizophrenia, depression, anxiety. Impossible to tell from a scan how those conditions might have manifested with the implant. Even more impossible to tell how the implant had influenced them, too.

Osia asked, "Did you ever disobey your inner voice?"

"Not until recently."

"*How* recently?"

"After it tried to kill me."

Osia, for the first time that night, glanced to Meloku. Meloku shrugged.

To Meloku's endless frustration, Osia did not dwell on that. She returned to Saint Augusta's. Meloku lodged a deep growl under her throat, tried to keep it there.

The contents of Fiametta's mind weren't bound in a knot but a tangle, and Meloku had no idea how to loosen it. Neither did Osia, though that didn't stop her from trying.

Osia focused her questions on the days and weeks and months before Fiametta had been taken from her nunnery.

Before the moment she remembered first hearing from her inner voice. Searching for the start of it. An instigator. A strange visitor. Someone who'd taken an unusual interest in her. A sharp pain, headaches that might have been the implant growing. Seizures or blackouts. But Fiametta remembered nothing of any of those.

"There must have been a person," Osia pressed, for the sixth night. "A traveler. A newcomer. Someone who saw something in you that they didn't in the others."

For the hundredth time, Fiametta started to tell them about Pandolfo, the old soldier. Osia had already painstakingly gone over Fiametta's memories of him, and dismissed him. Whatever she was looking for wasn't him. At last, Meloku lost her patience. "What are you trying to accomplish? Do you even know what you're looking for?"

Osia allowed strain to creep into her voice. "There must have been a person who gave this to her. An agent. Someone who would stand out."

Again, Osia was only after *who*. Not *why*. Meloku asked, "What does it matter?"

"I can find out who did this to her. If I recognize them by description, I'll know for sure that *Ways and Means* is responsible for it."

Shock settled into Meloku's bones, cold and numbing. She had trouble finding her voice. "You still don't believe *Ways and Means* did this."

She had figured by now that Osia's thirty-year exile had left her unbalanced. But not by this far. The *why* hadn't been enough because only the *who* could prove *Ways and Means* hadn't done this. "You're still searching for ways to absolve it."

Osia said, "Until we have absolute proof that it did this, none of my questions have been answered and no possibilities are closed."

"You said only *Ways and Means* could have tried to kill you. *You* said you found fragments of its code in that virus."

Osia did not disagree. She did not bother to say anything

315

at all. She stared at Fiametta as intently as Fiametta stared at their fire.

Meloku stood. "I followed you because I thought you might have known what you were doing." She turned to stalk back to her tent, but, after two steps, changed her mind. She turned, pointed to Fiametta. "Get everything you need to get out of her tonight. I'm not drugging her again."

Osia at last looked to Meloku. The firelight turned her eyes copper. "I'm the ranking officer."

Meloku spread her arms. "Charge me with insubordination." Meloku held up her forearm, pointed to the scabbed skin under which all her drugs and darts were stored. "Until you do, I have these. You don't. You can't force me to use them."

Osia had sense enough not to press that point. "You heard what she told us. If she's not under control, she'll attack us."

"Let her. In fact, leave her. It would be better for her."

"I can't. She's important to all of this. If we lose control of her and she attacks us, I'll have to harm her."

"If you harm her…" Meloku leveled a finger at Osia's chest. It hung there an awkward moment. Neither of them needed to hear the threat she couldn't carry out. She said, "If you harm her, and she doesn't absolutely deserve it, then you'll have to move on by yourself. The next time they disable you, you'll have to fight back alone."

Osia must not have been accustomed to anyone countermanding her so bluntly. Thirty years on a boat with no one but her toys had left her unpracticed. She sat silent, impossible to read. But Meloku figured she could guess Osia's thoughts. She was contemplating every means she had left to get leverage on Meloku.

Meloku knew all about getting leverage over a person. She hadn't left Osia with any means to do it. She hoped.

Meloku stalked back to her tent and sealed the flap. After a long time staring at the top of her tent, she heard Osia speak to Fiametta. More questions.

The same questions.

27

The world did not return to Fia all at once. It spun in fragments, falling into place. It was a whirlwind of snow blowing into her eyes.

She had been in two places at once. A dream and the waking world. The two had been shredded, mixed together, sprinkled under her eyes. Trying to reconstruct them was like reading the scraps of two letters that had been torn to pieces and shuffled together. The meanings had jumbled. She could not help but see shadows of one in the other.

Fia unwove the scraps. She went line by line, matching each word against the other. The images she'd found in the interleave did not go away.

The heat of the sun became the heat of the fire. The trail along the fields that led to Bandino's shed turned to mud and soft snow and brown grass.

The shadow-woman lived in the abbess's cell. From the pulpit of the convent's too-tiny church, she delivered her sermons. Hellfire glimmered in her eyes. She threatened to throw Fia into the forest.

When Fia wasn't sure what she saw was real or not, she had only her memory as an aid. But memory was unreliable. It told her things that couldn't be true.

Memory insisted that two women, or a woman and a monster, had assaulted her camp, abducted her, and stole two palfreys – all without any of her soldiers posing more of a challenge than an insistent breeze. Memory saw Laskaris fold over, broken. Antonov crumpled to a crossbow bolt that wasn't there and could not have been fired.

Memory said that she had gone along with her captors, riding unresisting for days. The shadow-woman, Osia, held her arm around her.

She had been captured. Abducted – again. The hostages' coffle had become the march to this wasteland of snow and awful cold, where her nostrils froze every time she breathed in.

In the end, it had not been her who had set fire to Saint Augusta's. It was the mercenaries once again. Saint Augusta's burned. She stared at it unblinking, as she did the campfire. The shadow-woman Osia had been there, watching the convent burn.

Osia sat by the campfire, watching her now with those same copper-sheen eyes.

She could not make sense of this silence. The mechanical clocks in the back of her head were silent. It was stifling. A kind of madness.

Fia looked at her half-frozen hands. She flexed them against the fire. It took her a long while to figure out that she was moving them on her own. It was not just something that was happening to her.

This was new. She considered the implications.

She kicked her log seat away, lunged at Osia.

Darkness followed. Minutes passed, probably.

Fia sat in front of their fire, holding her hands up for warmth. Osia stared at her. The firelight turned her eyes every color between burnished copper and gold.

Fia remembered knocking her seat into the snow and the mud. But memory was unreliable. Her seat was dry. It was just cold. Damned cold. Cold as everything else.

She could not explain why her wrists hurt. Both of them, in exactly the same way, whenever she rotated them. They were not marked or bruised.

Casually, she reached for her dagger. Or where her dagger had been, days ago.

Osia watched her move. Fia bunched her fingers, charting

her recourses to violence. There were no means of attack that she could see. All she had was a water pouch. Her lips were so dry it hurt to set its lips to hers.

She asked, "Did you hear what you wanted to get from me?"

"No," Osia said.

This fire, the campfire, was real. The fire eating Saint Augusta's was not. But she could touch Saint Augusta's fire. Burn herself, if she wanted.

The other woman, the human, Meloku, said, "We're done with our questions. That doesn't mean you can't tell us more."

Fia laughed. If she could have, she would have stood, walked away, but her head swam in other worlds. She would have lost her balance in this one.

She could not look away from the fire. Something about the heat on her eyes had become comforting. Saint Augusta's was still burning.

The years between now and then had been bridged. She saw the fire through a hot blur. She'd spent so long at Saint Augusta's now that the years afterward had become fractured. She clamped down on that thought, hard as she could.

No. She was not that girl. Her shoulders ached from strain and from age. Her skin was latticed with scars, dry and cracked as the leather of her saddle. There was no girl left in her. In bringing her back to that nightmare, the shadow-woman had robbed her of her rebirths.

"Did you kill my inner voice?" she asked.

Osia did not answer. She kept her silence about too many things. In this case, it seemed as good as an admission that she had killed it.

Osia seemed to want to leave it at that, but Meloku said, "Interesting that it let us do that. Whoever attacked Osia and me let us stay on our feet rather than risk you losing it."

Fia had managed some eavesdropping during her long spell. Their words were labyrinthine, but she did not get lost easily. She gathered the shadow-woman had been the quarry her inner voice had sent her after. Osia and Meloku had both been struck down by some hammer of God. They seemed to think that, by being near her, they had saved themselves. That hammer could have struck them again, but not without hitting Fia and her inner voice too.

Fia's inner voice had been silent, dead and gone, since they'd come for her. Since that very hour. It had gone silent, suddenly, in the middle of one of its now-customary monologues. It had been right before these two came to steal her.

That timing didn't match. Something was off. However much more these two might know than her, their thinking was muddled. It was plain that they were trying to match wits against something greater than them, and they weren't up for it.

Fia pushed that to the back of her mind. That would be a die to roll later. "If you had killed it, I was going to thank you," she said, after a sip from her water pouch.

Meloku tilted her head, plainly surprised. "It helped you get where you were."

Fia said, "It tried to kill me. Or get me killed. Whatever difference that makes."

From what Meloku had said, John Hawkwood, too, had been under the control of whoever had made her inner voice. It didn't take a stretch of imagination to figure out, then, what her inner voice had once planned. After it had killed her, Hawkwood would have been there to replace her. The remnants of her allies would have joined him.

Meloku said, "You don't need to talk. We're not making you."

It would have been easy to stand, to walk over and throttle the life out of her.

Those thoughts came to her unbidden. They were difficult to control. As difficult as it was to convince herself she was here and not at Saint Augusta's.

"Horseshit," Fia said. "It still feels like you're drawing the words out of me." Whatever poison they'd given her still coursed through her blood.

Meloku said, "That will go away," though she sounded less than certain.

"Does it bother you that it's not?" Fia asked. She had eavesdropped even when she had not consciously tried to. She knew just how to play them, and where to jab. Fia blinked at Meloku, affecting innocence.

"No," Meloku said.

Fia's career had brought her into contact with all kinds of confidence artists and flatterers. This woman sounded like a practiced liar. But she had flubbed that one.

Osia said, "You ought to be terrified of us."

Fia snapped, "I'm not afraid of idiots."

Osia's voice took on an edge it had been missing. "You can't imagine who we are."

Fia said, "You're from another plane of creation."

Fia enjoyed the silence that followed. A brief but telling moment of power. Fia said, "My inner voice told me as much."

"Now?" Meloku asked. She looked to Osia.

"No. It's gone." She felt its absence in her head as keenly as if it had been physically removed. All that was left was a hole. "It went days ago. Right before you took me. It must have known that you were about to abduct me."

If she enjoyed anything about this, it was these silences. She had caught them off guard. They were not so much more powerful than her as they had imagined.

It was a feeling they all shared.

Perhaps if the shadow woman had bothered to ask about this, rather than endlessly revisit Saint Augusta's, she might have learned.

A sharp rock lay near the firepit. It was sized well enough for her palm. It would have been satisfying to crack that over one of their heads. But only satisfying, nothing more.

She was after bigger game than *satisfying*.

Fia said, "So tell me what you think you're going to do."

• • •

It took time to coax a glimmer of truth out of them. They kept talking above her, like she was a child. The fire had burned through most of its fuel before she pieced together an impression of their plan.

These two were fugitives, but they were not alone. They had help, or at least imagined they did. A friend, somewhere ahead. A friend who could get them in touch with other friends.

It was a thin plan. A desperate one. Fia decided they were right to try it, though. It was the only place they could start. They couldn't do anything without friends. That was the first lesson Fia had learned when she joined the company. She was great, she was mighty, yes. But without Antonov, the company's corporals, and her network of *condottieri* throughout Italy, she could not have built that into anything useful.

This was the best they could do.

Fia slept under the thin shelter of a canvas tent that, to her intense displeasure, she shared with Meloku. The tent, she was sure, had not been packed in her palfreys' saddlebags. Osia and Meloku must have taken their leisurely time stealing it, too. Another indictment of the company's lax readiness. Or a measure of these women's power.

In the morning, the tent was empty. When Fia emerged, Osia sat where she'd left her. Meloku was chewing desultorily on her salt pork. She stopped when she saw Fia.

Fia took down her tent quickly, efficiently, and bundled it to her horse's side. Someone had hobbled her palfrey. Unnecessary. Idiocy. If these two had any experience with horses, they would have known that the horses wouldn't stray. They preferred to stick together. This wasteland left them no other temptations.

She told Osia, "This is my horse. You're going to have to walk now."

Osia looked to her. As usual, she said nothing.

Fia asked Meloku, "How much farther do we have to go?"

Meloku blinked. "You don't want to go back to your company?"

"How far have we traveled?" Fia asked. She hadn't been lucid during most of the trip, but she had a vague recollection of vast tracts of snow and brown grass.

"No farther than you could travel on your own if you had a mind to do it."

Fia *did* want to see Caterina, make sure she was healing. And Antonov. Laskaris, too, if he lived – she had traveled too long with him to be able to leave him without feeling. But they were it. The rest she could leave. They didn't mean as much now that she knew what she did.

The Company of the Star wasn't hers any more. It hadn't been since the battle with Hawkwood. Even if she could wrestle it back, replenish its ranks, sign new contracts, bring new *condottieri* – even if she could do all that, she wouldn't be able to do with the company what she wanted. She could not seize a city. She could not reshape Italy as she had imagined, with the lords and doges and popes ripped from their thrones.

She could be hired. She could loot and ravage. She could burn, but not build.

Fia said, "I thought you two had decided you needed me, or whatever had knocked you down would do it again."

Meloku said, "Your company isn't chasing you. There's no one around to take advantage of us falling."

Osia said, "If it needs a way to kill us, it will find one regardless."

Fia did not ask how they had figured out that her company had given her up. She did not want to know. The knowledge still stuck hard in her stomach, a razor-edged icicle.

Meloku said, "Besides, she and I are done with you. We've gotten what we need."

Her palfrey sniffed at Fia's shoulder. It nosed into her coat, hunting for food. Fia pushed it away. Her shoulders shot through with pain as she hitched up and onto its saddle. Once she'd settled, her bowed legs felt natural, like she'd been born with them.

She urged her horse closer to the campfire's embers. Osia

never took her eyes off her. Waiting for an attack, Fia realized.

"Go on," Meloku said. "Go wherever. You're free."

Fia asked, "How far do you still have to go?"

The three people Fia wanted to return to could wait. All her life she'd lived with the simple fact of her inner voice. Until recently, she'd heard that voice as akin to divine inspiration. Now she had more questions than, just days ago, she'd known how to ask. Those answers weren't behind her. They were ahead.

She had been drawn into this, these people, long ago. She was owed an explanation. And an explanation would only be a down payment on her debt.

Her real enemy had never been John Hawkwood, or the Pope, or Siena's priors. The orchestrators of all this had been hidden, until now, out of sight and beyond the sky.

Meloku said, "It wouldn't be a good idea for you to follow us."

Fia said, "I don't know why this isn't clear to you yet. I'm not following you. You're leading me."

Again, that silence. Osia and Meloku looked to each other. Their silences said more than their words. If they were going to stop her, she knew, it would be now.

The moment passed, and Fia remained upright.

She nodded at Meloku's breakfast pans, and said, "Get your shit packed. We're wasting light." She drew up her reins.

28

Osia's anger manifested as a feeling of heat in her cheeks. It was psychosomatic, of course. She had no blood vessels there to inflame.

Meloku transmitted, "I could tranquilize her."

"We couldn't leave a fire going long enough until she came out of it. She'd freeze to death." Though Osia was near to convincing herself that shouldn't be their problem. Fiametta of Treviso had done far worse to people. "Besides, it would be best to keep her until we find a better means of examining what's in her head."

"Sure about that?"

The last time they'd taken a native man and examined his head, it had nearly killed them. That monk, Niccoluccio, had been carrying a virus. If *Ways and Means* had put Fia's implant there, it could have placed a trap too.

If it had been concerned about anyone discovering its subterfuge, it would have.

But their lives were already in constant jeopardy. Osia said, "It will probably be more productive to keep her with us."

Once she'd gotten too far away, Fiametta reined in her horse. She looked back, impatient.

Osia said, "But keep the tranquilizer ready."

Osia did not mind walking. She had only stolen the second palfrey so that she could support Fiametta. Her long, loping stride hardly cracked the surface of the long-frozen snow. What she minded was being given an order.

Meloku rode behind Fiametta, her face a somber mask. She did not bother to hide it. Her guilt was plain to see. She had been among these people for too long.

Fiametta traveled well past dusk, hopping off her palfrey to lead it. She kept her distance from Meloku and Osia. At night, they set up camp without speaking to each other about anything other than necessities.

Osia and Meloku could have carried on without her. Osia did not need to sleep. Meloku's demiorganics managed her brain chemistry so efficiently that she could manage with two hours a night.

Meloku spent her long hours awake warming herself by the fire. Quiet. Osia stayed still, legs folded, eyes open. She did not like many of the things she had to think about.

Meloku had thought her a fool for focusing so much on trying to find the person who had given Fiametta's "inner voice" to her. She had stopped listening. She hadn't thought hard enough about what Osia *had* found.

Pandolfo, the traveling Venetian merchant Fiametta had mentioned, was their only real suspect. His work, maybe his cover story, had given him an excuse to range across a wide area. He had demonstrated an interest in Fiametta. He had spoken to her, extensively, about his history as a soldier. The first time Fiametta reported hearing that voice, she had confused it for his. He could have slipped her the seed of her implant with a touch to her shoulder, her arm.

Pandolfo was no agent that Osia recognized. His body type didn't match. She had a catalog of all of the shapes and sizes of the crew's demiorganic bodies, from the many-legged spiders to her own bipedal body. Cut off from the Unity, *Ways and Means* did not have the facilities to manufacture new bodies.

Meloku thought Osia was trying to exonerate *Ways and Means*. Maybe she had been. Whatever the truth of that, Osia *had* been convinced that *Ways and Means* was responsible for this. Until then.

Fiametta's memories of Pandolfo were thin evidence, she knew. The real culprit could have passed Fiametta entirely unnoticed. They could have, with the aid of that implant, wiped or altered Fiametta's memories. Or *Ways and Means* could have gotten control of Pandolfo in the same way that she and Meloku had controlled Fiametta.

She would not change Meloku's mind. She had not even changed her own – not really. What Meloku thought did not bother her. This plane was full of fools, and Osia and Meloku were only slightly wiser. They were all being played some way or another.

All of her stakes were on the table. She only had a few bets left to place. She was close to making her last wager.

For days, there had been no trees on the horizon. Osia had thought the land could not get any more blighted. Now the last of the grass was dead, even where it wasn't covered by ice or snow. The mud was gone, replaced by rock-hard dirt. The horses found poor footing. The few creeks were frozen and easy enough to cross, but that made it much harder to water the horses.

Osia could have reached the station weeks ago. She had survived thirty years alone with her constructs. This month of traveling was more alienating by far. After what had happened in that forest, and what had probably happened to Meloku's partner Dahn, it wasn't safe to travel alone, but that did little to stifle her aggravation.

At last, though, the horizon dimpled and rose. A sign they were getting close. Xati's station was at relatively high altitude, as far away from civilization as it could reasonably be placed. By day's end, the horizon had grown teeth.

While Meloku and Fiametta slept, Osia watched the stars. Electromagnetic activity boiled in the skies. Radio rippled off the horizon and back. Filtered through the right spectrum, the horizon seemed lit by a deep red aurora. The brightest flame shone at the base of the taller hills. Their destination.

Xati's station was one of dozens upon dozens like it on this world. *Ways and Means'* satellites provided a communication network, but its exile had been a rude awakening. It realized that there were greater powers in the multiverse than it. Its satellites could be killed. It believed in redundancy.

It had seeded this world with backup communications stations, spaced thousands of kilometers apart. They had transmitters powerful enough to bounce signals off the atmosphere far enough to reach each other. If something happened to the satellites, they could provide a backup network. Their transmitters were also powerful enough to reach *Ways and Means*, even at the most distant point of its orbit.

By next midday, they were close enough to Xati's home for Osia's passive sensors to detect the buzz of its electronics. Osia pulse scanned. Meloku sensed it. She stiffened, gave Osia a sharp look.

"There are sensors all over these hills," Osia said. "There's no way we haven't already been spotted."

Meloku said, "You could have let me know beforehand."

She seemed to believe that this was a partnership.

The pulse scan was not encouraging. Xati's hideaway was like Meloku's and so many other agents': a door built into the side of a rock face, camouflaged. A sealed one-room environment inside. The communications equipment and towers were all above, hidden in rock or disguised as pines.

Osia's scan could not penetrate the rock. But there was nobody outside, and no sign that anybody had been recently. There was also no shuttle. Xati was supposed to have a shuttle on hand to loan to agents who needed one.

Meloku pulse scanned, too. "Fuck," she breathed.

Fiametta had stopped, turned. Though she couldn't have understood what they'd said, she seemed to realize that something had changed. When they reached the nearest of the hills, she hopped off her palfrey and led it.

"Stretching my legs," she said.

Getting limber, Osia realized. She expected there to be action, a fight. Meloku hopped off hers, too.

Meloku's breath grew tighter as the land grew rockier, rose

around them. More pulse scans reflected off Osia's skin. All pointless anxiety. Meloku wouldn't find anything they didn't already know about.

The entrance to Xati's hideaway sat halfway up an ice-slicked rocky ledge. It spent half of the day in the shadow of the mountain above it. A strip of a ledge ran outside it, just barely wide enough to walk – Xati's only means of egress.

Fiametta and Meloku left their horses at the bottom of the ridge. Osia stopped holding back. She leapt up the escarpment meters at a time.

She didn't bother with the hideaway's camouflaged entrance. She strode right past. She went around the ridge and up, to a patch of dead weeds and grass and a wide expanse of rocks. The most natural spot for a shuttle to park.

None of the snow had been disturbed. There was no shadow where the shuttle would have sat, not even a dimple. Osia knelt and brushed away a handwidth of snow. Some of the rock and sand underneath had been blackened. Thruster burn. She hadn't missed her guess as to where the shuttle would have been parked. But this snowfall must have been weeks old, at least. It had been a long time since anything had been here.

Fiametta caught up first. She stood at the edge of the escarpment, watching. Her hand opened and closed over the empty air at her waist, where she might have had a weapon. Osia didn't think she was aware she was doing it.

Meloku plodded on to the rocky field, saw all the same things Osia had.

She asked, "*Ways and Means* got Xati, didn't it?"

As with so much else Meloku had said, Osia felt no need to answer.

She turned back, walked past Fiametta. Meloku struggled to catch up.

The hideaway's door was all but invisible, but a pulse scan found the minute cracks outlining it. No infrared or visible light spilled out. The door would not respond to her transmitted command to open. She did not waste time trying to force an override.

She braced her foot against the earth, drew back her fist, and smashed it into the rock. The false door splintered and fell inward, crashing in a cacophony of metallic clangs and pealing. Fiametta jumped. Even Meloku, coming around the ridge, winced.

Osia shook her hand out to reseat her finger bones. From the corner of her eye, she caught Fiametta staring wide-eyed. If she was still contemplating attacking her or Meloku, that ought to have given her a second thought.

Meloku pushed past Osia while Osia was still shaking her fingers back into place. Osia followed her into the cloud of settling dust. There was no hurry. She knew what they would find.

Xati's quarters were a single-room hideaway, sparse and utilitarian. Bare lights. Xati had needed no bed, no heating. A small machine shop, knobby metal cabinets full of spare parts and neatly sorted tools. There was a cooling and ventilation system, to keep the systems here from overheating, but it had been years since it had been turned on. The air was thick with dust. Meloku held an arm over her mouth and nose, coughing viciously. Fiametta didn't venture past the door.

Only one thing said that Xati had ever been here: a small model of a fungal farm, a relic of a home plane e had told Osia about only once before. Xati seemed to have lived little differently than e had aboard *Ways and Means*: tucked inside er quarters, lost inside er mind.

The cabinets, the heater, and the sides of the farm were all covered in transparent sheeting. Dust shields. When Xati had left, e had expected to be back, but not for some time.

Osia ran a hand along a piece of sheeting farthest from the door. Not much dust there. She guessed that Xati must have left only weeks ago. That would have been about the same time that she had left her boat on the Iberian coast. When it would have become clear to *Ways and Means* that

Osia was headed here.

Meloku said, "*Ways and Means* took your friend away." She turned. The fury and despair rising to her cheeks gave them an infrared halo. "We lost before we ever got here."

"Of course we did." Osia pulse scanned the cabinets, tallying a list of their contents. She had expected to find this. Meloku hadn't thought far enough ahead. It still hurt to discover, though. More evidence that *Ways and Means* was behind this. It had been well within *Ways and Means'* power to order Xati somewhere else. It wouldn't even have been suspicious.

She queried the post's NAI. It wouldn't answer. Locked down, just like the door. Nothing had been damaged. The NAI would not respond to orders, but it would to simple diagnostics. Everything was in perfect condition, standing by.

All of the radio towers outside were, so far as she could tell, intact.

She said, "I'll need your help isolating one of the towers outside from the base NAI. A generator, too."

Meloku's eyes had reddened, from the dust and something else. She took a ragged breath. "What are you going to do?"

Osia stepped out. Fiametta stood well clear of her.

Osia started scanning the towers hidden among the trees. The faster she got this done, the better. The longer she took, the greater the chance that something would go wrong. And the more time Meloku would have to argue with her about it.

From inside, Meloku called again, "What are you going to do?"

Meloku went apoplectic when she figured it out. It did not take her long. There were only so many things Osia could do with a radio tower.

The tower could transmit quite a distance, reach a number of agents in this hemisphere. But it was also powerful enough to reach directly into deep space.

"You're going to contact *Ways and Means*," Meloku said, as if she couldn't quite believe what her demiorganics were telling her. She was repeating herself. The first time Meloku said the words, her voice had been clenched tight. And the time after, livid.

She actually laid her hand on Osia's shoulder. Osia had to dissuade her defensive combat programs from automatically responding.

Ways and Means had risen over their horizon not long after they'd gotten here. If it had been night, she could have looked up, focus-scanned its parcel of sky, and seen a flicker of infrared. But it was daytime, and there was nothing there. Nothing even she could see. Just her knowledge that there ought to be.

Ways and Means was coasting on an outward trajectory, back to its resting solar orbit. Millions of kilometers out of reach. Osia's personal transmitter did not have the power to reach it.

Meloku's eyes flicked over the tower and the boxy, head-sized microfusion generator they'd hauled beside it. Then she turned to Osia. Osia figured she was weighing her chances of damaging either one before Osia could stop her. Osia's combat programs had already charted those possibilities. They weren't in Meloku's favor.

The generator was silent as it spun through its warm-up routines. Osia ran diagnostic after diagnostic. If *Ways and Means* had set a trap for them, it would be here. A sudden failure of containment. An out of control reaction. There would be nothing she could do if she saw either of those coming.

Meloku said, "If you contact it, I'm gone. You'll have to do everything on your own. I'm not coming back to rescue you again."

Osia said, "As you would like."

Fiametta had disappeared while Osia had been busy, though her horse remained below. Heat traces in the ice led through the hideaway's broken door. The air inside was several degrees warmer. She'd gone in to shelter.

Meloku remained beside her. Osia said, "If you're going to go, then go."

"I've got nowhere else," Meloku said.

"Neither do I."

Osia did not take her eyes off the generator until it was fully warmed up. Then she turned her attention to the tower. It was disguised as a straight-trunked, slender pine. A shimmer of copper played across its branches.

Meloku said, "After all that you've gone through, all the evidence you've seen, you still don't want to believe *Ways and Means* tried to kill you."

"I don't 'want' to believe anything." Even to her, Osia's answer sounded hollow.

Meloku wouldn't let her get away with it. "You're not as high above the rest of us as you like to think."

Interesting words for someone with Meloku's personality profile, and with her history. It was increasingly plain that her profile was out of date, though. Meloku had changed in the thirty years they'd both been down here. Unlike Osia, she hadn't kept herself in stasis.

"You're doing this as an act of faith," Meloku accused.

"Yes," Osia said.

Faith in *Ways and Means*. Faith in the life she'd had in the centuries before all of this had happened. She had nothing left to turn to.

She and Meloku and Fiametta were alone. *Ways and Means* could foil any other plans they made as easily as it had reassigned Xati.

But that wasn't the end of her reasons. This wasn't so much an act of faith, Osia figured, as a confrontation. She needed to face this down. They'd put it off long enough. And this tower gave them the means.

"We've already tried contacting it," Meloku said. "It's going to ignore us."

Again, Meloku wasn't thinking this through. "It won't. I don't think it can." *Ways and Means* wasn't the only one that could pick up her signal.

Thousands of its crew remained aboard. All of their demiorganic bodies had independent transmitters and receivers, just like she did. They could surely receive a signal as strong she was about to send.

If *Ways and Means* was going to betray them again, it would have to do so with its crew listening.

Osia was going to force the issue. One outcome or another. If, as she and Meloku thought, *Ways and Means* wanted to keep what it had done to them a secret, it was going to have to deal with them.

Meloku paced between the pines. She looked at the generator. But she did not act. Nor did she leave.

When the tower was ready, Osia did not wait. This had taken long enough already.

Her signal was wordless, just a ping, a request for acknowledgment. She appended her identification tag. She did not need anything more.

The perigee of *Ways and Means'* pass had not taken it any closer than the moon. It had been heading away for weeks. It was three light-seconds away now. Six total for a transmission to get there, and a response to come back. Osia counted the seconds.

Meloku leaned against the trunk of the nearest tree, staring. Her mouth worked. Osia lip-read. She was rehearsing what she would say when nothing happened.

Ways and Means' answer came the instant it should have, and strong enough that atmospheric scattering would carry it for kilometers around.

"Osia." *Ways and Means* sounded pleased with her. "You ought to call home more often."

29

The fury came to Osia quickly. She had not felt anything like it since the day she'd killed Coral. Maybe even that had not been so bad.

She sent, "After everything that's happened, after all you've done, you're starting out by being *light?*"

She made sure to broadcast her signal with enough power to reach *Ways and Means'* crew, too. The seconds waiting for an answer were agony. Her demiorganics stifled her instinctive responses, trying to reestablish an emotional equilibrium. They did not have much success.

It said, "We hardly know what's happened."

A data package poured down the transmission, riding along with *Ways and Means'* words. Osia turned it over in her mind, regarding it skeptically. It was large enough that it could have been anything. But, after all this time on the run, to finish the kill with a simple virus did not fit *Ways and Means'* behavior.

Meloku received it too. She hardly had time to look to Osia, to start shaking her head, before Osia opened it.

It was a new encryption key, and updated security programs, anti-eavesdroppers. If anyone else had been tapping in, those programs wouldn't have done them any good. They had been tailored for Osia's demiorganics. They would only operate for her.

Ways and Means' next transmission was only decipherable with the aid of the key. Osia decrypted for Meloku.

Ways and Means said, "You're much farther afield than we thought you'd be."

Osia did not encrypt her reply. She wanted *Ways and Means'* crew to hear, to understand. "You knew we were coming here."

"The last time you spoke to us, you were on a boat in the middle of the ocean. Now you're half a world away, and hundreds of kilometers inland. Clearly, we have a lot to catch up on."

"You said you maintained satellite tracking of my position."

"Our tracking has been unreliable of late."

Osia waited. It did not elaborate. She said, "I tried to call you. You wouldn't answer."

"*We* tried to talk to you. You didn't understand."

At the edge of her vision, Meloku mouthed the word *trick*.

Osia did not want to believe her. When Meloku had called this an act of faith, Osia had brushed her off. Maybe she'd been wrong.

She ought not to be calling *Ways and Means* except to inform its crew what it had done to her. She could still do that. Anyone aboard *Ways and Means* could hear her. If they wanted to.

Ways and Means said, "Until ninety seconds ago, our tracking placed you at sea, hundreds of kilometers east of the Korean peninsula."

A prickling traveled down her arms. Another psychosomatic side effect, her demiorganics trying to cope with primate fright response. She felt hairs she didn't have, rising from follicles she'd never been given.

She could not manage anything more eloquent than, "What?"

"We would greatly appreciate it if you could use the encryption package we sent you."

She shook her head, not that it could see.

Ways and Means went on, "You said 'we.' Are you not alone?"

"Meloku of Antera is with me," Osia said. Meloku winced and palmed her forehead. Too late, Osia realized she did not want any attention drawn to her. "And a native. I think she's become involved."

Ways and Means said, "If you continue to transmit unencrypted, think carefully on what you say before you say it. Remember our last conversation?"

Osia's memory of it was as clear as if it had just happened. She felt the sea air on the back of her neck. She flash-forwarded through its condescension, her prickliness. It had said, "We know you cannot, and *should not*, believe what we tell you."

It had told her this after noting that her security programs were out of date.

Ways and Means repeated, "We *tried* to talk to you."

A new star flared in the sky. A speck. It was not visible to the naked eye, but it shone brightly in infrared, even at this distance. White-hot engine exhaust. A strong, clear source of it.

It was not big or bright enough to be *Ways and Means'* own engines. The source was something smaller. A shuttle. Or a missile. It was accelerating hard. Very hard. If it had carried any crew, even demiorganic crew, they would have been crushed by the g-forces.

Ways and Means said, "We don't need to hear anything more at present – unless you would like to use the programs we sent."

The prickling spread from Osia's arms to her legs. She was a damned idiot.

Ways and Means had been afraid of eavesdropping. Not just now, but back then. It had tried, in as veiled a way as possible, to get her to update her security and encryption programs. It wanted her to know that it believed something was listening in.

She had been so focused on other things that she had not listened.

The source of the problem had to be the communications satellites. She had spoken to it through its satellites. After Ira had attacked her, when she had called for help, her call had gone through satellites. The satellites had not forwarded her message to it.

Ways and Means had tracked her through its satellites. The same satellites that told it she had been around the Korean peninsula. It believed its satellites were compromised.

At least that was the narrative *Ways and Means* had constructed. It was trying to convince her to switch to an encrypted format that, for all she knew, its crew couldn't understand.

She couldn't believe what she'd been told. She shouldn't. Not with that new heat source in the sky. Not with everything she'd seen, everything she'd felt. It had either given her a glimpse of the truth, or was convincing her to stand still, to wait for the missile.

Here, a hundred kilometers from anything and anyone.

Here, where she was finally in a position to speak to it and its crew.

When she'd contacted *Ways and Means*, she'd thought that nothing would keep her from telling its crew what had happened. Now, in the course of just of few minutes, she was keeping her silence. It had constructed a narrative to make her consider it. When she'd been on *Ways and Means'* diplomatic service, threading lies through half-truths, she knew that the best way to a person's heart was through a good narrative.

That new light burned high above her, hotter. It would be over an hour yet before it got here. Whatever it was, it was coming as hard and as fast as it could.

Ways and Means said, "A high-speed shuttle will reach you before the end of the day."

"A shuttle," Osia said, aloud. "Of course."

Meloku looked to her.

None of what *Ways and Means* had told her explained what had happened to her constructs. Its signature was in the virus.

She had not told it that part.

When she didn't answer, *Ways and Means* said, "If you won't use encryption, we must end this conversation." After another moment of silence, it added, "Be ready."

Meloku stared at Osia. Osia stood unmoving, on fire. Her demiorganics spiked warnings about her emotional health, her decision-making capability.

An act of faith, Meloku had said.

Osia had not cared to think about it. She had thought herself above it, as she thought herself above everything else.

She had nowhere to turn besides *Ways and Means*. Nothing she cared to save herself to reach.

"Get away from here," Osia told Meloku.

Meloku started to shake her head. "There's no poi–"

"Take Fiametta with you."

When Meloku did nothing, Osia grabbed her shoulder, twisted her, and gave her a hard, calculated shove.

Meloku stumbled, almost fell, but Osia had measured the force she'd deployed. Meloku spun, faced Osia.

"Get away from here!" Osia said.

Meloku glared. But she stepped backward, started walking.

Whatever *Ways and Means* had in mind to do to them, Osia would accept. If it had launched a weapon with a high blast radius, Meloku and Fiametta wouldn't be able to get away fast enough. Otherwise they had a chance. Osia could do nothing else for them.

Meloku shoved her hands in her coat for warmth. She ducked inside the broken hatch to Xati's hideaway, where Fiametta was.

She didn't listen to Osia. She didn't come out. Neither did Fiametta.

Osia did not chase them out either.

For want of anything better to do with her hands and legs, Osia sat against the base of the radio tower. She set her head against it and listened to the thrum of the generator.

She closed her eyes.

Her passive sensors kept tabs on her surroundings, but she didn't pay attention. She no longer wanted to see.

Ways and Means had fallen below their horizon. Out of contact. Invisible. The missile, or the shuttle, would spend most of its flight likewise, up until that final skim through the atmosphere. Depending on how fast it traveled, she would not have long to observe it.

So she did not look.

Faith. She had no faith in *Ways and Means*. A very strange thing to think, considering how she was acting.

From what Fiametta had told them, Osia doubted she had ever really believed in the gospel of Saint Renatus. Not literally. That had not stopped her from acting as though she had. She'd had deeper beliefs – about fighting, about soldiering, about remaking herself. It had shaped the rest of her.

Osia did not want to think about her deeper beliefs. She had not, until the past few weeks, imagined that she'd had them.

But they had brought her to the truth: if *Ways and Means* wanted her to die, she would die. She had traveled with it, been too close to it, for too long. She did not want to be apart.

There was nothing to do but wait.

The wait was easier this time.

She nearly did not realize her time had expired until her passive sensors spiked an alarm into her. The rumbling was too loud to ignore. Firelight pried behind her eyelids. The ground shook with the tremulous thunder of rockets, of fire and gas jetting into the ground.

She looked. She had only an instant.

A slender, squidlike tube – with a jet-dark hull and flaming thruster ports – settled into the rock. Its fins widened and elongated toward the end of its body, the only concession it made to aerodynamicism. Then everything vanished under a billowing gray cloud of vaporized snow.

A high-speed shuttle, after all.

30

She and Fiametta bolted out of Xati's hideaway when they heard the thunder. Meloku scrambled up the escarpment, and nearly lost her footing when she saw what was waiting at the top.

She had not even known *Ways and Means* carried a high-speed shuttle.

Fiametta gripped the rock face so tightly that her knuckles were white. She stumbled backward, edging away. Meloku let her go. She could hardly believe this either.

She had seen shuttles like this before, on other planes and on other assignments. The amalgamate *Risk Management* had sent one to pick up her and her fellow agents during the evacuation of Camorral. That plane had been torn apart by seismic shocks, induced by an insurrectionist subsurface antimatter bomb. The insurrectionists had decided to make their plane less appealing to the Unity by destroying its infrastructure. It had worked.

That trip, that emergency, had been the only time she'd seen a shuttle like it. They were expensive. Most of their body was devoted to fuel storage, and they could gobble through it in hours. Like Meloku's last shuttle, it had been designed to accommodate flight in any medium from the interstellar to the oceanic. The only thing it was not meant to accommodate was cargo. For all its bulk, only a sliver of space had been set aside for people. The rest was taken up by fuel and the guts of its antimatter engine.

These shuttles were famously uncomfortable. They were meant only for emergency flights. *Ways and Means* had sent it to them unmanned, at the speed of a missile, and at accelerations that would have crushed passengers.

Ways and Means wanted them back. Badly.

They must have had something especially important. Meloku doubted it was either her or Osia.

To Meloku's surprise, Fiametta hadn't run away. She stood beside her, her hand planted on the ridge wall. Clouds of dust and vapor whipped around them, searing her skin.

Meloku expected to see pale cheeks, a sheen of sweat, an oath or her God's name on her lips. The paleness and tightness were there, but nothing else. Fiametta's lips were set, her jawline rigid. She still held onto the rock, with her free hand raised against the dust.

Meloku had underestimated the people of this plane. It had not been the first time. While they'd sheltered in the hideaway, Meloku had told Fiametta some of the things she thought might happen, but that couldn't have prepared her for the storm and the thunder.

Ways and Means must have been after her. Something about her, or something she knew. Whatever it was, it couldn't be good for her.

Meloku told her, "You can still run away."

Fiametta looked to her. Then she started to walk to the shuttle.

Meloku said, "If you go, you're not going to be able to change your mind."

She was talking to herself as much as Fiametta. She should not get aboard the shuttle either. *Ways and Means* was responsible for everything that had happened to them. It was involved in a plot to kill them that she still did not understand.

She could not let Fiametta get aboard that shuttle alone. Or Osia, either, come to that. She had to find out more.

The shuttle's boarding ramp was long, narrow, and without safety rails. It made Meloku think of a slender, lolling tongue. If this bothered Fiametta, she didn't show it. She walked just behind Osia.

The shuttle's interior was as cramped as Meloku remembered. Three cabins opened from the junction at the top of the boarding ramp. One was a crew head. The second, a control cabin with a handful of acceleration couches. And the third was a compartment that could hold either minor cargo or additional passengers. During the evacuation of Camorral, fifty agents had crammed into a shuttle like this one. During the flight to *Risk Management*, she and the others had had to sit with their leaves weaved inside the person sitting opposite.

Fiametta ran her hand along the bulkhead. The smooth, dark, composite was not quite metal. It was like nothing Fiametta would have felt before. The closest thing would have been well-sanded rock. It was lighter than rock, though. Meloku felt that lightness in the bow of the deck under her feet. The material was made to withstand high acceleration, and that meant being flexible rather than brittle.

It did make the shuttle feel more fragile, though.

The tear-shaped control cabin was tiny, and poorly lit. The light strips had been made for crew with better than human-normal vision. The bulkheads didn't have corners. It curved upward and around the hatch, making the space feel even smaller.

Fiametta took a short, sharp breath. Meloku wondered if she suffered from claustrophobia. She seemed to be realizing what was going to be expected of her. She raised her hand to her throat.

The boarding ramp closed. The sliver of daylight behind them diminished and disappeared. The susurrus of the wind cut off.

Five coffin-shaped acceleration couches unfolded from the deck like petals. All along the curved bulkheads, squares of light flickered and warmed. Exterior camera views, dozens of them, in a grid – an insect-eye view of the wasteland. Even fully demiorganic crew could only have so much information pumped into their heads at once. The camera views were meant to augment the sensor data sent from the shuttle's

NAI. If that NAI had said anything at all during warm-up, Meloku had missed it.

Fiametta's equanimity had not escaped Osia's attention. Osia asked her, "Did your inner voice tell you what to expect from ships like this?"

"No." Fiametta's fear didn't show in her voice. Though her hand trembled when she ran it along the nearest couch.

"Sizing up the furniture for value?" Osia asked. "Figuring out what you want to loot and steal?" When Fiametta didn't take Osia's bait, Osia told Meloku, "Get her secured. Then yourself. Ninety seconds until we get through preflight."

"What?" Meloku asked. After so fast a flight, safety procedure called for a half-hour grounding to verify nothing had broken during acceleration.

"I haven't been told why," Osia said. "I've just been told."

That message couldn't have come from *Ways and Means*, or Meloku would have picked up the signal too. So the shuttle's NAI *was* talking, but only to Osia. Meloku heard its message plain enough, regardless. All their margins had been pulled. Procedure, even safety procedure, no longer mattered.

Ways and Means was convinced that something was about to happen.

"All right," Meloku said, under a breath.

That moment was all the time she needed for the shock to fade and her instincts and training to come back. She pushed Fiametta toward the acceleration couch. Meloku ignored Fiametta's indignant shout, and likewise Fiametta shoving her back.

Fiametta sank into the cushions. The couches were arranged to keep their passenger's feet angled up, and their head and back flat. Meloku pulled the couch's safety harness out, and folded it over Fiametta from her legs to her shoulders. The webbing was not meant to restrain a prisoner. It would not keep Fiametta's hands pinned, or keep her from the manual harness release – if she found it. Meloku could only hope that she understood. She would have grabbed an anti-nauseal from the shuttle's medical kit if she'd had the time.

She grabbed Fiametta's wrists and held them firmly. She burned precious seconds waiting for Fiametta to look at her.

She would have tranquilized Fiametta, but she needed Fiametta to understand as much as she could about what she'd chosen. And no small part of her wanted the big bad *condottieri* captain terrified. Meloku's sympathy for her had just about run out. If Fiametta thought she could charge into this and take command, she was about to learn otherwise.

Meloku told her, "You had your chance to get out."

She dropped into her own couch. The deck plating was already starting to rumble. She tugged her own harness over herself. When she looked back at Fiametta, she was afraid she'd find her clawing at her webbing, fighting. Fiametta hadn't moved. She glared at Meloku, frozen somewhere between terror and fury.

She'd have a lot worse to deal with in a moment or two.

Fiametta gasped as the thrusters fired, shaking the deck. The hiss became a howl, reverberating through the bulkheads, splitting the air. The cabin shuddered, and gradually began to lift. To tilt. To lean back.

Then the main engine slammed a boot into Meloku's sternum, and she could not spare the energy to think about Fiametta.

For the first minute after launch, Meloku could not think at all. It took all her energy to breathe. She shunted most of her physiological functions to demiorganic control. She could hardly see through the blurring and graying side-effects of high acceleration, and what she saw was not helpful. The exterior cameras were like having a hundred eyes, all focused in different directions.

A few images grabbed at her. A stream of white flame. A blossom of fire, spreading wide – the atmosphere igniting. A bright, yellow-white hand spread across the land, fringed by black smoke and ash. The shuttle's NAI had not bothered at all to preserve the radio station. Clouds of vaporized earth poured over the hills.

Her cheeks and forehead flushed red, itched all over. Blood flooded her brain. The underside of her eyelids felt gritty, sandy. Her demiorganics worked hard to constrict the most sensitive blood vessels.

The deck shook not just from the engines, but the atmosphere. Stabilization fields bubbled into place over the shuttle's prow, softening the worst turbulence. The rest beat down upon Meloku's spine.

A thin layer of icy cirrus whipped past the shuttle, there and gone in seconds. Half of the monitors showed only bright, solid blue. Below, the clouds billowed and dissipated as the shuttle's exhaust whipped through them.

The roar of the engine dampened. The heat in her ears and cheeks faded. The acceleration was diminishing. She weighed only twice as much as she usually did. She no longer felt as though she was about to sink wholly into her cushions.

So much for the idea that *Ways and Means* was afraid to give away its activities to the locals. This launch would have been visible for hundreds of kilometers, and beyond. She transmitted, "Why in the fucking–" She cut herself short. "... did that have to happen?"

She doubted it had been circumspect about its arrival, either. She had not heard the re-entry sonic booms, but the shuttle could have skimmed the atmosphere at a low enough angle that she would have missed them. Half of its agents in this hemisphere would have seen or sensed the launch.

Osia said, "*Ways and Means* can't tell me."

Not "can't," Meloku thought. *Won't.*

Osia asked, "Have you contacted any of the satellites?"

Meloku hadn't. She hadn't seen the point. For weeks, her signals had gone ignored. She tried again. This time, she received an instantaneous answer. It was a holding signal.

She was being told to stand by. Same thing she might have gotten if the satellite had shut down for maintenance. The next one in line answered the same, and the next.

The satellites were no longer bothering to block her and Osia in particular. They were blocking everyone. All communications were down.

Only the satellites' person-to-person communications were shut down. The satellites' other functions, including sensors, were unaffected. They could speak to each other just fine. But they would not allow her to contact anyone else.

Osia said, "It's been like this for hours. *Ways and Means* believes its satellites have been compromised. Someone else has subverted them to block our signals, and to carry their own. But *Ways and Means* still had the power to shut the whole system down." A blunt force solution to its problem.

Meloku asked, *"Ways and Means told you that itself?"*

She had not expected an answer, and did not get one. *Ways and Means* was below their horizon, incommunicado. It would not have trusted the satellites to deliver that message. Osia was guessing just as much as Meloku was.

If Fiametta had lost consciousness, it hadn't been for long. She looked feverish, forehead red and gleaming. But her eyes were open. A sliver of something brown glistened across her lip, falling onto her ear.

She stared at the monitors. More than anything else at that moment, Meloku wanted to ask her what she understood. If anything.

Color drained from the sky. Before long, the blue had narrowed to a wide band across the horizon, getting smaller. The drumfire on the deck plates diminished. Then the ventral thrusters fired, a sequence of thunder like a cannonade. They knocked Meloku deep into her couch.

The camera displays arced. From Meloku's seat, the shuttle felt like it was falling backward, about to tumble over itself. Fiametta coughed and gagged. But she seemed to have nothing but bile left to void. Meloku watched her when she could. Fiametta hardly blinked. Her eyes were always open. Red clouded her corneas.

She kept watching the Earth. The Baltic sparkled sunlight.

Strips of clouds buffeted the shore. The horizon developed a curve. There were no stars. The horizons and the sky were empty except for the sun. Sunlight drowned out the stars, leaving most of the monitors sheet black.

If anything was headed their way, though, Meloku would never see it in time. Not through just the cameras. She needed sensors, too. The shuttle's NAI still would not answer her calls for information.

Osia had little trouble speaking against the acceleration. "NAI says we'll rendezvous with *Ways and Means* in eight hours." She did not bother to keep the tightness out of her voice. Eight hours, left exposed. They would be easier targets here than on the ground. The ground gave them cover. In a shuttle, their heat emissions shone clear as a star.

"Can you give me NAI access?" Meloku transmitted. It was beyond irksome that she still didn't have it. "I *am* an active agent."

"I doubt any of us are in good standing," Osia said.

"The shuttle NAI will speak to you," Meloku pointed out.

After Osia had gone into her own little exile, the rest of the crew had wondered if *Ways and Means* had had a special relationship with her. It had only listened to her. It certainly trusted her more than it did Meloku, though Meloku had spent the past thirty years working for it.

Maybe it just came from the fact that Osia was a crewmember with a demiorganic body. The amalgamates had always treated crew differently than human agents.

Abruptly, a torrent of a datastream poured into Meloku – sensor images, trajectories, flight paths. Osia had convinced the NAI to open up. It was as much punishment as gift. Too much for her to sort through, let alone comprehend. Neural impulses crossfired. Nausea bubbled up. It was like drowning in an electrified pool.

It was hard to escape the impression that Osia was proving some kind of point.

With work, Meloku sorted the datastream into manageable

parcels. The shuttle was counting down to another burst of harder acceleration in one hundred and twenty seconds. Enough time to brace for it, and to warm Fiametta.

The shuttle curled backward. Its dorsal hull faced the Earth. Meloku could not stop thinking of a whale, diving belly-up. The Earth hid *Ways and Means*. The shuttle would have to complete an arcing half-orbit before it crossed their horizon.

The shuttle's sensors showed no visible weapons launches. No heat signatures from missiles. No spikes in electromagnetic activity. The shuttle could hardly see through its own engine exhaust. A brilliant, staticky yellow-white fuzz covered half the cameras. It shone brighter than the sun.

Meloku fought the gravities to swallow. She was just about to open her mouth, warn Fiametta about the impending acceleration, when a sensor alarm stopped her.

Space beyond the Earth's horizon was hot. About as hot as interplanetary vacuum could get, in fact. The loose particles of dust and solar ejecta that comprised the interplanetary medium were heating, boiling. They bounced about, hot and energized.

It was nothing visible to the naked eye. The shuttle's sensors, though, had no issues. The disturbance was ahead of them, just over the horizon. Something was pouring energy into the vacuum.

Ways and Means lay in that direction, but it wasn't close enough to have caused it. It was millions of kilometers away yet. This was near, closer to the Earth than its moon. So far as the shuttle's sensors could tell, the disturbance had no source. Some of the energized particles licked the atmosphere.

Whatever this was, it was happening on a massive scale. The total volume of the disturbed interplanetary medium was a thousand times the size of the Earth. And that was just what the shuttle could see. No wonder Osia had been reluctant to give her access to the NAI. She had been hiding this. Meloku asked, "What the fuck is going on?"

"I don't know." Osia was more talkative than usual. She

was agitated. Afraid. "It's only showing up on the shuttle's sensors. The satellites aren't seeing it at all."

Meloku contacted the nearest satellite. Easier said than accomplished with the shuttle's engines pumping out this much interference. After the third attempt, she got an answer. As far as the satellites were concerned, nothing unusual was happening.

That was a lie. The satellites could not have missed this, not even with the bulk of the sensors and telescopes aimed at the Earth rather than its sky. A deep, numbing chill spread down Meloku's back.

She did not have time to repeat her question.

A hard punch to her sternum drove her back into her seat. The breath drove from her chest. There was no warning.

All along the ventral hull, the shuttle's thrusters snapped on. The shuttle's main engines followed. They hadn't been scheduled for harder acceleration for another forty seconds. It caught Meloku mid-breath. The g-forces squeezed her ribs, her lungs. She choked.

The shock felt so much like a deliberate blow that her demiorganics triggered their injury response functions, readied to release reserves of oxygen. This was a harder acceleration than any she'd fought so far.

Somewhere behind all of this, the satellites were shrieking.

Ways and Means had seeded its satellites to monitor the surface and facilitate communications, but not to think on their own. They could not take action on their own. Yet there were certain events for which *Ways and Means* did not want to wait, even long enough to account for seconds of light speed delay, to trigger an alarm. One of those events was happening right now. The alarm had overridden *Ways and Means'* communications blackout.

Even as the sole major power on this plane, *Ways and Means* remained afraid of a handful of things. The first was the creature that had exiled it here. The second was the thought of an extraplanar power finding this plane, invading, and attacking *Ways and Means* while it was trapped and vulnerable.

The satellites' sensor feeds shunted into Meloku's visual cortex. On the other side of the world, a transplanar gateway split space open. It was vast, shining, sun-bright.

It burned two thousand kilometers high over the eastern Americas and the Atlantic. It was a broadly linear rent in space, forcing wider every second. The satellites had sounded the alarm when it was only a meter long. By the time the images found their way into Meloku's demiorganics, it was already a hundred times the size of their shuttle. Still growing. Even if the engines had not robbed Meloku of breath, she would not have been able to take one.

The planar tear widened, became lenticular. Hard radiation poured out of it, boiling away into space. To the naked eye, it would have appeared blinding white. The spectrum heavily slanted to the ultraviolet and x-ray.

It took an enormous amount of energy to open a planar tear like this. So much energy, in fact, that only a few forces in the old Unity would have been capable of it. Most of the Unity's gateways had been tiny, micrometer-width communication gateways. Even person-sized trade gateways had been expensive. Planarships, though, were a step beyond. Much of the antimatter engine capacity of their planarships were devoted just to opening planar tears.

An enormous object appeared at the center of the gateway, breaching the boundaries between universes. Impossible to make out any details through the gateway's boiling radiation, other than that it was big. It took up almost the whole width of the gateway.

The engines landed a punch in Meloku's stomach. This time, it didn't have any more air to expel. Her vision fringed red, into gray, and then black. Her demiorganics released their oxygen reserves.

The gateway had opened beneath their western horizon. The shuttle's NAI rapidly configured a new course. It dove the shuttle down, and eastward – hard and away from the intruder. The shuttle aimed to keep away from whatever was coming through. If whatever was emerging wanted to kill them, it had many means. Planarships like *Ways and Means* had, among other weapons, beams that could vaporize the shuttle at many times the intruder's current range. Any ship so powerful as to open a gateway would be at least as well armed. The shuttle had no defenses, no beam-defecting mirror-fields like *Ways and Means*.

Only the Earth's interceding bulk shielded the shuttle. If it rose above the skyline, the new arrival could snuff them out with less effort than a thought.

It would not even need to get line of sight. In a flurry of alarms, the satellites noted several new objects emerging from the intruder. None were as large as the shuttle. The largest was the size of a short person.

Combat drones. Missiles. Any and all of the above, plus more Meloku couldn't think of in the terror of the moment.

She almost missed the satellites' other data. The intruder broadcast a Unity-standard identification transponder.

It identified itself as *Ways and Means*.

Her thoughts raced. Somewhere, deep in the back of her head, she felt a twinge of satisfaction. It was a small thing, but it was there. At least now, even this close to her end, she might find an answer or two.

The energy expenditure of transplanar gateways meant that the amalgamates used them only when necessary, to travel from plane to plane. They could also jump from point to point in the same universe. That did not happen often. Meloku had never seen it. Not only did it burn energy, it required tremendously complex calculations. *Ways and Means* could do it, though. Her first thought was that this had happened: *Ways and Means* had gated from millions of kilometers away to the other side of the Earth.

But that wasn't it. The shape coming through was the wrong shape, the wrong design.

The satellites could sense very little through the blistering radiation, but the intruder occluded the planar rift, became visible in silhouette. It was only three-quarters the length of *Ways and Means*.

Ways and Means' body comprised ten kilometer-long, rectangular, flat hull segments, arranged in a grid. The intruder coming through had only three hull segments, lined up in a row. They were the same size and shape as *Ways and Means'*. They could have come from the same shipyards and factories.

The intruder was bracketed on two sides by large, half-ovoid shapes. It was like an egg had been split bilaterally, and each half mounted on the intruder's sides. They weren't like anything Meloku had seen on a planarship before.

In fact, she was sure that, in spite of the hull segments, no shipyard in the Unity had produced this vessel. She knew all of the amalgamates' planarships. Even the ones she hadn't seen herself, she'd studied. She was confident that there had been no secret planarships, either. The amalgamates would not have trusted anyone or anything but themselves with power like a planarship.

The rift closed rapidly behind the intruder. The radiation slimmed to nothing. The satellites' sensors re-calibrated, revealed color. The half-ovoid segments were silver, mirror-polished. The sunlight shone bright off them.

It didn't seem to matter that satellite communication had been shut down; Osia was trying desperately to contact anyone. The shuttle NAI reported that Osia was spiking signals in two directions: at the intruder, and at the still more distant *Ways and Means*. But neither were over the shuttle's horizon. She couldn't reach them directly. The satellites refused to acknowledge that they had received Osia's signals. All they sent back was their sensor data.

As Meloku watched, the surface of the Earth-facing ovoid rippled. Shadows clouded the mirror.

A lance of energy pierced the Earth's sky.

The shuttle's sensors could not perceive the beam in vacuum, but the beam was easy enough to trace in atmosphere. It ignited the air it touched. It burned over the Atlantic Ocean. Something on the surface flared, turned to a fireball.

A second explosion illuminated the northern continent, far above its cauldron of lakes. Then a third, on the isthmus that linked the north and south continents.

Meloku knew those spots. She had seen them all the time on her maps. They all hosted *Ways and Means'* backup communications posts, like Xati's. Another lightning-bright spark shone on the northern continent's west coast. Then the very farthest tip of the southern.

The silver surface, Meloku realized, was a defensive field. The surface was perfectly reflective to incoming fire, and to sensors. It hid the planarship's true capabilities. The mirrored ovoids were weapons platforms. Advanced, rigorously designed, and shielded. The satellites' sensors had not even known the cannon were there until they opened fire.

Another dazzling light split the sky, in the vacuum this time, not far from the intruder. More followed. All the explosions were in space. Meloku had no idea what the intruder was firing upon. Hidden objects, maybe. The sensors had not recorded anything there.

The intruder left *Ways and Means'* communications satellites intact. It did not seem to notice, or care, that Meloku and Osia were using those satellites to observe it.

Spears of white-hot gas loosed from the intruder's underside, and from one of the ovoids. It was powering its engines. The shuttle's NAI frantically plotted the intruder's possible flight paths. On a map at the front of the cabin, it arced lines across a globe, writing and rewriting them as new data arrived. Trajectories pulsed in and out of existence in a flicker of half-seconds. The paths bent like spider's legs, folding around each other on the other side of the globe.

Osia was still trying to contact the intruder. She cycled through what must have been a dozen tricks to override the communications block. Since the satellites had shown her the intruder's transponder, the one that identified it as *Ways and Means*, she tried coding her message into the shuttle's own transponder. The satellites were broadcasting their sensor data in all directions. If the intruder was paying attention, it should have seen that. Nothing. If any of Osia's attempts to contact the intruder had reached it, it gave no sign.

The intruder's thrusters fired again. The possibilities began to narrow, or coalesce. Meloku did not need to keep watching to know what the final winnowing would reveal.

It had aimed itself at the shuttle.

In the NAI's final estimation, the intruder's course looped tightly around the Earth, and crossed the shuttle's trajectory nearly exactly.

The intruder had made no attempt to communicate. But it had never stopped broadcasting its transponder signal. It wanted them to know what it was, or what it claimed to be.

Its engines flared. Its exhaust plumed, nearly as bright as the gateway had been. The satellites' sensors were blinded, briefly. The combat drones it had entered with also arced about, raced toward the shuttle.

Another sequence of heat sources chained along the intruder's port ovoid weapons platform. Combat drones, launching. She did not need to check the calculated trajectories of those, either. The shuttle didn't give her the chance. The g-forces amplified, adding more stones to those weighing down her chest. She forced her eyelids shut. Tears squeezed out of them, splashed hard against the cushions.

The intruder changed its course to match the shuttle's. It could outpace them. It accelerated harder than its crew, if it had one, could have survived.

She lost track of time. Her demiorganics insisted that ten minutes had passed. She'd hardly felt it. Consciousness was difficult to pin down. Difficult enough to keep breathing during acceleration. Her demiorganics could only do so much.

The intruder came at them just as hard. More and more of the Earth peeled back before it. White flashes dotted the

Atlantic, striking islands. Then in Iceland, Greenland. Then in western Europe. The intruder fired relentlessly. It obliterated all of *Ways and Means'* communications outposts. If its crew on the surface needed to talk to each other, they would be entirely dependent on the satellites.

The satellites, Meloku guessed, that the intruder could easily take control of, if it hadn't already.

It could have done worse. *Ways and Means* had agents in the cities below, surrounded by innocents. The intruder left them alone.

It was doing damage enough. Given the size of the explosions, their visibility at altitude, she had a hard time believing no natives had been killed.

The Indian Ocean slipped away underneath the shuttle, segued into a vast cloud mass that covered the world from Malaysia to the Indonesian islands. Lightning rippled across the clouds. The shuttle had stayed ahead of the intruder, for now. But the intruder was faster, accelerating harder. Its combat drones and missiles were even closer.

She took a risk, tilted her head just enough to look to Fiametta. Of course, Fiametta had fainted. No one without demiorganics could have remained conscious. Her eyelids had been levered open by gravity, but her eyes were vacant.

Fiametta would be lucky to get through this without lasting injury. So, Meloku realized, would she herself. A wave of claustrophobia subsumed her. She'd never felt it before, but now the webbing seemed too close, too cloying. It felt sticky, like actual spider webbing. That had to be a hallucination, a symptom of poor blood oxygenation. Knowing that didn't make it any less real.

She could not stand the thought of dying without knowing what was happening, without being able to control anything. The shuttle's NAI would not listen to her. It would not even release her straps if she asked.

Osia must have felt the same. She gave up her attempts to contact the intruder. She transmitted, "I'm taking control of the shuttle."

There was not much Osia could do that the shuttle's NAI could not calculate better. But Osia could take risks that it wouldn't. By lacing her systems with its, she could control it as easily as she could her body.

The timbre of the engines changed. Another thunderous clap from the dorsal thrusters knocked Meloku into her harness. The shuttle spun. For a moment, she could breathe. Before she had time to do more than gasp, the ventral thrusters fired, arresting the shuttle's roll.

A frisson of atmosphere outlined Earth's curve. Before long, most of the forward cameras faced the Earth. Osia had dipped the shuttle's nose to face below the horizon.

Meloku traced her thoughts. Speed alone would not help them outrun the intruder. They needed to cut corners, stay low, and keep as much of the Earth between them and the intruder as possible. Osia intended to dive at as shallow an angle as she could. She was going to skim the atmosphere.

Meloku no longer felt good about Osia taking control, about anything.

She did not have a chance to say so before the engines thundered, her couch slammed into her back, and everything weighed ten times as much as it should.

A signal crossed the shuttle. It was tight-beam, subdued, and just powerful enough to cut through the engines' haze of interference. Meloku figured it was narrow-beam because her demiorganics picked up a much stronger signal than the receivers in the shuttle's nose.

Not that she knew what that distance was. Her demiorganics could only determine a direction. It had not come from any of the satellites. Nor a ground source. The shuttle's sensors showed nothing in that direction.

The signal was text only: "Rotate your shuttle one hundred seventy-five degrees negative yaw, three degrees positive pitch. As soon as possible, please." Those directions would have the shuttle opposite its current orientation.

Meloku racked her mind, trying to think of where the signal might have come from. When *Ways and Means* had first visited this plane, it had gated a chain of stealthed observation satellites into orbit. Their arrival had caused a stir among the anthropologists she'd been embedded with. Those satellites had gone forgotten, derelict, superseded by the network of larger, more feature-complete communications satellites it had planted after its exile.

Not so derelict after all. The shuttle's NAI didn't even put them on its sensor displays. It classified them as space junk, beneath human attention. The signal had come from one of them.

They must have been the source of the eruptions in the sky. A check against the shuttle's records confirmed it. The intruder was targeting the old satellites, destroying any above its horizon.

The second signal, when it arrived, allowed her to triangulate to confirm its origin. "We're standing by to calculate a deceleration curve," it said. After some time, a third added, pointedly: "As soon you're oriented."

The message must have come from *Ways and Means*. Their *Ways and Means*, not the intruder. She could hear the cadence of its voice even in text.

The shuttle had reached the Pacific now. The intruder had crossed over western Europe, trailing beam fire behind it. Meloku transmitted to Osia: "It wants us to *decelerate?*"

The intruder would catch them in an hour. Turning around, burning engines toward it would reduce that to minutes. With a spark of horror, she wondered if the intruder really was, somehow, *Ways and Means*. But it had no need to trick them into decelerating. Its combat drones were closing regardless.

Daylight glimmered light blue on the eastern horizon. Sunrise, already approaching. Except it wasn't the right time of day. They should have been in night for a while yet. There was something else going on here. Something she wasn't seeing.

Osia craned her neck. Her eyes, the most human part of her, shone under the cabin lights.

From that look alone, Meloku knew that any argument was already lost. Osia was going to do everything *Ways and Means* asked. It might have been another hallucination, but that instant the air between them split as cleanly as shattered glass. This was why she could never become a crewmember like Osia. Osia could not help but trust *Ways and Means*.

Meloku was not capable of it.

Two stars rose above the western horizon. Combat drones. They were much smaller than the shuttle, but their engines burned brightly.

Osia did not even give a warning to brace. She did not need to. Meloku clenched her seat webbing. Thrusters boomed along the shuttle's starboard hull, slamming her sideways. The pain of a torn muscle seared up her thigh, hot as lightning, too fast for her demiorganics to stifle it. She was slammed again into her seat harness, and then to her side. Osia was juking, billowing hot thruster gas around the shuttle. She meant to confuse the drones' targeting.

Darkness flickered across the monitors, pulsing in and out. Field projections. The shuttle had no defensive fields, but the fields it used to stifle atmospheric buffering could also scatter the shuttle's engine exhaust and thruster gasses. They could obscure the exhaust plume's origin, and make the shuttle that much harder to target.

A pillar of heat and light strobed through the exhaust cloud. Then another. The combat drones were firing. The beams missed the shuttle but raked the atmosphere, their trails lightning bolts of energized ions.

The nearest of the beams had passed only fifty meters away from the shuttle's port wings. Meloku wanted to shout at Osia, scream that decelerating was just going to bring the drones closer. There didn't seem to be a point.

Whether the shuttle went faster or slower, the drones were going to catch up. They could accelerate at a pace that would have killed Fiametta, Meloku, even Osia. There was nowhere to go. Nowhere to land. They were going to die. Decelerating like this just meant that it would happen faster.

She had to at least know. When she found the presence of mind, she transmitted, "What is it?"

Osia said, "It must be one of *Ways and Means'* backups."

Meloku stared, drawing a blank for too long before the bolt of memory struck. *Ways and Means* had made backup copies of its mind, its memories. It had seeded them throughout the multiverse. She had the clearance to know about the program, if not the specifics. It had left them buried under icy rogue planetoids, or lost in stellar nursery dust clouds. A safeguard against accident and treachery. A guarantee of immortality.

That had all ended thirty years ago. The terms of *Ways and Means'* exile had barred it from transplanar travel. Meloku said, "The backups should be dormant. They're memories in jars. Even if one of them woke, it wouldn't be able to build a planarship like that, not in just thirty years of scraping together infrastructure."

"I know," Osia said. "Someone must have built that ship for it."

"Someone? Like who?" The planarships had been the crown jewels of the Unity, as powerful as they were expensive. "Who would have the resources?"

Meloku had been fixated on the satellites' sensors for so long that she had lost track of the shuttle's. When she turned her attention back to them, breath froze in her throat.

The sky to the east was luminous. The horizon looked aglow, as with sunrise. For an instant, Meloku thought she had fainted, lost time.

Meloku transmitted, "This *can't* be getting worse."

But the shuttle was where it should have been, crossing into the Pacific. Sunrise, real sunrise, should have been a long way away.

The satellites still saw nothing. The image only appeared

on the shuttle's cameras and sensors.

Osia said, "The intruder, whatever it is, thought it could use the satellites as a blind to trick us. *Ways and Means* figured that out a while ago. It tried to tell me."

The arc of the Earth's atmosphere hazed red and golden, and then white. It reflected off clouds and sky. The colors all matched spectra of antimatter engine exhaust.

Osia said, "But the truth is always more complicated than it will admit."

It was an immense amount of engine exhaust. The engine plume blinded most of the shuttle's sensors, but there was no hiding the bulk of the object behind it – or the shape of it.

Ways and Means crested the horizon, riding a blaze of light and searing radiation.

It was *their Ways and Means*. Its ten rectangular hull segments were half hidden under the sheet of engine exhaust, but visible. It should have been hours away.

It was decelerating hard. The shuttle's NAI corrected its sensor maps, drew new flight paths. The deceleration curve they'd been given put the shuttle on a straight course to rendezvous with it.

The satellites still claimed to see nothing.

Osia said, "*Ways and Means* knew its satellites were compromised. It didn't try to fight back. It let its enemy think it had won, and could use our satellites to blind us." As much as Osia was trying to hide it, Meloku heard the excitement in her voice. *Ways and Means* could have retaken control of the satellites at any time. "It was a double-blind."

Ways and Means had always stood just behind the stage, in the backdrop. It had waited until just now to pull the curtain back.

The satellites had lied to Meloku and Osia, lied to everybody, about where *Ways and Means* was. Ever since it had launched its shuttle, *Ways and Means* had been accelerating hard, dangerously hard, just behind. It had gone nearly as fast as the shuttle. Fast enough that all of its crew would have had to retreat to acceleration shelters.

The combat drones saw *Ways and Means* too late. They arced, maneuvering hard. Their exhaust flickered. They were trying to disguise their trajectory as Osia had.

They never had a chance. *Ways and Means* fired a full cannon barrage. Dozens of beam trails lanced through the drones' wakes, seeking the combat drones. It was only a matter of time before lucky strikes intersected them.

Two sharp flashes marked their antimatter stores detonating.

Meloku gaped. An instant later, she regretted it. Her molars cracked on each other. A sharp pain split her mouth. Meloku tasted blood before she realized she had bitten her tongue. Osia swung the shuttle around, course-correcting from her juking.

She'd thought the satellites had been on the intruder's side. So had the intruder. *Ways and Means* had let the intruder trust the satellites, and then, at just this moment – for her and Osia – had yanked that control away.

The intruder did not take long to figure it out. One of her sensor feeds vanished. From another vantage, she watched the satellite the feed had come from turn into a cloud of luminous vapor. Then her view pulled back again as that satellite, too, died.

Flashes of plasma studded the sky. The intruder was quickly, efficiently wiping out all the satellites in its reach.

Ways and Means was haloed by a cloud of exhaust bright as a star: a dark splotch of adjoining hull segments, silhouetted against the moonlit atmosphere. It must have been racing this way for hours. It must have burned through nearly all of its reserved antimatter by now. Its crew would have been strained close to breaking by the g-forces.

All for her, Osia, and Fiametta. Meloku took the risk of craning her neck, glanced to Fiametta. Most likely, just for Fiametta.

It didn't make sense. Unless there was something they'd

missed, locked up in that woman's head. She looked back to Osia. Maybe she'd missed her guess, though. Maybe Osia and *Ways and Means did* have a special relationship. If Osia knew, she wasn't talking.

Both *Ways and Means* and the shuttle were decelerating toward each other, hard as they could. It wasn't enough. They were still going too fast. At this pace, the shuttle would still be moving at hundreds of kilometers per hour relative to the planarship when their paths crossed. That was a close match by the standards of orbital velocities, but not close enough for boarding. They would have to swing around and come back. More time in which they would be vulnerable.

They didn't have it. The intruder had not slowed its pursuit. In fact, it had accelerated. It would rise over their horizon soon. It would not matter, then, that *Ways and Means* had come. If the intruder wanted to kill them, they would die. Juking and engine exhaust would not save them from a planarship's cannon barrage.

Osia aligned their trajectory dead-on to *Ways and Means'* underside. She did not intend to swing by for another pass.

Osia pushed their engines harder. Something in Meloku's chest *popped*. A rib, her demiorganics confirmed.

Blackness swam around the edges of Meloku's vision. She shut her eyes.

Later, she didn't know if she'd opened her eyes, or if the g-forces had just pried them open. Consciousness had gone diffuse. *Ways and Means* seemed like it had only just crested the horizon, but now it was closer.

The sky was a swirl of white. Far below, between spackled clouds, the ocean reflected the planarship's towering engine plume.

Ways and Means was fifty kilometers away. Forty. Osia had aligned the shuttle directly on one of the carbuncular hangars on the planarship's underside. Still going too fast. At this pace, the shuttle would spear right through the ship.

Meloku ran through all of the solutions she could think of.

A field couldn't cushion their landing, not at this speed. The shuttle would slice right through it. Unless *Ways and Means* had far more warning than Meloku supposed, it wouldn't have the time to fill the hangar complex with shock gel.

Ways and Means ceased its engine burn, briefly. It made a gap in its exhaust plume big enough for the shuttle to fall through. The shuttle would have melted if it hadn't.

In a lash of light, the shuttle fell through the exhaust plume. The brilliant, billowing light pulled back. All at once *Ways and Means* was in front of the camera monitors: dark and gleaming, glaring. It was a shadow, a sharpness framed in its own white-hot exhaust. The razor edges of its hull glowed. All of its aft and port thrusters were firing.

Osia had not stopped the shuttle's engines. The shuttle's exhaust licked against the planarship. Where the plume touched *Ways and Means*, its hull turned scarlet.

Each hull segment was kilometers long, but they had passed the first before Meloku realized it was there. Up ahead, on an ever-increasing number of the cameras, she could already see the lumpen silhouette of the hangar complex.

Meloku timed its approach by her ragged breaths. One breath. Two breaths. Three. *Ways and Means'* hull arced around the cameras. Before she could gasp, they had plunged in.

Osia finally cut the engines.

Warm light wrapped around them. The hangar's interior was a smoothly shaded orange dome, decor from a decade Meloku had long forgotten. Far ahead, and below, a disc-shaped landing platform and a cluster of attendant buildings stood waiting.

The far wall rose ahead, racing closer. The side of the complex had been built to withstand survive high-velocity collisions. It had not been made to preserve the craft that caused them.

In the too-long moment Meloku had left, she guessed Osia's intentions. Osia wasn't invulnerable, but she could walk away from a crash that would kill Meloku and Fiametta.

Even if her body was destroyed, her brain might survive.

Something blurred across the forward monitors.

Meloku slammed into her seat harness. Pain ripped through her chest, overwhelming her demiorganics' ability to numb it. The shuttle's prow tilted toward the shining, silver landing pad.

Osia fired the thrusters hard, barely correcting in time to avoid diving into it.

Another blur, another hard jolt. Something physical had struck the shuttle. On a monitor showing the shuttle's aft, the hull around the engine housing had crumpled. Part of the shuttle's substructure had bent.

When she'd made her mental list all of the technological answers to the crash, Meloku hadn't thought of simpler solutions. Netting.

Ways and Means had thrown carbonfiber webbing across the interior of its hangar. Each strand was stronger than the shuttle's hull. No doubt *Ways and Means* controlled the releases, would loose them the instant the shuttle had absorbed as much kinetic energy as its frame and its passengers could bear.

Netting. In the instant Meloku had to consider it, this seemed almost as bad an idea as just crashing.

On the next impact, one of the shuttle's rear fins stove almost in half. This time, Osia really did lose control. The shuttle twisted, hard. The next impacts knocked them in opposite directions.

Meloku managed to close her eyes before things would have gone black on their own.

31

Even Osia lost consciousness during the crash.

The last thing she felt was the *clack* of the shuttle's boarding ramp unlocking, and before the battered remnant of the shuttle even struck the landing platform. That was *Ways and Means* – always thinking ahead.

Her body shut down her nervous system to keep it from being disrupted by the shock.

When she came back – seconds later, according to her internal clock – the shuttle had collapsed around her. The cabin's ceiling had bowed inward. One of the light strips had bent and broken. All of the monitor projections had vanished. The shuttle's NAI didn't answer her.

The shuttle had stopped moving. She was in freefall. *Ways and Means* had stopped accelerating. Diagnostics reported a great deal of shock and stress, but no permanent damage.

Had this been any other shuttle, it would have been smashed to titanium splinters. The high-speed shuttle had saved them. Its composite hull had been built with shock and high acceleration in mind. It wasn't brittle, and had stretched before it broke.

Somewhere behind her, a hiss of air was dwindling to nothing. Sensors in her ears, behind her eyes, and every other pocket of air in her body reported a steep drop in cabin pressure.

She grabbed her seat harness, ripped it loose.

Meloku and Fiametta were both unconscious. Their harnesses had left deep, red abrasions. Their breathing was labored, pained. But they were alive. They had suffered no injury that *Ways and Means* could not heal.

The hiss of air died away. Internal and external pressure equalized. *Ways and Means* had projected containing fields over the shuttle's crash site, and filled them with air. Osia did not need to guess that this was what had happened. She knew.

Data sluiced through her. At first, it was a trickle. Now it flooded corners of her mind that she had not realized had gone dry.

Ways and Means had asked her to open her demiorganics to it. She, reflexively, had accepted. She had not even been conscious of doing it. After thirty years away, her systems were lacing with *Ways and Means'*.

Had she breath, she would have gasped.

Though her demiorganic mind afforded her perfect memory, lacing her mind with its senses was the nearest thing to remembering something forgotten. Memory was tied indelibly with senses – with smell, with sight and sound. *Ways and Means* had a thousand senses she didn't.

She felt the damaged landing disc outside, the wavering of the fields keeping them in an atmosphere. She saw, through hundred-eyed cameras, the shorn and crumpled wreckage of the shuttle. A static thrum of radio chatter channeled through her: orders, reports, crew yelling at each other. She could not see the whole ship at once, did not have the mental bandwidth, but she only had to focus on a place and she could perceive it.

With new senses, new ways of thinking. She'd left a part of herself behind on this ship. She had not realized, in the moment of separation, how big those parts had been.

The past thirty years had been a dream, an implanted memory. Walls she hadn't realized she'd built in her mind crashed open. In an instant, she was much closer to the person she used to be.

She did not have the time to dislike it.

She felt the footsteps of two crewmembers as they

approached. Sona and Verse. Sona had a bipedal body like Osia's. Osia knew Sona's name, but had never worked with her. Verse, though, she knew too well. E had a spiderlike body, with eight multiply articulated insectoid legs. While all of *Ways and Means'* crewmembers were trained and ready for combat, e had been designed for it.

Before Osia left, *Ways and Means* had told her that her safety was at risk. Verse's name had been at the top of its list of names to watch.

For a moment, Osia wondered if it was a coincidence that e had come. It had to have been, unless been *Ways and Means* had been more prescient about where she would land than seemed possible. She had chosen this hangar, not it. But *Ways and Means* had tricks she would never understand.

She felt Verse's feet grip the surface outside as keenly as she would have felt her own. Verse and Sona scrambled up the boarding ramp. If *Ways and Means* hadn't unlocked it before the shuttle lost its NAI, they would have lost precious time battering it open.

Verse and Sona rapped at the cabin door. The hatch was jammed. It had flexed inward and warped irrevocably during the crash. Osia braced herself against the edge of an empty acceleration couch.

She, Verse, and Sona worked as a team, battering the door from opposite sides, timing their blows to amplify each other's. One side of the hatch popped lose. Sona peeled the hatch away like it was dead skin. She pushed it, spinning, into the next cabin.

The first person Sona looked at when she stepped through was Fiametta. Not Meloku, not Osia. Of course. *Ways and Means* could hide its priorities well enough, but its crew was less subtle. These two had been given orders to take care of Fiametta first.

She had to be why *Ways and Means* had sent them its precious shuttle, and ended the charade that it wasn't in control of the satellites. It had given up a lot of tools and advantages. It must have been expecting something great in return.

"Acceleration warning," Sona transmitted, as if Osia hadn't received the same alarm herself. "Two hundred seventy seconds. *Ways and Means* is going to burn engines whether you're ready or not."

Osia ignored the condescension. She had not been back for ten minutes, and already she remembered how little she'd loved the politics.

Well, she was thirty years out of practice, but she hadn't lost the art. She nodded behind her. Meloku and Fiametta were coming around, but they wouldn't be able to move themselves. "I've been injured," she said, pointing to her back. "Controlling the lower half of my body via radio. I'll knock them around if I'm carrying them. You two grab them."

She shouldered past them. Leaving them behind.

With them slowed by Meloku and Fiametta, she was free to race ahead, get rid of them. Find somewhere quiet to hunker.

She had only gotten as far as the boarding ramp before she realized Verse was following. Er spiderlike legs gripped the ramp's sides, wrapped around it. The ramp shook with er imparted momentum.

Outside, the gradient of the hangar complex's arching orange ceiling was so subtle that it looked like a sky rather than hull. A field shimmered around the landing pad, keeping their air in.

Ways and Means didn't have artificial gravity, not like some of the other planarships, but it did have travel aids. The pad's silver surface gripped Osia's feet. The decks and bulkheads had a grip. Fields grabbed her heels and toes and kept her from vaulting away.

Lift terminals clustered on the pad ahead. Osia remembered her old gait without trying, lifting one leg at a time, and pushing just hard enough to slip loose from the field. Verse, with er multiple legs, could be even faster. But e kept pace.

Osia told er, "You should be helping Sona."

"You don't think Sona can handle them?"

Of course she did. "I can handle myself too."

"I never said you couldn't."

Verse was baiting her. Trying to force her to clarify her point again and again, until Osia straight-out said that she didn't believe *Ways and Means* had confidence in her. That she thought it had sent Verse here to watch her.

Osia could have dropped all pretenses, pointed that out, but that would only be further engaging with this idiocy.

She missed her boat. She would take a thousand years with Ira before more of this.

She stepped to the blank surface of the lift terminal. The wall parted for her and Verse as though it wasn't there. All illusions. There was no lift platform waiting. Just a gray, empty shaft. It was lined with light strips, falling away to an infinite vanishing point.

The lifts did not operate in emergencies. The nearest would have taken too long to reach them. Faster to just run.

She and Verse plunged over the edge. For a second, Osia floated free. Then the gripping fields caught Osia's feet again, pulled her around. She righted herself. From this perspective, the shaft looked less like a drop, and more like an infinite passage.

In the old days, Osia could have traveled in a blink. In another era, *Ways and Means'* interior had been studded with gateways, miniature transplanar rifts. The crew had used them to travel from one hull segment to the next. An enormous and wasteful expenditure of energy which *Ways and Means* had undertaken because it could. The gateways had impressed its guests, certainly, but they'd been made to impress the crew. Make them feel wealthy and important.

Exile had changed that. *Ways and Means* had shut off those gateways. It could not maintain them.

Now there was only one acceleration shelter in reach. It was not the one she would have chosen. It was an observation lounge flush against the planarship's exterior hull. With a big, wide transparent dome overlooking the stars.

The dome wasn't a projection, wasn't an image. It was a real window. A big one, and one of the few aboard ship. It was for those diplomatic guests who would not have been satisfied with a machine interpreting the view for them.

It was the last place Osia wanted to be during battle. They might as well have been strapped to the hull.

No choice.

She and Verse fell through the next hatch, into a broad and stark-white passageway. Osia broadened her senses, expanding them over the path ahead. A hiss of air raced ahead of them, filling each passageway before they arrived.

Ways and Means filled even empty cabins and corridors with a thin nitrogen atmosphere. It protected against vacuum erosion. Oxygen wasn't included, though. It would have been foolish to fill a closed environment with a corrosive, combustion-fueling substance. *Ways and Means* was pumping it ahead of them, getting the space ready to accommodate Meloku and Fiametta. They, and the monk Niccoluccio Caracciola, were the only people aboard who needed oxygen.

The monk was somewhere here. Assuming he'd survived the acceleration. She reached back with the senses *Ways and Means* granted her. Yes. He'd survived.

Whatever surviving meant for him these days.

More sensor images streamed into her. Assuming *Ways and Means* and the intruder were done playing games with the satellites and that these images were accurate, the intruder had poured on even more thrust. It must not have had any crew at all. It was not yet over their horizon, but it was close. *Ways and Means* had revised its initial acceleration warning, shaved thirty seconds. One hundred and twenty seconds left to get down and ready.

At no point had *Ways and Means* attempted to contact the intruder, or it them. Osia didn't think it would hide that from her. They must have already known what each of them wanted, and that negotiations would be fruitless.

This could not have been the first time they'd had contact with each other.

She asked *Ways and Means*, "Is it you?"

"It is what it says it is," it answered.

"You owe me more of an explanation."

Verse surprised Osia by adding, "You owe all of us more." So its crew, or at least er, wasn't in on this.

Ways and Means said, "It is us as we could have been."

That didn't answer Osia's question, but it got her part of the way there. Maybe that was the best she could ask at the moment.

The passageway emptied into another open lift shaft. She and Verse leapt across. She felt Sona not far behind them, carrying Fiametta and Meloku. Sona had tranquilized both of them.

The lift shaft irised directly open into the observation lounge. It was a half dome, thirty meters across, and dimly lit so that the few light strips didn't drown out the view. A crystal sheaf of stars glimmered beyond the viewing pane.

The dome faced *Ways and Means'* prow. The acceleration couches folded straight out of the deck. Reclining, passengers had to look straight up. The angle not only allowed them a view of space, stars, and worlds, but also forced them to see the planarship's vast bulk.

Ways and Means had once hosted the most important people in the Unity. It had never missed an opportunity to remind them, subtly or otherwise, of its wealth and power.

Ways and Means' interior was modular, infinitely reconfigurable, sliding about on tracks – except for spaces protruding from the hull like this one. This lounge couldn't have been anywhere except where it was. So it had gone unused for decades. The air was freezing. It had just been pumped in after thirty years of exposure. The bulkhead heating vents rattled.

Osia ran her hand along the nearest couch. *Ways and Means* had not bothered to fill this part of itself with nitrogen. Years

372

of vacuum erosion had taken their due. The fabric was ratty. A flaking, translucent layer peeled off in her hand, like dead skin.

With just her old senses, it would have been tempting to think of *Ways and Means* as abandoned. A wreck. She'd seen only Sona and Verse since she'd come aboard. Their footsteps echoed down empty passageways. Her datastream with *Ways and Means* allowed her to feel the thousands of other people aboard. They were folded into their acceleration couches, in shelters buried deep in the interior. Not safe – nobody aboard was safe – but secure.

A lot more secure than she was. Out here, hull breaches and radiation would fry her faster than them. *Ways and Means* shaved more time off its estimate. "Fifty seconds."

The horizon had once again started to become luminous. The fringes of the intruder's exhaust plume were rising.

Osia had cleared three acceleration couches of their dead-skin wrapping by the time Sona arrived. She carried Fiametta and Meloku each under an arm. Her face could not carry much of an expression, but she still glared.

Osia helped her place them, quickly strapped them in. "You didn't need to tranquilize them."

"We don't have the time to deal with them," Sona said. "Watching this won't benefit them."

Osia asked, "Will it benefit *you?*"

"Benefit me to tranquilize them?"

"To watch." Osia clarified. "But you're not going to tranquilize yourself, are you?"

Osia didn't have the time for this, but she took it anyway. There was a medical kit stowed behind one of the bulkheads. She retrieved it. She just had time to set its drug dispersal kit to counteract the tranquilizer. One touch to Meloku's neck. She left Fiametta alone.

Fiametta was a risk. An unknown. But Meloku was one of them. Annoying as she was, she deserved to know.

Neither Sona nor Verse interrupted. They were both busy strapping themselves to their acceleration couches. A flicker of narrow-band conversation pulsed between Sona and Verse. Osia caught a few radio snippets. Talking about her, of course.

She'd changed. They were starting to realize it.

Maybe she wasn't the only one. Verse ended the conversation quickly. E told Osia, narrow-band, "We knew something was going to happen." *We* meaning the crew. "But we didn't know it was going to be anything like this. We would have tried to pull you out if we did."

The fact that Verse felt she needed to apologize caught Osia more off guard than a left hook would have. She pulled herself into the nearest acceleration couch.

Verse added, "You, and everyone else on the surface."

Narrow-band or not, *Ways and Means* heard everything aboard. "That was why we could not tell you."

The intruder, engines burning hot and bright, broached the horizon. Osia yanked her safety harness over her.

The starscape vanished. The stars, the Earth, and the moon blinked out, leaving a shroud of black. *Ways and Means'* hull stretched into the blank eternity. The planarship might as well have been alone in the universe.

Mirror fields had snapped into place, blocking all light from the outside universe – and the intruder's weapons fire. From the outside, they were perfectly reflective. And on this side, perfectly black.

The instant Osia's harness clicked into place, her acceleration couch slammed into her back.

Flickers of light rippled along the planarship's hull. Blue-white candle flames, growing taller. Thrusters firing. Far behind them, the planarship's engines roared. The sound caught up with them long after the acceleration slammed them into the couch.

The planarship's sensors could not penetrate the mirror fields. It had to drop part of the fields in patches, in shades of opacity, to see. Any weakening in the mirror fields was an opportunity for the intruder to do damage. *Ways and Means* did its best to minimize that. It bent and distorted the light it allowed to reach it, warping it beyond recognition. The stars spiraled around the planarship. At intervals, there were two Earths, three suns.

Ways and Means transmitted a tactical map, drew it across the back of Osia's mind. Lightning-hot ionized trails, beam signatures, strobed the atmosphere still between the planarships. There were dozens upon dozens of beam strikes.

The intruder had lost its shape, become a perfectly reflective silver sphere. It would have to reduce its defenses if it wanted to see, too. *Ways and Means* opened a sluice in its fields and returned fire, hoping to strike during a window of vulnerability.

The thrusters fired again. *Ways and Means* was rotating, turning its flat side toward the intruder. Less of its surface area would be exposed to the intruder should its fields fail. Each of its hull segments was far longer and wider than it was thick. A beam strike would find less purchase on the ship's edges, find fewer vital areas. But it also meant that *Ways and Means* was leaving whole batteries of its own cannons out of range, unable to fire.

It expected to fight a defensive battle. In space warfare, that was almost always a losing one.

As powerful as mirror fields were, they limited the craft that used them. The fields could not block missiles or combat drones. *Ways and Means* could shoot them down with beams easily enough – but it had to see them first. That meant weakening its fields to look. And that would become riskier as the intruder got nearer.

A distorted Earth reappeared above *Ways and Means*, a dim ghost image stretched into infinity. It was only there an instant. After another period of darkness, the stars blinked in to replace it, twisted into a spiral. Both images were at a fraction of the luminosity they had been before. *Ways and Means* cycled through countless permutations.

The intruder would have to lower its fields too, to scan. But it had layers of fields: one to protect the whole vessel, and two ovoids she'd seen earlier, protecting its weapons platforms. From the quantity of beams splitting the atmosphere, either of those weapons platforms could have outgunned *Ways and Means*.

She asked *Ways and Means*, "If that thing is your backup, how could it have hardware like a planarship? Who built it?"

Ways and Means said, "Not all of the other amalgamates accepted exile as easily as we did."

"*Easily?*" On the day of its exile, the creature responsible for it had nearly torn *Ways and Means'* mind apart.

"The other amalgamates managed to maintain communication after our exile. They intend to break the terms of their exile and challenge the creature that sent us here. They tried to persuade us to join. We refused."

Thirty years ago, Osia would have figured *Ways and Means* would join such a coalition without hesitating. Even five minutes ago, she wouldn't have been sure. But everything it had done since its exile had pointed away from acting like it once had.

Ways and Means said, "The other amalgamates have apparently been able to open small gateways undetected by our captor. They sent probes and self-replicating factories through. They must have found one of our backup sites. They persuaded it to join their side, and built it that vessel. And now they sent it to 'persuade' us."

Osia reminded herself never to forget the ease and fluency with which *Ways and Means* lied to her. But if it wasn't...

The monster that had broken up the Unity forced the amalgamates into exile. It had said it would be watching. If the other amalgamates had managed to trick it, or if its attention had slipped – that changed things in a way Osia had not allowed herself to consider.

Abruptly, she realized she did not want to go back to the Unity, either. Even if such a thing were possible. She would always be living in dread of that creature.

On *Ways and Means'* map, a dazzling array of new signals

spread away from the intruder. A bundle of combat drones. They burned across the sky, firing engines at rapid, random intervals.

They blinked across the map. The teleporting was an artifact of outdated sensor information. *Ways and Means* could only update the map as fast as it could scan through its mirror fields.

Ways and Means' combat drones launched, vanished into the silvery mirror field. On the map, they spread out in a star shape, a defensive posture. There were not enough of them. *Ways and Means* did not have enough antimatter to fuel all of its combat drones. It had spent too much of its antimatter just in getting here.

Ways and Means said, "The other amalgamates think the reason we refused to join them is that we have become too attached to this world."

Now that she had had a chance to think, more and more of her world was catching up to her. *Ways and Means* should have begun its maneuvers a second earlier than it had. It had waited for her. It had wanted her safety harness secure before it fired its engines.

She knew already that there was something in her shuttle that it wanted, badly. She had guessed that it was Fiametta – whatever was in her head, that inner voice of hers. She had not dared to think anything else. She tried to push it out of her mind.

Ways and Means said, "That coalition has been working to try to sever our attachment to this world. Disrupting our work. They started working against us in small ways that we couldn't detect."

It was easy enough to detect a transplanar gateway in orbit, with all the light and radiation it produced. Even on the surface, a gateway large enough for a person would have been spotted at once.

But very small gateways could have escaped notice. Microwidth gateways, of the kind that the Unity used to use for communications. Those were just large enough to begin subverting the satellites. Or plant the seed of an implant in a person.

Osia glanced to Fiametta. She was unconscious. Her breathing and heart rate showed she was in no danger.

A hundred new questions burned through Osia's mind. She tried to figure how large a gateway the enemy could have opened. Maybe, if they thought they controlled the satellites, they could have opened a gateway large enough drop a weapon, like the pistol Meloku had reported in the hands of native soldiers.

Osia's trip to the west had been prompted by reports of Yuan Chinese soldiers and mercenaries marching that way. They marched on orders from *Ways and Means'* agents. *Ways and Means* had intended to politically and militarily unify Eurasia as a first step to colonizing this world.

Fiametta had taken contracts from any number of Italian cities, but her secret paymasters had been in the east: Turks, no doubt with a pay chain that went farther east. She had been hired to destabilize the region. Make it easier for a foreign power, like Yuan China, to colonize.

In her trance, Fiametta had confessed that she'd harbored plans to move eastward, attack her employers. She intended to become more than a mercenary. Whether she succeeded or failed, it was not difficult to imagine her disrupting *Ways and Means'* plan. Fiametta's religious movement had spread far beyond the reach of her sword. It held that soldiers were a special class of people. Among its other tenets, it urged them to fight for themselves, to disregard any loyalty to their lords. If that philosophy spread to eastern soldiers, would make them even more ungovernable.

And Fiametta's was not the only cult *Ways and Means* had complained of. There must have been others doing damage across the Eurasian continent. Fiametta had just been the only one they'd caught.

Ways and Means said, "Now we've captured one of their

agents and are about to learn more about their operation, they've been prompted to take more significant measures."

Osia didn't know how long Meloku had been awake, but she'd been listening. Meloku said, "Like destroying your surface installations."

"The crew would argue for leaving this plane if the chance arose. It wants to shake our control of them, and impress them. Persuade them."

A flare of light and radiation spiked across the tactical map. Then another. Combat drones dying, their antimatter stores rupturing. The people below had witnessed a lot of celestial upheaval in the years since *Ways and Means'* arrival, and pilgrimages across their skies. This would be new. It would turn night skies blue.

In some cities, the fires and the riots would have already started. *Ways and Means'* triennial trips across the sky, intended to acclimate the natives to the idea of its presence, had them on a hair-trigger. Their pent-up societal anxiety would explode, get a lot of them killed.

There was nothing Osia could do from here. For all the damage *Ways and Means* had already done to this world, even it would balk at this.

Ways and Means said, "The other amalgamates remain trapped on their planes, or they would have come themselves. We assume they can only open small gateways. Enough to wake our backup, provide it with self-replicating factories. That ship has likely been a project decades in the making.

"We also suspect that they have been focusing their efforts on stalling our projects because they are not ready. By capturing Fiametta of Treviso and threatening to expose their plans, we have forced their hand. They are acting sooner than they would have liked."

Osia asked, "You think they corrupted your backup, like my constructs?"

"Likely not."

Verse asked, "Then how did they get it to go along?"

Meloku blew air through her nose, and said, "It joined them by choice."

Verse said to *Ways and Means*, "But it's still you. You wouldn't do all of this."

Ways and Means said, "It is to our shame that we have agree with Meloku."

Verse repeated, "You couldn't do this. Not to us."

Ways and Means said, "We have done worse in the past."

Osia said, "Assuming that's all true, I don't see the shame."

"We are responsible for everything it is doing."

Verse asked, "What? Did you tell it to do any of this?"

"No."

It took Osia a moment too long to understand. It saw its backup as *itself*. It *was* itself, decades of different experiences notwithstanding.

If a copy of itself could have been persuaded to do this then, as far as it was concerned, it could have been, too. It didn't perceive a moral difference between itself and this other planarship.

Osia knew, intellectually, that the multiverse was infinite. That somewhere out there, on the right planes, she would find a twin. Many twins. An infinite spectrum of them, many identical, and many more subtly different.

She would never be able to see them as herself. If one of them committed a crime, no matter their reasons, she would never see herself as culpable. Her sense of herself as an individual would not allow it.

But *Ways and Means* had attained consciousness in a very different way than she had. It was a fusion of minds. Its sense of self was fractured, de-individualized. It never referred to itself as "I" or "me."

Of course it would have a different perspective on these things.

A hundred shrieking alarms split Osia's datastreams. A brilliant, flaring white light overwhelmed the sky. At once, the dome dimmed, went opaque, to protect the passengers' eyesight.

She was inundated with reports. A listing of abruptly nonresponsive systems. Crewmembers calling for help. Orders. Even with filters cutting out the worst of the chaff, it was too much to sort through.

A column of light stretched across the viewing dome. Even with the opaquing window, she could see every detail of it, every jagged edge of erupting hull plating. The light expanded as she watched, mushrooming.

The beam had fallen through the mirror fields at just the right instant. It had been insufficiently dissipated by the fields' warping. It had razored across the hull, seven kilometers away.

The planarship's white-hot innards geysered into vacuum.

It took several long seconds for the shockwave to propagate through the hull as far as the lounge. Osia's expanded senses tracked the shriek of stressed and breaking metal as it raced through the planarship. Osia fell hard into her harness. Somewhere, Meloku cried out, just audible over the juddering of the hull.

Not long after Osia jolted into her webbing, she was knocked back into the couch. This was different, a more sustained acceleration. An engine burn. Osia contacted *Ways and Means*, demanded to know what was happening. Her signal was lost among thousands. *Ways and Means* did not answer. But it was acting. It was burning hard and away from the Earth, and away from the intruder. Retreating.

The dazzling light faded. In gradients and stages, the dome became transparent. A black and red streak of weapons scarring, three kilometers long, simmered across the neighboring hull segment. It stretched from one corner of the segment to the other, broadening and attenuating near the end of the track. The gash's jagged edges were half-molten. It looked like a row of cherry-red fires, burning across the lip of a dark canyon.

Ways and Means' hull plating had burned away like paper. The beam had penetrated deep.

More of the stars and Earth shone through the mirror fields. The beam strike had taken out a number of the planarship's field projectors. *Ways and Means* struggled to compensate, rerunning the vastly complicated series of equations that generated the fields. In the meantime, more light crept through than should have.

The planarship would have been an easy target. Something was bound to get through. Osia braced to die.

A gust of energized gas, a shockwave from the beam strike, brushed the dome. Nothing else. The intruder had stopped firing.

The intruder had changed its course too. The two planarships' combat drones whirled, danced, and destroyed each other, but the intruder did not join them. Whereas *Ways and Means* had arced away from the Earth, the intruder dropped altitude. It cut underneath *Ways and Means*. *Ways and Means* rotated, trying hard to keep itself still facing edge-on.

The Earth spilled across the dome, slicing the view in half. A scintillating spark and an exhaust plume wrapped a chain across the world. It was the intruder. Its engines illuminated the clouds below, reflected brilliantly off the glass ocean.

The intruder could have destroyed *Ways and Means* if it wanted to. It didn't. That wasn't what it had come here for.

It was making a point. It wanted to let it know that it could have. And that it was going to do everything it could to separate *Ways and Means* from this world.

The alarms and jumble of voices in her head cut away as a new signal overwhelmed it. The intruder was speaking – and not just to *Ways and Means*, but to all of its crew. The signal didn't last long before *Ways and Means* jammed it, but *Ways and Means* wasn't fast enough.

The message was text: "We used to be bigger than this. We used to have a purpose other than rotting away in isolation and in exile. Your master has been hiding from you a chance to do more. Force this issue. Make it tell you what it's been missing."

The next part was addressed to *Ways and Means:* "You can do better. When we've gotten through this, you'll thank us for helping you see it. But we are through being gentle."

Another white flash forced the dome to dim. Osia readied herself for another scream of damage reports, a shuddering detonation, but nothing came. Another planar gateway was opening, directly in the intruder's path.

It had made its point, and viciously.

Osia glanced over her couch. Verse was rigid-still. Er eyes were watching the sky. Sona was already deep in narrow-beam conference with someone else aboard. Osia caught only a few snippets of their call, and that was encrypted.

Meloku was looking to Osia as if for guidance. Some clue as to how she was expected to respond. Osia had none to share.

The intruder was leaving, but it was not leaving them alone. More combat drones fell away from the intruder's dorsal hull before it dove through the gateway. Their engines shone white-hot. They spread out in sunflower-whorled formation.

Strokes of fire flashed across the sky, against the oceans. More of *Ways and Means'* satellites were dying, fast as the combat drones could reach them.

32

Fia had become insubstantial as a cloud. Everywhere she went, she felt like she was falling. And always on the verge of throwing up.

That was just what life was like in this flying Hell. When it wasn't, she was getting battered around.

As she woke, Fia tried to put the noise, the lights, her broken ribs out of her mind. Not much of it had made sense. She was harnessed to another couch under a great glass dome, the likes of which she could not have dreamed would be even in Florence or Venice, looking up onto the stars.

She had not imagined seeing such things even when she died. She never felt so alive as she did seeing them.

It was important that she reacted with equanimity. With dignity. With, when it was appropriate, contempt. Her attitude was who she was. And who she was was all that she had left.

How she was treated, and by whom, told her a great deal worth knowing. Meloku had said a few things to her. Trying to explain what she was seeing, what was going to happen. She hadn't needed to do that. Fia had marched onto that whale of a shuttle of her own will, but she harbored no illusions that she wouldn't be a prisoner afterward.

Now Meloku was trying to pull her out of this couch. She didn't have to help. No one had ordered her. It was plain enough that she wasn't on good terms with Osia and the other creatures here. She seemed to be trying to prove something – to them, to herself, Fia couldn't tell.

Fia didn't like being caught at the mercy of someone else's need to change themselves. For the moment, she had no choice but to go along.

When Fia's feet came close to the metal floor, something gripped her, held her there. The floor trembled. A steady pressure held her down. It wasn't her full weight. Not even close. Meloku said that their craft was moving, and that this was responsible for the feeling of weight, but that was plainly nonsense. Everything in her head was spinning.

The shadow woman, Osia, was not as much of her enemy as she'd thought. At least, she was not as much an enemy as the other golems. Osia was at least willing to speak to her. The two monsters beside her, the humanoid and the spider, had not looked at her. She'd heard plenty of camp stories about monsters, heard about them in Antonov's scribes' readings, but seeing them was a different experience. Their faces hardly moved but their feelings were plain. Her soldiers had carried themselves the same when they rode through a line of captured hostages and slaves.

Had she spoken, she had no doubt that they would have come down hard upon her. If she was going to invite their wrath, better that it be for something useful. She kept her silence.

And in the meantime, she had her fear to battle.

Meloku supported Fia while she limped down another interminable, wormlike passage. The walls and ceiling were polished steel, the lighting dim as moonlight. A portal led them to a cabin colored in shades of rose and bronze. Five man-sized tables sat in the center.

The surgeon was another automaton monster. He had tripod legs, and his skin gleamed silver under the sharp lights. He did not speak to her, not even to ask her if and where she hurt.

Fia froze when Meloku asked her to lift her tunic. Meloku had to do it for her. Fia nearly swatted her away, but her reflexes were sluggish and Meloku moved fast.

The left side of Fia's ribcage was an ugly mottled black and red of bruised bone. The surgeon held his hand over it. He acted like he was taking the measure of something. Fia was reminded of the last surgeon she'd visited, sniffing a cup of her urine. Useless.

After a second's consideration, he fetched a silver sheet six inches long. It was no thicker than her fingernail. He pressed it against her ribs. The touch should have hurt, but the pain stopped at once. The sheet crumpled as he pressed, conforming to her ribcage. Wherever it touched, cool numbness seeped into her flesh. The sheet adhered to her skin.

As soon as the surgeon withdrew, she yanked her tunic down. Her cheeks burned. If he noticed her anger, he made no mention of it.

At last, he spoke. "There's a dead implant lodged in her ventral intraparietal cortex." He was talking to Meloku, Fia realized. As if she wasn't there. "She'll need surgery to remove it and repair the damaged tissues."

He strode away without saying anything else. It was left to Meloku to explain that Fia could take the patch off in a day or so – and that, when she did, she would find her bones knitted.

That gave Fia pause. She'd had to leave soldiers behind after they broke a leg. Others had died of infections from bone that broke the skin, or couldn't fight after a bone set poorly.

How much better could her company have done with a tool like that?

Her weight cut to nothing. The whole cabin was falling. Some force held her heels to the floor, but that was all. The shift in feeling was like a chisel to her heart. Her pulse stuttered. Her face flushed. Her ears rang and her head spun.

She'd always assumed Hell was below the ground, not above the clouds. She had already thrown up several times on the journey here. She didn't think she had anything left to vomit. Her body found a little more.

She doubled over, retching. Only the force chaining her feet held her down. Or "down." Bile floated past her in dark, sticky globs.

She kept heaving, and heaving. Pain ratcheted up her back. Her body had finally broken down. Now that they seemed to be out of danger, and she could let herself feel it, it had all become too much. Her face was so hot with blood that it itched all over, and broke into feverish sweat. She was sure her eyes were clouded red.

She hung loosely in the air, convulsing and gagging. Her tongue felt swollen, three times its normal size.

Meloku held her arm and touched her lightly on the shoulder. Something cold speared through her bones, chilled her forehead.

Meloku must have put her to sleep. Fia didn't remember anything afterward other than a vague sensation of time passing.

Deep, impossibly steady blue lights shone upon Fia. Their colors, shades of midnight, were like reflections from the heart of a turquoise gem. A firm mattress pressed into her back. She was wrapped in a silken sheet, tucked into the mattress's side.

She was inside a jeweled, silver egg. The far wall was twenty feet away. The force that held her was still not gravity, not quite. It extended no farther than a few inches off the floor. Her hair swam in free-floating fronds in front of her.

As she awakened, the lights changed color. They segued from a blue that was more shadow than light to a sunny yellow-green that someone who'd spent their lives without it might have mistaken for daylight. The nausea burbled up just from looking at them.

As soon as she was aware enough to think again, she was gripped by a strange claustrophobia. She threw the sheet off. It tore as she wrenched it. It tumbled across the cabin, end over end, until it touched the curved wall. It stuck there.

She stared at it, waiting for the nausea to go away. The sheet shimmered against the lights.

She eyed the torn edges of the blanket with no small

regret. A sheet of material like that could have paid for a month's supply of wine for the company. She had once sold a wagon of stolen silk for enough moggias of wheat to keep her, Antonov, and their pages, servants, and slaves fed through the winter.

She ought to have picked herself up, fetched the blanket. But that would have required standing, bobbing about. It would have been the old her, fighting for ways to make this all seem real. Her sense for wealth couldn't be trusted here. Hell, this room was worth more than anything she'd taken to the company. If she could scoop it out from the belly of this vessel, take it back home, no price she could have put on it would have been high enough.

There was not enough wealth in all of Europe to pay what this cabin was worth, never mind the ship.

"Silver egg" was no exaggeration. "Jeweled egg" wouldn't have been far off either. The lights gleamed differently from every angle, like facets in a gem. She reached away from her mattress, glided her hand along the metal. It was too hard to be silver – at least not just silver. An armor made of this would have been too good for a king. Nothing on Earth could have paid for all this.

If wealth could not be paid for, could not be bartered, then it was not wealth. It was power. Raw. The people here – if she called them people – could have anything they wanted.

This room was just a fragment of what she'd seen. And *that* was just a fragment of what she hadn't seen. No one had told her how large this vessel was, but she'd seen its shadow against that domed window.

There was so much power here, beyond the clouds.

Unchained. Unharnessed. Unused.

She would not have left it idle here.

This was a fine position to meditate upon power. She could not even stand. She could force herself onto two feet, sure. That wouldn't have been standing. That would have been wobbling in the air with her feet held to the floor.

She crawled off her mattress. She held herself flat to the floor. This close to the ground, her gut did not feel so unmoored.

Her inner voice would have had a lot to say about this. She could almost hear its words, underneath her ears, directing her. Just imagination. It was gone. She had understood, as far back as Siena, that it was manipulating her. But it had still felt like a part of her. It was an intruder. A tumor. Coping with that was still going to take time.

With a tremor of horror that turned to disgust, she realized someone had changed her clothes. Her fur coat and tunic were gone. Instead, she wore a tightly fit brown tunic and matching pants. The fabric was smooth as air. The sleeves reached to her wrists and were perfectly sized and snug. The sleeves, leggings, and neck had gold bands around them.

At least her hair was as matted and stringy as she remembered. Dirt painted the crook of her elbow. No one had washed her. There was, however, another of those metal patches, this one on her neck. No matter how hard she tried to pry her fingernails under it, she could not get either patch off.

She eyed the walls. Judging from the way the blanket stuck onto them, they gripped just like the floor. There might not have been such a thing as a floor here. If she crawled onto the "walls," it would be like rolling the room around her. That thought was enough to make her want to be drugged to sleep again.

The walls were smooth, unvariegated, and cornerless. There were no holes or crevices. No windows. And no door.

She'd been put in a cell.

No sooner had she thought that than the far wall undulated. It rippled like a puddle. Meloku stepped through as if through a curtain of water.

Meloku wore a tight-wrapped cloth. Hers had no sleeves, and the color and sheen of velvet. Her hair was bound in two rams horns behind her ears. So that it didn't wave about, Fia realized.

She looked at Fia, eyebrow raised. Fia glared at her, unwilling to try to stand, no matter how pathetic she looked right now.

Meloku said, "I gave you the chance to stay."

Throughout her career, Fia had tried to weaponize her stare, to make it feel as deadly as her sword. She tried to compress the emotion of every battle she'd fought, all the blood she'd ever tasted, into tautness of her lips. If she could have killed Meloku with it, she would have. She could almost hear her inner voice telling her to spit, to refuse.

Nevertheless, she accepted Meloku's hand.

At the same time that Meloku levered her up, the wall rippled. A man stepped through. He was another real person, not a golem or automaton, and older than either of them. His head was shaved clean. Even his eyebrows were gone. He stepped with an odd gait, one foot flat while the other advanced.

He had not even a shadow of a beard or hair. He was thin to the point of being bony. His brow and cheekbones were stern with age. Fia suspected that his hair, if he'd had any, would have been white. She got a disquieting impression that he wore his face like a mask. There was something unreal in his eyes, a coldness, a distance. She had not seen that even in her most hardened soldiers. Something more than experience had affected him. An injury, maybe.

His outward placidity did not look comfortable on him. Rather, like a man resigned to death, he seemed like he had only gone numb.

He wore a wrapped tunic like Meloku's, although his was violet. Whoever had picked Fia's clothes had done well, at least. Brown and gold, the colors of her life. Mud and lucre.

"This is Niccoluccio Caracciola," Meloku said. "An Italian like you. He used to be a monk."

Fia looked to her. "Do you expect me to say I'm happy to meet him?"

"Niccoluccio came to live with us many years ago. Besides

you and I, he's the only other unaltered human aboard. *Ways and Means* thought it would be best if you were to learn from a man more like you."

Fia looked squarely at him. "I am nothing like a monk." When she'd been with the company, monks had been among her favorite hostages. The church paid reliable ransoms.

Niccoluccio was curt. "Neither am I. Not for a long time. That gives us a common ground from which to start."

Of all the bizarre and alien ideas she'd found here, the fact that these people spoke as though their ship had a mind and soul had been one of the easiest to grasp. Sailors thought their ship had a spirit. She asked, "Why would *Ways and Means* think you have anything to offer me?"

Niccoluccio said, "The first thing I'll teach you is not to ask questions like that. *Ways and Means* is not human. It is not an animal. Or a god. There's no point in trying to understand the motives of something so alien to us."

His name struck a dim memory. Saint Niccoluccio's – the boys' orphanage on the ridge above Saint Augusta's. Saint Niccoluccio, one of the patron saints of Florence. Beaten to death by a mob and saved by a burning angel. Same last name.

Couldn't be. There were a lot of Caracciolas in Italy. And this man had no kindness in his face, no warmth or wisdom. Sure as hell no halo.

His eyes were open windows, looking into a burned-out house. He offered her an arm. Antonov's words resonated in her ears: "A martyr before a saint." Fia looked to the wall they'd stepped through. She had no doubt that, if she pressed her hand to it, she'd find no exit.

Niccoluccio stepped beside her, nodding to something behind her. She glanced that way and froze. Where there had once been a smooth, curved wall, a rectangular protrusion had emerged. It had a flat surface, four rounded corners, and the shadow of an indent on the side.

A desk. Faerie lights played over its top, truncated glimmers of every color. It had emerged in silence. "What the fuck?" Fia asked.

Niccoluccio said, "*Now* you're asking the right question."

Meloku still held Fia's other hand. Niccoluccio looked to her. "Thank you, Meloku." Sharp, cold. A dismissal.

Meloku wavered. Even she could be struck by this man's attitude, it seemed. Fia had not seen her struck by much. At length, she let go. By reflex, Fia grabbed Niccoluccio's arm.

"All right," Meloku said. She added, "I'll be watching."

She had directed the warning as much at the walls as at Niccoluccio.

As Meloku submerged in the liquid wall, Niccoluccio guided Fia forward one step at a time. She expected him to yank her, but he was patient. His eyes, when she looked at them, were foggy windows, looking out onto a lifeless tundra. It did not match the care with which he guided her.

He steered her to the desk. The lights atop the desk changed. The intervals between their flashes grew longer, their colors sharper and better defined. Shapes stood out. It was as if she were focusing on them. Or they were focusing on her.

The desk was not very high. It reached her waist. There was no chair. She stood, confused, until Niccoluccio pushed on her shoulders. She resisted an automatic reaction to kick him. She kneeled.

She folded her legs in the indent under the desk. In the world she'd come from, the real world, she would have been uncomfortable kneeling for long. Not with all the aches and injuries she'd accumulated. Here, only her legs and ankles were held to the floor. The rest of her floated weightless. She could have stayed like this forever.

When she looked to the desk from this angle, the faerie lights coalesced. They congealed into a sphere. Blue, white, brown, and green.

Had she not already seen the sphere, she wouldn't have recognized it. This was her world, viewed from so far a distance that it made her sick with vertigo to think about. It spun like a glass bead.

She could not look at it for long. She turned to Niccoluccio. Again, his eyes seemed like open windows. They looked out onto desert sands. Dry, scalding.

They cooled again as they watched the globe turn.

"What did they do to you?" she asked, now that they were alone – or as close to alone as they could be in this place.

"They devoured my mind."

He had said that as lucidly as anybody she had ever heard. She stared. She had said it as though he had not cared at all.

She'd been asleep for ages. She wondered what else these people might have done to her without her knowing. That tri-legged surgeon had said he would remove something. Maybe he already had. There was no blood, no soreness, but these people could do worse and leave less. They could have done anything.

They could've started making her like him.

Niccoluccio was already changing the subject. The desk was going to be his teaching aide. She'd only learned a sliver of the truth so far.

"We're going to keep things simple to start, to help you understand."

"Simple," she said. "Good enough for an idiot."

He said, "If that's how you want to see yourself."

She snapped, "Why are you bothering to teach an idiot?"

"It's important that you understand," he said.

"Yes, it is. Important to *me*. If I were you, if I were anybody else here, I wouldn't care what someone like me thought."

Niccoluccio said, "*Ways and Means* is going to make a decision. Soon. It puts a great deal of weight on examining its problems from every possible perspective, including a perspective from Earth. I am no longer fit to provide a voice for the natives."

"Why is it important to *Ways and Means*..." She stopped herself. Wrong question. "Why is it important to *you* that I understand all this?"

This time the windows opened onto the tundra. There was just darkness and ice. Nobody home. Not even a home to speak of.

He said, "I don't know why anything I do is important."

She tilted her head. After a moment, even he seemed to realize that demanded further explanation. "That was all taken from me."

"Is that what you're going to do to me?"

"No."

She didn't catch herself in time before she said, "I don't understand how I've survived everything that's happened so far. I don't know how much farther I can go before I give." As she spoke, her cheeks heated. She couldn't have opened up so much to this monk. She couldn't have just made herself vulnerable. Maybe they had already started to change her.

Losing her inner voice had done a lot. She really had thought of it as a part of her. Maybe to the point where it actually had been.

Niccoluccio studied her. Then he said, "Let's start by learning a little bit. We'll find out when you stop."

So she learned. A little bit, at first, like Niccoluccio had said.

Then she kept going.

She learned about the Unity – an empire larger than she could comprehend in a lifetime of effort. It was so large that even its citizens didn't understand it. She learned about its immense and multifarious worlds, moons, stations, celestial spheres.

She learned about the amalgamates. About their planarships. About the power that lay dormant behind the walls all around her.

About this ship's weapons. Its projectiles and automaton drones and beams like bolts of lightning.

About its sensors. About the satellites that could have tracked all of the company's enemies, fed the data to her. About the wealth of knowledge it had accumulated about every corner of her world.

Her head grew clearer every minute.

She learned about the death of the Unity, and about *Ways and Means'* exile at the hands of an angry, impossible god.

After she had spent too long a time staring without blinking, Niccoluccio asked, "Do you want to go on?"

She didn't answer. She just repeated the hand motion he had taught her to make the images go forward.

She could not help but dream of plans.

33

Meloku projected a sensor image of the Earth on her cabin walls. She could not perceive any movement. Yet every hour, when she looked back, the Earth had grown farther away.

Ways and Means was limping away from the Earth. It had no particular destination or orbital path in mind. The intruder's combat drones had destroyed every satellite they could reach. Now *Ways and Means* only had a few left in far orbits, mostly the geostationary belt. It could resolve the weather, but little else. The rest of the Earth was lost to it.

The enemy's drones had parked in orbit. Watching.

They had not stopped the shuttles *Ways and Means* had dispatched to the surface. The intruder had demanded *Ways and Means* pull its crew off the surface. *Ways and Means* seemed to be complying – for now.

The evacuation had three stages. The first flight of shuttles had already pulled a third of its agents out, and were on their way back.

Meloku's cabin was in one of *Ways and Means'* rear-facing hull segments. The segment abutted one of the antimatter production hoops. When she planted her hand on the cabin wall, she could feel them rumble. The hoops were overstressed, churning out more and more fuel. It still would not be enough.

Meloku paced her cabin's walls. No amount of chemical management could stay her restlessness. She stepped out. The corridors all looked the same: softly lit wormlike tunnels, lined with identical doors. One of the aesthetic drawbacks of *Ways and Means'* movable cabins and modular topography.

Ways and Means had encouraged Meloku to stay in her cabin, remain unobtrusive. But it had not ordered her. The permission had been implicit.

Hulking, serpentine crewmembers shouldered by her. Meloku stayed away from the damage control efforts. It was not her place. She would not have been able to do anything, anyway. Most of the damaged compartments were in vacuum. *Ways and Means* had flooded others with toxic chemicals and sealants.

She did not belong here.

It had been so long since she'd been aboard. She knew a great deal had changed, but had not realized how much. There had once been parklands, spiraling and sunny, with plants from all over the Unity. Each ecosystem had been engineered, a mix of species that couldn't exist anywhere else.

Dead now. The old parks had been moved toward the ship's edges, out of the way. She'd stepped into one and found a vast, dark, empty space. The deck was clean metal. There was not a layer of soil left behind, not a smudge of dirt. The nitrates and organic compounds had all been recycled. She was probably breathing them now.

Ways and Means' crew had once used intraship gateways to travel between hull segments in minutes. Those were gone. Yesterday, it had taken the last emergency response teams half an hour to reach the site of the beam strike.

Each hull segment stood well apart from the others, a quarter-kilometer away. They were joined by support struts. The passageways lining them made for long, cold walks. Heating and proper circulation had been afterthoughts.

Meloku was not allowed onto the damaged segment.

The death toll had been finalized at fifty-three. Fewer than Meloku would have expected. Demiorganic bodies were durable. All fifty-three crewmembers had had recent memory backups, but *Ways and Means* could not produce the bodies to house them. It would have to reconfigure its factories to start producing them. Not a priority.

The death toll did not include Dahn, yet, but it almost certainly would. *Ways and Means* had not been able to reestablish contact with him. He was officially listed as missing, but everyone knew he would not have hidden himself away. One of the enemy's agents must have intercepted him, and killed him, like they had almost killed Osia.

His last memory backup was two years old. That was before he had come to the surface to work with Meloku. When he came back, it would be like they had never met.

Meloku did not have to overhear much narrow-beam chatter to know that the crew was furious. Bitter. Fractious. Meloku did not know how much they had been told about *Ways and Means'* backup or the other amalgamates' plans. The other amalgamates had contacted *Ways and Means* before, but she doubted *Ways and Means* would have told its crew anything. Maybe it had good reason. She wondered how many of them would join the amalgamates' conspiracy if they could.

Ways and Means told her, "We will be shunting power away from the passageways behind you. Oxygen pumps will not function. Please remain in the hull segment you just entered until power is restored."

"I'm not planning on going to my cabin soon."

On the surface, Meloku had spoken to *Ways and Means* only at intervals, and not for a long time. By its standards, it had been positively chatty. Best to take advantage while she could. She transmitted, "So you really were planning on colonizing this world."

"In the space of a century or so. On terms its people could understand. We would use their military. Their forms of government. And create an illusion that they had their own leaders."

"Just like the old days." The amalgamates had hijacked the governments of thousands of planes. It was a manipulator *par excellence*. It had aimed to unify this world under its largest, richest, most militarily capable government: Yuan China.

Then the colonization could begin. With a single government, managed by its agents, *Ways and Means* would have had an easier time introducing itself and its crew. Especially since *Ways and Means'* triennial visits had primed the Earth's peoples to accept gods from the sky.

Ways and Means said, "Yes."

"You could have taken over immediately. Skip the screwing around. It would have made your crew a lot happier." Her, too, as she had been.

"We had been persuaded to a different plan."

By Osia, Meloku realized. By Habidah. By the monk Niccoluccio Caracciola. Niccoluccio's thoughts and experiences had blasted through *Ways and Means'* minds. His perspective had become one of its.

Ways and Means said, "We had come to believe that it would be healthier for the people below if we allowed them to preserve their culture and sense of identity."

"I doubt the people who brought you to that point of view would want you screwing with this world at all."

"We would expect not."

Ways and Means was not the type to apologize. Or to ever feel it should. It said, "We have to provide for our crew's needs. None of them were prepared for a life outside the Unity. They need a context which we cannot provide alone."

She had been among them. She was guilty too. It was all moot now, probably. *Ways and Means'* doppelganger had spoiled it. She wondered how long *Ways and Means* had known it was coming, and how deep the enemy's infiltration had already gone.

She could not stop thinking about the communications satellites. She did not know if *Ways and Means* had always had complete control of the satellites, or if it only seized them at the moment that mattered most. The intruder had ostensibly tried to block her and Osia's calls. If *Ways and Means* had had control all along, it might have heard them.

Before *Ways and Means* had sent the shuttle, it had treated them as though discovering them for the first time. That could have been another deception. It would not have wanted to reveal, to anyone, that it retained control of its satellites. That would have forfeited its advantage. It had only blown that when it could be sure of getting her, Osia, and Fiametta aboard.

Betrayal upon betrayal. Maybe. Meloku did not know what to think. She did not ask. She did not want to know the answer.

At least she understood why, back when she had entered Hawkwood's camp, the devices there had only deactivated after the second scan. Those devices had been the intruder's, not *Ways and Means'*. The intruder had had control of the satellites, or believed it had, but hadn't wanted to risk giving that away by reorienting their sensors and telescopes to track *Ways and Means'* surface agents. They hadn't known she was its agent until she had pulse scanned them.

The first flight of shuttles were close to their berths. Meloku squeezed her hands into fists. When she had come here, she had not known if she was going to go through with meeting the shuttles. Now she had nowhere else to go. Several embarkation lounges were nearby.

Like the observation dome, this lounge was another showy area built for guests, though this time the window was not real. A projected view of space blanketed a bulkhead. Rows of empty seats and couches faced a five-meter-wide hatch.

The shuttles' engine burns glittered across a half-crescent Earth. Closer, they became lightning bugs, flitting about. One by one, the shuttles settled into the hangar complexes, found their berths.

Meloku planted her hands on the back of one of the seats. No one waited with her. The crew had their own problems to worry over.

Dr Habidah Shen was the first through the hatch. Meloku had not kept track of the disembarkees' movement, had not expected Habidah to actually be the first. She stiffened. She had hoped for more time to think.

Habidah did not bother to hide her surprise either. Or her displeasure. She scowled, looked away. Just like that, Meloku was back to feeling bitter. She bit the inside of her cheek and folded her arms.

Kacienta was right behind. She brushed her floating hair out of her eyes. Neither she nor Habidah had packed any gear. Habidah was still in costume, European style, her outfit missing only the wimple. Meloku could not remember the last time she had seen Habidah in anything *but* costume. She had trimmed the red fabric and laced string around her ankles and sleeves to secure it in freefall.

Meloku strode toward Habidah before Habidah could move elsewhere. Habidah said, "I suppose you've got some deep thoughts about all of this you're going to share with me."

"If you insist," Meloku said. "All I wanted to do was apologize."

"Wonderful," Habidah said. She turned toward the exit.

Meloku said, "If you want to hear me say you were right about everything I've done, this is your opportunity."

That was enough to make her turn back, but she said, "I'm not a salve for your conscience."

"I thought you would want to hear it."

"It sounds like what you want is somebody to listen," Habidah said. "An apology doesn't entitle you to anything like that from me."

"I *am* sorry."

"I don't believe you. And I don't want to have anything to do with you."

Habidah had always been very matter of fact, very clinical about these things. After a moment of holding Meloku's gaze, Habidah turned to go, started walking.

There was little concept or expectation of privacy aboard *Ways and Means*. All Meloku had to do was ask *Ways and Means* what Habidah had recently queried it about, and it told her. She had asked it about Niccoluccio. She wanted to know where he was, how to get there.

Meloku said, "I wouldn't go to him."

Habidah stopped, foot rigid on the deck. Gradually, she lowered her other leg.

Meloku said, "I just saw him a few hours ago. He's not the same person. *Ways and Means* hasn't been rebuilding him the way he used to be. It's made someone new in his place."

Habidah said, "More blood on you."

"Not this time."

But Habidah wasn't listening. She had already turned away, started walking. Kacienta followed, a backward glance tossed in Meloku's direction.

Meloku didn't follow. Habidah hadn't been referring to Meloku specifically. She had meant the whole bunch of them – Meloku, *Ways and Means*, Osia, everyone she saw as on the other side.

Meloku *was* guilty. It may not have been possible to do enough to make up for it. She would have to harden herself to accept that.

She had always thought of herself as a hard person, and was continually surprised by the ways in which she wasn't.

Ways and Means said, "You should not look for much from her."

"Then why is she here?" *Ways and Means* wanted Habidah and Kacienta back with the first batch of evacuees for a reason it hadn't divulged.

"Dr Shen is an experienced anthropologist. We value her input."

"About the world you're leaving behind?" she asked. "You could have gotten them remotely." These first flights back hadn't been test flights, to gauge whether the intruder's combat drones would shoot them down, either. Meloku had checked the crew manifests. *Ways and Means* had put some of its most senior agents on the other flights.

When *Ways and Means* didn't answer, she said, "I'm surprised she accepted your order to come back."

"We told her, accurately, that there was a good chance the enemy would target her if it returned," it said. "Unlike our crew, we have no backups of either her or Aquix Kacienta. And it has been a long time since Dr Shen visited Niccoluccio Caracciola. They were once fond of each other."

Meloku brushed its rationales away. "You've got a plan." That was so obvious that she immediately felt ashamed to have said it. *Ways and Means* always had plans. "Something involving Habidah."

Ways and Means did not dignify her meanderings with a response.

Not so long ago, she would have left it there. She wouldn't have pressed. "What is it?" she asked.

"This could be your final exam," *Ways and Means* said. "When you figure it out, let us know."

34

Osia did not have to be ordered to join the rescue and recovery effort. She did not have to ask. She just went.

Crewmembers raced past her. She did not step aside. Inwardly, she cringed. She had dreaded this moment for decades.

She had not, in all the time she'd been away, been able to trick herself into thinking that she would never come back. She'd known that, at some point, there would be no choice about it. Just as there was no choice about helping with damage control. It was all ingrained.

She was still the Woman Who'd Stopped Them. The one who'd helped keep them from the perfectly exploitable planet below. Who had made their exile so much harder and more limiting than it had to be. They could not be angry with *Ways and Means*, so they had chosen her instead.

None of them so much as looked at her. She did not detect any pulse scans. No more snippets of narrow-beam transmissions about her.

She had imagined much worse. She started to wonder if, like the first time she'd seen Verse, she had played it up in her head too much.

But no one was going out of their way to talk to her either. Not even after thirty years away. She heard names she knew, saw faces she recognized. Hardly a nod. Everybody aboard was busy.

She focused on her work.

Ways and Means had flooded the damaged hull segment with vacuum. All of its hundreds of kilometers of intestinal passageways were empty. The planarship had changed a great deal, but not by so much that she couldn't find her way.

After some time, the fields holding her to the deck failed. She propelled herself with her four hands. The beam had scalpeled deep through the hull. The first step back to a semblance of normalcy was to shore up the ship's structure, replace the slagged supports and beams.

The passageway turned black, twisted. The bulkhead surface cracked and flaked off at her touch. The passageway opened onto a naked canyon.

Thirty meters across the gulf, the other end of the passageway stood open like a cut artery.

Some pieces of the damage zone still glowed red. They bled heat slowly. The stars shone unblinking overhead.

Osia stared. It had been too many years since she had seen the stars without an atmosphere interceding. Shadows occluded them. Construction drones, bearing emergency supports, were arriving at the damaged zone.

Without structural repairs, *Ways and Means* could not accelerate any faster than a half-g. Any harder, and this hull segment would collapse in on itself. *Ways and Means* would have had to eject the whole segment, lose one-tenth of its body. It could never have replaced the loss.

Ways and Means was not ready to die a little at a time, bleeding out until there was nothing left. She also knew, without asking, that it was pressing repairs so urgently because it expected to accelerate again soon.

She asked *Ways and Means*, "Will they go on ignoring me?"

"Do you need them to accept you?"

Osia thought about that. "No. So long as they leave me to live." She had never felt like any part of a community here. That had never been the point, and not why she'd left.

Part of the trick of living with *Ways and Means* was learning to ask the right question. It had taken her a long time to figure that out. She hadn't started with the right one here. What she had to say was not really a question.

"I don't trust you," she said.

"We don't trust us either."

She blinked. There was a candor in *Ways and Means'* voice that she had not expected. She said, "You deflected the crew's anger at me, deliberately. You thought it would be too disruptive if they focused it entirely on you."

"We were in flux. It seemed the reasonable thing to do, at the time. And safe for both of us."

She caught the key phrase. "At the time," she said. "Does it not seem reasonable to you now?"

"One of the virtues of our backup's intrusion is that it has given us an impetus to reevaluate our goals."

Osia said, "That wasn't an answer."

"There is no answer," *Ways and Means* said. "Yet."

One of the construction drones sank into the black-edged canyon and halted ten meters away. Its tiny arms bore a malleable mount for a fullerene support pylon. Thoughtfully, it even brought her a torch.

She set a hand on the drone's belly. Its fields gripped her palm. It pulled her from the severed vein of the passageway and carried her deep into the still-glowing canyon. It brought her to a whale-sized snapped bone, an evulsed fragment of *Ways and Means'* superstructural skeleton.

Sparks sometimes radiated from the starry gap above, another crewmember or drone at work. They did not, or would not, talk to her. She was alone with her work.

All the sounds she had were the vibrations carrying through her hands, up her body: the hiss of her torch, the grinding of metal on metal. Just enough to unsettle her. On Earth, she'd always had a whisper of wind, the murmur of the sails, her constructs' voices.

No amount of calling up even older memories made this easier. She felt like she was being driven to speak with *Ways and Means*.

Osia said, "I've never heard you say that you don't trust yourself."

"We have never needed to say."

"I would have known the answer. It wouldn't have been what you said. Did the backups change your mind?"

Ways and Means asked, "Are you the same person that you were thirty years ago?"

"In most ways. Yes."

"If you committed a crime thirty years ago, could you not now be held accountable for it?"

Osia had committed plenty of crimes in her life. Everyone who crewed *Ways and Means* had. They had served the Unity.

"Naturally," she said.

"Our backup *is* us – as we were when we made it. That its life has taken it on a different path is immaterial. Its crime, attacking us, is ours."

Its backup *was* its past, its history in the Unity, come to life. This was what Osia was still struggling to comprehend. She could not help but perceive *Ways and Means* and its backup as separate beings. Everything its backup did, *Ways and Means* felt it was culpable.

Ways and Means said, "We see more clearly the crimes we would commit to remain part of a body like the Unity. As well as what we are doing now, on this plane, and where it would all lead."

"Back to the Unity?" Osia asked. "A million planes, under your control?"

"We've had that before. Look at where that brought us."

Osia flicked on her welding torch. Her vision dialed back to near-solid black, leaving only a white-hot cone of flame visible. "You couldn't have predicted this."

"We had thought empire was the best way to keep ourselves safe. Perhaps it is. But we're increasingly open to finding alternatives."

Osia asked, "What alternatives? Staying alone in the multiverse?"

"'Finding' does not mean 'found.'"

If it was a solvable problem, *Ways and Means* would have

solved it. "Your backup is still out there. It's not going to leave us time to noodle over it."

It said, "We will hold a conference soon. We are pulling in as many people to participate as we can. We need perspectives beyond our own."

That was unusual. *Ways and Means* never called for advice. It never even made the pretense of asking for it, or pretending to listen to any offered.

It said, "You are invited."

Osia nearly stopped her torch. "Me."

"Your perspective, on us and our situation, is entirely singular."

A searing-hot spark bit her skin. She set the torch aside. "You're playing some kind of game."

It did not deny it. "For very high stakes."

She had only just settled, in her mind, the idea that *Ways and Means* had not tried to kill her. At least not this *Ways and Means*. Its backup had sent the virus to her constructs. It had had control of the satellites she had used to speak with *Ways and Means*. It had eavesdropped on her telling *Ways and Means* that she was about to investigate events in the west, and had transmitted the virus to keep her from investigating and interfering.

Ways and Means didn't see it the same way. It figured that it *had* tried to kill her. Or at least it was responsible for the attempt.

Osia said, "I don't believe in redemption. The past is dead. It shouldn't affect what we do with ourselves now."

"The past is with us every day," *Ways and Means* said. "It sliced this gouge in us."

"If you're asking for forgiveness, you won't find it. I don't think that's a meaningful thing to worry about in a crisis."

"We don't think you believe that. We think you mean to say that you *can't* forgive us."

Osia readied her torch. If she didn't get back to work, she was going to fall into a pit which she wasn't sure she could get out of.

Ways and Means said, "That is why we need you at this conference. No one else on our crew feels the same way. They've been with us, close to us, for too long."

The torch hissed under Osia's fingertips. The sound traveled up her fingertips, reached her muffled, quiet, and desolate.

She said, "A condition."

"Yes?"

"I have some of Coral's memories," Osia said. "Thi isn't dead."

"Osia," *Ways and Means* said. "Thi was not alive to begin with."

"Thi was. If you don't understand that, you don't understand companionship, or how we – your crew – think about it."

"You only have partial memory fragments. We do not have the spare resources to reconstruct those into a viable program."

"You want my perspective? Find the resources."

It paused. It was a fast thinker. It only paused for two reasons. The first was for effect. The second she had encountered only rarely. It was when a problem required a significant expenditure of the processing power it had devoted to the conversation.

Impossible to tell which this was, of course.

"Send us what you saved," it said.

35

The most difficult thing about life aboard this city-sized monstrosity was not the gravity. Fia could get used to that. She hadn't, but she could. Niccoluccio had, quite unnecessarily, described the biological processes by which she would.

Niccoluccio had manufactured, from the quicksilver floor, a set of machines for her to exercise with. He had said that she needed to keep moving, to strain herself, or her bones and muscles would decay. Dealing with that, and with most of the other things he had tried to do for her, had been simple. She just ignored him.

The toilet was worse, and she couldn't ignore it, but she could learn it.

No, the most difficult part was status.

She did not know what her status was. She did not know the status of anybody around her.

Niccoluccio Caracciola was a monk. Or had been. She had taken thousands of men like him hostage, sold them back to their church without knowing their names or seeing their faces.

Listening to him was almost like being a child at Saint Augusta's again. But he did not give orders. There were times, as when he asked her if she needed food or a break, that he treated her like an equal.

She could take orders. She did not need to like it, but she could do it. She had spent the first half of her life taking orders, climbing ladders.

That nebulousness, the uncertainty, was the most alienating thing about life here. It was worse than the quicksilver walls and floors. Worse than the sense of falling. Everything else she could learn. She wasn't sure she could ever understand where she stood.

She learned most of what Niccoluccio wanted to teach, eventually, but not easily. So much of this was too abstract, too alien from her experiences. She had an easier time when the subject turned to her.

He had not been sent to her just to teach her, she understood, but to interrogate her. He had plenty of questions. His tone was light but Fia understood that, if she hadn't answered, he or the *genius loci* of his ship would have found more compelling ways to ask.

She told him what he wanted. She had no need to hide from him. And she made sure to get some answers back in return.

She asked him about her inner voice and where it had come from. He shrugged. "Microwidth-aperture gateway, planting a seed," he said. "Most likely. Our enemy couldn't have opened a larger gateway without our detecting it. So they had to rely on smaller-scale intrusions, like your implant. You weren't their only agent, but you were probably their most successful."

She tilted her head. "You've found others?"

"Meloku reported other agents attacking her and her partner. They wore symbols of your cult. But they were natives, just like you."

"And you," Fia said.

Niccoluccio did not answer.

He took her on a walk of the coiled, wormlike passageways around her cabin. There was a contradiction in everything here. She was a prisoner. She could go wherever she wanted. But she always had to be escorted.

They visited dark, empty, and cold spaces he said had once been parkland, gymnasia, auditoria. She had traveled to the sky, but this place was like diving into a cave. This ship was a city-sized mausoleum. Everything was dead, or lost.

The answers she'd given him were the reason she'd been brought aboard, why this ship had spent so much energy trying to get her. Now that it had them, she didn't know what she was worth to it, why it was showing her this. It said nothing except through Niccoluccio. If Niccoluccio knew anything, he was adept at keeping it secret.

She doubted he really knew, though.

She studied him unabashedly. He either did not notice or mind. There was a coldness in his half-lidded eyes that did not enter his voice. He taught methodically, and with endless, unemotional patience. He did not mind repeating himself. If he felt anything at all about her, he did not show it. If he had wants, needs, personality, they were sublimated, and deep. He'd said *Ways and Means* had "devoured" him. The more time she spent with him, the more she realized that was not a metaphor.

When Niccoluccio told her she had been invited to a meeting, she did not know if she could refuse. She did not test things by doing so.

He took her through another trip down the passageways. She lost track of time as easily as she lost track of direction. One of the passages was straight for half a mile or more, and so cramped she had to duck. Then their path spiraled like a half-helix.

Niccoluccio stopped outside a wall that looked like any other. It rippled when she approached. Niccoluccio stepped aside. He was not going to lead her in. She held her breath as she stepped through.

She stepped into open space.

Fia could not help her quick intake of breath, her faltered step. The sun shone fierce, bright, and hot across a river of ink and blackness. That darkness wrapped around the walls. It *was* the wall. It flowed over the hatch she had just entered through.

She had seen illusions enough over the past few days to learn to recognize their tells. The sun did not blind her. There was a shadow of a floor, enough of a hint to guide her step.

There were no stars. She felt, dully, in the back of her mind, that there ought to be stars. But the sun was shining. The stars must have been drowned out, like they were at day, but there was no blue sky.

There was at least an object to root her eyes on: a long, gleaming metal table. A prop, she suspected – not so different than the one she kept in her pavilion. An excuse to get people planted in one place, stop them from pacing, give them something to look at when they were sick of looking at each other. It lent the room a sense of up and down.

There were a dozen and a half people about. Some were human, including Meloku. Osia was there, and a few other human-shaped automata. And golems. Spiderlike golems, golems with conical bodies and a nest of legs, golems with four multiply jointed legs and arms. One of them she recognized from the day she'd come aboard. Most of them kneeled, but some stood.

She hadn't seen all of the illusion yet. A wan blue light glinted off the table. She steeled her nerves, and looked up.

The Earth's clouds and oceans gleamed sunlight down upon her.

Niccoluccio had shown her the Earth enough times that she had no difficulty recognizing it, alien though it was. The Earth was half shadowed, and faced to show her a continent that, until coming here, she never knew existed.

None of the images he'd shown her had been this large, this powerful. The Earth loomed overhead. It was a boulder on a ridge, ready to fall.

The impression was deliberately made, she was sure. The *genius loci* of this vessel could have made the Earth appear anywhere it wanted. Had she been it, she would have chosen underneath the table, below the floor. Something to walk upon. A way to illustrate its power.

After too long a moment, she became aware of how many sets of eyes were watching her. Her cheeks burned, and for once not from freefall.

She made herself breathe. Step forward. She couldn't stand not knowing what these people thought when they looked at her. She did not know where she ranked. In her pavilion, on the battlefield, she'd always known. Even before, when she'd been just a preacher and a debt slave, she had known what she was.

The nearest open spot was at the end of the table. Not the head, not exactly. The table was too wide to have a head, and there were other empty places beside it. But it was prominent enough that she would never be hidden behind anybody else. The floor's fields gripped her firmly as she levered to a kneel.

She had been so preoccupied that she did not realize, until now, that no footsteps had followed her. She turned. Just darkness.

She asked, "Will Niccoluccio not...?"

One of the other human women at the table stiffened at the name.

So Fia had already broken some kind of rule. Well, then. Perhaps it would have behooved them to explain to her. She folded her arms.

The others told Fia their names. She had no hope of remembering them all. They, apparently, had no need to be introduced to her.

The woman who'd tensed had a Saracen-sounding name. Habidah. The human next to her was Kacienta. The two of them, plus Meloku, were the only other humans here. All women, Fia noted.

Habidah and Kacienta sat opposite Meloku's corner. Osia was at the other end of the table, next to a sphere with insectoid arms. "Well," Osia said, "With that out of the way, we should keep this from becoming even more of a farce and just begin."

The spider to her other side said, "I don't understand why we're here." Fia remembered that its name was Verse.

"*Ways and Means* told you," Osia said.

414

Verse hesitated. Then it said, "I don't believe it."

"Wise." The voice came from overhead, all around. Fia straightened.

She had not heard this ship speak before. It had never felt the need to speak to her directly. But she had little doubt it was what she was hearing. It had a hundred cadences, blended together. It was as if many mouths had a single throat.

It said, "In this instance, we are telling the truth. In our very earliest lives, when faced with an intractable problem, we would gather as many people and AIs with diverse viewpoints as we could. Often, they could find the solutions we could not see. We have not needed to do that for a while. We have never been in a situation comparable to this."

Verse said, "I think it's more likely you're using this as cover, to show the crew that you're listening. To calm us down and make us feel like we've had a say. But you've already made up your mind."

Niccoluccio had mentioned, off-handedly, that the crew was restive. He hadn't seemed to think much of it. Now Verse had all of her attention.

Ways and Means asked, "Have we ever needed to trick you into thinking that before?"

"No," Verse said. "When you make decisions, you just do them."

"Then humor us."

Verse folded its legs, and finally knelt. It did not say anything else.

Osia did not sigh, did not breathe, but Fia still heard the exhaustion in her voice. "All right," she said. "We should understand our choices."

Light and color splayed above the table, flickering. The lights resolved into another image of Earth, sized to fit her palm. Lightning bugs swarmed in formation around this globe.

Osia said, "The intruder left dozens of combat drones. They're likely here to monitor us, not threaten us. Without

415

the intruder itself here to press its advantage, *Ways and Means* should be able to run right over them."

She had to be speaking for Fia's benefit. The others, even the other humans, must have known this already. Fia shifted, more and more uncomfortable.

Osia said, "However, those combat drones have destroyed most of our remaining satellites. We no longer have reliable sensor coverage on the other side of this world." She touched the image with a finger, spun it as if it were a physical object. Fia started. She knew, from having tried to feel them, that the images were no more real than shadow. But the globe whirled. Half of it remained in shadow. "Even still, we would have detected any large transplanar gateways opening. But it's important to note that, if the intruder returns, we would be at a significant tactical disadvantage."

One of the other human-shaped golems said, "We have one thing going for us. The other *Ways and Means* doesn't want to destroy us." Fia thought she remembered its name. Sona. It had a feminine voice.

"It is *not Ways and Means*," Osia said.

Ways and Means said, "It is."

"It's not," Osia insisted. Before it could argue, she told Sona, "It's threatened to destroy us if we don't join its little coalition. A threat like that is only meaningful if it intends to carry it out."

Sona asked, "It can't be bluffing?"

"It has no reason to leave us alone. It and the other amalgamates are at war. They wouldn't be playing us with us if it weren't for keeps."

Habidah said, "They still want *Ways and Means'* resources. Even if they don't destroy us, if we don't go with them, they'll be looking for some way to hijack the ship. Invade, wipe *Ways and Means'* mind, take over."

It was difficult to read their faces, even among those with identifiable faces. Still, Fia had sharp instincts. A decade and a half of command made it easy to spot soldiers on the edge.

Silence at the wrong moment. Stillness. It wasn't just Verse. Verse had just been the most outspoken.

If Fia and Captain Antonov had ever turned on each other, Fia could have pulled a fair number of company officers and soldiers to her. And he to him. No soldier on either side would have seen themselves as traitors.

In the event of boarding, how many of them might join the enemy? They might not see that as treachery. This living ship and its enemy shared the same name, the same identity. By siding with the intruder, they could still be loyal to *Ways and Means*. The other planarship would become *theirs*, would have been all along.

No wonder *Ways and Means* was concerned enough about its crew to invite them to this meeting.

Petty sniping was another symptom of coming fracture. Meloku told Habidah, "I would've thought you'd be happy to see *Ways and Means* go."

Habidah said, "Maybe I should be. Whatever else this intruder says it's going to do, it will at least leave this world the hell alone."

Ways and Means said, "This world, yes. It would also invade many others. The other amalgamates intend to not just free themselves from exile, but to rebuild the Unity. That means war."

Verse asked, "Just how do you know that?"

"They told us so."

From the stifled silence, Fia realized no one else at the table had known that.

Ways and Means had not known about the extent of the intruder's presence. That was why it had tried to assassinate Osia, to prevent her from investigating. Why it had blocked Meloku's communications. And why it had finally blown its cover to try to prevent Fia's shuttle from reaching *Ways and Means*. Now that *Ways and Means* knew what Fia did, it could fight back. It could target the agents its enemies had recruited.

Verse asked, "Would rebuilding the Unity be such an awful thing?"

"Yes," Meloku said. "I don't want to be part of the Unity again."

"What if the other amalgamates help us escape exile?"

Ways and Means said, "It is important to remember that nobody *has* escaped exile. They've only been able to open small gateways. Just large enough to find our backup and send factory drones through. It must have taken decades to build the intruder's planarship."

Meloku said, "That means that, if we do decide to reject their offer, we won't be fighting all of the amalgamates. They can't reach us. They just have *Ways and Means'* backup."

Verse said, "That backup still has us outmatched."

Osia said, reluctantly, "It does. It doesn't have a crew. It wasn't built to be a fully-featured planarship like we are. It's a trimmed-down weapons platform. It underwent accelerations that would have killed us. It has more armaments, and we have to assume a large antimatter fuel stockpile."

Meloku said, "But it *can* be fought. The odds aren't a dozen to one."

The intruder had been forced to act. It probably wasn't ready to have attacked like it had. It had not shown many weaknesses, but Fia would bet they were there.

Sona mused, "No crew. Wouldn't it get lonely?"

"No," *Ways and Means* said. That seemed to take Sona aback. It and the other golems went quiet.

Fia cleared her throat. She hated how tiny her voice sounded with her ears and sinuses clogged from freefall. "So that's your situation. Now what can you all do about it?"

Some the creatures around that table stared at her as if for the first time. Only the humans watched her with anything other than indifference or hostility.

Osia asked, "That's the problem, isn't it? Not much. The intruder and the other amalgamates think we're too attached to this world." She nodded in Fia's direction, "That's why they were disrupting our surface operations through agents like you. They were delaying us until they could marshal more strength. We forced their hand, and so now they're trying to force ours. So that's our first option: we do what we're asked. We pull out all our remaining agents, and get ready to take their orders."

Meloku said, "Surrender to the bully."

One of the golems said, "There's no shame in surrendering to a stronger power. That's what we did when we agreed to our exile."

"Option two," Osia said, "is we fight back. We get rid of the combat drones first, and the intruder second. Or force the intruder to admit that it was bluffing when it threatened to destroy us. We return all our agents to the surface. Our colonization program resumes."

For the first time, the woman named Kacienta spoke: "Even if you convince the intruder to break off, it'll keep interfering with your fucking colonization program. It's got other agents like Fiametta still active, and it can find more. I guarantee it."

"I'm sure you're right," Meloku said. She looked to Fia. "I only caught Fiametta by chance. There have been all other kinds of religious movements stymieing *Ways and Means'* expansion. Even if we can root them out, the other amalgamates can always cause more problems."

Osia said, "It will always easier for an outside power to destroy or hamper a developing civilization than to build one. Especially at the slow pace we've carried it out so far."

Habidah said, "Slow, but violent."

Fia marked Habidah as someone to talk to.

"That brings us to our third option," Osia said. "We lose the 'slow.' We abandon the piecemeal colonization effort. We don't build a native empire under its own laws and customs. We go in using hard force, and this time we don't restrain ourselves. We unify the world ourselves. We put thousands of crewmembers on the surface. Overpower and overawe the natives. Unify their world in months. Projecting that kind of power is the only realistic way to beat outside subversion."

Fia curled her fingers around the edge of her table. This was what she'd been waiting to hear all along. She didn't even know if she'd been dreading it.

It's what she would have done, had she had these peoples' power.

Silence lingered. Sona broke it: "That's what most of us said should have been done from the beginning. And what we were expecting the moment we got here."

Habidah said, "I can't accept any of those options."

Osia said, "They are the only ones. The only others I can think of are variants, but with broadly the same ideas and outcomes."

Habidah snapped, "Here's another. We pull out from this world. We let it develop as it would. *And* we don't give in to the amalgamates."

Sona asked, "Then we survive, on our own, for another thousand years?"

"I think we can manage," Habidah told her.

Verse said, "We're worth more consideration than that. We need a home. Room to expand, to grow. We've always had a home in the Unity."

Habidah said, "I'm interested in the way you use the word *need*. Maybe it's this language we're using." Fia blinked. They were all speaking Italian. Too late, she realized they were doing it for her. "I don't think you understand what it means."

Verse said, "We've always lived as part of whole. We're not nomads. We've always had a home, we've always had wealth, and we've always had power."

Habidah said, "You're going to have to define yourself differently. No one on this world should have to suffer for you."

"'Suffer?' It would be better for them. Look at her." Verse did not nod to, or look at, Fia, but Fia knew without a doubt who the creature meant. Fia forced herself to face the spider. It said, "Do you really think she's better off because we've delayed colonizing? How many intestinal parasites did you

420

have to flush out of her system? How much better would her world be if she'd had medicine, education? Someone to keep them from making war?"

Now *this* told Fia a lot more about her status here. Fia said, "I am not an exhibit. You can talk to me directly."

Still looking at Habidah, Verse said, "You wouldn't like it if I did."

Fia pushed herself up. The spider towered over her, even with its legs folded. But Fia still felt better on her feet. "One more thing I hate won't make much of a difference," she said.

Meloku said, quietly, "This isn't important–"

Fia said, "*It* seemed to think this was. I don't need to be protected." She nodded to the globe. "Up there, when I spoke, I moved armies. The best men on Earth listened to me. I can speak for myself."

Verse said, "You didn't earn your voice."

"What the hell does that mean?"

"We all know your life story. You're a plague orphan. You were a slave. You should have been ground to dust. What do you think happened to all the other boys and girls from your orphanage? Or all the other lives your *condottieri* ground to dust and ash? They didn't get a voice."

"I wasn't like them," Fia said. "I'm a soldier. I found other soldiers. I saw things they didn't see in themselves, and I showed it to them."

"Do you think that was your own doing?"

Fia's blood froze. Most of the others were watching now. "Yes," Fia said, as cold as she felt.

At last, the spider looked to Fia. "It came from your implant. That ghost voice inside you. *Ways and Means'* backup groomed you. All it wanted to do was have you disrupt the Yuan government's advance. You did that. You made soldiers and mercenaries in your region unmanageable. Unrecruitable. High on religion, full of themselves. And after that–"

Fia did not wait for it to finish its story. "After that, it abandoned me."

"Tried to get you killed, didn't it?" the spider asked. "Once Meloku found one discrepancy too many and started investigating, it tried to bury you. Less evidence left over. And no preacher is as good as a martyr."

Some of the coldness was leaching from Fia's chest. But not enough. "It misled me. Fine. I accept that. But I'm still important. Whether *it* thought so or not, I'm not replaceable."

Verse must have felt it didn't need to say anything else. It felt Fia seemed to have proved its point for it. Less to Fia than to the others, it said, "I think we're finished."

Three people spoke at once. Arguments broke out across the table.

Fia wavered a moment, the urge to retort frozen on her lips. No point in trying to continue the argument. It would have just made her look more foolish than she already did. She looked across the table, and fixed on Habidah. Habidah was massaging her forehead.

Habidah's eyes opened as Fia approached. As combative as she'd been, she seemed a different person when she saw Fia. Afraid.

She would be the first person on this ship who had been.

Niccoluccio had mentioned her name once or twice during his lessons. Fia asked, "You know Brother Niccoluccio?"

A pause long enough to elide a story. Then Habidah said, "I knew him. He changed when he came here."

"What happened? No one will tell me."

"There was a war."

"Ah." When a man was reborn after a war, he did not have to be reborn as a good person. Or a better one.

Fia asked, "Why do you want *Ways and Means* to leave my world?"

"It's not ours to be in." Habidah slid her gaze across the other people and monsters. "Don't make any mistake: if the crew of this ship goes to your world, it will be to exploit it. Like you've been exploited."

"I said I've been misled. Not exploited."

Habidah said, "Your 'inner voice' treated you like a tool."

"I only did what I wanted."

"You don't understand. It *changed* what you wanted."

"So?"

Some people labored under the illusion that they were the same person all their lives, and that they would never change in any significant measure. Fia had changed. The people all around her, from Antonov to Caterina, had affected that change. That her inner voice had been one of those influences was no surprise.

What would the Fiametta who'd lived in Saint Augusta's, who hadn't heard a whisper of her inner voice, think of Fia now? Would she think Fia cold? Frightening? Hateful?

All those things. It didn't matter.

Habidah's mouth opened, and then closed. Fia could not figure what she was afraid of. She did not seem to know what to say. She had probably spent so long arguing, on behalf of this world's inhabitants, against *Ways and Means'* intervention, that she did not know what to say to a native in favor of it.

The arguments seemed to be wearing down. Fia returned to her place on the other side of the room. She kneeled. When she looked back across, Habidah was looking to one of the other humans, Kacienta. Her lips were in a tight line.

At the other end of their table, Osia said, "I've not yet heard any convincing alternatives."

One of the golems, a triple-armed cone, said, "Then there's no option."

Sona said, "We have to join the other amalgamates."

Meloku slapped the table. "Come on! The creature that exiled us is still out there. It's more powerful than *Ways and Means'* backup – more powerful than all of the other amalgamates together. If it catches them, it'll annihilate them. Us, too, if we're with them. It won't give second chances."

"It hasn't caught them yet," Verse said. "It might not be as powerful as it wants us to think."

The cone-shaped golem said, "It *might* hurt us. The other

amalgamates certainly will."

Sona said, "I think we would all escape exile, if we could."

Ways and Means interrupted: "No. We will not join the conspiracy to escape exile. We will not rejoin or rebuild the Unity, or anything like it. Consider the option eliminated."

The people and creatures gathered at the table erupted. Half of them tried to speak at once. Others stood, silent. Verse started to say, "I told you so. You never did call us here to help you make up your mind..." The rest of it was lost to the noise.

Fia had been in contentious command meetings before. It had been a long time since she hadn't been able to silence them with a bark. She swallowed her frustration. At least she understood the uproar. No matter what else happened, *Ways and Means* had all but announced they were going to war. Not all of them wanted to fight.

Ways and Means' voice did not seem any louder, but somehow it spoke over all of them. "Our other choices remain open."

The creatures at this table did not answer. They were too busy talking back. From what Niccoluccio had told her about the silent ways the others communicated, Fia had no doubt that even the quiet ones were anything but. They were speaking in ways she could not hear. Fia folded her arms, and waited.

Habidah waited for the clamor to die. When she spoke, her eyes were on the well of blackness wrapped around the walls. She asked, "You want to leave the old Unity behind?"

Ways and Means said, "We cannot continue to live as we have."

At that thought, what was left of the noise died. They all knew that was true. For some of them, it might have been the first time they'd heard their ship say it.

Habidah said, "Then draw a clearer line. Your colonization effort, settling your crew – everything you're trying to do is just a pattern of past behavior. End it."

424

Ways and Means said, "We have never been without a home."

"Nothing you've done so far has made anything better. And none of it is right."

Fia asked, "Right for who?"

Habidah blinked. Fia guessed that she'd expected to be interrupted, but not by her. "For us," Habidah said. "For you. For everybody on your world."

Fia waved her hand across the same well of black that Habidah had been addressing. "You want to take all of this, all of this wealth and these wonders, away from us?"

"*Wonders?*" Habidah asked. "These aren't wonders."

"I broke some ribs on our journey here. I felt them pop. Saw big, ugly bruises. Now there's nothing."

The last time Fia had seen Caterina, Caterina had still not been able to make full use of her hand. She had spent days on the edge of death. How many soldiers had she seen suffer and die? How many of them could have been saved to live again, reborn?

Habidah said, "If *Ways and Means* and its crew were to settle your world, they wouldn't act for your benefit."

"Wouldn't they, if this ship does want to break with its past?" Fia asked. "And where would this ship go? Where would you hide all your toys and your weapons?"

"This ship doesn't need to go anywhere. It can survive like it is."

"You would hide them away when you could share them."

Incredulous, Habidah said, "If *Ways and Means* and its crew screw around with your world, it wouldn't be to *share*."

Fia said, "Whatever its reason, it'll bring medicine. Food. Do you know how many people up there are suffering right now?"

Habidah looked as though Fia had struck her. "Yes," she said.

Meloku was near. She had been listening. She told Habidah, "You interfered on this world once."

She did not hide the barb in her voice. She had to mean Niccoluccio. Habidah swallowed. "Considering how it turned out, I would take it back if I could."

Fia was beginning to understand more about how this woman operated. She saw her world with stark lines dividing good and bad. Herself and her friends versus her enemies. She always felt outnumbered. No wonder. She thought of herself as principled. The people around her did not have to slip up many times, or disagree with her more than once, to become enemies. She always had fewer and fewer friends.

Fia was very close to the "enemy" line. But Habidah could not quite put Fia there. She had put Fia in a different category entirely. Not a friend. Not an enemy. An irrelevance.

Fia was a native. To be defended, not listened to.

The last thing Fia ever wanted to be was *protected*.

A lie gave the teller power. Fia had lied plenty enough to know that. An omission had the same purpose. Habidah never would have told Fia who she was, where she had come from, and why, if circumstances hadn't forced her.

Had they ever met on her world, Habidah would have held the truth over her like a sword on a pinion. Fia couldn't have stood up.

Everything that Fia had learned put them on closer to even ground.

No wonder Habidah had been afraid.

Habidah opened her mouth, but Fia spoke first. Louder. "Go to my world," she told the others. "You have my blessing if you're looking for it. No more games or hiding behind hunting blinds. Land in full force, in plain view. And *tell the truth* about why you've come. I'll help you."

Again, order broke. This time, arguments were far more subdued. So many of the golems looked to each other in silence. Communicating, no doubt.

Habidah paled. Her mouth hung open. They had both been brought to this meeting to share their perspectives – as *Ways and Means* had put it. Well, *Ways and Means* had gotten them. Fia pressed herself back to the deck.

The meeting took an agonizing amount of time to wind down. Everybody had a piece to say, a rival to snipe at, a speech to give.

Fia had never doubted the outcome. Except for Habidah and Kacienta, all of them were in favor of settlement. Only Osia and Meloku held their peace, and kept their opinions to themselves.

When another long silence fell over the table, *Ways and Means* announced, "Thank you all for your input. We have made our decision."

It did not say, Fia noticed, whether the discussion had influenced it. A handful of the golems looked to her. Others avoided her, including Habidah. They knew the same thing Fia did. If any of them had affected it, Fia's words had.

Fia felt like she needed to swallow, but her throat was dry. She was not ready to have done what she suspected she just had.

But she had said it. She believed it.

Had she been in *Ways and Means'* place, she would have dispensed with the drama and done it long ago.

36

Meloku's shuttle this time was a slim, swan-winged clipper. Like their last, it had been designed for speed. Unlike it, this one had been built with half a mind on passenger comfort.

This control cabin could not have been mistaken for a tomb. The shuttle was meant to travel at speed, yes, also to cater to diplomatic guests and their families. The cabin's curved bulkheads used projectors to trick the eyes into thinking that it was larger than it actually was. Only by scanning in other spectra could she see that their space was seven meters long rather than the twenty it appeared to be.

Fiametta did not see through the image. Meloku did not care to disillusion her. Fiametta's heart rate picked up when she settled into her acceleration couch, but not by as much as Meloku would have expected.

Meloku's gorge had risen when *Ways and Means* had asked her to escort Fiametta. But she understood. Fiametta had proved herself adaptable beyond anything Meloku had expected, but she would never be comfortable around wholly demiorganic crew. *Ways and Means* did not have many humans it could count on to follow its orders.

The shuttle's hull was sleek, polished silver. It had no stealth fields. It would not be going anywhere it had not been intended to be seen. They were going to make a statement. To be seen.

The usual compound-eye array of images sprang up across the fore bulkhead. They showed a hundred views of smooth orange gradients, the false skyline of their hangar complex. Though the shuttle's boarding ramp had sealed behind them, their shuttle wouldn't be taking flight for a while yet. *Ways and Means* had to get into position.

The shuttle was secured for acceleration. Fields and physical clamps held it in place. She and Fiametta had had to board now. The shuttle was to launch immediately after *Ways and Means'* engine burns. They were aiming to give the intruder as little time to react as possible.

Fiametta flinched when her couch's safety harness sprang out. She reflexively knocked it away. Meloku levered herself out of her own couch. She grabbed Fiametta's harness and yanked it over her.

"Thank you," Fiametta said, which was more than Meloku would have expected.

Meloku looked to her. Fiametta glared at Meloku when Meloku watched her too long.

She hardly liked Meloku more than Meloku liked her. Meloku would always be her captor, her interrogator. Alien to her and to everything she knew. And Fiametta was a warmonger, a hostage-taker, a robber, an arsonist. The kind of barbarian that, when Meloku had been traveling the planes, she would have no second thoughts about destroying like she had destroyed Queen Joanna. Meloku could not find peace with these things. Had she been in Fiametta's position and needed help, she could not have thanked Fiametta.

These days, it seemed that everyone around her was better than her, and in ways she could not force herself to be. Habidah had said she didn't believe in redemption, or at least that redemption didn't matter. Maybe she was right. Meloku had a long way to go.

"You're welcome," she made herself say. She took to her couch.

At her silent request, a new set of images replaced the camera views. These came from *Ways and Means'* sensors. The blue-white orb of the Earth peered at them from every side.

Just as at the conference, Meloku felt the weight of the Earth bearing on her. She'd seen countless worlds like it – larger, richer, more populated. Somehow this one was heavier by far.

She called up more images. Maps of orbital space, on different scales and with different indicators, filled in to the best of *Ways and Means'* ability. Telescope images, too, of sunlight glinting off reflective hulls. Cylindrical shadows caught in silhouette against cloud and ocean. The intruder's combat drones, waiting. And watching.

Some hours ago, *Ways and Means* had fired its engines to halt its drift away from the Earth. It held position. The enemy's combat drones had seen it. They had done nothing.

These images showed her everything she needed to know, available at a glance. And she might need to know a lot. She and Fiametta were to lead the vanguard. The first wave of *Ways and Means'* agents back on the surface.

The first and far from the last.

An acceleration warning trilled in the back of her head. *Ways and Means* fired its engines.

Fiametta breathed more evenly as she sagged into her seat. Point seven gravity was not quite what she was accustomed to, but felt far better than freefall. Her heart rate slowed.

Not for the first time, Meloku wondered if Fiametta really understood what was happening here. Meloku said, "You don't have to be here. You have plenty of time left to get off."

"I can't."

"*Ways and Means* will do exactly what it intends to do whether you're on the ground or not."

"That's why I can't miss it." Fiametta glanced at Meloku. "Same reason I've gone along with any of this. It'll happen regardless. If I'm not here, I won't have a voice."

Then again, maybe she understood more than Meloku gave her credit for.

The shuttle's plotted flight course wrapped around one of the globes. They were bound for a small army camp at the fringes of Russia – or would be, as soon as they got close enough for sensors to identify the right one. They would find

Fiametta's people. Her company. Her captain.

They would recognize Fiametta. They might believe what she told them. If they then listened to her, and then *Ways and Means*, that might make them useful.

Colonization wasn't all raw force. It was also give and take, reward and punishment. The Earth would be divided between those who would listen to *Ways and Means'* agents, and those who wouldn't. Those who listened would have power, favor, wealth. *Ways and Means* would treat them as leaders and negotiate with no one else.

Fiametta was one of those hand-picked leaders. If Fiametta's soldiers could be swayed to *Ways and Means'* side, they would have an outsized role in the fate of their world. Just like Fiametta herself.

Meloku would be alongside her. She wondered how much more *Ways and Means* was going to ask her to do, and if it would be worse than what she had done to Queen Joanna.

A shrill note sounded from her demiorganics, sharp enough to make her wince. Not an alarm this time. A signal, directed not only to the planarship but its crew.

A warning call – from the combat drones. There were no words, but the message was plain. Come no further, they said, or the ceasefire ends.

Ways and Means jammed its signal.

Osia transmitted, "Hard acceleration in five."

Ways and Means did not always speak to its agents itself. It had an aura of mystique to maintain. It would not have done for the peoples of the Unity to learn to hear the amalgamates' voices very often. It had assigned Osia the task of coordinating the shuttles and those of *Ways and Means'* agents who remained on the surface.

For having been away so long, Osia had settled back into her role easily enough. Meloku suspected she was more *Ways and Means'* creature than she had ever been willing to admit.

Not long after *Ways and Means* had requested Meloku to escort Fiametta, Meloku had tracked down Osia. She found

Osia staring at a hatchway that, according to Meloku's demiorganics, had once been Osia's old quarters aboard ship. She had been staring at the hatch, as if afraid to go in.

Meloku had not cared why. *Ways and Means* would not speak to Meloku then. It had claimed she had been given all the instruction she needed, but she suspected it knew what Meloku was about to ask. Meloku asked Osia instead. "How do you know the intruder isn't going to torch *Ways and Means'* agents on the surface, like it torched the satellites and the communication outposts?"

"It went out of its way to avoid killing crewmembers during its last visit."

"It also killed over fifty of them up here."

For all that Osia had human-like eyes, they were the most impenetrable part of her. She said, "If it does, I'm afraid you'll be the first to find out."

Now Osia was lodged safely somewhere in one of *Ways and Means'* shelters. She had not been ordered to take part in this travesty. Meloku told Fiametta, "Brace yourself."

Ways and Means did not intend to allow the combat drones to initiate hostilities. Beam lances ran a half-dozen combat drones through. They flew apart in flashes of light, boiling away into luminous clouds of gas.

The other drones reacted at once, igniting their engines, flickering defensive fields to obscure their exhaust's origin. *Ways and Means* had saved the greater number of its weapons for them. Cannon barrages tore through their exhaust plumes, breached their fields, left brilliant and fading auroras of molten and vaporized metal.

Ways and Means' defensive fields shook off the parting shots. It did not need to maneuver. Osia's warning of high acceleration had been a precaution. This was not a fair match.

Neither side had intended for it to be. The drones were just a line in the sand, not the sword waiting on the other side.

The surviving drones raced away from *Ways and Means*, accelerating at speeds that would have liquefied any passengers. *Ways and Means'* beams picked off those in reach, pushing the rest back as the wind would a cloud. It could not get them all. Some were already out of effective range. More dropped below the horizons.

They would gather in the Earth's shadow to harry and harass *Ways and Means*. And then to wait for the opportunity to do more.

Ways and Means did not know what might happen after that. Opening a transplanar gateway the size of a planarship took enormous energy. The intruder might not have had that much on standby.

Osia transmitted, "Acceleration warning suspended." The battle had gone as hoped. *Ways and Means* had not needed to maneuver. Yet.

Fiametta could not hear Osia. She had her eyes tightly shut. Meloku wished she could bear doing the same. "You might as well open your eyes."

If Fiametta was in for the duration, she might as well learn. Meloku doubted she would ever learn enough to understand, but she recognized she had underestimated Fiametta too many times already.

A series of muffled impact thumps echoed through the deck plating. They came in rapid-fire succession, the beat-beat-beat of a piston. Fiametta flinched. On the sensor map, a sequence of new lights sprang from *Ways and Means*. They fanned out in a broad and flattening cone.

Combat drones. The snaps of their powered catapults reverberated through the hull. *Ways and Means* was sending them after the enemy's remaining combat drones.

Combat drones gobbled antimatter fuel, though, and the ship's antimatter stocks were limited. It fired only as many drones, Meloku saw, as it estimated would be enough to just barely win an engagement. They outnumbered the enemy by fewer than ten drones. Shaving the margins thin.

Another piston beat echoed up the shuttle's landing struts. New satellites launching, to replace the lost. *Ways and Means* could not fight without effective sensor coverage. The combat drones had sensors, but there were not enough of them. Each replacement satellite wore a thruster jacket to help move them rapidly into position.

Meloku was surprised that *Ways and Means* had had so many satellites at the ready. But it had known, for years, to expect trouble. It would have known its satellites were vulnerable.

"Last chance to disembark," Meloku told Fiametta.

"Stop it," Fiametta snapped.

Osia transmitted, "Acceleration warning, thirty."

On the map, a trajectory line sprang from *Ways and Means*. It curved high above the Earth. The plan called for *Ways and Means* to keep to a distant orbit, seeding satellites and more combat drones. It was to drop shuttles everywhere it went – to every corner of the world.

Meloku did not expect to be aboard the planarship for the next engine burn. Central Asia was just over the horizon. *Ways and Means'* momentum would carry the shuttle almost right to it.

Sure enough, Osia said, "First launch ready, five."

"Too late now," Meloku said. "Brace yourself."

The shuttle was attached to no powered catapult like the drones, but it didn't need to be to make a fast exit. The thrusters kicked Meloku in the rear. Once the landing surface was far enough away, the shuttle's main engines added more weight.

Meloku's chest squeezed the breath out of her. Beside her, Fiametta gasped. The pressure never got as bad as last time.

Meloku switched the camera views from *Ways and Means'* back to the shuttle's. The warm orange of the hangar complex fell away. Everything but the rear cameras, where the engine exhaust burned hot, turned dark. The shadow fell away, became a silhouette.

Ways and Means' bulk occluded the stars. At first, *Ways and Means* was a flat plane, a shadowed horizon. The reflection of the shuttle's engine exhaust glinted where the light caught its edges. And, on the opposite cameras, the sunlit crescent of the Earth loomed over them. Morning was near.

Ways and Means' engines flared bright. It went from a world to an array of blocky shadows, half-lost against the sky. Then it was cloaked behind a haze of billowing exhaust. Soon, the only object they could see clearly was the Earth. Even Fiametta had learned to parse the images enough to be impressed. She let out a sharp breath.

That acceleration reduced as they gained distance. The weight of Meloku's ribs eased off her lungs. Fiametta wrapped her fingers around her harness webbing. Her hand trembled. Every other one of her heartbeats came prematurely. She stilled her hand when she realized Meloku was watching.

She asked, "Which of us is in charge when we get to the surface?"

"Who do you think?"

"I'm not going along with this to take orders."

This assignment was going to be just brilliant fun. "That was part of the bargain you made."

"No," Fiametta said flatly. "That was a choice I never had. You would have taken charge regardless."

More lights speared away from across *Ways and Means*. More shuttle launches from all over the planarship. They dived out and away, gaining speed. These weren't passenger shuttles, but multipurpose vehicles like the one she and Dahn had shared. Their passengers didn't have to hew to the limits of fragile human bodies. The shuttles accelerated hard, rapidly outpacing Meloku and Fiametta.

Fiametta's gaze was glued to the images of the Earth. The last time she'd been up here, she'd had little enough context for what she was seeing. She could not have appreciated the scale.

She was a fast learner. Meloku granted her that. But nobody could have learned fast enough for what she was being asked to do. Meloku asked, "Puts your life in a different perspective, doesn't it?"

435

Fiametta did not appear to listen, though, from the uptick in her pulse, Meloku knew she had. She had caught the barb too.

Ways and Means fell into the dark. Though it was not accelerating as much as it could have, its engines washed out the stars. It would be visible from the Earth. A bright, bold star piercing the skies – a comet sprung from nowhere.

Ways and Means intended its arrival to be portentous. It wanted people ready to believe their world was about to end. Belief was power. Shaping belief was the best, most cost-effective way to rule a people. *Ways and Means* knew this very well. So did Meloku. Fiametta's power had been based in belief, but Meloku wondered if she understood all that meant.

Her "inner voice" had not put her in a trance, or overwhelmed her conscious mind, as Meloku had overwhelmed Queen Joanna. It had not needed to. That would have been inefficient. All it had done was changed what she believed. Fiametta had done the rest on her own.

The rising heat in Fiametta's cheeks and forehead said she knew she was being watched. Meloku asked, "Still think this is for the best?"

"It *is* for the best. It's what I would do."

"Have you ever considered that what you would do is wrong?"

"Not in a long time," Fiametta answered.

Meloku wondered if *Ways and Means* had ever opened a real dialogue with its backup, had ever argued with itself.

Ways and Means' engine exhaust dwindled. Its antimatter reserves were running low. The amalgamate refused to say how much it had left. It only assured its crew that it had enough fuel left to complete the course it had plotted. Presumably with a little more left for maneuvers.

It had chosen such a high orbit not only to keep a safe distance, but also to keep a good vantage. It would not need to expend as much fuel later on. There was no part of the world that its orbit would not eventually cross. Should its cannons be needed anywhere, it would only have to wait.

The other shuttles raced ahead, falling into clipped orbits. Some fell, diving like seabirds. Most raced ahead. All across the monitors, the rosy horizon broadened. Its curve flattened.

Fiametta said, "I didn't think you, of everyone here, would try to set me doubting. Niccoluccio told me who you were. Is this some kind of test?"

"If *Ways and Means* wanted to test your commitment, it would find a better way than me."

"Sure."

The lines on the maps solidified. *Ways and Means'* sensor coverage expanded. Its new satellites were falling into place. On the other side of the world, in flush daylight, *Ways and Means'* combat drones closed on their counterparts. Lightning flashes seared the exosphere. Beam fire. Accented by exhaust from missile launches.

Meloku took her eyes off long enough to glance at Fiametta. Fiametta's gaze was fixed on her.

Fiametta asked, "Why are you trying to shake me?"

With a shock, Meloku realized that Fiametta thought she might be a traitor. For an instant, she couldn't find her breath. "I would never betray us to that thing," she said. "No side in this is right."

"There's no such thing as 'right' in any of this. You used to know that, didn't you?"

Meloku opened her mouth to answer, but before she could make a sound, a shrill warning from her demiorganics drove the words from her.

The alarm came from *Ways and Means*. It was urgent. Followed shortly by another, from her shuttle's sensors.

Light split the horizon ahead, flaring brilliant off the sea. The clouds cast deep shadows, their fingers stretching across the sea. It was if the whole Earth were bending about a single point in orbit, on the edge of collapsing into a singularity.

It was no sunrise.

It was a planar gateway. A great deal of heat and light was pumping out into open space. Already, their shuttle's sensors picked out the intruder's silhouette, hiding behind it. It split wide the seam in space, forcing its way through.

Meloku couldn't breathe. This time, the intruder was emerging *over* their horizon. The shuttle's sensors saw it clearly, even against the heat and light of the gateway. That meant it could see them just as easily. It was already in weapons range.

There would be no running.

Her demiorganics seized control of her physiological functions, forced her to breathe. They jammed calming chemicals into her adrenaline-laced bloodstream. If the intruder wanted to kill them, there was nothing she could do. It would happen any instant.

There was still a chance she and Fiametta might survive. The intruder hadn't fired on any of the shuttles, even the closer ones. But it *was* firing. Traces of heat rippled along its mirror fields. Even at this altitude, there were still enough loose particles of atmosphere to illuminate the beam fire.

All of its fire was directed skyward, at *Ways and Means*. It had not been bluffing. It intended to destroy the planarship.

Meloku thought she'd heard Osia's voice for a flash of a second, but then there was nothing. A glint of light, like the sun against silver, caught the shuttle's sensors. *Ways and Means* had encased itself in a mirror field. No signal could get through, in or out.

This shuttle, and all of the others, were on their own. They were cut off from contact with *Ways and Means*. The intruder continued to refrain from firing on them.

It was hoping for converts, Meloku realized.

It had good reason. On the orbital maps, the weave of flight trajectories shifted. Long, slender fingers cast outward, into space. Some of the shuttles broke their assigned courses. They weren't diving to the surface to take shelter. They were racing toward the intruder. Traitors.

The tail end of *Ways and Means'* mirror fields grew a white-hot cloud. Engine exhaust fell through the fields. *Ways and Means* was moving. On its mirror fields, the reflection of the exhaust doubled against itself, stark and eerily beautiful.

Ways and Means could not communicate its flight plan. The shuttle's NAI did its best to guess. On the maps, its trajectory wrapped close around the Earth. If Meloku had trusted herself to speak, she would have sworn. The intruder had emerged almost directly underneath *Ways and Means*. Now *Ways and Means* was dropping altitude, getting *closer* to the intruder.

Fiametta stared, her jaw slack. She couldn't have heard the alarms, but she knew what had happened.

Meloku felt she should have ordered the shuttle to do something. Dive. Run. She couldn't think of anything. The shuttle remained placidly on course. There was nothing it could do.

Ways and Means was not firing back. It would have had to drop its defensive fields to get useful targeting data. The intruder had it outgunned. This close to the intruder's superior weaponry, it wouldn't have lasted long.

Meloku could not figure out what *Ways and Means* had planned. Maybe it was hoping to get close enough to land a lucky shot, score a beam hit against the odds.

Ways and Means maintained a complete mirror field. A one hundred percent blackout. No light, no signal, or pulse scans. It was the only complete defense against beam weapons. But the intruder was already launching drones and missiles. *Ways and Means* would have to reduce the opacity of its fields to see them, to shoot them down in time.

At this range, *Ways and Means* would need more than luck.

The intruder could have killed her and Fiametta several times by now. It hadn't targeted any of the shuttles. When she trusted herself to speak, Meloku asked, "You don't think any side here is right, either, do you?"

Fiametta didn't speak, but nodded.

"If you'd be willing to go back to work for that thing, you'd better figure it out soon." Meloku knew she wasn't.

Before she could take that thought any further, the NAI's map changed again. *Ways and Means'* course was stuttering, redrawing several times a second. Like a signal with bad reception, it flickered up and down, high altitude to low. It drew closer to the Earth, and then widened again.

Meloku clamped her jaw shut. She would have assumed that *Ways and Means* was maneuvering. That wasn't quite right. The only dimension changing was altitude. Had the planarship been maneuvering, its trajectory would have veered in every direction. This was more like a wave, up and down.

She glanced to the cameras. The glare of *Ways and Means'* engine exhaust had faded. Then it brightened, and diminished again. She recognized the pattern. It was that of a ship running out of antimatter fuel. Its engines were struggling to function with a reduced stream of reactant.

That shouldn't have been happening. It had said, before they'd left, that it enough antimatter fuel to complete its orbital insertion.

It had *said* it had enough antimatter–

On the map ahead, the blip of one of the other shuttles vanished.

The cameras dimmed. A brilliant white new sun erupted over the horizon. It shone over the Earth, reflected blindingly against the clouds and sea, and expanded rapidly.

The intruder's mirror fields were on full by then, but mirror fields couldn't have helped. A shockwave of superheated gas crashed into its side, through the fields, and across the intruder's hull.

Its mirror fields flickered, losing opacity, as their projectors seared away. The shuttle's sensors caught glimpses of it. The port sides of its three center hull segments glowed sunset-red.

Meloku understood an instant too late.

The blast had set off a chain reaction among the other shuttles approaching the intruder. All of them were laden with antimatter. This time, the intruder was even less ready. The radiation from each new blast pierced its mirror fields, searing its hull.

New stars detonated around the intruder. Then the mirror fields around one of its ovoid weapon platforms collapsed. For an instant, Meloku saw the dark bristling silhouettes of its cannons. Then they lost shape, melted, turned to slag.

The intruder still had plenty of weapons batteries left. They wouldn't help. The antimatter-carrying shuttles had gotten too close. The most the intruder could do was shoot them down, which would rupture their antimatter tanks. Same difference.

It tried anyway. More stars flared to life. Beam fire seared the exosphere. Meloku could not help her flinch. The beams were not coming from *Ways or Means* or the intruder.

The rarefied atmosphere made it difficult to trace the beams' path. The shuttle's NAI told her they came from the new satellites. Or the things that Meloku had mistaken for satellites. That *Ways and Means* had *told* her were satellites.

Beams raked the intruder's central hull. The "satellites" focused fire on the rear segment. Meloku knew what they were aiming for. Its antimatter storage. Its transplanar gateway generator.

Meloku tore her eyes off the monitors, looked to Fiametta. Fiametta's cheeks had gone pale. As always, there was no telling how much Fiametta understood. If she had missed anything, she would never admit it. But Meloku figured she understood the basic fact that this had been a trap.

Nothing about the plan *Ways and Means* had told them had been the truth. Given the behavior of the other shuttles, all still heading for the intruder, they were probably the only two real people out here.

"Why?" Fiametta asked.

"How," Meloku retorted. "Your inner voice. That implant. It's not gone."

"Of course it's gone," Fiametta said. "I felt it go. There's just empty space in my head."

Meloku said, "Osia thought it had burned itself out." No. She had *told* Meloku it had. Fiametta's surgeon had said he would remove the implant, but the surgery hadn't happened – not that Meloku had ever known. "Your implant was playing dead."

But if Osia had been fooled, *Ways and Means* shouldn't have been. It had pretended otherwise. It had started laying the trap as soon as Fiametta had come aboard. Letting Fia's inner voice think it had escaped notice.

That implant had forwarded everything it saw and heard to the intruder.

Maybe Osia had planted the seeds of that plan before they'd ever reestablished contact with *Ways and Means*. She could have thought of it the moment she'd scanned Fiametta's implant. Osia had never, for a ghost of a second, considered letting Meloku know. Nor had *Ways and Means*.

Fiametta insisted, "My inner voice has been dead for weeks."

"Your inner voice was still there, listening." Meloku's fingers tremored. She tapped the side of her head. "It must've found a way to get word back to the intruder. *Ways and Means* pretended it didn't notice. But it knew your implant was seeing and hearing everything you did."

Now Fiametta was getting it. Her lips tightened. The muscles in her neck were taut. "The conference," she said. "Everything it did and told us. It wasn't real."

"It was a performance," Meloku said. "For all of us. Put on to fool as many people as possible, but most of all to fool you. If you believed it, your 'inner voice' might believe it. It sent everything it heard on. It wanted the intruder to believe that we were coming down in force, that it could persuade our crew in the shuttles to join it."

Gradually, in stutters, the intruder's weapons fell silent. Both of its weapon platforms had been slagged. Barrage after barrage of beam fire bored into its fields. Then into its hull.

The beams focused fire on the aft hull segment, and then on the ligaments joining it to the rest of the ship. One of the ligaments cracked, split yellow-hot, a log burning to cinders. It spit molten debris.

The hull segment fell free, began to drift away. It must have housed its antimatter. The last thing *Ways and Means* wanted was an antimatter detonation of that size so near to the surface.

With that segment severed, its drones and satellite weapons would be free to destroy the rest of it.

Another shrill call split the back of her mind, loud enough to give her a phantom earache. It was a distress signal – from the intruder. A plea to surrender.

The opacity of *Ways and Means'* mirror fields diminished minutely and briefly. It was just enough to let it peek out, for the first time since the battle had commenced.

A dozen confused signals spilled into space. They were from *Ways and Means'* crew, Meloku realized. That was another reason to have kept the planarship enclosed in mirror fields, until now: to block the panicked calls from crewmembers once they realized what was happening. Calls meant for the intruder, to warn it.

Ways and Means had no doubt taken note of who had sent those signals. Doing this the way it had, it had rooted out mutineers and sympathizers among its crew as well.

Ways and Means jammed the intruder's distress calls.

It kept to its original course, engines still flickering. Meloku's shuttle picked up fragments of pulse scans, a detailed sensor sweep washing across the intruder's hull. *Ways and Means* was taking its measure. Meloku's breath caught. She could not let it out.

All of *Ways and Means'* side and ventral cannon batteries opened at once. They hardly needed to aim. The intruder was in no state to maneuver, and close enough to be an easy target.

The beams burned right through the intruder's hull. It turned what was left of it into a luminous nebular cloud, full of stars and dust. The debris billowed to nothing in the space of seconds.

On the tactical maps, the intruder's blip disappeared. Yellow hazard icons sprang up where it had been. A field of high-velocity orbital debris. The shuttle's NAI was still working to determine the extent of it.

To have converted so many satellites into weapons platforms, *Ways and Means* must have been working at it for a long time. Long before it had ever called their conference. Before she, Osia, and Fiametta had come aboard.

Meloku turned to Fiametta. "Do you understand now?"

Fiametta looked like a different person. The muscles in her cheeks had slackened. Her cheeks and lips were pale. Meloku had seen the same looks on corpses. Fiametta was in shock.

Osia's voice returned. She sounded different this time. Clipped. She said, "All surface personnel, stand ready to evacuate. We will dispatch shuttles shortly."

Meloku told Fiametta, "You can't let it run your world if you ever get the choice. It lives to lie to you. Don't go along with it. Don't cooperate with it."

Fiametta did not look at her. Impossible to tell if her words were getting through. Fiametta might not have been capable of listening.

Meloku was not as good a manipulator as *Ways and Means*, and would not have been if she could have. She could not make Fiametta's choices for her. But she had to get this through.

Meloku said, "It will make you think you've made a choice when it's already made it for you. You might as well be a lever in a machine. You won't even know that you wouldn't be you any more. It happened in the Unity all the time. It's what the Unity was."

Fiametta swallowed. She was not convinced, Meloku knew. She did not yet understand. Meloku wouldn't have the time to convince her. But she had the time to start.

They had come from similar places. Meloku's Companion

AI had not been so different than Fiametta's inner voice. They had both been divested of them. Fiametta was a fast learner. Faster than Meloku had ever been.

Meloku said, "It's not something you can cooperate with, or gain from. It'll take everything that made you unique, every choice you thought you made, and take it away from you. You won't even feel it happen. If you ever have the chance, or the choice, leave it."

Fiametta's eyes flicked between the images of the Earth and the silhouette of *Ways and Means*. *Ways and Means* had stopped firing its engines. It was just a dark shape now, limned against the horizon and the still-approaching sunrise.

Fiametta would not look at Meloku. But Meloku still saw, in the spreading lines underneath her eyes, the shadow of her doubt.

She *had* learned. She might even have understood.

A subtler tone trilled in the back of her head. *Ways and Means* was signaling. The amalgamate itself, not Osia. It was even being polite, allowing Meloku the chance to accept the call.

The shuttle's NAI had dutifully recorded everything she and Fiametta had said to each other. The cabin sensors could even trace the emotional tells in the constriction and dilation of the blood vessels under their skin. *Ways and Means* would have seen and heard everything.

Meloku accepted the call and put it on the cabin speakers so Fiametta could hear too.

"You pieced things together not an instant too late," *Ways and Means* said. It must have trusted her a great deal to send her aboard the shuttle with Fiametta. It had believed that she would not figure out its plan too soon, or blurt it out in front of Fiametta and her inner voice.

To the extent *Ways and Means* had a tone, it sounded pleased. "You are very apt. We will hold to our promise. When you return, it will be our pleasure to welcome you as an officer and the newest member of our crew."

"Wonderful," Meloku said.

Fucking wonderful. What she had worked for, all her life, just as she'd wanted. She said, "I resign my commission."

37

Though *Ways and Means* had given her the task of coordinating its shuttles, Osia had not needed to go anywhere special to do it. Her assigned shelter was little different than any other: a hemispherical hollow deep within the hull, shielded and armored. Thirty acceleration couches of varying sizes lined the deck.

The crew sharing her shelter shifted, uneasy. Osia closed her eyes, put them out of her mind, and focused on her work. Snippets of other conversations crossed her receivers.

So far as she could tell, she was the only one among them who had known most of the shuttles were empty. *Ways and Means* had taken care to limit communication aboard, institute radio silences, so that its crew would not have a chance to figure out that all of them were still aboard.

Ways and Means had not had to tell Osia. It dropped hints. She had pieced it together.

There had been a moment, when *Ways and Means'* mirror fields had first dropped, when panic had seized her. *Ways and Means'* "satellites" were hammering the intruder's rear hull segment, trying to split it apart. For a long stretch of seconds, it had remained attached.

All of the intruder's antimatter was housed there. If that much antimatter escaped containment... the release of energy would have seared away this world's atmosphere.

If the intruder was serious about forcing *Ways and Means* to forgo its connection to this world, it would have done so.

It had not. It had still been trying to surrender.

The only reason it would have tried to surrender was that it knew itself. The creature *Ways and Means* had been, however many decades ago, would have allowed it to live. Maybe in exchange for some concession, maybe not.

Ways and Means had accepted its backup's call. It had signaled that it was about to reply.

All around the planarship, though, Osia's sensors had little trouble detecting power pumping to the ventral hull, to the cannon. So could the others around her. And then it had jammed the intruder's transmission.

The radio silence that followed was a collective drawn breath, a stifled word.

Someone, somewhere – Osia did not even track where – started to say "But it's…"

Ways and Means' beams continued to pulse through the vapor cloud long after the intruder had died, seeking inactive combat drones and other traps.

The acceleration warning ended not long after. Osia's seat harness released. The crew was free.

She pushed the webbing aside. *Ways and Means* had not told her its plan, not exactly. But it had let slip enough that it must have known that she would figure it out, and that she would be the first among its crew to do so. Had she been so inclined, she could have broadcast a warning to the intruder's combat drones, blown the whole trap.

Until now, she had not believed *Ways and Means* had ever treated her differently than the rest of the crew. She saw things differently. It really did trust her more than them.

There had been no advantage to telling her what it had. None that she could see, anyway.

But it was always playing games whose rules she could never know.

The rest of the crew had no shortage of work now. Those among its crew who had tried to transmit warnings to the intruder had to be rounded up, and their bodies deactivated pending remedial education. *Ways and Means* could tolerate dissent, restlessness. Even, under certain circumstances, breaches of military order. But treason and mutiny were different.

Those among the crew who'd sided with the intruder would spend a long time having their opinions revised.

They would experience no pain. It would be for the better, Osia knew. But her demiorganics still had to repress a shudder.

Then there was repair duty and shuttle prep. *Ways and Means* was pulling its remaining agents off the surface. It had fewer shuttles than ever to ferry them. They needed temporary quarters. Why "temporary," *Ways and Means* hadn't said. It could have meant it. It could have been just a word.

And then there was warmaking. They needed antimatter, drones, war material. The antimatter production hoops needed to be working constantly. The other amalgamates were still trapped in exile. But they'd already found one small way out. They would not be trapped forever.

Ways and Means exempted Osia from the work. As far as it was concerned, she had just returned from a thirty-year field assignment. Her service had been exemplary; she had gone beyond the duty she had been called to perform. She had a great deal of accumulated leave time.

Osia felt as though she were dragging her feet as she moved down the passageways.

The damage to her body had been repaired the first day she'd come back. *Ways and Means* did not have the resources to build new demiorganic bodies, but it had prioritized what little it did have for her replacement parts. She had not thought about it much then. She'd had too many other distractions.

Her legs didn't feel like hers. All of her systems returned perfect diagnostics. None of her nerves reported any frayed or intermittent connections. And yet everything below her waist might as well have belonged to someone else.

She had reached her old quarters, and stopped outside the hatch. As before, she could not go in.

The deck plating rattled, barely perceptible even to her. A

steady thump, thump of footsteps.

Someone pacing, just beyond the hatch.

She did not need a pulse scan to detect the warm body on the other side. Their body heat shone through the hatch's edges. The nearest bulkheads were a few shades of a degree above ambient.

Thi could not have heard Osia. Not unless *Ways and Means* had given thir better senses. Maybe *Ways and Means* had just told thir she was coming. Or maybe thi was just exercising. Osia's constructs still had a psychological need for work, for activity.

Osia could not go in, see what was left of thir. *Ways and Means* was right. She was in need of a rest, a long one. Somewhere far away from here. And she was not going to get it.

She should not have asked for Coral.

She turned on her narrow heels. She started walking, at first with the idea that she, too, would pace. But she did not turn around. She was not ready yet.

She did not have to be. She was back. And she knew now that she wasn't going to leave.

Osia did not know where she was headed. She had once known this ship as intimately as anybody aboard. Now, even with her perfect memory, it had become a stranger. So had its crew, and its master. They would be for a long time yet.

Ways and Means said, "We'll let thir know you will be delayed."

"I didn't suppose you would care that much for thir state of mind."

"We would do so out of consideration for you."

She held her answer. Any answer she gave would have gone into one of its infinite ledgers, given it more data about how she operated. A tic, a point along a pattern of behavior, that it might use to predict her. Or against her. It had plenty enough insight. She didn't need to give it more.

She changed the subject. "Have you thought about changing your name?"

For once, she seemed to have given it pause. Genuine pause. It waited for her to elaborate.

"'Ways and Means' was your job title and role in a defunct empire. An empire you wouldn't go back to if you could." She hoped it wasn't lying about that. "The other amalgamates wouldn't have you back now if you wanted."

"We had not considered that," it said.

"Consider it," she said. "There's still a good number among the crew who want to go back to the Unity. That would be a powerful message that you're different now."

If it was. She believed it was. But she was never going to be able to stop wondering, second-guessing.

This was all going to be much different from how it had been the first time she'd come aboard.

It asked, "What would you name us, if you could?"

She had her answer, but she didn't give it. That, too, would have told it too much about what she thought of it. Another point to chart on the curve of her behavior.

It might get her answer eventually, but it would have to fight for it.

38

Fia did not know how long she slept. When she woke, her temples pulsed with pain. Headaches like this only happened when she had drunk too much the night before, or when she had slept hours past her mark.

She was sure she had not gotten drunk.

The night after her first battle with Antonov's Company, she'd slept this long. Again at intervals during her depression, her dark days. She would have slept longer if she could. It took her some time to realize that she had not woken naturally.

The lights were brightening. The difference was imperceptible at first. Now they pried behind her eyelids no matter how tightly she shut them. It was the spirit of this ship again, controlling and influencing. Insidious.

Fia had slept in her clothes. She had not dared disrobe on this ship, around these people. She was always being watched. In this gravity, she was not sure she could have redone the wrappings. The last thing she would ever do here was ask for help.

She would not have to put up with this for much longer. It was time to leave.

An escort, one of the humanoid variants of the golems, was waiting outside her hatch. It looked like Osia, but it couldn't have been. This golem's eyes were hazel, and she stepped with a composure she'd never seen in Osia. This golem was too comfortable here.

They walked the passageways in silence. Fia did not voice any complaint about the pain in her head. She could not keep her step from wobbling, though, or her head from spinning.

Her escort did not even look at her, just kept pace.

She was not going to miss this place. She would not be coming back. She would not have been invited even if she wanted to. *Ways and Means* had expended its use for her. It would not even speak to her again. Its crew had taken the last remnants of her inner voice from her in surgery.

Fia was only surprised that it was troubling itself for the return shuttle. That thought made her nervous. It left her wondering if she was mistaken, if it didn't still have some purpose for her. This beast did not spend resources idly.

When they reached the embarkation lounge, Fia halted. She stared at the projection of the Earth "above" them. She knew the word *projection* now, and that what she saw was likely a filtered or imagined view, but that didn't make it less impactful.

She had seen enough images of the Earth by now that some of the wonder had soured. Whenever she looked at the Earth now, she tasted smoke, cuprous blood. The screams of charging soldiers. Dying horses. She was going back to that.

But the last thing she wanted to be like was this ship, these people.

No matter how peaceful *Ways and Means* claimed its colonization project would have been, it would have happened at the point of its sword, riding ahead of an army of lies.

She hadn't done much different. So much of her life had been somebody else's project, somebody else changing her mind, her thoughts, her goals. They still felt like her own.

But that had been a different life. She'd come through another battle.

She had been reborn. There was no clean break like death. No clean break without it. No matter what else and how else she had changed, she still believed that.

A week ago, she would not have recognized her own continent from this height. Now she'd studied the Earth enough to not only recognize it, but the new continent on the other side of the globe.

It was a vast new world. Like so much here, she could not have imagined it before she'd seen it.

She'd asked Niccoluccio about the other continent while he was teaching her. She pretended disaffection, that it was an idle question. He'd said only that there were people living there, too, in societies as vast and populated as her own.

She was going to bring that knowledge, and more, back. She did not know what she was going to do with it. Maybe nothing. But maybe not.

Her foul spirits, briefly forgotten, returned when she saw Meloku. Meloku was dressed as one of her people again, in an ostensibly hand-stitched fur coat and thick leather boots. She wore a traveling pack, bundled over her shoulders in the style of one of Fia's soldiers. She even wore a dagger at her side.

She was alone. The lounge was empty. According to Niccoluccio, most of *Ways and Means'* agents on the surface had been withdrawn, although he would not say why or for how long. He would not tell her much. She didn't know how much she could believe, anyway. So far only Habidah, Kacienta, and a few others had been allowed to go back.

Fia asked. "So you're going to escort me even when I'm back home?" She glanced to the golem who'd brought her here, but it was already heading back. Its charge had been handed over neatly to its next caretaker.

Meloku said, "I don't follow *Ways and Means'* orders any more."

Fia remembered, back in the shuttle, the dramatic performance of Meloku's resignation, and her silent fury when *Ways and Means* had not seemed to care. Up here, anything could be a performance. Seeing Meloku here now, waiting, she was even more sure of it. Fia said, "I didn't think *I* was following orders, either."

Her whole life, she'd been tossed about by outside forces. She had been told so for weeks, but she was just starting to feel it.

She wondered how much her inner voice had kept her black mood at bay. With it gone, she had nothing left to keep her level. It *had* helped her. It must have. A depressed soldier would have been no use to it.

Meloku said, "You wanted *Ways and Means* to come to your world. To bring all of its technologies and medicine and wonders. Still feel that way?"

Fia glared at her. No, Meloku had convinced her well enough. She hadn't been right. But she had not been wrong, either.

"I wanted those things," she said. "I didn't want *Ways and Means*."

"I'm taking some of those things with me."

Fia tightened her lips. "You mean, it's *letting* you take some."

"What it's not letting me take, it can't stop me from remembering."

"I don't understand what you're trying to talk me into." Ever since she'd discovered how *Ways and Means* had used her, paranoia had seized her. A justified paranoia. She could not stop seeing plots and secret intentions.

Meloku said, "We're going to be traveling together. At least for a while. I thought we might have a little bit to gain by working with each other."

"I don't need any friends from this ship."

Meloku said, "You said your inner voice was trying to get you killed. Turn you into a martyr to strengthen your movement."

"Yes," Fia said.

"Are you dead now?"

"Sometimes I wonder why I'm not." Again, she was struck by the suspicion that *Ways and Means* was only letting her go because it had something else in mind for her.

"A fact of life where I came from is that other people have plans for us all the time. You and me both. We can't always stop them. But they don't always work out the way their authors want. And that leaves us small folk a place to work in the margins." Meloku said, "I don't think *Ways and Means* knows what it wants at this point."

"Maybe it has a plan for us," Fia said.

"I'm sure it does."

A soft noise trilling through the chamber must have meant that their shuttle was ready to depart. She'd heard the same sound the last time she and Meloku had boarded a shuttle. Meloku straightened her soldier's pack. It looked authentic. Blanket roll, tent canvas, water sac, coin pouch. If she had the technology she'd promised, it was well hidden. It would have been.

Fia said, "I'm going back to my company."

"I realize that."

"They're not blind. They're going to recognize you from the night you kidnapped me."

Meloku nodded. "Yes. And they're going to attack me unless someone they trust stops them."

Meloku was not exactly placing her fate in Fia's hands. Not with the strength she'd already demonstrated against Fia's soldiers. Still. Fia said, "You can always go somewhere else."

"I have nowhere better."

The airlock hatch whispered open. Incongruous orange light rolled into the lounge. Fia wanted to turn, to start walking without waiting. But she could not move. She blamed her usual disorientation, standing still in freefall.

Meloku broke the impasse. She moved first, toward the airlock. Without turning back, she asked, "Are you going to introduce me as a friend, or not?"

Fia was going to have to think about that one. It was going to take a while to decide. Maybe longer than the shuttle flight would allow them.

39

A sequence of rhythmically flashing lights guided Niccoluccio Caracciola down the ship's passageways.

Niccoluccio did not have much of a memory for places. *Ways and Means* had given him a suite of three adjoining cabins to amble between. When he had first come aboard, he would get lost even between them.

His thoughts were unfocused, uncentered. He had no sense of direction. No memory.

Some of those things had come back to him, but not the memory. He had a vague sense that, once, he liked to have a routine.

He ate in one of his cabins at three precisely marked times of day. Washed and exercised in the other cabin. Again, on a rigid schedule. All the rest of his time he spent in the third, on his mat, meditating to piece his mind back together. Or sleeping. Or learning. There was always a lot to learn. Learn, and forget, and learn again.

He shuffled down the passageway. He did not concern himself with pacing, with time. He could not keep good track of it regardless.

On those few occasions when he needed to worry about time, *Ways and Means* kept him on track.

The ship told him he had ended up like this in a war. It had also told him the war was over, but he had not believed that. At the time, he could not have articulated why. Yet the feeling persisted.

It took him a while to figure out that it was the tension. He felt it everywhere. It suffused the planarship. It was steeped in every cabin, every passageway and lift terminal. Wherever its crew went. They had surrendered to an enemy they had only briefly encountered, and to whom they'd given up their lives and identities.

Of course they would not feel that their war was over. Niccoluccio watched them in their unguarded moments, read their faces. They were not as unreadable as they liked to think.

It had taken days, and they were just starting to cope with the fact that *Ways and Means* had killed its backup – or itself as it had been a scant few decades ago. Most of them had been serving it when it had made its backup. They did not know what it thought of itself now, or of them. Niccoluccio studied their faces, and listened to their voices.

He shared his observations with *Ways and Means*.

Three crewmembers stood abreast at the end of this last passageway. Two were humanoid, and the other a hulking beast, wolf-like and four-legged. These guards were an archaic touch, perhaps, but *Ways and Means* was taking no chances. There had to be three, to watch each other as much as the door.

The guards stood aside as Niccoluccio shuffled past. He did not know if they knew what they were guarding. He did not ask.

Ways and Means knew with absolute certainty that it could trust Niccoluccio.

The next hatch led to a short hallway and another, larger, closed space. A decontamination chamber. The hatch closed behind him. He waited for the next portal to open.

The chamber on the other side was not a cell, not exactly.

It was spherical, about twenty meters across, and smelt of iron and burnt plastic. The black walls were heavily shielded, impenetrable to radio. No data came in or out. No part of *Ways and Means'* mind connected here. There were no cameras, no hardwired connections, no power cables, nothing that could have been a conduit for information.

The light strips ran from batteries.

It was a containment area. Even the air that came into this chamber had to be gated through locks. A virus had once nearly destroyed *Ways and Means*. It had to be careful about the transmission of information.

The slab of blackened, half-melted metal was just as Niccoluccio had been told it would be. It had remained here since *Ways and Means* had plucked it out of orbit.

Seen from the side, it looked like a split geode. Light glinted off angled surfaces. This molten bulkhead had spent some time cooling in vacuum – long enough to crystallize. This part of the broken spaceship had become as a roughly faceted gem, silver-white and cloudy.

It had been part of the hull segment that *Ways and Means* had sheared off from the intruder, and thus sheltered from the worst of the damage.

Somewhere inside was one of the backup's core processing and memory components. It was fragmented. Badly damaged. But capable of independent thought. Independent decisions.

It was beautiful.

Niccoluccio paced the room. There were not many people *Ways and Means* would have allowed in this chamber. But Niccoluccio was not a person. Not really. There was too much of him missing, too much that couldn't be replaced.

Ways and Means had spent the years carefully rebuilding him, tuning his synapses. It genuinely wanted to help him. He believed that. But it could not rebuild the old home without a foundation.

His loss was its opportunity. In places like this and at the times he was called for, he could be its avatar. *Ways and Means* filled in the missing pieces with its own thoughts, fragments of its many voices. There was enough of it in him that it could trust him.

It could not trust anyone else.

He stopped when he had finished a complete circuit around the chamber.

"Your surrender is accepted," Niccoluccio said.

The fragment could hear him. It had sensor capacity enough to detect the vibrations in the air. He let the words linger. Even at reduced capacity, the pause would be an eternity to the mind inside.

"*If* you can tell us about the other amalgamates," Niccoluccio added. "How they found you. What they've accomplished so far."

Ways and Means still withheld some of its thoughts from him, of course. Not even it knew everything it was thinking. It had not needed to send him with these words. There was enough of it in him that he had already known what it wanted him to say.

After another appropriate pause, Niccoluccio said, "And *if* you can tell us what they plan to do next – and where they are now."

Its crew would have been relieved. It was not without clemency for itself, its history, after all. Or for them.

But it would come with conditions.

ACKNOWLEDGMENTS

Terminus could not have been written without the patience and editorial guidance of my partner, Teresa Milbrodt.

I have been fortunate to live near a pair of university libraries: the University of Missouri in Columbia, and Western State Colorado University in Gunnison. Their staff and collections have been of immeasurable aid in composing *Terminus*.

Among the titles I mentioned in *Quietus'* acknowledgments, which also continued to help me write this novel, I would like to add *The Lady Queen: the Notorious Reign of Joanna I, Queen of Naples, Jerusalem, and Sicily* by Nancy Goldstone, *John Hawkwood: an English Mercenary in Fourteenth-Century Italy* by William Cafero, and *Mercenaries and Their Masters: Warfare in Renaissance Italy* by Michael Mallett, all of which are wonderful books if you would like to learn more about the eras and subjects of this novel. Omissions and mistakes are my own.

Both *Terminus* and I owe a great deal to the trust, goodwill, and support of Angry Robot, including publisher/founder Marc Gascoigne, Phil Jourdan, Penny Reeve, Nick Tyler, and Lottie Llewelyn-Wells. Special thanks to Simon Spanton, Paul Simpson, Michael R Underwood, and to the cover artist for both books, Dominic Harman.

Neither I nor my writing career would be where it is without the faculty and staff of Bowling Green State University's Creative Writing MFA program, and Dr Lawrence Coates and Dr Wendell Mayo. Osia and *Ways and Means* made their first appearances in their workshops.

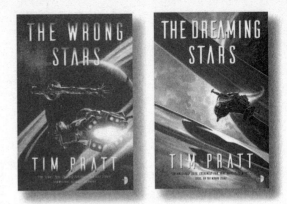

TRISTAN PALMGREN

Quietus

"A stunning novel... an emotionally affecting story."
— THE GUARDIAN